Borrowed Time

Edie Claire

Dedication

For all my minister friends.
Let the record show: You guys *rock*.

Acknowledgments

With many thanks to Dru Quarles, MD, for her medical expertise; to Key Tronzo, tap dancer extraordinaire, for inspiring the character of Rose; and to Ellen Bowermaster Welch, MLS, for daring me to write a book about a sexy librarian.

Chapter 1

Sarah Landers wasn't looking forward to the mail coming. She never did, except at Christmas, and the stale heat of midsummer that currently bathed western Pennsylvania was a far cry from Christmas. Not that she considered a mildly muggy, 87-degree day to be hot. She had grown up in southern Alabama. She knew hot.

She stood at the narrow window beside her front door, twisting a lock of her long straight hair first clockwise, then counterclockwise, around her index finger. It was a nervous habit of longstanding, and though she had learned to squelch the urge in public, private moments such as this found her vulnerable.

She didn't want to collect the mail. But bills had to be paid; household matters, attended to. She couldn't just let it sit.

The box-shaped truck pulled away from her mailbox and rattled off around the rest of the cul-de-sac. There was no rush. She could go out after the truck was gone.

She turned, and as her eyes swept over the spacious, nearly empty living room before her, her chest swelled with pride. By many people's reckoning, the fifty-year-old split-level fell far short of a suburban showplace. But its sound infrastructure, funky floor plan, and grossly outdated interior fit her like a glove. It was the first real house she had lived in since she was a teenager, and for the last three days, she had been reveling in her newfound quarters with an enthusiasm as close to reckless abandon as she ever got.

Which was to say, not very.

Her belongings hadn't filled a fraction of the available floor space. Two of the bedrooms were completely empty, and she liked them that way. Emptiness meant solitude, as did owning her own patch of earth. Apartment living had been more practical for a single woman, true, but the feel of grass beneath her bare feet was a simple pleasure she had missed.

The mail truck's motor revved, and she turned again to see it move out of sight. She drew in a breath, opened the door, and stepped out.

Strong sun beamed from almost directly overhead, and she raised a hand to shield her eyes. When the droning hum of a lawn mower met her ears, she dipped her chin as well. She didn't want to talk to anyone.

She cast a glance to her left. All was quiet with the young, two-income family next door. Numerous plastic three-wheelers and yard toys lay where they had been discarded, heating up in the summer sun. An obese black Labrador lounged on its back in the shade, acknowledging her presence with the partial lifting of one eyelid and a single, lethargic thump of its tail.

She turned her head the opposite direction and found that dwelling, too, to be perfectly still. The septuagenarian inside was the only neighbor she had met thus far, and Sarah had liked her immediately, as she did most elderly people. Rose was an active, intelligent woman with better things to do than pay attention to her, which was exactly what she wanted. Sarah had read horror stories about nosy neighbors in suburbia, and she was determined not to fall victim. Her home was her sanctuary.

She was halfway to her mailbox when the sound of the lawn mower grew suddenly louder. She raised her head just enough to see the front of a green push mower emerging from behind the brick ranch across the cul-de-sac. She averted her eyes.

Of all the neighbors she had caught sight of, she wanted to meet the man in the brick ranch the least. She had glimpsed him through her front windows—getting in and out of his beat-up car, reading the paper on his porch, talking to passers-by as they walked dogs and pushed strollers—and he showed every sign of being just the sort of person she did *not* want around her sanctum. A chatty, gregarious busybody.

She quickened her steps, keeping her head down until she arrived at the mailbox and could safely turn her back. Then she popped open the metal door and peered inside. Only a small pile. That was good. She reached in and pulled the papers into the glare of the sun.

The bill on top was from the phone company. The envelope underneath made her stomach lurch.

Sherman and Sylvester, Attorneys at Law.

She flipped the envelope to the back of the pile. A furniture catalog addressed to Resident. A flyer for a carpet-cleaning company. The phone bill again.

Sherman and Sylvester, Attorneys at Law.

She exhaled, her mind racing. She could avoid the letter if she wanted to. Throw it away unopened; pretend it didn't exist. She had done the same many times before; her skills as an ostrich were unparalleled. But this letter, she knew, should hold no surprises. She had heard the news already. Destroying the hard copy wouldn't change what was to happen.

Apparently, nothing could.

She ripped open the envelope, dragged out the letter, and uncrumpled it with an irreverent flick of her wrist.

Dear Miss Landers.

They always called her Miss Landers. Never once, over the considerable course of her patronage, had they ever called her Sarah. She knew the formality to be both a show of respect and a subtle show of disapproval. They were kindly Southern gentlemen, but they had never quite understood where she was coming from, and that had seemed to bother them. She could sympathize. But she could not explain.

As discussed in our conversation of July 12th, we must reiterate that due to the denial of your writ of mandamus to the Alabama Supreme Court, the ruling of the Circuit Court regarding the condemnation of your property on Angus Road in Lee County shall stand, and said property will be acquired imminently by the acquiring authority of Lee County, Alabama...

Had the attorneys had multiple rows of teeth and cartilage for bones, she might have convinced them to take her case further. She suspected there might still be another appeal, another angle to pursue. But Sherman and Sylvester had scruples. They had told her at the outset that she had no case— that the proper procedures for eminent domain had been followed and that the compensation offered was more than just. They insisted that they had given her request their best shot—tying up the proceedings in a succession of carefully orchestrated legal knots, literally buying time. But the game was over now. They could hold off the inevitable no longer. She would only be wasting her money.

As if she cared about that.

Your legal access to the property will cease as of the 25th of July as previously stated, hence we strongly recommend that you remove any personal belongings from the house and grounds immediately, as demolition may commence at any point thereafter—

She refolded the letter and forced it back into its envelope. *Demolition.* The county would build its precious bypass, no matter what stood in the way. They would destroy the house. Bulldoze the grounds. Level everything and pave it under a sea of asphalt. Maybe they wouldn't find anything. Maybe they would seal up the whole accursed place like a tomb, locking all evidence of the past in an impregnable, government-maintained vault.

Or maybe her life would be over.

She slammed her mailbox shut and whirled around, only to find her gaze colliding with that of the man with the lawn mower. He was only a cul-de-sac's width away from her now. She started.

His steps slowed. He offered a smile. He waved.

The blood drained from her face.

He was wearing grimy cutoffs, old sneakers, and no shirt. He was the same man she had seen before, fully clothed, interacting pleasantly with others. But knowing that couldn't stop the ripple of anxiety that coursed through her now. He was young—in his late twenties, early thirties, perhaps. Not excessively tall for a man, but still several inches taller than her. His tanned skin was drenched with sweat; his muscles gleamed in the sun. Deep brown eyes and a crown of tight, shiny black curls bespoke a Mediterranean descent. Greek, or perhaps Italian. Dark. Powerful.

Menacing.

She attempted to muster her wits, but her pulse pounded.

She returned his wave with a stilted gesture and started back toward the house, cursing her timidity even as she fled.

It was the letter, that was all. It had messed with her mind a little, but she would be fine.

The lawn mower's engine rattled to a halt, and her pace quickened. Surely the man hadn't stopped mowing just to talk to her. Shouldn't it be obvious she wasn't amenable?

She reached her front steps and lifted a foot. She didn't want to be rude, but why should she feel obligated to interact with someone just because she lived near them? All she had wanted was some space and a garden—a homeowner had a right to be outside without being harassed.

She jogged up a few steps. The flower beds beside her walk would be perfect for planting tulip bulbs in a few months, but right now, she would have to settle for autumn mums. Tulips wouldn't come up till spring.

She might not be here then.

Footfalls sounded from her driveway. She took another step up, keeping her gaze trained on the ground. A couple more yards, and she would be safely inside again.

Everything went black.

Chapter 2

Sarah's head hurt. A sharp, prickling pain spread over the back of her scalp; the bones of her skull throbbed. Everything was still black. Where was she?

She tried to open her eyes, but they didn't seem to be working. She wondered if she was dead.

"Are you all right?"

Her lids flew open.

Dark eyes peered at her from a fuzzy face. A halo of bright light rippled around its writhing, curly edges—black locks as alive as Medusa's, brimming with prismatic beads of moisture. A drop of liquid struck her squarely in the nose.

She had to be dead.

She closed her eyes again, her heart pounding. It was *him*. He had come back for her.

"Go away," she said, or at least she thought she did. He answered her, but she couldn't make sense of the words. Her hip ached, her head was still being bludgeoned. Over and over. *Bam. Bam.*

"Stop it!" she forced out, trying to curl up and dodge the blows. She couldn't seem to move. "Dee! Where are you?"

"Open your eyes!"

The order pierced the haze of her mind like a gunshot. She obeyed.

He hovered over her, his face close. She wondered if he looked as he did then, or if hell had transformed him into the demon he deserved to be. But she couldn't tell. Her eyes wouldn't focus.

"Stop hitting me!" she ordered, straining to see. After a few seconds of concentration, she succeeded.

The man hadn't moved. He simply stared back at her, his

eyes wide with concern. Her breath caught in her throat.

It wasn't *him*. It was the man with the lawn mower.

"Take it easy," he said slowly. "Nobody hit you. You collapsed. You fell backwards and hit your head." His gaze moved to the painful part of her skull, and his eyes flickered with alarm.

Sarah's brain struggled for sense. She was not dead. But she had to have lost her mind. She remembered walking up the steps, hearing this man's footsteps behind her. She had awoken with her head hurting. But she couldn't have passed out as he said. Never in her life had she passed out—she had felt perfectly fine just seconds ago.

Had he struck her?

Her heart thumped violently against her breastbone. She raised a hand toward the part of her head he was staring at, and her fingers struck liquid. Warm, sticky liquid.

The man grabbed her hand and replaced it at her side. "Don't worry," he said mildly, attempting a smile. "I'm sure it's nothing serious. Head wounds just bleed a lot, that's all."

Head wounds bleed. The familiar, unwelcome images flashed through her mind in warp speed.

No! Her stomach roiled. She tried to sit up, but the front yard spun.

"Don't do that," the stranger instructed, "Stay down. Just let me take a look." He removed a handkerchief from his pocket and dabbed at the most painful area of her scalp.

She jerked, and he winced. "You're going to need stitches," he announced. Then he looked toward her house. "Is anyone else at home?"

Her breaths came ragged and heavy as she willed herself to concentrate, to be logical. She was all right. She had a little cut, that was all. How she had gotten it she wasn't sure. But there was no need to panic.

She swallowed and found her voice. "No one else is home now, but Rose is next door," she said, eager to bring in a third party—just to be on the safe side.

He shook his head. "She's at the senior center. She's there every Saturday morning." He looked over his shoulder toward his own house, his expression pensive.

Her pulse pounded in her ears. This man couldn't have hit her. Could he? Her front steps were in plain sight—at least potentially—of half a dozen houses. It was ludicrous.

He turned back to her, put his handkerchief in her hand, and pressed both firmly against her head. "Just try to keep some pressure on it," he instructed. "I'll bring my car over and run you to the ER."

The man's voice and hands were gentle, and a part of her longed to trust his good intentions. But the larger part remained apprehensive. If she had tripped or stumbled, why couldn't she remember that? What if he *had* struck her? What if the whole purpose had been to get her into his car?

Cold dread surged. She jerked up. "I'm not—"

She couldn't finish the sentence. His face swam before her eyes. Her head felt as though it would split. The pain in her hip was searing. She lay back down and turned away from him. Maybe this was it. Maybe she was in hell after all.

A hand rested lightly on her shoulder. "I know you're confused," the stranger continued, "but I promise you've got nothing to fear from me. I'm only trying to help you. That cut needs stitches, and you could have a concussion. I'd be happy to drive you to the hospital, but if you're uncomfortable with that, I can call an ambulance. Just tell me what you want me to do, and I'll do it."

The candor in his voice nagged at her common sense, and she tried again to think straight. Surely, her suspicions were absurd. They were not two strangers meeting on a deserted roadside—they both owned homes here, and everyone around them knew who he was.

She shifted to study him. He was dark, yes. His eyes, his skin, his hair. But he was nothing like the man she remembered. His expression was sympathetic; his manner, kind. He was just a man. A neighbor. A good Samaritan.

She mustered her strength and reared up.

"Easy," he responded, steadying her with a hand on the back. "You'd be better off lying down."

She clenched her teeth and struggled to her feet, putting a

hand on his slick, bare shoulder for support. She didn't want to touch him, but she knew she couldn't get up otherwise. Another wave of dizziness arose as she stood, but she removed her hand anyway.

"I'm sorry," she apologized. "It seems I lost my head for a moment. I appreciate your help, but I'm fine now, so please, go finish your lawn. I'll just go inside and lie down for a while."

He watched her with bewilderment, his hands poised as if he expected her to crumple again. "You have to have that cut stitched up," he insisted. "Furthermore, if you do have a concussion, the worst thing you can do is fall asleep."

They were standing close together now, and as her gaze met his she felt another stab of uneasiness. His brown eyes were piercing.

She turned her head.

"Please," he continued. "Either let me take you to the ER, or let me call an ambulance. But you can't just pretend this didn't happen."

She almost laughed. But she knew that doing so would make her look hysterical, and she had disparaged her sanity enough already. Furthermore, he was correct. The handkerchief she was holding was soaked through. The cut was deep. She couldn't just ignore it.

She threw another glance in his direction and wished he had a shirt on. His appearance made her nervous, but that wasn't his fault. Men with physical strength always intimidated her, never mind that such a phobia was both politically incorrect and pathetic.

She decided to imagine a shirt on him. *A crisp yellow shirt, with red polka dots… There.* He was no different from the multitudes of men she assisted on a regular basis at her job—just a little younger. He was offering her a ride to the ER, and she needed one. She couldn't safely drive herself.

He's a nice person. Everything will be fine.

She extended her free hand. "My name is Sarah Landers," she explained, working to keep her voice steady. She couldn't meet his eyes again. Her overactive heart seemed to be pumping half her blood straight out of her head, and she was growing dizzier. "I would appreciate that lift to the ER. Thank you."

He reached for her hand with a smile, but the expression disappeared as she swayed on her feet.

Strong arms moved in and caught her. "Sit down," he instructed, guiding her onto the retaining wall at the edge of her driveway. "Unless you want a matching cut on the other side."

She shrank under his touch, every muscle tensing.

The instant she was safely seated he released her, then moved back a step. "You'll need some ID and your insurance card," he said, looking toward her house. "Tell me where your purse is, and I'll get it for you."

Suspicion flickered, but was doused by a surge of nausea. There were easier ways to get a woman's purse. She would not be stupid. "It's on the kitchen counter, by the microwave," she responded weakly.

He nodded. "Don't move." He ascended the steps, and his eyes landed on her scattered mail. To her horror, he stretched out a hand and began to retrieve it.

"No, don't!" she shouted, her voice rattling her skull with pain.

He stopped and looked at her curiously, then picked up the last envelope and added it to the pile. "It's all right," he answered, making an obvious effort not to look at what was in his hands. "I'll just put it inside for you."

She couldn't seem to breathe. He was in and out of her house within seconds, and when he reached her he paused only to lay down her purse before heading back across the cul-de-sac. "I need to grab a shirt and my keys," he explained as he moved. "Please, just wait there. Don't try to get up again."

She sat and watched helplessly as he sprinted to his own front door, then disappeared inside.

Her limbs began to tremble.

The triage nurse pulled the bloody towel away from Sarah's head. Her lips pursed, and she studied Sarah's scalp with narrowed eyes. "Yes, you'll definitely need to have that stapled." She replaced the towel with a sterile pad and put her hand back into position over the wound. "How did it happen?"

The question shouldn't have caught Sarah off guard, but it did. The ride to the hospital had been nerve wracking, and she was still out of sorts. Her neighbor had insisted on helping her out of the car and into the building, and it was all she could do to convince him to let her approach the desk on her own. She had thanked him and told him to go home, assuming that once he was gone, her sense of being safely in control would return. But her limbs were still shaking.

"I'm not sure," she answered. "I was outside, and the next thing I knew, I was on the ground."

The nurse, a plain, competent-looking woman in her forties, eyed Sarah skeptically. "You passed out?"

Sarah took a deep breath, trying not to be affected by the predominance of the color white. The smell. The steady drone of distant voices, the intangible aura of fear. She had not set foot in a hospital in nine years. She had forgotten.

She wanted to forget.

"I'm not sure what happened," she repeated. "I've never passed out before, and I felt fine at the time. I think I probably tripped over something, but if I did, I don't remember it."

The nurse studied her with a practiced eye. "Did you eat breakfast this morning?"

"I ate the same thing I always eat."

"Were you changing position, like rising from a chair?"

"Just walking up some steps."

"Did you have any idea it was coming? Feel funny in any way?"

Sarah shook her head, but regretted the motion. Her skull throbbed.

"Is there any history of loss of consciousness in your family?" the nurse asked, moving to scribble something on a chart. "Anyone with seizures?"

Seizures. The images erupted in Sarah's mind as sharp as the day they were real. Walking close to her sister's stretcher as it approached the double doors of the ER, the paramedics bouncing its rubber wheels over the threshold. *Bump. Bump.*

Dee's eyes opening, then rolling back in her head. Her spine contorting, her arms and legs jerking. Every muscle of her body in spasm.

"No," Sarah answered, nauseous again. "There's no epilepsy in the family."

Just one antidepressant overdose.

"Did you wet your underwear when you fell?" the nurse continued. "Bite your tongue?"

"No," Sarah whispered, her voice cracking.

The nurse offered an appraising stare. "Did anyone else see what happened?"

Sarah started to answer, but the response stuck in her throat. She did not want the man across the cul-de-sac any further involved in her affairs. "A neighbor," she said offhandedly. "He drove me in, but I'm sure he's gone now."

The nurse's eyebrows rose. "And what was his name?"

She hesitated, wondering how she could have neglected to glean that particular information. "I don't know," she explained, trying not to sound as sheepish as she felt. "I only moved into the neighborhood a few days ago."

The nurse appeared dubious. "You don't know his name?"

Sarah's heart beat faster. "No."

The nurse's brow creased with concentration. Her eyes bore into Sarah's. "You need to be honest with us, Sarah. If you're afraid of someone, we can help get you to someplace safe. Just tell us the truth. Did someone hurt you?"

She flushed with alarm. The last thing she needed after acting such a fool was to have her neighbor harassed for his kindness. "No!" she protested. "I don't even know the man. He was mowing his lawn. He said I collapsed and fell. He brought me here, and he left. Could we just leave him out of this? Please?"

The other woman's face blurred before her eyes.

"Take it easy, Sarah," the nurse said calmly. "We're going to go ahead and move you to a room now. Then you can lie down for a minute."

We're going to move your sister to the ICU now, a man in blue scrubs had said. *You can see her as soon as she's stable.*

Dee had never gotten stable.

"You need to relax," the nurse continued. "You've lost a lot of blood. It's normal to feel light-headed. The doctor will be in to see you shortly, and they'll give you something for the pain."

Yes, we'll give her something for the seizures. Just take it easy, honey. Hang in there. We'll do everything we can for her. I promise.

Sarah dropped her aching head into her hands. She didn't want to remember. She couldn't bear to feel that horrible pain—again. She missed her sister. Missed her so damned much. Still.

In spite of everything.

Chapter 3

Sarah crossed her wrists and rubbed her upper arms. The treatment room was freezing. The circumstances of such a visit would make her anxious no matter what she was wearing, but the skimpy hospital gown ensured that she felt both cold and vulnerable as well.

Three excruciatingly long hours had passed. She had been alternately poked, prodded, and ignored. Her head wound had been closed with six staples. A phlebotomist had drawn four vials of blood. She had been hooked up to an EKG machine. She had waited interminably to be slid into a CT scanner like a sardine. She had been offered juice and some crackers. She had tried to keep her mind on the present.

The nausea had subsided, and her skull had ceased to throb after the first dose of painkiller. But her mind was still uneasy.

The doctor who examined her had at once declared that her injuries were caused by a fall, with the brunt of her weight landing on her hip and her head striking something hard—evidently the corner of a concrete step. Her assertion that she must have tripped over something seemed no more plausible to him than it had to the nurse, and despite her denial of any foul play, she could tell he was not convinced. Only after returning from a long and unexplained absence did he inform her that there was no doubt she had suffered a loss of consciousness, and that because her history held no obvious explanation, a complete work-up would be necessary.

Now at last, all the ordered tests had been completed. She waited only for the doctor's final visit and, hopefully, her discharge. She eyed the plastic bag that contained her clothes, her frustration warring with her better judgment. She wanted to get dressed; she wanted to leave. Had she been convinced that the tests were unnecessary, she might have. But despite the doctor's comforting words, the intensity of his gaze had disturbed her. She got the feeling he was looking for something specific. She wanted to know if he had found it.

She stared at the faded clusters of star shapes on her gown, mentally outlining where the pattern repeated. There was little else to look at. *Hospital gowns are like the emperor's new clothes*, one of her favorite elderly patrons had told her. *They only give you the illusion you aren't naked.*

Her lips drew into a smile, but the emotion she felt was bittersweet. Less than a week, and already she missed them. The large-print crowd at the Johnson County Library could always make her laugh. Leaving Kansas City had been difficult, but she was determined that if her past was going to catch up with her, it should happen among strangers. Pittsburgh's Eastern Allegheny Regional Library was vast and well-funded, and in her field, not many women were offered upper management positions at the age of twenty-six. No one had questioned her motives in moving.

The air conditioner switched on, and her smile faded as an arctic blast swept down her back. Swearing under her breath, she slid off the bed, collected another gown, and put her arms into it like a coat. Then she hopped back up and huddled. Not much longer, she assured herself. Then she could go home.

You might as well go home now.

A fresh crop of goose bumps arose. She could recall the other doctor's every word, even after nine years. He had been thin, African-American, and young. Perhaps a resident. She could see the sadness in his eyes; sense his helplessness. *I'm sorry. But there's nothing more we can do.*

She closed her eyes. It was no use. No amount of mental distraction could keep the sights and sounds of the hospital from taking her back. She didn't want to relive the day that Dee had died—she didn't even want to recall their last few, cheerless years together. Her only comfort came in remembering her sister as a child, as she had been before the trouble started. Frizzy-haired and mischievous. Wacky, imaginative, fun.

That was her Dee. The sister she had loved.

A knock on the windowed wall interrupted her reverie. She looked up, and her eyes widened. It was the man from across the cul-de-sac.

"Hello," he greeted, opening the door and popping his head through. "Care for some company?"

Her pulse pounded. She couldn't believe he was standing there. No matter how helpful he had been, he had no business coming into her exam room, particularly when she was half dressed. She had a sudden desire to dive behind the bed like a child, to scream at him to go away. But as the significance of his presence dawned on her, she became mortified on a new front. "Please tell me you haven't been sitting in the waiting room all this time," she asked, her voice tight.

He slipped on into the room, but remained by the door. "I haven't been sitting in the waiting room all this time," he answered, offering a smile that was warm, yet somehow sly.

Her heart continued to pound. "You went home?" she asked hopefully. She was certain her discomfort was obvious, but if he sensed it, it had no effect on him.

"No," he responded lightly, still smiling. "I've been visiting other patients. But I checked in now and then to see when they might spring you. They tell me it should be soon."

Her limbs began to quiver again. Rationally she knew the man intended no harm, but she didn't want him near her, regardless. His appearance was too disquieting. He had put on a clean shirt, but he was wearing the same cutoffs and sneakers in which he had mowed his lawn. Tiny bits of cut grass still clung to the hair on his calves, and he was so tanned that not even the incandescent lights overhead—which gave her own skin the pallor of a corpse—could sap his vim. He seemed so out of place in the tense, sterile setting of the ER that his presence was like a mockery.

"So, what was the verdict?" he asked, his voice cheerful. "Did they figure out why you passed out, or do they still think you were assaulted by a diabolical neighbor?"

Her stomach twisted. His tone was teasing, and there was a twinkle in his eye, but her horror at his allusion was not assuaged. She remembered the doctor's long absence earlier, and drew in a ragged breath. "What did they say to you?"

His smile only widened. "Don't worry about me. I know people. It was my fault for not introducing myself." He stood up straight and stepped over to her, hand extended. "My name is Adam. Adam Carmassi."

She felt obliged to stretch out her arm, but no amount of willpower could keep it steady. Her hand was cold as ice.

They shook.

His own hand was warm; his grip, firm. "Sorry I didn't say so earlier," he continued, stepping back again, "but the blood gushing out of your head had me a little rattled. You're lucky I didn't pass out myself."

Her eyebrows rose. Comfortable with gushing blood or no, she did not believe men like him passed out. Then again, she never thought she would have, either. "You seemed perfectly calm and collected to me."

He grinned. He had a nice smile, and she could see why he might indeed "know people." The masculine features that evoked anxiety in her were the same sort that made other women's heads turn. His frame was solid and muscular. His jet-black hair was wild and unruly, and his high cheekbones and square jaw line were accented by a perpetual shadow of stubble. But most striking were his eyes. Deep brown and thickly lashed, they exuded a fetching mixture of intelligence and verve, and she found her attention drawn to them involuntarily, even as the rest of his appearance disturbed her.

"I appreciate your bringing me here," she reiterated, attempting to put some authority in her voice as she shooed him. "But you really don't have to stick around. I'm fine now. Go home and finish that lawn."

"Sorry," he quipped. "Carmassi ER Transport is a comprehensive service. The ride home is part of the package."

She tensed further. As much as she would like to chalk up his actions to neighborliness, spending three hours in a hospital on a Saturday for the sake of a stranger had to cross the line. She would be a fool to think he didn't want something.

She flushed. Then she shivered again.

Resisting the urge to rub her arms, she bucked up her voice with a bravado she didn't feel. "I think," she insisted, "that Carmassi ER Transport needs to reallocate its resources to Carmassi Landscaping, before the latter gets a reputation for walking off the job. Don't worry about me. I already called a friend to pick me up. She's on her way now."

"All right then," he responded. "If you're sure you don't need anything."

She let out her breath out with a whoosh. "I don't. And I won't," she assured, perhaps too adamantly.

His eyes held hers, as if he could see right through her. She turned away. Her relief at his leaving had to be obvious. If her suspicions of his motives were also, he would surely take offense. Few men appreciated being shot down romantically before expressing an interest, and she had no idea whether Adam was even single. She never apologized for being straightforward with her own intentions, but she didn't want to be rude either, particularly when he had been so helpful.

"Thank you again," she said more politely. "I'm sure I'll be seeing you around the neighborhood. I owe you some donuts or something."

He turned and opened the door. He didn't seem offended. But in his face she perceived the same emotion she had seen when looking up at him from the ground. He seemed worried.

"You don't owe me anything," he answered.

Sarah picked up her comb and gritted her teeth, knowing that even if her head wasn't throbbing, combing the hair around her wound would be painful. But she vowed not to complain. At least she was home. After her discharge from the ER she had greeted her house's already comfortably familiar interior with a rush of relief, locked the door behind her, and headed straight for the shower. Her hair was now free of blood. But the stain on her psyche persisted.

The news she had waited for was mixed. All her test results had been normal. Her blood sugar was fine, her heart had its electrical act together, and there was nothing in her skull that shouldn't be. But while she was happy to know what hadn't caused her to pass out, she could not stop wondering what had. The doctor had suggested that her loss of consciousness was a fluke related to stress, but he had no idea how preposterous that theory was. If stress alone could make her faint, she would have spent most of the last decade unconscious. One formal letter from Sherman and Sylvester was nothing, and neither was a senseless episode of fear over a man. Those things were mere nuisances.

She grasped her hair near the roots, hoping to blunt the pull of the comb, but its first tug brought a stab of pain so sharp her knees weakened. Realizing she was due for another painkiller, she headed for the kitchen and extracted the plastic prescription bottle from her purse. She had just swallowed the pill when her eyes alighted on the mail.

The small stack lay on her kitchen counter. The phone bill was on top. Her heart skipped as she extended a finger and nudged it. The letter from Sherman and Sylvester lay underneath, its return address still intact, despite her indiscriminate ripping.

Heat flared in her cheeks. Adam Carmassi had seen the envelope. Whether or not he had paid attention to it, she didn't know, but the invasion of privacy still rankled. His barging into her hospital room had been awkward, but no one knew about her business in Alabama. No one. As up front as she always tried to be about the fact that her parents had died young, she never told people that she still owned the family estate—much less how hard she had been fighting to keep it.

She picked up the letter and turned it in her hands. Adam couldn't have read it. He hadn't had time. And why would he want to? People got mail from lawyers all the time. Most of it was uninteresting. She was being paranoid.

She stepped to the trash can and tossed the letter in.

We strongly recommend that you remove any personal belongings from the house and grounds immediately. The lawyer's words tormented her as she watched the paper flutter onto the remnants of her breakfast. A pit of heaviness settled in her stomach.

This would be her last chance. Only a few days remained. A

part of her did want to go back, to see what was left, to make sure she had taken everything with any kind of sentimental value. But another part of her knew better.

"I can't," she mumbled, whirling around. "I just can't." She moved quickly to the middle of her living room, as if putting physical distance between herself and the letter would relieve her guilt. It didn't. Her eyes drifted to the framed picture of her parents that sat on her bookshelf, and her mother's light-blue eyes reprimanded her even as the smile, and the melodic voice Sarah remembered, were soft. *You didn't leave the quilts, did you, Sarah? You know how hard your great-grandmother worked on them, and the Texas Star won a blue ribbon once...*

She tore her eyes away. Yes, she had left the quilts. She had left the chest with Dee's and her baby clothes. She had left the portraits her father painted when he was a teenager. Where could she have put it all at her aunt's house? Or when she was at school? It hadn't seemed important—the mementos had seemed safe enough. She figured she could get them anytime.

She had not. She hadn't set foot on the twenty-acre fallow farm, the long and winding gravel driveway, or the wide wooden porch steps in more than five years. Even her trips before that had been hasty ones—periodic visits with her aunt to collect necessities, check up on things. She had no idea what shape the house was in now, and she was afraid to know, even as she chastised herself for failing to safeguard her parents' property.

Her aunt had perceived how difficult being at the farm was for her. Karen had even thought she understood her niece's reluctance. She hadn't. No one could possibly understand the horror that house held for Sarah—the crippling fear that twisted her gut, even now, at the thought of it.

She could salvage no more of her family's belongings. She couldn't drive all the way to Alabama and back—she had just started a new job; she couldn't ask for time off already. Flying was a problem in itself; but even if it weren't, she knew she couldn't face another visit. She had barely coped when her aunt had been there to support her, and since Karen had divorced Sarah's uncle, the woman was technically no longer family.

Going back to Alabama alone would be no catharsis. It would be a nightmare.

Pulling her fleece bathrobe tighter around her, Sarah walked to the thermostat and turned off the air. Not even a steaming hot shower had dislodged the chill that being in a hospital had driven into her bones. If a different emergency room in a different state could bring up such vivid memories of Dee's suicide, what would seeing the house itself do to her?

She shuddered. Thinking of her family as they had been, putting her last days in Alabama out of her mind, was the only way she had eventually come to terms with what had happened. But she *had* come to terms with it. She was managing just fine.

The doorbell rang.

She jumped. She hadn't heard it ring before, and it was amazingly loud. She made a mental note to see if the volume could be adjusted, but she made no move toward the door. She wasn't expecting anyone, and she was not in the mood to buy Girl Scout cookies.

The bell rang again, and her resolve weakened. What if it was Rose, from next door? What if the woman needed something? Taking care to stay out of sight of the window, she approached the peephole and put an eye to the glass. It was Adam Carmassi.

She stepped back.

Why was he here? Surely all the necessary pleasantries of their business had been concluded. She didn't want to talk to him again. She didn't want to talk to anyone.

She returned to the living room. He would go away eventually. If pressed later, she could always say she was in the shower. It was almost true.

The third ring was a triple. She covered her ears. Surely chimes that loud could be heard even if one was in the shower. Now he was being rude.

Irritation surged, and the heat that came with it was welcome. Why was she cowering in her own home? If she didn't want neighbors ringing her bell on a whim, she should make her wishes clear from the outset. She tightened her bathrobe another notch, stepped up to the door, and swung it open. "Mr. Carmassi," she said formally, "Do you have any idea how loud that thing is?"

He responded with another disarming grin. "Sure I do. That's why I knew you'd answer."

She stared at him. His knowledge of the inner workings of her house was disconcerting, but it shouldn't surprise her. She had spied him conversing in friendly terms with half the neighborhood already. Why would the previous occupant be any exception?

"What do you want?" she asked flatly, determined not to encourage him.

"I wanted to make sure you were okay," he said, his own voice remaining pleasant. "That you didn't get any bad news after I left. Are you all right?"

She swallowed. "I'm doing fine, thank you. The tests all came back normal." Her fingers found the door handle. "I appreciate your concern, but please, don't feel like you have to keep checking on me." She watched his reaction carefully as she spoke. She needed to get her point across, but she didn't want to make an enemy of him—or any of the neighbors.

"I was glad to see you got home safely," he continued. "It must be convenient to have a friend who works for a cab company."

Her face paled. She cleared her throat. "Yes," she confirmed, "very convenient."

She had lied about calling a friend to drive her home. She had moved to Pittsburgh only seventy-two hours ago—she didn't have any friends. Other than her new coworkers, the only people she knew by name were the woman next door and her real estate agent. She had planned to call a cab all along. She hadn't planned on having her homecoming spied on.

She stepped out of the way of the door. If he was sharp enough to know she had lied to him, he should be sharp enough to figure out why.

"Did you move from someplace else nearby, or are you new to Pittsburgh?" he inquired, firing off the question as if he feared it would be his last.

He was correct. "I'm new to the area," she admitted, adding

no details. She pulled the door up to her side.

He moved backward. "I see. Well, if you ever need anything—directions, pizza coupons, extra-strength Tylenol—don't hesitate to ask, it's a friendly neighborhood. Any of us would be happy to help."

The door began to close. "Thanks for the advice," she responded. "And for your help this morning. Goodbye."

His return goodbye was muffled by two inches of wood. She turned around and leaned her weight against the closed door. Adam Carmassi wasn't stupid. He would get the message and leave her alone. Maybe his gregarious nature would be an asset. Maybe he would tell everyone else to leave her alone, too.

She let out a breath and crossed to her bookshelves. It had been a harrowing day, and she was still on edge. But there was nothing wrong with her that couldn't be fixed by some down time with a good read. She had done little else the last week besides pack and unpack boxes, many of them loaded with books. Perhaps she had overdone it.

Her fingertips grazed the spines of her favorites, then came to rest on *Watership Down*. Perfect, she thought, removing it. An escape into fantasy would be welcome.

She turned toward the bedroom, and her gaze moved again over her collection of family pictures. Their visibility was no accident. She had shelved the pictures as she always did, prominently at eye level. Her childhood had been a happy one, and the early images—especially her parents' wedding portrait and the picture of her and Dee with Santa Claus—always brought comfort. Her nuclear family was gone now, but her uncle and three of her grandparents were living; and their portraits, if not their communication, reminded her that she was still a part of something.

The small photograph on the far right was different. It had been taken at Dee's high school graduation, and though Sarah had been careful to replace it in its proper position each time she moved, she could seldom bring herself to look at it. Now, with the memory of her sister's suicide fresh in her mind, she found her eyes drawn to the smiling, eighteen-year-old face.

Dee had died just a year later. She had suffered emotional

problems even before their parents' deaths, and she hadn't had the strength to cope. She had been counting on Sarah, but she hadn't trusted her. If she had, maybe things would have been different.

Sarah turned from the picture and clasped the book to her chest. She couldn't change the past. All she could do was remember her sister fondly. That, and keep her promise.

Don't worry, Dee, she thought, repeating the assurance that had, over the years, unwittingly become her mantra.

I won't tell anyone.

Chapter 4

With one arm, Adam Carmassi launched a foam basketball across his living room and up toward the plastic hoop that hung off the top of his coat closet door. The ball missed the basket by a good ten inches, dropped silently to the floor, and rolled out of sight.

He made no move to fetch it. He hadn't even noticed he'd missed.

Instead he rose and walked into the kitchen, where the leftovers he had been heating up sat in the microwave cooling down. The buzzer had gone off five minutes ago. He hadn't noticed that either.

What he had noticed, and the source of his continued restlessness, was the look in Sarah Landers' eyes.

She had beautiful eyes. Large and almond shaped, with deep-blue irises that shone brilliantly against her pale skin and dark hair. But the emotion he had seen within them was anything but beautiful. At first he told himself it was anxiety—over her health, the fall, the sight of her own blood. She was alone in an unfamiliar city. Of course she would be uneasy, even frightened.

But he knew it was more than that.

He popped open the microwave door, but didn't remove the plate. He simply stood, staring sightlessly at the mound of macaroni and cheese inside, the image of her eyes still front and center in his brain.

Terror.

From the moment she had first looked at him, even as she still stood by her mailbox, she had been oddly hesitant, and wary. When she regained consciousness after the fall she had been nothing short of terrified—and for all he knew it was his own approach, his misguided attempt to break the ice, that had pushed her over the edge.

She had been afraid of him.

He slid the plate out of the microwave, jabbed a finger at a tepid shell of macaroni, and slid the plate back in.

Afraid of *him*.

He touched a button. The microwave began to whir.

There were people who didn't like him. It was inevitable in his line of work, no matter how hard he tried. Anyone who expected him to be perfect was bound to be disappointed. But overall, he had a way with people. He prided himself on being able to get along with most anyone, even those who disagreed with his views. He had a short temper which occasionally got the better of him, but as far back as he could recall, even when he had been a hulking grade schooler—big for his age with wild curls down to his shoulders—no one had ever been afraid of him.

Why was she?

The words she had uttered repeated themselves in his mind. *Go away! Stop it! Dee, where are you?*

He couldn't shake them. Couldn't dispel the sour twinge of worry that had obliterated his appetite. She wasn't his problem. Not technically. He had done what any responsible person would do for a neighbor, and he'd been summarily thanked and dismissed. No further action was required. Yet his stomach remained in knots.

It shouldn't, he reasoned. Sarah was a stranger to him; her situation had nothing to do with what had happened with Christine. He should not even be reminded of it. The two women had nothing in common, either in appearance or personality. Sarah was unaffected and independent. Aloof. Witty. Proud.

Terrified.

Just like Christine had been.

The microwave buzzed.

Adam breathed out heavily. The fear that had haunted his wife's eyes would always be his cross to bear. He had seen it; but he hadn't paid attention. He had been too distant, too self-absorbed, too willing to pass it off as more baseless, effeminate drama. He could never forgive himself for that.

Sarah Landers was afraid of something, too. Deathly afraid. He knew that with certainty, even if he did barely know her. He couldn't pretend he hadn't noticed.

Stop hitting me!

He jerked as if someone had struck him, opened the microwave door, and pulled out the plate.

"Someone hurt her," he said aloud, confirming the suspicion he had been loathe even to contemplate. The thought of any woman being brutalized by a man sickened him. Yet the theory made sense. Such a history would explain her wariness, her fear of a well-meaning stranger. Perhaps even her loss of consciousness. She could have moved to Pittsburgh just to get away from someone. She could be hiding from him right now.

Adam sunk a fork into his macaroni, but made no move to take a bite. Instead he left the kitchen, crossed to his desk, and picked up the phone. He couldn't contact Sarah himself again—not tonight, nor even tomorrow. Any more overtures from him would only alarm her further.

But that didn't mean he was powerless. He wouldn't let himself be.

Not this time.

Chapter 5

Sarah gazed out her front window the next afternoon, scanning the cul-de-sac for signs of life. She saw none; not even at Adam's house. She chastised herself for spying on her neighbors and turned away.

It was a dreary Sunday, with constant, sticky rain choking the stagnant air. For the sake of her health she had sworn she would do nothing strenuous, including more unpacking, but the vow was proving difficult to keep. She couldn't walk outside; she couldn't garden. Worse yet, a stubborn residual headache made her eyes hurt after even a few minutes of reading, and her cableless television offered nothing besides baseball and two-star movies—diversions far too weak to displace the grim replays of yesterday from her mind.

The clang of the doorbell surprised her. She stepped over and peered through the peephole.

Her eyes were met with a bold splash of fuchsia—a shiny running jacket with matching shorts. The legs exposed were lean and tanned, and from the waist down, one might have guessed the woman attached to be a fit forty-something. The deep crows' feet and sagging cheeks on the face above were more telling, but if the woman hadn't announced her age quite proudly at their first meeting, Sarah would never have guessed her neighbor to be seventy-three.

Sarah stood still a moment, hesitating. She liked Rose, and the prospect of having some intelligent—and unintimidating—company to converse with was tantalizing. But she was not in the habit of inviting guests inside her home. She had always guarded the privacy of her apartments with zeal, instructing visitors to meet her in the lobby or, better yet, scheduling social meetings elsewhere. But she had no lobby now. And she could hardly entertain in the rain.

She took a breath. There was no need to be defensive. Surely, in a house this large, she could accommodate one elderly guest without feeling vulnerable. The foyer could serve as a lobby, and she could offer Rose a seat on one of the bar stools at the kitchen counter. The sunken living room and bedroom beyond could remain private.

She swung open the door with a smile. "Rose! How are you? Won't you come in?"

The older woman smiled back, displaying a set of teeth far too perfect to be real. "I hope this isn't a bad time to visit, but I just wondered if you'd gotten moved in all right." She stepped inside and extended a foil-wrapped parcel.

Sarah shut the door and accepted it.

"It's zucchini bread," Rose explained. "I'm overrun with zucchini this year. Consider it a belated housewarming gift."

Sarah studied the heavy loaf in her hands dubiously, not sure what to do with it. Potato pancakes and carrot cake she had heard of, but making bread out of a vegetable was new to her. Nevertheless, the gift afforded the perfect opportunity to steer Rose toward the bar stools. "Thank you, but it's hardly belated. I haven't even finished unpacking yet."

She led her guest toward the kitchen and placed the concoction on the counter. But when she turned around, Rose was no longer behind her. The other woman was already stepping down into the living room.

"I've always loved this floor plan," Rose mused, surveying the area with admiration. "Harold had no decorating sense, of course. Martha didn't either, for that matter. But this house has its own sense of character."

Sarah's heart pounded, even as she cursed her paranoia. She knew that by most people's standards her desire for privacy was over the top. No matter how uncomfortable Rose's prying eyes made her, she could hardly scream at the woman to get back up the steps. She needed to relax. Everything would be fine.

"Would you like a drink?" she offered hopefully.

"No thank you, dear," Rose replied pleasantly. Her eyes scanned the full wall of bookshelves, then fixed on Sarah's collection of family portraits. She smiled broadly and stepped toward them.

Sarah froze in place.

"Are these your grandparents?" Rose asked, pointing to the nearest frame.

Sarah took a breath, forcing herself out of her trance. Everyone had family pictures; there was no reason hers had to be kept behind closed doors. Inquiring about a hostess's family was a perfectly ordinary thing to do.

She put one foot in front of the other until she reached Rose's side. The portrait in question was an old photograph of her father's parents, taken before he had been born. The bright young faces in the picture bore little resemblance to the maniacal couple who had swooped into Sarah's life at her father's funeral, bemoaning their agnostic son's certain descent into hell. She preferred not to recall the latter.

"Those are my father's parents," she explained. Then she pointed to the portraits nearby. "My mother and father are in the middle, and her parents are to the right. My parents died when I was a teenager." She kept her voice even. Whenever anyone brought up the topic of parents, she attempted to beat them to the punch—before they put their foot in their mouth.

To Sarah's relief, Rose did not overreact to the revelation. She merely nodded, letting her eyes drift over the rest of the photographs for a few more seconds before speaking again. "My own mother died when I was twenty. My father married again, but my stepmother and I never got along. In retrospect, it was my fault. I was hell on wheels."

Rose's tone was casual, matter-of-fact. Sarah felt herself smile a little. "Surely not."

The older woman flashed a wicked grin. "You have no idea, my dear. Get to know me better, and I'll tell you all about it." She leaned forward, taking a closer look at Sarah's parents' wedding picture. "Was it a car accident?"

Sarah swallowed. Most of the time, she didn't mind talking about her parents. Deep down she knew that being open—at least about the things she could be open about—was therapeutic. But today her baseline of anxiety was already high.

"No. It was a private plane, piloted by a friend. They were on their way back from a conference—they were both university professors. Some combination of pilot error and mechanical failure. We never knew for sure."

"I'm sorry," Rose said sincerely. "I'm sure it's harder when it comes as a surprise. I've lost a lot of loved ones, but I've always had warning. I even got warning of my own death; but then, that turned out to be greatly exaggerated."

Sarah's eyebrows rose. She was grateful for the change of topic, but had no idea what to say.

Rose snickered a little. "I got all ready to die eight years ago. They told me I had ovarian cancer. So I called my first husband's mistress and told her I forgave her, then sold some stock, took a cruise, and had a one-night stand with a widower from Des Moines. Wouldn't you know it—as soon as I got back and got under the knife, they told me the pathologist had made a mistake. My ovaries were fine. I was going to live after all."

Sarah was silent a moment, absorbing the story. "You must have been ecstatic. And furious."

"Damned right I was furious!" Rose said sharply. "I called that worthless tramp right back up again and told her to go straight to hell."

Sarah cracked a grin. "I meant furious with the pathologist."

Rose waved a dismissive hand in front of her face. "Oh, no. My second husband was a urologist—I know doctors are only human. It's not like the ovaries were doing me any good anyway."

Her eyes moved to the picture of Dee.

Sarah tensed again. "My sister committed suicide shortly after our parents died," she offered, anticipating the next question. "And no, it wasn't an easy time for me, but I managed."

Rose's gray eyes fixed studiously on Sarah. "You're a fighter," she said, her tone admiring. "I would have guessed that. Takes one to know one." She returned her gaze to the pictures. "Where did you grow up?"

A flicker of suspicion swept through Sarah's brain. Rose's

questions weren't out of line, but the timing was curious. Could Adam have sent Rose over to check up on her, perhaps to determine whether she had family nearby?

She forced herself to dismiss the notion. Why would he?

"I grew up in Alabama," she explained, doing her best to sound nonchalant. "Around Auburn University, mostly. My parents both taught there."

"A Southern girl," Rose said with approval. "Lovely. I've never known anyone from the deep South before. You'll have to make me some grits someday. Are any of your relatives still there?"

Suspicion flickered again, but Sarah doused it. She had no reason to keep her dearth of nearby relatives a secret. "I'm afraid I'm not a big fan of grits, myself. But I do make a mean country-fried steak. As for relatives, my father's parents still live in Alabama; my other grandmother and my uncle live in Georgia. That's about it."

She didn't tell Rose that she hadn't seen or talked to her father's parents since her sister's funeral, nor did she mention that her maternal grandmother had been in an Alzheimer's facility for years and that her uncle was a grade-A asshole. The point was the same. She had nobody local.

"And what about you?" she asked swiftly, determined to redirect the conversation. "Do you have family nearby?"

Rose stepped away from the pictures and nodded. "I never had any children of my own, and both my husbands are gone now. But I do have stepchildren from my second marriage. They were grown when Dean and I married, but they adopted me anyway. So did the grandchildren—and the great-grandchildren." She smiled. "They're a delight when they visit, but I have to admit, I prefer living alone."

"So do I," Sarah said quickly, sensing a kindred spirit. "I work with people all day long, but in the evenings, I enjoy my solitude. And my books."

Heartened, Sarah turned back toward the kitchen and gestured for her guest to follow. Her plan was to put the zucchini bread in the refrigerator, offer Rose another drink, and then hopefully engage her in a rousing discussion of good literature.

But those things never happened. One second Sarah was walking across the room. The next, everything went black again.

"Sarah? Sarah! Wake up now. Nap's over."

Cold hands patted her cheeks. A voice, sharp and insistent, stirred her brain back into consciousness. She focused her eyes on Rose's tightly pinned hair, a hodgepodge of dark brown and mousy gray streaks, then moved her gaze to the other woman's thin, smiling lips. The face was upside down.

"Well, thank heavens," Rose said flippantly. "Fainting spells I can handle. Comas are another matter. Are you all right?"

Sarah was lying in a crumpled position on the gold, seventies-era carpet, which to her good fortune was made of extra-thick shag pile. Her hand flew immediately to her head, but the wound hurt no more than usual. The only part of her that ached was the hip opposite the one she had bruised yesterday—and that pain was mild. She shifted her weight to sit up, realizing only as she did so that her head and shoulders had been resting on Rose's lap.

"I'm so sorry," she sputtered. "I didn't fall on you, did I?"

"Not entirely. I wouldn't say I caught you either, but I did keep you from banging your head again. How do you feel?"

Sarah struggled to her feet, and Rose went with her. "I feel fine," she said truthfully. Unlike before, she felt neither dizzy nor addled. Those symptoms had probably come from the head wound, not the—.

Her heart began to race. *The whatever it was.*

"What happened exactly?" Sarah asked, marveling at how easily the septuagenarian had gotten to her feet. Rose must have moved quickly to break her fall; it was a miracle neither of them had been hurt.

"You turned around, took a few steps forward, and then started to sway," Rose answered, gesturing for her to have a seat on the couch. Sarah complied, and Rose sat beside her. "I only got to you a foot from the floor. If you'd fallen forward, I wouldn't have had a chance."

Sarah's face flushed with embarrassment. "You must be quite an athlete. Thank you."

Rose's pale eyes, though worried, sparkled a bit. "I've been a professional dancer since the fifties, dear. I ought to be."

Sarah's eyes widened, and she opened her mouth to ask another question. But Rose interrupted her. "How many times has this happened?"

The suspicion Sarah had been battling shoved itself to the forefront. Rose did know what had happened to her yesterday. Had she not just said "banging your head *again?*"

Sarah allowed herself a deep breath. So, her new neighbors *had* conferred. Adam had told Rose about the episode, probably encouraged the visit. Perhaps he knew that Rose would be a more welcome guest than he.

Sarah's heart continued its pounding. A part of her felt duped. Her privacy, her anonymity violated. But another part of her was warmed. Two people she barely knew had conspired in what they believed to be her best interests. She couldn't help but be touched.

"This is only the second time," she answered. "I guess Adam told you about the other one."

Rose nodded, admitting her knowledge without apology. "He was worried about you. Now, so am I. When are you supposed to see a doctor next? Do you have some sort of follow-up scheduled?"

Sarah hesitated. The ER physician had instructed her to follow up with her PCP, but even as she had nodded her assent, she knew that she probably wouldn't. She didn't have a PCP, and besides, she didn't plan on having any more problems.

"I'm sure it's nothing," she assured, standing. She walked toward the kitchen again, bracing at every step for another surge of blackness. None came. Physically, she really did feel fine. "Are you sure you won't have something to drink?" she asked, pleased at the opportunity for a rewind.

But Rose was nobody's fool. "Passing out twice in as many days isn't nothing," she said firmly, rising herself. Her forehead puckered; her gray eyes turned steely. "What are you, a man? Women are supposed to have better sense about such things. You need help, you get it. Simple as that. Now, who's your doctor? Or don't you have one yet? No—of course you don't."

She marched to the kitchen counter, picked up a notepad and a pen, and started writing. "I have the perfect internist for you: Dr. Charles Payne. He's young—well, young to me—he knows his stuff, and he treats old ladies with respect. What more could you ask for?"

She ripped off the sheet and handed it to Sarah. "His number's in the book. Try to get in soon. You'll feel better when you get some answers. The number at the bottom is mine. If anything like this happens again, call it. Or else just yell loud. I'm only a stone's throw away."

Sarah accepted the slip of paper. "Thank you."

Rose stared at her skeptically. Her tone turned earnest. "You shouldn't be driving, you know."

A heaviness settled in Sarah's middle. This couldn't be happening to her. She was healthy; she always had been. The blackouts were something temporary—something she ate. She *had* to drive. There were no two ways about that.

"I have to drive," she responded flatly.

Rose's eyes remained hard. "That's what I told my stepkids. They didn't buy it either. 'Rose,' they said, 'you're probably one of the healthiest seventy-year-olds in the state of Pennsylvania, but you can't see worth a damn, and you know it.' I can see just fine, of course, as long as I'm looking straight ahead. But when it comes to seeing things to the side, I can't tell an Irish Setter from a fire hydrant. I told the kids I didn't plan on running down either one, but they kept after me until I admitted that my driving was a risk to innocent people." Her eyes bore into Sarah's. "And right now, so is yours."

Sarah's face felt hot. All at once, she wanted to be alone again.

"I appreciate your concern," she responded, working hard to keep her voice from faltering. "But I'm sure I'll be fine by tomorrow morning. I've just been working a little too hard lately, that's all."

Rose's lips didn't smile, but there was a twinkle in her eye. "So like me," she said heavily. Then, without instruction, she turned and headed for the door. "Well, I've got to get going. If you need anything at all, just give a yell." She opened the door and turned around. "Whether you drive or not is entirely your decision, my dear. By the way, what does your car look like?"

Sarah's brow furrowed. "It's a blue Civic."

Rose nodded, then gave a devious wink. "Right. I'll go warn the neighbors."

Chapter 6

Sarah walked up the steps from her garage, entered the kitchen, and tossed her purse and keys on the counter. There, prominently displayed, lay the slip of paper she had left home this morning without. The name of the doctor she was supposed to call—the name she had been wracking her brain to remember.

She slid her new phone book out of the drawer. It was five-thirty in the afternoon. She still had a shot. Her fingers fumbled with the thin pages, and she let out a muttered curse. Her hands were shaking. She was as jittery as a wind-up toy on a tile floor.

You had no business driving.

Don't you think I know that?

She had been battling with her conscience all day. This morning, her stubborn side had won out. The side that had insisted the risks of her driving were both minimal and greatly outweighed by the inconvenience of the alternative. Hadn't the taxi that brought her home from the hospital been overpriced, filthy, and twenty-five minutes late? She couldn't afford to be late to a new job, she had told herself. Rose had been overreacting. She had been downright snarky.

She located the listing for Dr. Payne. She began to dial.

Her stubborn side had been all talk. Not five minutes into the commute she had found herself holding the steering wheel in a death grip, her knuckles white with tension, her foot poised to release the accelerator the instant she felt a twinge of anything. The drive had been the longest twenty minutes of her life, and the return trip had seemed even longer.

Are you insane? You could have hurt somebody! How selfish can you be?

The doctor's line began to ring. She took a deep breath. Her hands were still trembling.

She wasn't driving again. No way, no how. Not until some doctor figured out what was happening to her, and how to keep it from happening again. She didn't have to pass out to be dangerous. As uptight as she was, she could be hazardous with a can opener.

The ringing stopped just as a loud knock on the front door sent her leaping from the floor. She exhaled with frustration at her jumpiness.

"You have reached the offices of Drs. Payne, Ladbrook, and Abernathy. Our offices are currently closed. Operating hours are Monday through Thursday, nine—"

Too late. She hung up the phone. The knocking noise came again, this time louder. She moved to look through the peephole. It was Adam Carmassi.

She stepped back. Despite everything he had done to help her, her instinctive reaction to him was still apprehension. He just looked too blasted much like the man in her nightmares. But she would have to get over that. They were neighbors, and such irrational fear was no longer acceptable. A show of irritation at his pounding on her door, however, was justified.

She put her eye back up to the peephole and saw that his hand was raised to knock again. She let him finish the next few pounds, then pulled open the door. She didn't ask why he hadn't used the bell, or why he felt compelled not just to knock, but to beat her door into submission. She was pretty sure the look on her face expressed her feelings.

His hands dropped to his sides. "Sarah," he said, his voice gruff. "Could I talk to you for a minute?"

She surveyed him dubiously. His face was flushed, his eyes intent. If he had looked at her during their first meeting the way he was looking at her now, she would have run away screaming. Knowing better, she held her ground. She looked back at him levelly and said nothing.

He moved back, rubbed his hands briefly over his face, and cleared his throat. When he spoke again, his tone was even. "I'm sorry. I guess I should have used the bell."

She made him sweat a moment longer. "Is my house on

fire?"

He cracked a grin. "No. Not as far as I know, anyway. Can we talk? Please?"

Her anger softened. There was something about his smile that comforted her, though she found it difficult to qualify. When his face was alight with humor, he looked like no one but himself: the wisecracking Good Samaritan. His asking Rose to check on her yesterday had been a genuine act of chivalry, and she did appreciate it. The least she could do in return was let the man say his piece in the air conditioning.

She stepped aside and swung open the door, but placed herself carefully to discourage his entering any farther than the foyer.

He complied beautifully. "Rose tells me you passed out again yesterday," he said as he stood, breathing hard. "Did you see the doctor she recommended?"

Sarah stared at him. She wasn't sure what to say—whether to thank him for his concern, politely ask him to leave her alone, or both. Had they not had the same conversation at least once already?

Before she could answer, her phone rang.

"Excuse me," she said, shaken. She moved mechanically toward the unfamiliar sound. Almost no one called her cell phone—she always gave out her work number. The call had to be either an emergency or a mistake. Keeping one eye on Adam, she picked up the phone from the counter.

"Hello."

"Hello? Is this Sarah Landers?" The young man's voice was unfamiliar, but his accent—even five words of it—pegged his geography. He was a Mississippi boy.

Her pulse quickened. She answered in the affirmative.

"This is Josh Myers. I'm an intern here with Sherman and Sylvester in Montgomery. I just got back from your farm out by Auburn. Mr. Sherman asked me to run by and take a look at the place—see if it looked like you still had any stuff left out there. He figured I ought to give you a call."

Sarah watched nervously as Adam began to drift out of the foyer. "I'm sorry," she interrupted, "but this isn't a good time—"

"This won't take long," the young man insisted, unfazed. "But you need to know that whatever you got left in that house after next week is going to auction. If that's fine by you, then there's no problem, ma'am. But I know some people would rather—"

Her blood ran cold. "Auction?" she repeated. "They were supposed to destroy the place. It was condemned."

"Well, yes, ma'am," the voice drawled. "But they don't just bulldoze a whole house and throw a little dirt on it, you know. If there's anything inside worth selling, the county's going to want to make a buck. Now, I'll be honest with you—it didn't look to me like there was much left worth selling, at least not that I could tell from the outside. But Mr. Sherman told me to make sure you knew how it was going to be handled, because some people don't care for other people picking through their things like what happens at some of these auctions—"

The images shot through her mind like daggers. Pushy women huddling over her parents' antique vanity, picking through her mother's costume jewelry with chipped fingernails. Smirking men, pocketing her father's screwdrivers. Her great-grandmother's quilts heaped into a filthy box, being dragged up to the podium. People everywhere, swarming the grounds…

She felt sick again. She hadn't thought about what would happen to the things she left behind, much less how it would happen. Like a fool, she had envisioned it all simply disappearing. It would be one thing for her family's belongings to be boxed and given to charity. But for the wretched county to—

"Ma'am? You still there?"

She collected herself. "I'm here," she answered. "Is there anything I can do to prevent a public auction? Legally?"

He was silent for a moment. "Well, you don't really need the law. As long as the place is still yours, you can clean the stuff out yourself and leave them nothing to sell. But you've only got eight days left, ma'am."

"Eight days," Sarah mumbled.

"Mr. Sherman did tell me to make clear that you'll have to

handle any arrangements like that yourself," he continued apologetically. "We're a law firm, you know—not a moving company."

A moving company. Hope flickered.

"Thank you for calling, Mr. Myers," she finished.

"Sure thing."

She replaced the phone on the counter, her eyes fixing on the phone directory. She could hire a mover, have them bring everything left in the house up here. She still had time.

"Sarah?" Adam asked. "Is everything all right?"

Her chin jerked up. She had forgotten him. He was standing on the opposite side of the counter looking at her with the same perceptive brown eyes that had rattled her on their first meeting. He had heard everything she'd just said.

Her heart thudded in her chest. *Get rid of him. Now.*

"Everything's fine," she said briskly, walking around to face him. "Refresh my memory. Why did you come over?"

His dark eyes studied her face, and despite the mask of concern he was wearing, a grin played on his lips. "Righteous indignation."

Her eyebrows arched. He had lost her. "What?"

He took a breath. "Rose called me this morning and told me that you'd passed out again. She also told me that she wasn't sure, but that she thought you had driven yourself to work. She was under the impression that you weren't taking what had happened seriously enough. When I saw you pulling into your garage just now, I got angry, which is why I pounded on your door. I apologize again for that."

She shook her head in disbelief. "You got angry because I was driving? You barely know me. Why would you care?"

He stared back at her. "It's my job to care."

"And what job is that? Neighborhood busybody?"

"No. I'm a minister."

Her eyes widened. He might as well have told her he was a woman. Or a lion tamer. Or an alien.

"Oh, please," she retorted without thinking. "You are not."

His gaze remained unflinching. "I don't know whether to take that as a compliment or an insult. What would you guess I do for a living?"

Her eyes surveyed his muscular form, his dark skin, the unruly black curls. "I don't know," she floundered. "Something with the Mafia?"

He didn't smile.

A pang of remorse hit her gut like a bomb. Her personal religious bias was one thing, but that had practically been an ethnic slur. What was she thinking?

Before she could speak again, however, he surprised her with a chuckle. "I've got to say, I've been accused of a lot of things, but organized crime is a new one."

"I'm sorry," she said sincerely. "I didn't mean that the way it sounded. It's just—" she hadn't a clue how to explain herself. Her exposure to ministers, of any kind, was limited. She had never been a churchgoer. Her father had reacted to his parents' lunacy by renouncing organized religion as a whole, and her mother, who had been born into a long line of non-practicing Catholics, had never bothered to argue with him. Reading fiction had left her with an image of ministers as fragile, middle-aged nerds, even though the few she had met in the flesh were actually plump, Bible-thumping types with loud voices and judgmental stares. Neither portrayal was consistent with lifting weights, much less stripping half naked to mow a lawn.

"You don't look like a minister," she defended meekly.

He looked down, making a pretense of surveying his khaki slacks and cotton shirt. "Well, what would you suggest? I'm a Methodist, and Protestants don't do the collar thing. I'm not even wild about ties. I'd wear jeans to work if I could, but the ladies in the office frown on that, and the last thing I need is to tick them off, believe me."

She digested his words slowly. The man really *was* a minister. No wonder he hadn't been around on Sunday. No wonder he knew people at the hospital. No wonder they had believed him when he said he hadn't assaulted her.

She breathed out with relief. She had been suspicious of the man's over-the-top interest because she assumed he was after her body. But he was getting paid to be nice.

"I'm…really sorry," she stammered. "I must look like the world's biggest bigot. I just—" Words failed her again. "I had no idea."

He offered a shrug. "No big deal. You forget about the door-pounding thing, and I'll forgive the dig at my Sicilian grandmother. Deal?"

She paled.

He laughed out loud. "Just kidding. Grandma Carmassi was born in the Bronx. But she does have a penchant for Godfather movies."

She narrowed her eyes at him, though with a grin. His good humor was infectious, and she suspected that, under different circumstances, his wit could be highly entertaining. But right now, she wanted to be left alone. "All right," she said evenly, crossing her arms over her chest. "So you're a minister and I'm a librarian. Now that we have our professions straightened out, I can help you discharge your duties. You raced over here to tell me I shouldn't be driving because it isn't safe for the public. Check. I agree with you. It was stupid, and I won't do it again until I'm sure I'm okay. Now, is there anything else?"

He looked back at her with an expression she couldn't quite read. At some level he seemed amused by her, but at the same time, there was a grimness in his eyes. "Did you see a doctor today?" he asked quietly.

Her pulse sped up. She avoided his gaze. "No, I couldn't get an appointment. But I'm going to call again tomorrow."

"Passing out twice in forty-eight hours could be serious, Sarah."

His voice was deadly calm. Intense. She didn't like it. "I said I would get an appointment. What more do you want?"

"I want you to take this seriously."

"I *am* taking this seriously!"

He stared at her for a moment, and she stared back. All at once she had the strong impression he wasn't thinking about her at all. He was thinking about something—some*one*—else.

He turned his head. The moment ended.

When he looked back at her, his expression was cheerful. "I'd be more than happy to drive you to work tomorrow, or to the doctor's office—whatever you need. My hours are flexible; it's no trouble. I make a passable chauffeur; just ask Rose."

Sarah's heart skipped a beat. Now that she no longer feared his intentions, she had to confess she was tempted. But she hadn't moved to Pittsburgh to make friends. She had moved to Pittsburgh to get away from them. "I can't ask you to do that."

"You didn't. I offered. I'm also offering to introduce you to a friend of mine—a member of my church—who's an internist. She's a very sharp woman; if you're not already set on Rose's doctor, I know you'd like her. Plus, if you're worried about taking too much time off work, I know she wouldn't mind trying to fit you in around lunchtime tomorrow. What do you say?"

She had nothing to say. She needed a ride. She needed an appointment ASAP, and one at lunchtime would be perfect. Furthermore, she had a strong preference for female physicians. But none of that really mattered. She couldn't keep taking favors from Adam, even if he was a minister. She didn't like being dependent on people.

She opened her mouth to decline, but he interrupted. "As long as you don't need to leave here any earlier than eight-thirty…" he began.

She was on the excuse in a flash. "Oh well, I have to be at the library by eight. And it takes at least fifteen minutes to get there."

He donned a wide grin. "No problem. I'll pick you up around seven-thirty, just to be on the safe side."

He made a beeline for her door.

It took her a moment to realize she had been duped.

"*Reverend* Carmassi," she called out, following him. "Are ministers supposed to lie?"

He let himself out, then tossed a response over his shoulder. "No. But I was pretty sure you'd interrupt me before I finished."

She watched as he jogged across her lawn, seemingly anxious to get out of earshot while ahead. She smiled briefly, then clenched her jaws in thought. Perhaps she could accept a few friendly favors in a crisis, provided she kept her guard up.

Tomorrow, hopefully, she would get a diagnosis and could resume driving. Everything would return to normal, and she could go on with her new life in Pittsburgh, isolated and self-sufficient, just like she had planned.

For however long it might last.

Chapter 7

"So, any chance you're looking for a church?"

Sarah glanced at her watch. Four minutes. She had been in Adam's car all of four minutes before he'd delivered his pitch—just as expected. And he'd looked itchy after two. It was amazing he had restrained himself until this morning.

She cleared her throat. "I think we should get something straight," she began, prepared. "I don't go to church. I never have. I'm not an atheist or anything, but I'm just not into it. I respect your decision to be a minister, but I don't want to be lectured about hellfire and damnation any more than you want to hear about the Dewey decimal system. All right?"

His face showed no expression. It took him a moment to answer, but when he did, his voice was sober. "And what if I *am* interested in the Dewey decimal system?"

She tried hard not to smile. She knew that if she was to spend any amount of time in his company, there would have to be ground rules. First off, for her own comfort, was "no evangelistic badgering." She did find religion interesting, in the academic sense, but she had absorbed far too much of her father's cynicism to make Adam's recruitment efforts worth either of their time. Second, and most importantly, they would have to maintain an emotional distance. For both their sakes.

"I think we understand each other," she responded. "Do you happen to have the number of that internist you mentioned? I was going to call her as soon as I got to work."

"No need," he announced. "Melissa said she'd see you at noon. It's all set. But you do need to call the ER and ask them to fax your records over." He retrieved his wallet from the dash, pulled out a business card, and handed it to her. "I thought I'd pick you up at the library at a quarter till twelve.

Hopefully, we can get you back to work by one. Sound okay?"

Discomfort scrambled her insides. Adam seemed intent on pushing her boundaries. "It sounds fine, thank you. But you don't need to do me any more favors. I can handle things myself from here on out."

He nodded, but his smile was sly.

She sounded like a broken record.

Sarah watched as Melissa Gardner, M.D. flipped through the faxed pages stuck inside Sarah's medical chart. From the questions asked before the exam, Sarah knew that the doctor had already read the report from the ER. The current perusal was at least her second pass.

Sarah waited nervously, her eyes fixed on the ceramic broach pinned to the doctor's white lapel. The painted face of a golden retriever stared back at her, tongue lolling. The pin was hopelessly gaudy, yet somehow endearing—as were the black sneakers and white gym socks that poked out from beneath the doctor's too-short slacks.

Melissa was not a physically attractive woman. She was short and stocky, with dull brown hair and a complexion that bore witness to an acne-plagued adolescence. Her sober manner and severity of expression suggested intelligence and perfectionism of the first order, despite her choice in fashions. But behind the doctor's thick-lensed glasses, her bright hazel eyes shone with compassion.

After what seemed an eternity, she raised her chin. "All right, Sarah," the deep alto voice began calmly, but firmly. "Here's what I see. You've lost consciousness twice in a short period of time, which in itself isn't unusual for a woman your age. What is unusual is that your history, and the tests that were run, all seem to be pointing away from the more common causes. That leaves us with the more uncommon ones. And I'm afraid they're not always easy to diagnose."

Sarah swallowed. "Like what?"

"I'm concerned about your heart. Specifically, some sort of arrhythmia. The EKG you had was normal, but the problem with an EKG is that it only records over a short period of time. If an arrhythmia is intermittent, it can go undetected."

"An arrhythmia," Sarah repeated. Her heart sped up as she spoke, then began to thump violently against her breastbone. The irony of the response did not escape her.

Melissa nodded.

"That can be serious," Sarah murmured. Dramatic stories of young athletes dropping dead loomed large in her brain.

The doctor nodded again. "Yes, some arrhythmias can be very serious. But they *can* be treated. There's no need to panic—we just need to figure out exactly what's going on."

Sarah willed her heart to slow down.

Willing didn't work.

Melissa began scribbling on the chart. "We'll get you set up with a 24-hour Holter monitor. If your heart shows any disturbances while you're wearing it, we'll know. I'd also like you to have an echocardiogram, so we can check your heart for structural problems."

The words blurred in Sarah's head. *Don't panic. Can be treated.* More tests. More time. Naively, she had been hoping that today would be the end. She had been hoping that the doctor would hold up some colored test strip, say "aha," and send her home with pills. Or better yet, announce that there was no problem— that the last four days had been nothing more than some bizarre, delusional mistake.

"What about driving?" Sarah asked. "I haven't had an episode for two days. Isn't there a chance that the problem was only temporary?"

Melissa's sharp voice left no room for argument. "Of course there's a chance. But not a good enough one to risk your life getting behind the wheel of a car. Not with a history like this."

Sarah's stomach felt like she'd been sucker-punched.

"You should avoid being in any situation where a sudden loss of consciousness would be dangerous," the doctor instructed. "I'm not saying you shouldn't cook dinner or do stairs, but now isn't the time to be cleaning out your gutters. And you shouldn't be operating a lawn mower, much less a car. It's just too risky, Sarah. If you do have an arrhythmia, you stand a very good chance of at least having some dizzy spells. You could also pass out again with no warning—just like before. Do you understand?"

Sarah breathed out slowly. "I understand."

"Lastly, you'll need an EEG, to rule out a neurological problem. You'll need to schedule that soon—it can take a week or so to get in."

A week. A week of dirty cabs. A week of turning down Adam's well-meaning offers of assistance. Over and over.

The doctor seemed to be reading Sarah's mind. "You're very lucky to have a neighbor like Adam," she said, her tone warming. "He told me you're new to the area. I know that worrying about your health now is inconvenient, to say the least. But you can count on him to help you out if you need it—he's a wonderful person."

"He's been very helpful," Sarah responded, thinking of how determined he had been to get her an appointment quickly. "Very concerned."

Melissa looked up. She seemed to have caught Sarah's unintentional emphasis on the last word. "Well," she responded gently, "I'm sure that's because of Christine."

Sarah's eyebrows rose. "Christine?"

The doctor offered a sad smile. "His wife. She died of a brain tumor. Most people don't take symptoms seriously when they're young—they just assume they're healthy, and that it must be nothing. Adam doesn't think that way anymore."

Sarah's stomach ached anew. "How old was she?"

"I don't know exactly; I never met her. I assume late twenties. It happened over a year ago, before he came to the church I go to."

"I see." A pall enveloped Sarah. No one should die of a tumor in their twenties. No spouse should have to live through it. She had no idea Adam had suffered so much, so recently.

A look of discomfort passed over Melissa's face, as if she wondered whether she had said too much. She averted her eyes. "We'll get that Holter monitor on you as soon as possible. And I want you to call the office right away if you feel even the slightest bit of dizziness or lightheadedness. If it happens after hours, or if you pass out again, head straight to the ER." She paused. "You live alone?"

Sarah nodded.

Melissa considered a moment, then bit her lower lip. "It would be better if you had someone with you. But if that's not possible, you should at least arrange for someone to check on you now and then. Make sure a neighbor or friend has a key to your house. And keep a cell phone within reach. Don't take stupid chances. All right?"

Sarah nodded again. But her mind was far away.

She gazed up at the wall clock in her still unorganized office. It was six o'clock. Adam would be waiting.

She gathered her things and rose. She hadn't intended to let him drive her home—not after driving her in, then transporting her to and from the doctor's office. She had intended to call a cab. But Melissa's words had left her reeling, and she had gotten out of his car without remembering to argue.

Yes, some arrhythmias can be very serious.

She didn't know what to feel. She didn't want to overreact. She didn't want to under-react. A part of her didn't want to react at all.

You could die, Sarah. With no warning at all.

The last words had never left the doctor's mouth. But they had hung in the air nevertheless.

I could die.

It was ridiculous. Silly. She was twenty-six. A mere five days ago, she had felt perfectly fine. She had plenty of problems, but poor health was not one of them.

She pushed open the door of her office and walked out into the hall. The library had closed an hour ago; the building was practically deserted. What would happen if she passed out right now?

She paused a second. She regrouped. She walked forward.

The workday had been completely unproductive, and if she had been her own boss, she would have fired herself. She hadn't been able to concentrate on library business no matter how hard she tried. Instead she had spent much of the day looking up and calling moving companies. To her distress, none had seemed eager to sign on for the clearing out of an unknown amount of furnishings from an abandoned home where no one would be available to supervise, and when she mentioned the necessary time frame, a few had even hung up on her. It was summer; everyone was moving. Why hadn't she planned further ahead?

She reached the library's front door. She opened it.

You never plan anything far ahead. You don't even have a will.

A flicker of fear raced through her brain. She had never even thought about making a will. Not because she didn't have money—both her parents had been heavily insured against accidental death, and Dee's suicide had made her their sole beneficiary. She had more assets than she knew what to do with, and once the county compensated her for the property it was seizing, she would have even more. If she were to die without a will, who would inherit it all? Her uncle?

Her teeth gritted. Her parents had not worked hard their entire lives just to pad Dwight Bird's retirement account. The man was so miserly he had tried to place his own demented but still physically active mother in a third-rate nursing home so that her care wouldn't drain all her savings before she died. If Sarah hadn't stepped in and insisted her grandmother go to a specialized Alzheimer's facility, the poor woman's mind would have deteriorated even faster than it had.

Uncle Dwight wasn't getting jack.

She had to write a will. Immediately. She couldn't risk leaving her grandmother without an advocate, without some care plan in writing. The woman existed now as little more than a vegetable; her son would shove her in a drawer if Sarah weren't around.

If I weren't around.

She breathed in with a shudder. If she were gone, her family's graves wouldn't be tended. Dee's favorite flowers wouldn't be put on her headstone every winter. No one would ever visit them again…

A coldness pierced her.

No one visits them now.

She stopped outside the double doors, staring blankly into the nearby bushes. Guilt pummeled her insides. It was true. She hadn't visited the graves in years. She had paid for flowers to be put out—but she had no way of knowing if they had been. She hadn't taken care of the farm. She hadn't preserved her family's belongings. Now, in a matter of days, the house and everything in it would finally, completely, be gone. And so, dead or alive, would she. Run out. Run away. Like a rat from a burning barn.

She felt herself shivering. She *had* to go back. But how could she? She couldn't face that house again. She couldn't stand in that living room, remembering—

A man's hand clutched her arm.

Chapter 8

Adam Carmassi jumped back as if he'd been struck. If he hadn't moved so quickly, he probably would have been.

"I'm sorry," he soothed, holding up his palms. "I didn't mean to scare you. But the way you were—. When you didn't answer me, I thought you were about to pass out again."

Sarah stood several feet away, staring at him, breathing heavily. Her blue eyes, stricken with terror mere seconds ago, now flooded with remorse.

"It's not your fault," she said, her low, normally melodic voice reduced to a croak. "I just wasn't paying attention. I didn't…hit you, did I?"

"No." He would have liked to crack another joke. Make her smile, put her at ease. But nothing seemed funny. The second he had touched her arm, she had whirled on him like an animal in a trap, terrified beyond all reason, ready to defend her life. Almost expecting, it seemed, to lose it.

What the *hell* had happened to her?

They didn't speak for a while. It was unlike him, but for once, he could think of nothing to say. The doctor visit had clearly upset her. On the drive back to the library earlier she had done nothing but sit and stare out the window, and when he had asked her how it went she had dutifully answered—but in the guarded, listless tone of someone who doesn't care to think about what they're saying. *I need more tests. I won't be driving for another week.*

When he had tried to press, she had retreated, and he had given up.

Temporarily.

"Are you…ready to go?" he asked tentatively now, gesturing toward his car.

She nodded.

He studied her as they drove. He seemed incapable, in fact, of not doing so. The more time he spent with her, the more intrigued he became. Sarah had a strength about her that was incredibly rare in someone her age—a fierce independence, a determination to overcome. The sort of person on whom societal forces like peer pressure and materialism had no effect. She held herself outside of all that, piloting solely by her own sense of reason. And yet she was a paradox. Because in moments like the one he had just witnessed, her eyes betrayed a soul so haunted, so vulnerable, that one wrong move could shatter it like glass.

In those moments, his desire to help her swelled almost to a compulsion. It was in his nature to want to help anyone, but his zeal in Sarah's case was unusual. He knew plenty of ill people who needed transportation to doctor's appointments, and he was willing enough to provide it when asked—once in a while. But coercing a hesitant woman into accepting him as a regular chauffeur was not part of an ordinary day's work. Nor was taking advantage of a personal friendship in order to schedule a medical appointment over lunch.

He was overcompensating with Sarah, and he knew it. He had failed miserably with Christine, and that guilt still tormented him. It would continue to torment him whether he helped Sarah or not, and he knew that, too. But analyzing his motives didn't change what he was feeling. Not when the sight of Sarah's troubled eyes wrenched his insides like a dishrag.

As if reading his mind, she straightened. "I'll call the cab company as soon as I get home and work out a standing reservation. Dr. Gardner said that I should ask someone to check on me at home now and then, and I'm sure Rose wouldn't mind popping over in the evenings. But that's all I need at the moment. You've done far more for me already than I could ever have asked for. Thank you."

He looked back into her stony, determined face. Her false bravado wasn't fooling him—she could barely talk without her voice quavering. But she did seem bound and determined to shut him out.

He couldn't let that happen.

"Actually," he said with mock seriousness, "I'm still a couple points shy of renewing my good Samaritan license. I could help a little old lady across the street, but I can't move fast enough to keep up with Rose, and all the other seniors in the neighborhood still drive. That's why you've been such a find for me. It's okay if you take a cab to work, but if I could ferry you to just one more doctor appointment—that would be all I need. Any chance you'll have another this week?"

She stared at him, her almond eyes narrowing slightly. He could tell she was fighting a smile. "Are you always like this?" she asked.

His eyebrows arched. "Like what?"

"So…unministerlike."

He grinned. "And how would you know what other ministers are like? You said you'd never been to a church."

Amazingly, she grinned back at him. "Touché."

"You want to hear—"

"No."

"I was going to ask if you wanted to listen to the radio."

"No, you weren't. How dumb do I look?"

He could answer that question in a heartbeat. There wasn't one dumb thing about her. She was bright, articulate, and wise to his tricks. She even shared his sense of humor.

A queer sense of dread passed over him. Lighthearted moments with Sarah had been few and far between, but when she smiled at him, she seemed uncannily familiar. Almost as if they were old friends. As delighted as he was to know that he had cheered her, that particular sensation disturbed him.

He started talking again. "You look quite intelligent, actually. Which is why I was hoping you wouldn't let a little pride get in the way of your common sense. You don't like being dependent on other people—I get that. Most people don't. But how's a do-gooder like me supposed to get any satisfaction if everybody else in the world is completely self-sufficient? I mean, really. Have a heart!"

She rolled her eyes playfully, then let out a sigh. He watched as a lock of her long, straight hair drifted over her shoulder, then splayed across her chest.

With an effort, he moved his eyes back to the road.

Sarah was a difficult woman not to look at. Never mind that she made no attempt to attract the opposite sex. She wore no makeup, and her clothes, although flawlessly professional, were quite intentionally boring. But none of that mattered. It would take a man much blinder than Adam not to spy the subtle curves of her lean figure beneath the dowdy fabrics; not to be entranced by her smooth, almost feline movement. The very fact that she *didn't* decorate her body lent her a beguiling aura of earthiness, a fresh-faced, natural grace that drew the male eye like a siren.

He would definitely have to watch himself.

"Will you ask me if you need another ride somewhere?" he continued, keeping his tone light. "Please?"

She paused before answering. "Yes, I will. Thank you."

There was a new softness in her voice, and the sound of it warmed him. But the pleasure was short lived.

"The doctor—" she began, "I mean Melissa, your friend, told me about your wife. I'm sorry, Adam. Very sorry."

The temperature in the car around him seemed to drop. He felt as though he had stepped into a rain shower.

"I just want you to know," she continued, "that I understand what it's like to lose someone unexpectedly. I don't know if Rose told you, but I lost my whole family nine years ago. My parents and my sister. I know that's not quite the same thing, but still, I think I understand. You're young. You had plans. Now you feel cheated."

The rain around him turned to hail. Biting, driving pellets of ice. He knew he should say something, but he couldn't speak. Sarah thought she understood about Christine. But she didn't. No one did.

"I know you think I'm upset about my health," she offered. "But the fact is—" Her voice broke off.

With one glance he knew her thoughts were no longer with him, and the knowledge brought instant relief. Christine's death was the last thing he wanted to discuss with her. Sarah had been about to say something about herself, something important.

Seconds passed. She turned her head and stared out the window. He had almost given up hope of her completing the statement when she whispered, almost inaudibly. "I haven't visited their graves in years."

Her voice was suffused with guilt, and a cold twinge of pity twisted in his stomach. He swallowed. "Would you like to?"

She nodded.

He asked the next logical question. "So, why haven't you?"

She made no response.

He waited as long as he dared. Pressing her wouldn't work, but the moment was too precious to lose. He was searching for the right thing to say when she spoke again.

"I was supposed to take care of their things, but I never did that either. Next week it's all going to an estate auction."

Her voice was distant now, almost matter-of-fact. But the anxiety on her face was plain.

She's afraid to go back there, Adam reasoned, his mind racing. He remembered all too well the phone conversation he'd overheard the day before, though it had made little sense at the time. What was there in her hometown to be afraid of?

Perhaps *he* was there. The man who had hurt her. The man she had mistaken Adam for as she lay in her driveway, bleeding and delirious.

A flash of anger shot through him, and his teeth clenched. But he forced himself to concentrate, to keep the ire from his voice. He had to be careful what he said.

"It sounds like you've still got the weekend," he suggested. "Where are we talking about?" He knew she came from Alabama; he hadn't forgotten a single nugget of the information Rose had passed along. But it wouldn't do for her to know that.

She gazed sightlessly out the window, her mind still not fully in his company. "Auburn, Alabama. It's too far to drive in a weekend, even if I could drive."

"You could fly." No sooner had the words left his mouth

than he remembered that her parents had died in a plane crash.

"I don't fly," she confirmed, still not looking at him. "I mean, I haven't. Maybe I will someday. But I can't now."

He took a deep breath. The tone of her *maybe* struck a chord in him. It was a tone he used himself whenever he talked about hang gliding, bungee jumping, or any of the other dangerous amusements he longed to try. The calculated risk had always made them seem foolish, even indulgent—particularly when he had been married to a woman who depended on him so much. But his own fear wasn't absolute. Under the right circumstances, he knew he could be coerced. In fact, in the back of his mind, he was counting on it.

Sarah had every right to be leery of flying. But he was willing to bet she wasn't as afraid as she'd convinced herself she should be.

"Desperate situations call for desperate measures," he began. "It sounds to me like if you ever needed to fly, it's now. Wouldn't settling your unfinished business at home take a load off your mind?"

She turned her face farther away. It was a long time before she responded. "I would like to go," she said finally. "But it's impossible. Even if I did fly, I would still need to drive to get around down there."

Adam gazed at the quarter of her face that he could see, and the pain entrenched there stabbed at him like a knife. She was terrified, yes, but not about flying. She was afraid of the man who had hurt her, and her fear was preventing her from following her heart—from setting things right with her conscience. The conflict had to be torture. The driving thing was just an excuse.

He didn't think about what he said next. Didn't stop to consider, to debate. It was foolhardy, idiotic, and totally inappropriate, and perhaps because he knew that, he said it all the more quickly.

"I could drive you around."

Slowly, Sarah turned her head and stared at him. "In *Alabama?*"

He returned his eyes to the road. She had to think he'd lost his mind. Perhaps he had. His heart beat wildly, but he covered with a casual shrug. "Sure. Why not? I've never been to Birmingham. I was going to look for an E-saver flight to Chicago this weekend, but one's as good as the other."

He didn't add that he already had plans in Chicago. He had arranged to spend his long-awaited weekend off with a college friend, stroll The Loop, and take in a Cubs game. But none of that was set in stone. In fact, now it sounded boring.

He didn't look at her, but he could tell she was still staring. "You don't fly to Birmingham to get to Auburn," she corrected offhandedly. "It's quicker to drive from Atlanta."

He shrugged again. "Same difference. I've never seen Atlanta either, outside of the airport."

She was silent. He imagined he knew what she was thinking—she was struggling to find the proper words to tell him just how absurd the offer was. Minister or not, no man in his right mind would fly across the country just to be helpful to a new neighbor. Not without an ulterior motive.

He stole a glance at her face.

That was exactly what she was thinking.

He couldn't blame her. She wouldn't believe the truth, even if he could explain it. What he really wanted was to spend more time with her, to get to know her better, to earn her trust. Only then could he get inside her head enough to assuage that wretched look of fear in her eyes—and perhaps some small portion of the guilt that haunted his own.

"You can't be serious," she stated.

"Of course I'm serious," he answered, thinking fast. Convincing her that his motives were pure would be a challenge. No woman as attractive as she was could be unaware of the effect she had on men. She would never believe that he had no ulterior motive. His only shot would be to convince her he had a different one. Like, say, avarice.

"Who wouldn't jump at the offer of a free weekend away?" he proclaimed, cringing inwardly at his own brazenness. The ploy was both presumptive and rude, but if it worked, it would be worth it. "I love traveling; I just can't afford to do it much, and playing chauffeur to you would be a small price to pay for the chance to see a new part of the country. You'd have to give me a chunk of time to see the sights by myself, of course, but other than that I could drive you anywhere you wanted to go. You pay for my plane ticket, my motel room—and I don't mean some dive, I want something nice with a pool—and the rental car. I'll pay for my own food. What's there to see around Auburn?"

He assessed her reaction. She seemed flabbergasted. He decided to keep talking.

"Isn't the Civil Rights Memorial down there somewhere? In Birmingham?"

She blinked at him. "It's in Montgomery."

"Is that close to where you're going?"

"More or less."

He smiled to himself. Five whole seconds, and she hadn't said no yet. Clearly, she was tempted. A man who could be bought would seem like a man she could control. But he doubted she was convinced yet. And her house was only three doors down.

"You don't have to give me an answer right now," he offered. "I know it would be an expensive weekend for you. And you're probably worried about the flight. But you don't have to be. Air travel is still the safest way to go, statistically, and I'm good company on a plane. I got my brother—who is the world's most paranoid conspiracy nut—safely to LA last year, and he hadn't flown since nine-eleven. It's all about distraction."

He pulled into her driveway. She remained sitting stiffly, her face thoughtful. He caught her eyes and grinned at her. "Honestly, I'd love to go. But don't feel obligated just because I want to see the South. You don't owe me anything. If you decide my services are too expensive, I can still do Chicago as planned. No big deal. Just let me know by tomorrow so I can get an E-saver ticket."

She looked back at him, her expression searching. She was considering it, he could tell. The thought of having someone with her, even someone she barely knew, seemed to be mitigating her fear.

The man she was afraid of was in Alabama. He was sure of it.

But she didn't trust him yet, either.

She moved to get out of the car. "Thank you for the ride. I'll take a cab tomorrow. As for the—"

He was quick to interrupt her. "If you do need a ride anywhere else, call me. As for the trip, please, just sleep on it. I'll check back with you tomorrow. Goodbye, Sarah."

She stood a moment with her hand on the car door, looking at him with a gaze so studious he felt a strong urge to squirm. But his game face didn't falter.

She smiled superficially, returned his goodbye, and closed the door.

He watched her as she walked up the steps and into her house, her slender legs moving nimbly, her long, shiny hair bouncing along behind her. Whatever turmoil was going on inside of Sarah, her carriage was never meek. Her shoulders were always drawn back, her spine straight, her head held high. When she was still, she seemed fragile. But when she moved, she was lissome. The contradiction was fascinating.

Her image stayed with him as he backed his car out of her driveway, across the cul-de-sac, and into his own.

Excellent actor or no, he was going to have a hard time convincing Sarah that his interest in her was purely platonic.

He sure as hell couldn't convince himself.

Chapter 9

Sarah rang the doorbell. Her heart pounded against her sternum, and her hand went reflexively to the knobby leads taped to her chest. The thin wires were hidden under her shirt, and to an uneducated observer, the Holter monitor clipped to her waistband looked much like a MP3 player. But she felt like a cousin of Frankenstein.

The door opened within seconds. Adam greeted her as if he were pleasantly surprised.

"Do you have a minute?" she asked, once again willing her heart to slow. Willing alone never seemed to work, but she didn't have an alternative. It had been twenty-four hours since Adam had offered to accompany her to Alabama, and she owed him an answer. She was here to give it.

"Sure," he answered, gesturing for her to come in.

She entered the house's living room, then looked around, baffled. She was hardly knowledgeable in matters of interior design, as her own outdated house would attest. But the look of Adam's living quarters was so far off the mark, even she was struck. The room was furnished with dilapidated antiques, from spindly end tables to a scratched-up secretary, and the assorted high-backed couches and chairs were upholstered in faded patterns of roses and trefoils. The wallpaper consisted of dainty floral stripes, and the worn carpet was mint green. If she had to give the atmosphere a name, the best she could think of would be "little old lady."

He offered a wry smile. "What? You don't like my decorating?"

She couldn't think of a polite answer.

He chuckled. "I know, it's hardly me, but no one at the church has offered to redo it, and there are things I'd rather spend my money on. Besides, who knows? The next pastor in here might like the place."

She began to understand. "You don't own the house, then."

He shook his head. "No, the church does. I just live here. Would you like a drink?"

She threw him a wary glance. "Do you stock the refrigerator yourself?"

He grinned. "I have orange juice and diet cola. Take your pick."

"Juice, please. Thanks."

He dodged through a doorway into a small kitchen, and Sarah continued her perusal of the living room. With the exception of the plastic basketball hoop in the hall, it didn't look like it saw much living. Her eyes moved toward the wall over the couch, and a large silver frame caught her eye. She stepped forward for a closer look.

It was Adam's wedding portrait.

He and Christine looked young, barely in their twenties. The couple stood before a church altar, he with his arm wrapped tightly around his bride, she nestled into his side, both of them beaming with happiness. Adam wore a dignified-looking, classic gray tux, but with his black curls flying and a youthful glow to his face, he looked more Bohemian than clerical. Christine's white gown was equally traditional and modest in cut, though her petite figure, delicately boned and curved in all the right places, could only be played down so much. Her short, golden-blond hair framed her face in perfect, wavy curls, and her large, light-brown eyes were as gentle as those of a doe. Her cheekbones were high; her lips, full; her complexion, peaches-and-cream.

She was most the beautiful creature Sarah had ever seen.

"Here you go."

Sarah jumped a little. Adam had returned with her drink. As she took the proffered glass and stepped away from the portrait, melancholy enveloped her. He and Christine had looked so happy. The pain of losing her must have been unbearable.

"Your wife was very beautiful," she offered awkwardly. He

had seen her looking at the picture; it seemed inappropriate to say nothing.

His eyes flickered away from hers, his discomfort obvious. "Yes, she was." He turned and took a sip from his glass.

Sarah decided to change the subject. Her own history, if nothing else, had afforded her some insight into other people's grieving. Sometimes talking about the person you had lost felt good; other times, it didn't.

She spotted a set of diplomas on the wall behind the dining room table and crossed over to read them. "Master of Divinity, Pittsburgh Theological Seminary," she quoted, lightening her tone. "Well, what do you know? You weren't lying after all."

Her eyes moved to the second one, and her levity dampened. It was also from the Pittsburgh Theological Seminary. *Christine Reed Carmassi. Master of Arts, Religious Education.*

Adam cleared his throat. "We went to school together," he explained, making an unsuccessful attempt to sound cheerful. "We met in college, actually, then we both went to seminary. But she wasn't a minister, per se. Her interest was Christian education."

The sadness within Sarah deepened. Not only had Adam been married to the most beautiful woman on the planet, but he had found his soul mate as well.

Found, and lost.

She looked into his dark eyes. The pain within them was profound, and the sight brought an immediate moistness to her own. But she squelched the impulse, suspecting that he would dislike being the object of pity as much as she had when her own wounds were fresh. Reminders of loved ones didn't have to be sad.

"Beautiful *and* smart," she said with a smile, walking toward him again. "What possessed her to settle for you?"

His eyes brightened instantly. "Temporary insanity, I suppose."

"Must have been." Spirits bolstered, she took a long swig of her drink. She had been concerned that being alone with him in his house would be unsettling, but his physical appearance no longer unnerved her. When she looked at him now, all she saw was a genuinely kind person who had suffered a tragic loss—much like she had. "Can we sit down somewhere, maybe?" she asked.

"Of course." He started to wave her toward one of the antique chairs, then reconsidered. "Why don't we go downstairs? It's a little more—well, normal."

She shrugged in agreement, and he gestured for her to follow him down a narrow staircase off the kitchen. They stepped out into a finished basement that occupied the entirety of the house's footprint, the ground-level back wall having sliding glass doors that opened onto a concrete patio. The furniture downstairs was much like her own: inexpensive, mismatched, and chosen for comfort. An unimpressive entertainment system occupied one corner, the expected weight set, another. One wall, she noted with satisfaction, consisted entirely of bookshelves.

She sat down on the generously padded couch without being prompted, and he settled on the arm of a recliner opposite her.

"So how have you been feeling?" he asked. "Any more episodes?"

She shook her head. "I've been fine for three days now. Melissa says that if the rest of the tests come back normal, it will be okay for me to travel—as long as I'm not alone." Her hand itched to fiddle with the taped-on leads again, but she refrained. If he had noticed the contraption already, he had been tactful enough not to mention it. "That's why I'm here. I wanted to talk about what you suggested yesterday—about my paying your way to Atlanta."

His hand went to his mouth, and he rubbed his chin. It seemed almost as if he were trying to cover a smile. "You made up your mind?" he asked.

Sarah paused. His idea had seemed preposterous at first, and in many ways, it still did. If anyone had told her a week ago that she would voluntarily embark on a plane trip with a man, she would have laughed out loud. But this had been no ordinary week. What was left of her life had been turned upside down, and if her only chance to right it meant facing two phobias at once, so be it. Moving to Pittsburgh had taken strength, but she had found it. She would find the strength to do this, too.

"Yes," she answered. "I have."

She tried not to show any hesitancy. She could not completely discount the possibility that his offer might be romantically motivated, either consciously or subconsciously. But she had been careful not to encourage him in that direction, and his behavior had always been courteous. Whether he was attracted to her or not, she was certain now that she had nothing to fear from him. On that score, the long talk she'd had with Rose last night had put any lingering misgivings to rest.

Adam is an absolute lamb, my dear, the older woman had insisted with a dismissive flick of her wrist. *You couldn't be safer than with him. He's honest, and he's kind-hearted—he would never take advantage of a woman. Believe me, I know a skirt chaser when I see one. Hell, I was married to one. Adam's more like Dean, my second: discerning men who look for substance.*

Sarah didn't doubt the assessment. Rose was a very shrewd woman, and she had been Adam's neighbor—and his friend— for over a year. Melissa seemed equally fond of him, and even Sarah's own instincts, distorted as they were by her past, avowed his integrity. But his stated motive in making the offer still baffled her.

Do you really think he wants to go with me just because it's a free trip? Sarah had asked, frustrated. *Does he like to travel that much? Because if he's not planning to jump my bones, I really don't see what else he could get out of it.*

Rose hadn't laughed. Instead she had pondered the question, almost long enough to worry Sarah. But eventually, she had answered. Sort of.

Adam is the adventurous type, there's no doubt about that, but you can't always tell what's going to float a man's boat. When he flew to Seattle last fall I told him he should look up my sister—that she made the best lasagna west of the Mississippi and had a thing for Italians. I was only joking, of course. What young man wants to spend his vacation having lunch with an old widow? But damned if he didn't drop in on

Rhoda, and she got such a kick out of him she keeps pestering me to send him back.

Rose had fixed her gray eyes on Sarah then, her voice bittersweet. *I can't pretend to read the man's mind. But I do think that his getting away from here for a few days, spending time with someone his own age, would be good for him. He may seem content on the outside, but he's still carrying so much sadness…too much sadness.*

"Well?" Adam prompted, interrupting Sarah's thoughts. "Do I get a free trip, or don't I?"

She cleared her throat. It would be difficult, but she knew what she had to do. The offer he had dropped into her lap was too convenient, too fortuitous, to reject. Since leaving the doctor's office she had thought of little else besides the gravesites she might never visit again and the keepsakes that her absence would see thrown to a flock of bargain-hunting vultures. She couldn't rest until she had said one last goodbye—and proved herself brave enough to do right by her family.

"Here's the situation," she answered, keeping her tone professional. "I may need more help than you realize. I'll want to move some things from my parents' house to a storage unit. Nothing really heavy—but I don't think I could do it all by myself, either. It may take most of the day on Saturday. If you want, you could take me back to the motel in Atlanta and drop me off as soon as we're done, and then you could have Saturday evening and Sunday morning by yourself to see the city. But you might not have much more time than that. Is that a problem?"

He watched her for a long time, still half hiding his mouth behind his hand. "What about Friday night?" he asked.

"What about it?"

"Will you need me then?"

"I'm afraid so." His disappointment reassured her a little. If he wasn't interested primarily in sight-seeing, he was doing a darned good imitation of it. "Even if we go straight to the airport after work, we won't get to Atlanta before nine, and it's another two-and-a-half-hour drive to Auburn."

"Is the drive interesting?"

"No, not in the dark it isn't." She began to worry. She wanted to be honest with him, but if he withdrew his offer now, she wasn't sure what she would do. To survive such a trip, she would need more than just a chauffeur. "If you want more time alone," she suggested, "I could try to hire some moving help locally—"

He raised a hand. "I'm not complaining. I'm just getting the details straight. As far as I'm concerned, we're on. I can carry some boxes, no problem. Go ahead and buy the tickets."

Sarah smiled. But she tried not to smile too broadly.

"Anything else I need to know?" he asked.

"No," she responded. "That's all for now."

He didn't realize the appropriateness of his question. She didn't want him to know any more about her plans. On this journey, his ignorance was precisely what would make him so valuable. His alien presence would be her mental shield—firmly anchoring her to the here and now. She knew she couldn't set one toe inside that house without someone at her side to ground her, and though Adam was less than ideal, he would have to do. Returning bodily to the accursed place was bad enough, but slipping mentally into the past—reliving what had happened there—would be unendurable.

"Are you going to be okay with the flight?" he asked, studying her with concern.

She felt a flush of warmth. The more familiar the dynamic between them became, the odder it felt. When it came to nonprofessional relationships, she was out of practice. She didn't have male friends, at least not any who weren't old enough to be her grandfather.

"I'm a little nervous," she said honestly. "But I'm not really worried about the danger. My parents died in a four-seater operated by a private pilot; I know how risky that is relative to flying commercial. Driving is riskier too, and I've spent plenty of time crisscrossing the Midwest in a compact car. The only reason I've put off flying for so long is—"

Her voice cut off. It was more information than she wanted to give.

"What?" he prompted.

She didn't want to say it. He would misunderstand.

I'm afraid to do it alone. The words were on the tip of her tongue, but she fought them back. How pathetic would it be to tell him the truth? That in all the years since her parents had died, he was the first person who had offered to fly with her? That despite all the mental exercises she had put herself through, poring over statistics and battling superstition, she still couldn't face the thought of boarding an airplane by herself? She knew what would happen. No sooner would the plane begin to sink down from the sky than she would find herself mentally reliving her parents' last moments, imagining the horror they must have felt...

She had never been able to do it. But she believed that she could now, as long as someone was there to distract her. Someone who understood.

"I don't know why," she lied. "I guess I'm just a procrastinator."

He offered a smile. It was a we-both-know-I'm-not-buying-that smile, but it was a kind one, nevertheless. His eyes twinkled as he looked at her.

She felt suddenly antsy. "Well, thank you for the drink. But I need to go. I have plans to make."

She rose and handed him her empty glass, then headed up the staircase and picked her way through the antiques toward the door. He followed at a polite distance, but seemed reluctant to let her leave.

"So," he chatted, "What kind of weather can we look forward to down there?"

"It'll be hot."

"It's hot here."

She laid a hand on the doorknob with a chuckle. *"Right."*

"Will you call me with the details?" he asked. "Do you need a ride anywhere in the meantime?" His voice was merry; his enthusiasm about the trip, plain.

She pondered Rose's assessment. Maybe he was just happy to get away. From what she had seen of his belongings, he wasn't rolling in the kind of discretionary income required to travel for fun. As much as she had acted the lunatic lately, it was difficult to imagine him enjoying her company. But perhaps the company didn't matter to him. She of all people could empathize with the desire to experience someplace new, any place devoid of painful reminders.

At least one of them could enjoy the trip.

"Yes," she answered, pulling the door open. "And I don't think so, but I'll let you know."

"Great. Goodbye, then."

She returned his goodbye and closed the door behind her.

Chapter 10

Adam watched as Sarah attempted to settle herself in the middle seat, her body pulled as far away from his—and the window—as she could manage. He was glad the aisle seat was empty, but he feared it might not stay that way. The plane was still loading.

"I don't remember these seats being so small," she commented, her voice strained. Her face was pale; her manner, anxious. He had been trying to make her comfortable with small talk ever since he had picked her up at the library, but his efforts were failing. She was strung so tightly that he was almost nervous himself, and he loved to fly.

"That's probably because *you* were smaller," he quipped. "Unless you used to fly first class?"

She looked at him as though he had called her a spendthrift. "Of course not," she retorted. Then her eyes filled with alarm. "You don't normally fly first class, do you?"

He laughed out loud. "Um, no. I consider myself lucky not to be in cargo."

She seemed to relax a bit. Then she pulled the emergency instruction card out of the pocket in front of her and began to read it. He really wished she wouldn't.

"Would you like the window shade open or closed?" he asked, determined to distract her before she hit the part about procedures for a water landing. She looked up at the window, but didn't answer. The question appeared to be a tough one.

"The way I see it," he explained calmly, "you have two options. You can either focus on the realities of the flight, we can talk about it, and you can try to enjoy the fun parts, or we can both pretend we're somewhere else and avoid the topic completely. It's your call."

She thought for a long time. But before she could answer, his fear was realized. The occupant of the aisle seat arrived.

"Hello, there!" the man boomed. He thrust a large duffel bag into the overhead compartment, then dropped his over six-foot, over two-hundred-pound body into his seat, spreading one long leg and one meaty arm well into Sarah's territory.

She shrank into the center of her cushion like a clam.

Adam sighed. Mercifully, the man did not appear interested in engaging Sarah in conversation. He merely clicked his seat belt into place, unrolled the magazine he was holding, and began to read. Yet the proximity of any large, unfamiliar male seemed enough to put Sarah at stroke risk. Her blue eyes had already been wide, but now she sat stiff as a board—her pupils dilated, her hands clenched so tightly that her knuckles blanched.

"You know, Sarah," Adam said smoothly, unbuckling his seat belt. "I think it would be better if you sat by the window. Then if you do decide you want to look out, at least you'll have a good view."

She looked at him with frank relief—and appreciation. "Thank you," she whispered, adroitly pulling up her legs and maneuvering behind him and into his seat as he rose. "I think I would like to see the view."

She zipped up the window shade and turned to stare out at the tarmac, her body pressed against the side of the plane as if she wished to escape through it. Adam moved into the middle seat and exchanged a polite smile with the stranger. The two men fidgeted a moment, attempting to jockey their equally broad shoulders into semi-comfortable positions.

Adam tried not to sigh again. It would be a very long flight.

"I think the last plane I flew on was a DC-9," Sarah remarked, polishing off the last drop of her complimentary coffee.

They had been in the air for over an hour now, and much to Adam's surprise, the time had passed swiftly. Sarah had weathered takeoff like a soldier, stony-faced, but resolute. Once they had broken through the clouds into the azure sky above, her nerves had seemed to settle, and for the last half hour, she almost seemed to be enjoying herself.

"How do you know?" Adam asked. Her sudden desire to lead the conversation was another surprise, and a pleasant one. Perhaps it was the caffeine hitting her veins, or perhaps a delayed effect of her anxiety. Either way, he was enjoying it. Not that he minded holding up more than his half of a conversation—he prided himself on being good at that. But being granted a little window to her soul was a promising step forward.

"Because I'm pretty sure there were only five seats in a row on that one," she answered. "From what I remember of the outside, it was either a DC-9 or a 737. But 737s, like this one, have six seats abreast."

He cracked a grin. "So even though you haven't flown since you were a kid, you've been reading about airplanes?"

She smiled back. "I've spent most of my life in libraries. I've read about everything."

He couldn't resist. "Even theology?"

Her gorgeous eyes narrowed at him. "Yes, that too. But I'm *not* going to discuss that particular subject with you, so forget it."

"I thought you said you weren't interested in religion."

"I'm not."

"So why do you read about it?"

She uttered a growl.

He chuckled. "Okay, sorry. What else do you like to read about?"

She thought a moment. "Travel. I'd love to see Europe. And China. The Sydney harbor in Australia, with a side trip to Tasmania. The Amazon. A glacier. There's not much I wouldn't like to see."

Adam straightened. Her voice, in the blink of an eye, had changed. She had begun by sounding upbeat, almost playful. But her tone had quickly deteriorated to a wistfulness, a soberness, that chilled him. She wasn't listing the destinations as though she were looking forward to seeing them. Rather, she seemed to be bemoaning what she knew could never be.

Was she that worried about her health? She had insisted to him before they left that the additional tests Melissa ordered had shown nothing wrong. His own uneducated assumption was that her problems were the result of previous trauma, though he hadn't voiced that. With a flash of fear, he wondered if she were hiding a grimmer truth.

"We're talking entirely too much about me," she said, her voice back to cheerful again. "I want to hear about you. Why do you like to travel?"

He wrestled with the desire to call her health claims into question, but decided against it. He was supposed to be keeping her in-flight attitude positive. "What's not to like?" he responded with a shrug. "Flying, driving cross-country. Seeing new things, meeting new people. I'd like to get to all fifty states, but I still lack thirteen of them. I've only been overseas once, on a mission trip to Ghana. But I'd love to travel more. As for Sydney, I've wanted to climb the Harbour Bridge ever since the 2000 Olympics."

"So you're a thrill seeker," she announced.

The designation startled him. "Well, no, I wouldn't say that."

The pilot's voice came over the PA system, announcing that the plane was beginning its descent into Atlanta. Sarah immediately turned and shut the window shade with a snap.

"Do you like roller coasters?" she asked briskly, a new note of anxiety in her voice. Had her parents' plane crashed on landing?

"Sure, I love them," he answered, assuming she was inviting distraction. "But I haven't been on one in ages."

"Why not?" she fired back. "There's a whole new generation of thrill rides out there now. Some really do make you feel like you're flying. I read that at Kennywood in Pittsburgh, there's a ride where you free-fall on cables from a 180-foot tower. Have you done that?"

She was talking fast, as close to babbling as a normally reticent individual could get.

"You mean the Sky Coaster," he answered, making sure his

own voice stayed light. "No, I haven't. But I've always wanted to."

"Then why haven't you?"

The plane's nose pitched downward, and his ears popped. Sarah pushed her back flat against the seat, her hands clutching the armrests. He knew he should keep her talking, but she'd picked the wrong topic. The last thing he wanted to do, right now, was explain to her how much Christine had loathed any amusement that smelled even halfway dangerous, how she had nearly gone into apoplexy when he told her he wanted to try out the Sky Coaster. He hadn't done a lot of things he'd wanted to do when they were together, and since she had died, the thought of running straight out and doing them seemed disrespectful.

"The timing just wasn't right, I suppose," he hedged. Then he came as close to a lie as he cared to get. "Besides, I couldn't find anyone who wanted to go with me, and things like that aren't as much fun if you're alone."

She looked at him. Her face was anxious, but not miserably so, and her grip on the armrests had slackened. "Yes," she offered. "I know how that goes. Still, you should try it sometime. I'm sure it's safe, and it would certainly be something to remember."

The plane's engines revved. Adam raised his voice. "You have plans to go to Kennywood this summer?"

She seemed shocked. "Oh, no."

He laughed out loud. "Well then, you've got some nerve jumping on my case!"

The plane lurched, its nose tilting still farther down, and Adam anticipated Sarah's reaction with dread. But she seemed to be holding her own. "I suppose I am a hypocrite," she agreed. "I read about all the rides, and they sound like fun, but I can't see myself ever actually going on any of them."

"And why not?" he baited.

Her eyes flashed with an emotion he couldn't put his finger on. "It's not that I'm afraid of the risk," she insisted, her voice firm. "I'm not. Really. It's just that I don't feel like—"

Her voice broke off, and Adam waited with frustration. Her

unfinished sentences were maddening.

"It's just not for me," she concluded.

Adam gritted his teeth. That was *not* what she had been about to say. What she had been about to say would undoubtedly have helped him understand her better. But every time the woman got close to accidentally saying something meaningful, she caught herself just in time. It was an irritating talent.

"Well, if you ever *do* decide to try the Sky Coaster," he ordered, "give me a call. I'm not afraid of it either—I just need a little push. You don't have a high-pitched scream, do you?"

"I wouldn't know," she answered. "I've never screamed."

The landing gear came out with a thump. Sarah's face paled for a second, then flushed. She leaned away from Adam and pushed the window shade back up.

He watched her curiously as she gazed out the window, her forehead nearly touching the glass. Around her he could see the myriad lights of Atlanta, twinkling through the darkness below. Her lips curved into a smile.

"Makes a pretty picture, doesn't it?" he offered.

She made no response. But the unexpected joy in her face spoke volumes. She continued looking out as the plane lowered, drawing back only when the first touch of wheels onto asphalt brought a jolt to the cabin.

"The engines will get louder again while we're braking," he advised, unsure how much about landing she remembered.

She sat back in her seat quickly, her slender fingers with their short-trimmed, unpolished nails holding the end of the armrest between them in another death grip.

He watched helplessly, fighting a natural desire to cover her slight, trembling hand with his own. He knew better than to touch her. Her reaction to his innocent gesture at the library was not something he wished to see repeated, particularly within the confines of an airplane. If he were to win her trust, it would have to happen from a distance. The irony of him, a stereotypically demonstrative Italian male, being chosen for such a challenge did not escape him. But he wasn't complaining.

"Just a couple seconds more, and we'll be stopped," he assured. The plane shuddered and roared, then finally, slowed. The lights of the airport terminal appeared outside the window, then began passing by at a leisurely pace. They had landed.

Adam watched as Sarah let out a long, slow breath.

"Are you all right?" he asked.

She looked straight ahead rather than at him. "I'm fabulous," she answered. Her cheeks were a healthy pink again; her face was glowing. "I did it."

He smiled. "Yes, you did."

She breathed heavily, the rise and fall of her chest drawing his attention, not for the first time, to the soft, clingy shirt she was wearing. Before he could force himself to look away, he was startled to feel her hand squeeze his wrist.

"Thank you," she said, releasing him so quickly he wondered if he'd imagined it. The gesture was a reflex, and a stiff one, but it was still significant. She *was* beginning to trust him.

"You made the whole thing so much easier. I appreciate that," she continued. "I'm sorry I was so uptight. The way back will be better, I promise."

"Does that mean we can debate theology next time?"

"No. But it does mean I won't chatter in your ear like some brainless twit." She glanced at her watch. "How long till they let us out of here?"

He suppressed a grin. Sarah the Independent was back now, in all her glory. "Unless you want to break your leg jumping onto the tarmac, you'll have to wait until we get to the gate. I suggest you relax. We're in the back of a full plane—it's going to take a long time to unload everybody."

She sank back onto her seat cushion.

"I'll get you to Auburn tonight, don't worry," he finished, his voice optimistic. "With the time change, we might even make it to the motel by midnight. Provided no one loses our luggage."

Her expression clouded. "There's no hurry," she said distantly.

Adam clenched his jaws. For all of thirty seconds, she had

been happy. One mention of their destination, and her face had drained of joy.

He knew better than to ask what—or who—she was dreading. But he had every intention of finding out.

Chapter 11

Sarah drew back the thick motel curtains and squinted into the sunshine. Not a cloud was in sight. The day would be hot, hazy, and brutally humid, like every other July day in southern Alabama would also be.

She raised her freshly brewed cup of coffee to her lips and took a long swig. Within seconds her stomach protested, the dull ache that ordinarily festered there being punctuated by a new, sharper pain. Most likely, her ulcer was coming back.

She wasn't surprised.

The drive in from Atlanta had seemed endless, and she had hardly slept even when her head did finally hit a pillow. Adam was being nice enough, but keeping all knowledge of her past from him was proving more taxing than she had thought. The man wouldn't give up, and a half hour into the ride she had had no choice but to feign sleep. She couldn't rebuff any and all polite inquiries without seeming paranoid, but she hadn't yet devised a competent cover story, either. That brainstorm hadn't come until around 3:00 AM, when she had stumbled out of bed and scratched the idea down on a piece of motel stationery before she could forget it.

She knew that Adam didn't understand why she had waited so long to come back. He had to think her a horribly neglectful daughter, and when he saw the state of the farmhouse today, he would probably think her unstable as well. *Why didn't you just sell the place?* He would ask. *What use has it been serving, abandoned all these years?*

They were legitimate questions, but honest answers were not an option. She would say whatever she needed to say to satisfy his curiosity. Then she could conduct her business in peace, and they could go home.

Her eyes swept over the courtyard, where a man was removing his shirt in preparation for a dip in the pool. She noticed that he was well built, as she did occasionally with men who were a safe distance from her at the time. Only after he finished pulling his shirt over his head did she realize it was Adam.

She turned away from the window.

Half an hour. In half an hour they would meet in the lobby as planned, and the day's ordeal would begin.

She took another sip of coffee, and her stomach cramped.

"So," Adam asked jovially, gazing at the vista through sunglasses as he drove, "how long did you say it's been since you were down here?"

She turned her head away with a sigh. Not only did the man waste no time, he was as subtle as a ton of bricks. Last night she had pretended to fall asleep on that question. Now she was stuck, but at least this time she was prepared.

"Five years," she responded. "That's when my aunt and uncle divorced. After that, things got complicated."

"Oh, I'm sorry. Complicated how?"

She took a breath. The mix of fact and fiction she was about to deliver could be tricky. "My aunt was wonderful to me after my family died. She supported me through that summer, helped me get settled in at college, and brought me back to their house for holidays and school breaks. But Uncle Dwight, my mother's brother, was and still is a narcissistic clod. Shortly after I graduated from college my aunt finally gathered enough gumption to divorce him, which was good for her but unfortunate for me. She and I lost touch, and I was left to deal with him directly."

She stole a glance at Adam and was puzzled by the worry on his face. The whole point of the story was for him *not* to be concerned. Furthermore, she hadn't even gotten to the sticky part.

"Why don't you get along with your uncle?" he asked.

"I told you," she answered, working hard to keep her voice

casual. "Because he's a jerk. My mother never could tolerate him either. He's the epitome of egocentrism. Everything is all about him, all the time."

"Does he still live here?"

Her eyebrows arched. It seemed a strange question. "No, he never did. He lives in Atlanta."

Adam opened his mouth as if to ask something else, then changed his mind. He seemed confused.

She decided to finish laying out her story before she got confused herself. "I wanted to sell my parents' house from the beginning. I just couldn't see myself ever living there again, and neither my uncle nor my grandmother wanted to live there, either. But the decision wasn't mine alone. Legally, I had to have my uncle's approval, and he insisted we should try to rent it out instead. Of course, he never did anything *about* renting it out, so it just sat there. Every time I visited, even when my aunt was still around, he and I would argue about it. After she left, he paid someone to board up the house and change the locks. He kept telling me he would get a new set of keys for me, but he never did."

Adam said nothing. His eyes were on the road, his brow creased into a frown of concentration.

"I should have come down just to visit the graves, but I couldn't bring myself to do it, knowing that the house was here, falling apart, and that I couldn't even get inside it. I never intended to wait so long between visits, but the idea of fighting with my uncle again was so off-putting…time just got away from me."

"Which way do I turn?" Adam asked, hesitating at an intersection.

She pointed towards the cemetery.

He turned the car, but didn't look at her. "You mentioned an estate auction. What's that all about?"

Sarah nodded. At least this part was easy to explain. It was true.

"It turns out that Lee County settled the sale issue for us by condemning the whole farm under eminent domain. They're building a new section of the bypass, and it's supposedly going to cross right over the property. I tried to protest it, but I lost. Now I've only got a few days left to recover whatever I want from the house."

"You got the keys from your uncle, then?"

She stiffened. Such pesky, unanticipated details were likely to keep plaguing her. "Yes, he finally mailed them," she lied. "Turn in here—it's just over the hill."

The car pulled into the cemetery, and as her eyes moved over the familiar rows of upright stones, another ache gnawed at her middle. Adam didn't speak as she directed him through the narrow, snaking lanes and showed him where to park.

"I'll be about fifteen minutes," she said, keeping her voice strong as she stepped out of the car. "You can wait here or you can drive around, whatever you want to do." *Just don't follow me. All right?*

Adam stood up and shut the car door behind him. He removed his sunglasses, then wiped his brow with the back of his wrist. "You were right. It *is* hot down here."

She smiled a little. "This is nothing. It's still morning."

He looked at her, but didn't smile back. "If you're sure you want to be alone, I think I'll take a walk around. But don't worry about me. Take all the time you need."

She assured him that she would, he replaced his sunglasses, and they parted company.

She ambled a bit, avoiding the actual plot in question until he was a distance away. It was silly, she supposed, but she didn't want him anywhere near her family's resting place. It was one thing to lie to a person as you rode along in a rental car. It was another to do it while standing over your mother's grave.

As the double-wide, gray granite headstone came into view, she held her breath. But as soon as she neared it enough to confirm the presence of a vase of flowers at its base, she exhaled with relief.

Her parents' plot was well tended. The grass was cut, no weeds were growing, and the headstone hadn't been chipped. The flowers she had paid for in January were holding up well, and there were no signs of vandalism. She walked up to the stone, placed a hand on its sun-warmed surface, and smiled.

Beth and Stephen Landers would be pleased. They hadn't wanted anything fancy, just dignified. They had died unexpectedly in their prime, but Sarah had always taken comfort in knowing that their lives to that point had been full. Both had been respected in their fields and well liked by their students, and one university association, after raising a significant amount of money in their honor, had even named a scholarship after them. They had died doing what they loved, and they had lived with no regrets.

Perhaps that was why, whenever she visited their grave, her sadness was tempered by a sense of peace.

She lifted her eyes, and her stomach roiled. She put a hand to it and turned.

Dee's grave was not directly beside their parents'. It was ten yards or so away, beneath a tree. Sarah began to walk toward it. Her limbs felt heavy, and her mind began to race.

Be calm, she ordered herself. *You're not a teenager anymore.*

She reached the smaller, heart-shaped stone and stopped her feet before it as abruptly as a soldier. *Deanna Elaine Landers. Born March 11, 1983. Died May 23, 2002.* A spray of purple silk orchids adorned the stone's base, just as requested. The burial plot, too, was perfectly tended. But this time, Sarah didn't smile.

Her sister's grave would never bring her peace.

Unlike the death of their parents, Dee's passing had been no accident. Dee had killed herself because she didn't think she could trust her sister, and that was something Sarah could never forget. It was also something she couldn't easily forgive.

She bent down and adjusted the flowers. Purple orchids had been her sister's favorite. A macabre choice for a girl, but that was Dee. Always wanting to shock people, shake things up. It had been a tough job with parents as liberal as theirs, but somehow Dee had always managed. Like when she had painted the walls of her room with alternating black, green, and magenta stripes. Like when she had refused to go to college. Like when she had turned down a decent-paying clerical job with the university to work the counter at Hardees.

Like when she had started dating *him*.

A flash of light on metal arose in Sarah's mind, forcing its way in as if thrown like a javelin. Smooth, shiny chrome. The glint of moonlight. Wheels in mud. Dee's ragged, heavy breathing. His cruel, twisted face.

Sarah jerked upright. She opened her eyes wide and scanned the cemetery, forcibly replacing the images with real ones. *Sunshine. Green grass. Headstones.* Her pulse pounded in her ears.

It's not then, it's now. Cut it out.

A motor revved on the road nearby. She shuddered.

That's not him.

She whirled around, looking for any reassurance of where she was, who she was. But all that surrounded her were graves.

"I'm sorry, Dee," she said out loud, casting a cursory glance back at her sister's headstone. "I can't stay here any longer. I'm sorry."

Her feet headed toward the car in double time. She stumbled over a foot stone.

Maybe he's behind you.

"Stop it!" she snapped, whispering through clenched teeth. "You're *fine*. Just fine."

She reached the car and pulled the door handle with a jerk. A hot blast of air struck her full in the face—the result of a mere ten minutes of baking in the Alabama sun. She leaned in and looked for the keys. She didn't see any.

"Adam!" she called, straightening for a look around. "Adam?"

He was nowhere in sight.

She cursed under her breath. It might have been nine years, but nothing in the cemetery had changed. It looked exactly the same. The stones, the sun, even the houses that bordered it were no different than they had been on the days of the funerals. The whole purpose of bringing another person along was to make sure that what was happening to her now wouldn't happen. She would *not* relive that time again. She would *not* allow the images to pop up unbidden, overtaking her conscious mind. She would *not*.

She leaned against the closed car door. The side-view mirror gleamed in the sun.

Chrome fender. Moonlight.

"Adam!"

"I'm here." His calm, deep voice floated over from just behind the car. "I was taking a break in the shade." He gestured to a clump of trees nearby. "But frankly, the shade doesn't help much. Are you ready to leave?"

She looked into his friendly, sweating, Pittsburgh-origin, present-day face, and the frantic beating of her heart began to ease. "Yes," she answered. "Let's go."

Chapter 12

Adam turned on the car's air conditioner full blast, adjusted the vent toward his face, and leaned in for extra oxygen. The humidity was oppressive. He'd seen cooler days in Ghana.

He studied his passenger as surreptitiously as he could, concerned. Her reaction to the cemetery was unexpected. Visiting a loved one's grave could be a somber occasion, but somber hardly described Sarah's reaction. When she called his name she had sounded frightened, and he had sprung up half expecting to see someone confronting her. But she had been alone. Alone and terrified.

"This seems like a well-kept cemetery," he commented as they pulled out. "Was everything all right?"

"Everything was fine," she said sharply, looking away from him.

Adam squelched a sigh. It was incredibly frustrating that Sarah was still as likely to consider his concern for her a threat as she was to be comforted by it. Every time he thought they were getting closer, she would slam the door in his face again.

He had to be patient.

"So, where to now?" he asked, making an effort to keep his voice casual.

She paused before answering. "When you visit a new city, what do you do? Do you make up an itinerary, or do you prefer to just drive around and see what's there?"

The question surprised him. "I like to just drive around."

She seemed relieved. "Well, why don't you do that, then? I'm not quite ready to go to the house yet."

His eyebrows rose. "You got it. Sounds like fun."

Touring the small town of Auburn was indeed fun. He drove through Toomer's corner with its stately live oak trees, explored the quaint downtown and picturesque campus, and tooled around Jordan Hare stadium to catch a glimpse of the War Eagle. Then he swung about the town's outskirts for a view of the poultry farm, pig farm, veterinary school, and rodeo ring. He would have liked to have gotten out and walked some, but Sarah, who sat stiffly in her seat hardly paying attention, didn't seem amenable. He could have left her in the car, but since he didn't entirely trust her not to drive off with it, he decided to stay in the air conditioning. If he was going to be moving boxes in the heat of the day, he might as well preserve his strength.

"Would you like to stop and get something to drink?" he asked finally, spying a commercial area with plenty of options. He was parched.

Sarah looked around. "All this is new," she announced with more cheer. "A lot of things have changed since I lived here, but this is all new even since the last time I visited. Sure. Let's stop."

He pulled into a mom-and-pop chicken outfit, and they both ordered pink lemonade. Once inside the nearly deserted building, Sarah seemed more comfortable. She told him how much of what they had seen was new and explained a little of the university's history. But her narrative was oddly devoid of any personal references—no people she cared about, no places for which she felt sentimental.

He listened with a practiced ear. Sarah's low-pitched, musical voice was pleasant to hear no matter what she was saying, and when she was relaxed and confident, her clear blue eyes were equally captivating. But he knew darn well she'd been lying to him.

Her explanation of the situation that had brought her here didn't add up. If her mother "never could stand" this maligned uncle, why had she left him legal control over her property? Wouldn't his guardianship have ended when Sarah turned eighteen? And if selling the house truly had been Sarah's goal, why would she have protested the county's buying it?

The particular issues at stake were, quite obviously, none of his business. And yet, he couldn't help but wonder why she was trying so hard to mislead him.

"It must have been interesting going to high school in a small town swarming with college students," he said casually, content for now just to keep her talking. He didn't like being lied to, and the deception stung a little. But he'd never been one to take offense easily, and in this case he was willing to give Sarah the benefit of the doubt. She wasn't trying to hurt him; she meant only to protect her privacy. He could hardly blame her for that.

In the meantime, the lemonade was excellent and the aroma of frying chicken was making his mouth water, even if it was only midmorning. "Easy for a teenager to get into trouble, I bet," he teased.

She smiled a little. "It would have been much more tempting if my parents hadn't *expected* us to misbehave. My form of rebellion was choosing to be a bookish, tee-totaling square. Dee had it tougher."

Adam started at the name.

Sarah continued, not noticing. "The straight-laced routine wasn't for her, and since my parents were full-fledged hippies, she couldn't do that either. So she set her sights on 'trailer trash.' She was very intelligent, but she pretended no interest in anything even halfway intellectual."

"Your sister's name was Dee?" Adam asked before he could stop himself.

Sarah snapped to attention. "Yes. It was Deanna. Why?"

Adam's mind replayed the unpleasant image of Sarah lying flat on her driveway, the blood just beginning to trickle through her dark hair. *Stop hitting me! Dee, where are you?*

"Adam," Sarah insisted, "Why are you staring like that? What's the deal with my sister's name?"

His mind raced. He took a deep breath.

Dee. He had assumed that the assault Sarah had been reliving was a recent event. But her sister had been dead for nine years.

"You said her name before," he explained carefully. "After you passed out and hurt your head. You asked for her like you were looking for her, and you seemed to think that someone was hitting you."

The blood drained from Sarah's face. "I was delirious," she said defensively. "Who knows what I was saying?" She took a sip of lemonade, but her complexion hadn't half the color of the liquid in her straw. "I do still dream about my sister occasionally. I'm not surprised her name would pop up."

Adam let out a breath. Despite the bravado in Sarah's voice, the hand that held her straw was trembling. She was like a china doll—a beautiful, yet rock-hard shell teetering gradually toward the edge of a curio shelf, boldly facing obliteration below. Every fiber of his body wanted to scoot back both their chairs, sweep her up in his arms, and hold her until the trembling stopped. But he knew he couldn't touch her.

Not unless she wanted him to.

"Sarah," he said, quietly but firmly, catching her eyes. "Please tell me what you're so afraid of."

She held his gaze for only a split second. Then she straightened her back, tossed her long hair over her shoulders, and folded her hands in front of her.

"I'm not afraid of anything," she announced coolly. She was obviously fighting to appear self-assured, but her efforts were wasted on Adam. Her words meant nothing when he could see raw terror swimming behind her eyes. "I just don't like being here. My parents died while I was living here, and my sister killed herself in the very house we're about to visit. You expect me to be having a great time? To be enjoying this?"

The attempt to make him feel guilty missed its mark. She hadn't started shaking because she missed her family.

"I know someone hurt you," he pressed, trying his best to sound supportive rather than threatening. "I could tell by the way you acted that day—and I don't just mean what you said. You were afraid of *me*, and everyone knows I'm a pushover. I'm telling you this because I can see that you're spending a lot of energy trying to cover it up, and there's no reason for you to do that. If you want to tell me about it, fine. If you don't, you don't have to. It's up to you."

Her eyes held his for several seconds—appraising, watchful, keen. Behind their brilliant blue irises, her mind seemed to be turning cartwheels. When she spoke again, her voice was calmer.

"Someone did hurt me," she said quietly. "But it was a long time ago. I suppose it's possible I flashed back to that after I fell. Both times I had head injuries, so it wouldn't be surprising."

She took another sip of lemonade. Adam said nothing.

"It happened when I was fifteen. Dee and I were at a pub she liked to go to—the grill made great burgers, so a lot of high school kids ate there. But the night I got hurt, a few twenty-something locals got really drunk. When the manager asked them to leave, they got belligerent. Dee and I decided to take off, but we never made it to the door. Somebody slugged somebody, and then it was chaos. One of the drunks was staggering around, swinging his beer mug and yelling, and he hit me with it. I really don't think he meant to hit *me*; I just happened to be there. But it was a dead-on hit to the side of my face, and I wound up with a fractured jaw. It took a long time to heal."

She stopped and took a breath. She studied Adam again. "Last week, when I came to in my driveway, my head throbbed. It felt like someone was pounding on my skull with a hammer. I was confused; I thought maybe you had knocked me out. I know that sounds paranoid now, but it was just a gut reaction."

Adam listened carefully, his breath measured. She'd come up with a darn good explanation for what she'd said in the driveway, he had to give her that. But she was lying again. No way was the terror he kept seeing in her, the near-panic he had just witnessed at the cemetery, caused by an accidental injury she'd received more than a decade ago. There was something else. And whatever it was, she still wasn't comfortable sharing it.

"So there's nothing here, in Auburn, now," he asked, "that you're afraid of?"

Alarm flickered in her eyes even as her face remained impassive. "Of course not. What gave you that idea? I told you, I have some unpleasant memories here, that's all. Surely you can understand."

Adam didn't think he understood much of anything. But he

had forced the issue as much as he could. For now.

"I'm sorry about what happened," he offered. "I can see how a memory like that might pop up under those circumstances." He polished off his lemonade and threw both empty cups away. "So," he said with forced cheerfulness, "what do we do now? Were you going to rent a trailer, or do you think the trunk of the car will do?"

Sarah stood. Her complexion had still not regained its full color, but her expression was resolute. "I'm not sure. I thought we might go to the house first and have a look around. Then I can decide what we'll need."

"Sounds fine," he said agreeably, smiling with a lightheartedness he didn't feel. Sarah was not the first badly traumatized person he had ever met; nor the first he'd tried to help. He was a professional counselor of sorts, after all. He had been trained in how to deal with others' grief and suffering, how to empathize without taking the pain on himself. He had gotten pretty good at it, actually.

But with Sarah, none of his usual tricks were working. Every time he looked at the woman, her pain gnawed at his very bones.

She slipped out from the behind the table and walked toward the door. He hesitated. Then he followed her.

Chapter 13

"Turn here."

Sarah held the aged leather key chain in her lap. She was aware that she was fidgeting, pressing each of the keys hard between her fingers, first in turn, then together. But she had to vent her anxiety somehow.

Adam had tried to talk to her on the drive out, but she supposed she hadn't been cooperative. He had seemed fascinated with the scenery—field after field of rolling hills; large, modern brick homes interspersed with aged wooden ones and trailers of every description. The pastures in which beef cattle grazed seemed particularly interesting to him, and he had marveled at the one-room shacks whose skeletons stood in their midst, crumbling and long abandoned, except by the occasional cow.

The car turned. Her muscles went taut.

The house's long, winding lane loomed before her. A shudder wracked her spine.

You are NOT going to react this way, she ordered herself.

"Looks like my uncle is a little behind with the bush hog," she commented, watching as weeds higher than her head engulfed them. And not just weeds. There were bushes in the yard. Saplings. The drive itself was peppered with so much breakthrough flora that in places the gravel beneath was obscured. Adam moved the car ahead slowly, the taller weeds between tire paths bowing to its fender, then scratching along its underbelly.

She couldn't even see the house.

She stole a glance at Adam. He looked as horrified as she felt.

"I was expecting as much," she lied, keeping her voice

steady. "My uncle kept telling me not to worry about upkeep, that he was taking care of it. But I always suspected he wasn't spending a dime on the place."

Adam was quiet for a few seconds, apparently having to concentrate to discern drive from non-drive. "Your uncle sounds like a real piece of work."

"Indeed," she agreed. So he thought the man was certifiable. What did it matter, so long as he didn't think she was?

"How far back is the house?" he asked, straining to see over the horizon of seed pods that capped the towering weeds.

"It shouldn't be much farther now," she assured, not having a clue. Nothing in this mess seemed familiar. She could be anywhere.

She wished she was.

"There," he announced finally, looking ahead. "I think I see it."

"Just keep following the drive," she instructed, still not seeing anything. "It will fork right in front of the garage; you can park there. The house itself will be off to the left."

When a small wooden building rose up before them, she hardly recognized it. Clapboard walls once painted white had peeled to a dirty gray. The whole lower right quadrant of the garage door was gone. The window in the storage loft held only shards of glass.

Adam parked the car and gazed out the driver's side window without speaking.

Sarah cleared her throat. The reaction she had feared had begun. Her heart was in overdrive. Her hands were sweating. A heavy weight descended onto her shoulders; her stomach burned.

You're going to take this in stride, she commanded. *You're going to keep Adam talking, and you're going to pretend it's no big deal.*

"What a mess!" she exclaimed, opening her door and hopping out. "Don't get me wrong, this was never a show place, but it's amazing what a few years of neglect will do, isn't it? Maybe you'd better not look when we get to the house—it could be a real disaster."

Adam stepped out of the car. Her chatter hadn't elicited a

smile. His face looked grave.

Her eyes drifted over his shoulder.

She could see the second story of the house behind him. Every inch of paint was peeling. Half the window panes were broken. The other half were gone.

You can do this.

"Amazing," she repeated tonelessly. "The attorney I hired to deal with the eminent domain told me the place had been vandalized—he didn't say to what extent."

Adam made no comment.

She put one foot in front of the other. She marched up what had been the front walk, pushing weeds out of her face as she moved. She could hear him following her. She reminded herself of her plan.

"Where did you live when you were little?" she asked. "What kind of house? Were you born in Pittsburgh?"

It took him a few seconds to answer, but when he did the very sound of his voice, with its alien northern timbre, reassured her. He was real. He was of the present. So was she.

"I was born in Slippery Rock, but I went to school in Plum, not far from your library. We had a typical Pittsburgh house; two stories and a basement, steep yard. My brother and I would have killed for a big flat area like this—it would have been great for football."

She almost grinned. The man was made of tact. "I suppose it would work better if it was mowed first."

"For football, yes. But I wouldn't be so quick to cut these weeds if I were ten. They'd make for one wicked game of capture the flag."

The playful tone in his voice soothed her further, and she imagined that her pulse was slowing. She wasn't alone, and she wasn't seventeen years old. Everything would be fine.

She reached the front steps. She climbed them. An empty chip bag crunched under her foot. She took a deep breath and looked around.

Trash was everywhere. The floor of the wrap-around porch was littered with cans and bottles of every description, rumpled grocery sacks, fast-food take-out containers, and cigarette butts.

Chunks of porch rail had broken off and were lying in the weeds. The adjoining windows were covered with plywood. The plywood was covered with graffiti.

She remembered having the windows boarded up. She had received a few angry letters from the county—something about a hazard or a nuisance—and she had hired somebody to seal the place tight. But she had no idea, now, how long ago that was.

She directed her eyes straight ahead. It didn't matter what was on the porch. There was nothing here she wanted. All she had to do was look for the storage chest in her parents' room. Then she could look for her father's paintings in the attic. She didn't have to go into her room. She *wouldn't* go into Dee's. She could walk through the living room and pretend it was nothing more than a hallway. And then she would turn around and leave.

As simple as that.

She fitted her keys in the locks. She pushed open the door.

It stuck at first, then swung forward on stiff hinges, releasing a cloud of dust from its swollen frame. *Don't look. Just go to the master bedroom.*

Keeping her eyes on the floor, she stepped forward.

The room was lit only by the sunlight pouring in from the open door. But that amount of light proved plenty.

The floor was covered with every kind of refuse imaginable. Beer bottles. Pop cans. Candy wrappers. Pieces of cloth. Pieces of wood. Pieces of things she couldn't identify. She couldn't help herself. She raised her eyes.

The living room, and what she could see of the dining room and kitchen, was unrecognizable. The furniture she remembered was gone. The recliners. The couch. Every stick of the entertainment center. The floor rug. The paintings on the walls. The dining room set. Only the heaviest, most oversized pieces remained—the china cabinet, the buffet. The only ones, she thought with repulsion, that couldn't be lifted through a smashed-out window.

She returned her eyes to the floor. Nausea overtook her.

"Sarah?" Adam said gently, his voice coming from

somewhere behind her. "Are you all right?"

She swallowed hard.

"No, I'm not all right," she answered honestly, forcing out each syllable in the strongest tone she could muster. Her shock was giving over to anger, and she welcomed the feeling. Anger she could use. "I'm furious. But it's too late to do anything about it now. I'm just going to check on two things, and then we'll leave."

She stomped away from him, kicking debris from her path as she headed up the stairs. She kept her eyes down. She had to. If she hadn't, she would have tripped over a half-full two-liter of root beer. A discarded pair of track shorts. A broken radio. What looked like the cover of one of her parents' old record albums.

Nausea surged anew. She blurred her focus and walked faster.

She wanted to tell herself that the family chest would still be there—the steamer trunk that had come through Ellis Island with her father's relatives so long ago. But she wasn't foolish enough to be hopeful. It was a valuable antique. And even if it had survived, even if the vermin who had handed everything else out her windows had considered it too heavy to bother with, it would almost certainly have nothing inside it.

Unless, of course, she or her aunt had locked it. Had they? she couldn't remember.

She reached the landing and moved quickly to the right. She tried not to look in her room, but her peripheral vision wouldn't obey. In a flash she could see that her furniture, too, was gone. Everything was gone.

She closed her eyes tight outside Dee's room, walking forward blindly, delivering a vicious kick to anything that touched her feet. She reached the master bedroom doorframe. She swung around inside it, her breath held. She opened her eyes.

A bulky wooden bed frame stood in the center of the room, devoid of mattress and box springs. The heavy wooden vanity had been pulled away from the wall, its drawers standing open and empty. Trash was everywhere. Dirty clothing was everywhere. She didn't look to see if it had been her parents'. She didn't want to know.

The chest was gone.

She lurched forward to open the door to the closet. It held more of the same. Wadded, dirty clothing on the floor. One forlorn, misshapen hanger suspended above.

It's gone. All of it.

No quilts. No baby clothes. No keepsakes. *Nothing.*

Her head felt hot. All her blood seemed to have pooled there, flushing her cheeks and leaving her limbs cold. She was walking in a nightmare. A nightmare of her own making.

She whirled around to leave and collided with Adam. He was standing in the doorway behind her so quietly she had forgotten him. She bounced off him as if he had shocked her, then pushed past him through the door. Forget the plan. His presence couldn't stop her from feeling. Nothing could.

She walked to the end of the hall and looked up. The drop-down attic stairs weren't hidden, but there was a chance they might be missed.

The handle was beyond her reach, and she looked around for something to stand on. But before she could search far, Adam appeared at her side. He reached up, pulled on the handle, and slid the wooden steps down into place.

"Thank you," she mumbled, not sure if her unsteady voice could be heard. She tested the steps with a bounce, declared them stable, and ascended.

Sweat trickled down the side of her neck. It was hot. The whole house was sweltering, but the air under the roof was like an oven. She moved off the ladder and surveyed the attic on her knees.

Her mother's neat stacks of boxes had disappeared. What remained was a sea of torn cardboard, strewn clothing and books, loose papers, and broken Christmas decorations. Every box had been gutted. A smaller proportion of these belongings seemed to have been desirable enough to steal, but the broken-out windows at both ends of the attic treated her to a cruel image of the family's artificial Christmas tree sliding over shards of glass and plunging onto the lawn below.

That was all the windows treated her to. No air whatsoever was moving through them. The heat was stifling, and moisture, heavy as dew, tainted everything in sight with the acrid scent of mold.

Dad's paintings, she reminded herself. They might still be here. They were amateurish. Who would want them?

It was hard to see in the semidarkness, and she had no idea what living creatures might be sharing the space. But she didn't care. She crawled off on hands and knees, searching.

She was only vaguely aware of Adam appearing at the stairwell. "What are you looking for?" he asked. "Can I help?"

Sarah answered, but her voice seemed to be coming from someone else. "Paintings. I'm looking for my father's paintings."

She picked through the debris with determination. Sweat rolled down her back as she bent; drips fell from her face onto her hands. She sifted through the reams of jumbled paper. College notebooks, textbooks. Old letters. A dot matrix printer. A bird cage. Clothing that looked familiar—perhaps hers. Moth stains. Mildew. One torn Hawaiian lei.

"Sarah?"

The tone in Adam's voice stopped her cold. She turned to see him sitting a few yards away, holding something toward her. It was a canvas board.

She scuttled toward him and grabbed it, then moved into the light.

Sunset at Taos. Orange, reds, and yellows. Pueblos stacked to the sky.

"It's his!" she stammered, her lower lip trembling. "I remember it."

He picked through the pile some more, then turned back to her. "Okay, I've got three others, two on canvas and this one. Were there any more?"

She took the portraits from his hands. They all were damaged to varying degrees. Torn on the edges, even moldy where bare canvas remained. But her heart leapt with joy at the sight. "This was his dog, Lucky Day," she explained, holding up a stiff rendition of an English Setter in a broken plastic frame.

"It was my favorite. The others were all landscapes. He loved New Mexico."

"Is this all?"

She nodded. Drops of sweat flew.

"Then let's get out of here before we both pass out," he said shortly, taking the other three paintings from her lap. He held them away from his body as he moved towards the stairs, and as she followed she could see why. His shirt was drenched.

When she mounted the stairs he held up his hand for the dog picture she still cradled in her arms, and she gave it to him. Her legs were wobbly, and she had to put both hands on the steps to steady herself. When she reached the bottom, he slid the stairs back into place.

She looked at him. His flushed skin was shining, and drops of sweat clung to every dark ringlet of his hair. "Here's my suggestion," he offered. "Let's lock up, go back into town, and get some food and something to drink. Then you can decide where you want to go from here. How does that sound?"

She nodded, reminding herself that he wasn't used to the humidity. Not that even a lifelong Southerner could have tolerated that attic much longer—it wasn't only humid, it had to be well over a hundred degrees.

He headed down the hall before her, still carrying the paintings. She focused on them and only on them, ignoring as best she could the nightmare to her left and right. *Five years.* All the damage she had witnessed had been done in that much time. The bulk of the looting must have occurred before she had the windows sealed. But was there still an opening somewhere—an opening big enough for a person to squeeze through? Was her house still party central for every degenerate in the county?

She followed Adam back down the stairs and into the living room. He made a beeline for the door, and she attempted to follow him. But keeping her eyes on the paintings had a price. Her foot caught on something, and she stumbled.

Adam whirled around. "Are you okay?"

Her left hand had landed on a crushed paper bag. Her right was touching someone's underclothing. She jerked both hands back, pulling her foot from the broken drawer in which it had lodged. If she had stood with her eyes closed, she might not have seen what lay on the floor by the fireplace. But she didn't want to fall again. And as she pulled herself to her feet, her open eyes took in every detail.

A twin mattress, crumpled and stained, lay flat on the floor. On one side lay scattered mounds of empty beer cans, cigarette butts, and discarded condoms. On the other side, propped at an angle, sat what had originally been attached to the wall above the mantel. A long, rectangular mirror.

"Let's go, Sarah."

She couldn't move. The dreaded thoughts shuffled front and center. She was *here*. Here where everything had happened. The one place, physically and mentally, where she had sworn she wouldn't allow herself to be. The couch was gone. The rug was gone. Nothing in the room looked the same. But it was the same, because there was a mattress. Right there where the couch had been. The same thing had been happening in the same spot, over and over, all this time.

"Sarah—"

"DON'T TOUCH ME!" She jumped away from the hand. Shudders rocked her body. She could see him as if it were yesterday. His vile skin exposed and sweaty. His abhorrent tattoo. His sadistic glee.

"Sarah?"

He was out there, somewhere. Still. Nothing had changed.

"Sarah, look at me. Please."

She wasn't better. She wasn't in control. What happened that night couldn't be erased, because she hadn't forgotten it. She couldn't forget. Every miserable image was engraved on every miserable cell in her miserable brain.

Images swarmed before her eyes like cockroaches. Dee, sitting on her bed, laughing, raving about the guy she was so hot for. Him standing at the door, whiskey bottle in hand, bare to the waist, displaying his muscles like a gift. His hideous, smirking smile. The sweat on his suntanned back. The bobbing of his oily black curls—

You can't tell, Sarah! You can't!

Dee's voice pounded in Sarah's head. Her temples throbbed. Her feet itched. The walls of the house seemed to undulate around her.

Why had she come here again? Why?

Her eyes searched for the open front door, and she lurched toward it like a madwoman. She knew that Adam was in the room, and she knew that he wouldn't hurt her. But it didn't matter, because she couldn't stand the sight of him, either. It was too much. Too close. She had to get away. She had to get away from everything.

She plowed forward over glass, metal, and trash—leaping as necessary, hustling toward the door at full speed. She reached it and ran through, and then she kept going. She jumped off the porch and into the weeds, parting the brush with outstretched arms. She heard Adam calling, but she ignored him. She was looking for a safe place, and she wasn't stopping until she found it. There had to be a safe place.

Somewhere.

There had to be.

Chapter 14

Adam stood on the porch, looking out. He would say his blood was boiling, but in heat like this, that statement would be true even if he weren't furious.

Damn that mattress.

The horror of finding one's family home in shambles was bad enough. He could see how deeply the carnage was affecting Sarah, but up until just now she had held herself together. Her reaction, in fact, had been more controlled than his own would have been. Everything her parents had owned had been either abused, defiled, or stolen. Whether she blamed her uncle or herself, an eventual outburst of anger was understandable, even expected. But the outburst he had just witnessed hadn't come from anger.

"Sarah!" he called. "Stop!"

The only sound that returned was the rustling of weeds.

He dropped the paintings onto the porch and took a quick, deep breath. The heat in the house had made his every muscle go limp. But the look on her face just now had been worse. It had made him feel sick.

Something terrible had happened to her here. She had been remembering it as he watched, and it was clear that the sight of the mattress had been the catalyst.

He jogged down the steps and began to follow the trail of trampled weeds she had left in her wake. The task wasn't difficult.

"Sarah!" he called as he moved. "Let's go, all right? I'll take you back to town."

He heard nothing.

Her trail led around the side of the house. He followed it to where it passed near the back porch, then left it to climb the steps. The landscape sloped gently downward from where he stood, and he soon located his quarry. The tops of the weeds were moving about a hundred yards away.

This time he didn't call to her. He just headed out.

Perhaps she had been reliving her sister's suicide. Perhaps Sarah had found Dee's body in the very spot where the mattress lay, or perhaps the mattress itself had been Dee's. But he didn't think so.

The weeds ahead gave way suddenly, and he found himself standing in a narrow, freshly bush-hogged trail. He would have liked to have stayed on it, but as it stretched to the left and right, he knew it would take him no closer to Sarah. He reentered the weeds on the other side and kept moving.

He hated the thoughts brewing in his head. It was hard enough to imagine the suffering that losing three family members would inflict on a teenaged girl. To think that there might have been more… It was inconceivable.

Yet from his first encounter with Sarah, he suspected that she had been maltreated by a man, and nothing she had said since had changed his mind. The barroom brawl story hadn't explained her terror at the cemetery, nor could it explain her reaction to the mattress and mirror. Most people, faced with such a spectacle in their own home, would feel a mixture of anger and disgust. But Sarah's eyes had filled with horror. The nature of her response had chilled him, and empathy had driven him toward her. But he had been several feet away, still, when she had shouted at him. Shouted at him not to touch her.

She had been reliving a rape.

His heart pounded, and the vessels in his temples throbbed. He was angry. He was so angry he felt like he would explode, and if the heat around him didn't abate soon, he was certain he would. He wanted to murder a man, and he didn't even know who. He wanted to strangle the life out of him.

Nine years. If Adam was right, what had happened to Sarah had happened at least that long ago. And she was still profoundly affected by it. Had she ever had any counseling? Had it happened before her parents' deaths? After? Even with professional help, how could any girl experience such trauma on top of the loss of three loved ones and ever be whole again? Particularly when she lacked any semblance of faith?

"Sarah!" he shouted, his frustration clear in his voice. He thought he had come far enough to intersect with her trail, but there was no sign of it. The landscape had leveled, and he could no longer see downhill. Where was she? How far would she run before realizing what she was doing?

He had to find her. Not only was she emotionally distraught, but the jury was still out on the state of her health. Running around in this heat could be dangerous for her.

It was about to be for him. He needed a drink of water so badly he was on the verge of lightheadedness.

"Sarah!" he called again. "I know you can hear me. And if you don't answer me in the next twenty seconds, I'm going to assume you passed out again, and I'm going to call the police and an ambulance and get them all out here looking for you. Is that what you want?"

He stopped abruptly, cursing under his breath at the anger he could hear broiling in his own voice. Sarah had run because she was frightened, and he was a hot-headed idiot. How could she possibly understand that he wasn't angry at her, but at what had been done to her? No wonder she wasn't answering him.

"I'm here."

He froze. Her voice was coming from somewhere to his left, downhill. "Where's here?" he called more gently.

"By the pond."

Adam swiveled his head. He had seen a patch of stagnant water from the porch earlier, but he couldn't see a thing now. Just weeds, bushes, and more weeds. He moved toward the sound of her voice, and in a few seconds, found himself on another plowed lane.

"Sarah?"

She appeared at his left and walked toward him. She looked wilted, like a cut flower. Her hair was damp, and her blue cotton shirt was plastered to her lithe frame. But to his surprise, she seemed eerily calm. Too calm. Only after her eyes surveyed him did she adopt a worried expression.

"I'm sorry," she said softly. "You didn't have to chase after me. I just needed a minute to collect myself, that's all."

Adam didn't answer. Her flight did seem to have drained her of whatever emotion she had been running from, but he himself was far from collected. He couldn't look at her without imagining what she'd suffered, and he couldn't imagine what she'd suffered without feeling rage.

"You're angry with me, aren't you?" she asked, not sounding afraid so much as remorseful. "Don't worry, I don't blame you. I make one lousy hostess."

"I'm not angry with you," he reassured hastily. Then he took a long, slow breath. Damn, he was thirsty. "I just get cranky when I'm dehydrated. Are you all right?"

She nodded. Then she moved back in the direction she had come, walking up to a survey stake that had been driven in the ground beside the plowed area. She ran a finger over its cryptic markings, tossing her head in the direction of the pond behind her. "Would you believe that we used to swim in that?"

Her voice was casual, light, almost jesting. But even as she talked, a shudder wracked her body; her limbs trembled.

Adam pulled his eyes away from her long enough to glance in the direction indicated. The small pond at which the mowed trail ended was anything but inviting. Its edges were clogged with mushy vegetation, and half its surface was coated with a thick green slime.

He could think of no response.

Sarah continued to study the stake. "There was another one of these uphill, closer to the house. What do you think they mark?"

Her hands were still shaking. Her voice cracked.

Keeping a respectable distance between them took every ounce of self-control Adam possessed.

He breathed in deeply. The question might seem as idle as her last one, but he didn't think it was. Was she wondering whether her house was directly in the path of the new road? Did she want to make sure it would be destroyed?

"I have no idea how to read survey stakes," he answered honestly. "But no matter where the road cuts through, I'm sure the county will raze the house. They won't want the liability."

Sarah showed no reaction to his statement. She remained standing perfectly still, looking out into the weeds with a pensive expression. He allowed her reverie to continue as long as he could stand it—which didn't prove to be long. If he had to bake in this sun one second longer, he wasn't going to be able to think straight.

"I could really use something to drink, Sarah, and I'm sure you could, too. Can we go now?" He made an effort not to sound testy. Unfortunately, he failed.

To his amazement, she looked up at him with a grin.

"What?" he asked. "What's so amusing?"

"Nothing," she answered, moving toward him. "I just like that you've got a temper. It proves you're human." She walked around him, carelessly brushing his shoulder as she passed by.

His reaction to her touch was involuntary; but with an effort, he squelched it.

"Did I ever claim not to be?" he questioned, keeping his eyes carefully away from her sweat-soaked shirt as she headed uphill through the weeds.

"No," she answered thoughtfully, not looking at him. "But as much as you've done for me the last week, you might qualify as a guardian angel."

He absorbed the comment. He decided he liked it.

"Does that mean you believe in angels?" he challenged, following her.

She chuckled over her shoulder.

"Nice try, preacher man."

It took three large pink lemonades, six chicken strips with honey barbecue sauce, a clean shirt, a touchup of deodorant, and twenty minutes of air conditioning to make Adam feel like himself again. But now that he was ensconced in a restaurant booth with frigid air blasting straight down on his head, he was comfortable enough to resume worrying about Sarah.

To his chagrin, she had said nothing further about her outburst in the house. She had said nothing about the house at all. She had passed the drive into town sitting quietly in her seat, staring at the paintings she clutched in her lap, slowly shuffling them to admire each in turn. When he had asked about them, she had explained that her father had wanted to be an artist when he was young, but that his parents hadn't approved, and he had given it up. She then thanked Adam for helping her find them, speaking of the success as though retrieving the paintings had been her one and only goal for the visit.

"Well," she announced after finishing off her red beans and rice, "I've done everything I needed to do here. All I ask is that you get me back to Atlanta and drop me off at the motel I picked out. I'll relax by the pool with a good book and you can have the rest of the weekend to yourself."

Her voice was amiable, almost chipper, as if she had just spent the last few hours gardening or chatting with friends. Adam marveled at her capacity for denial.

"I'll be spending tomorrow morning with my grandmother," she continued. "She's at an Alzheimer's care home a few blocks from the motel. I can walk over in the morning, but if you could pick me up in the lobby at noon I figured we could go straight to the airport afterward. Does that sound okay?"

He couldn't answer immediately. He was too frustrated. He realized now that despite Sarah's quip about his guardian angel status, she wanted nothing more from him. He had served his purpose; he was dismissed. She didn't want to share her problems with him. She didn't even want him to know she had any.

But he did know. And he hadn't spent the morning sweating himself to a raisin because he wanted a free trip to Atlanta. He had made the journey because he cared about her. Exactly why he cared and whether or not he should was not the point. The fact was, he could no more stop himself from caring, from trying to help her heal her obvious emotional wounds, than he could walk away from a starving man while toting a canteen and a ham sandwich.

"Sarah," he began, attempting a matter-of-fact tone. "After you lost your family, did you get professional counseling?"

She stiffened, as he knew she would. But her defensive

reaction didn't last. She stifled it in a heartbeat, returning to her false front of equanimity. "Of course," she answered. "My aunt took me right after Dee died. I was a mess."

"How long did you go?" he pressed.

"All summer. Why? You don't think it worked?"

He smiled. Her dry wit amused him, even if she did use it like a weapon. "Sarah," he said frankly, "after everything you've been through, I think it's a miracle you can tie your shoelaces. You're a very strong person."

She looked back at him with genuine appreciation. "Thank you."

"You're welcome." He forged ahead. "But there's a difference between being strong and being superhuman."

Her eyes flashed a brief distress signal, but her voice stayed light. "Meaning?"

"Meaning that no normal mortal could go back to the house where she had grown up with parents who died so tragically and where her sister had committed suicide; find all her family's possessions looted, misappropriated, or destroyed; and come away from the experience with a smile on her face talking about spending the evening with a good book."

Her jaw muscles clenched. "Did it ever occur to you that I just might not want to share my personal life with you?"

The barb hit its mark, and for a second, Adam's resolve faltered. But with an effort, he shrugged it off. He would not take her defensive tactics personally. "That would be fine," he said agreeably, "except that I don't see anyone else around. And frankly, you could do a lot worse. I'm a good listener."

"You're also a minister," she said heavily. "Which means you have an angle."

Adam's eyes widened, perplexed. He was used to his profession being an asset; people usually felt safe trusting him with their confidences. "And that would be…"

"You know perfectly well," she admonished. She was smiling at him now, and her tone was teasing, but he could sense the candor behind her words. "Saving my soul from eternal damnation in a lake of everlasting hellfire. Or boosting your church roster…whichever. You may start out all nice and undemanding, but eventually, you plan to start sliding in the pitches. Come to this, check out that. It's for your own good, and oh, by the way, here's the collection plate."

He studied her a moment, speechless. For an intelligent person who read so much, she had a terribly warped view of religion. He wondered where it had come from. Regardless, he couldn't fix it today.

He smiled back at her instead. "No," he said finally, pretending to have made a tough decision. "You can go to some other church if you want, but the last thing I need is a parishioner who can watch my every move out her front windows. I prefer to keep my personal life separate from my job." The last line was such a crock, he could hardly deliver it with a straight face. He'd never had any personal life separate from his job.

She eyed him skeptically. "So, you're not the least bit interested in saving my soul?"

He contemplated, taking his time. Her brilliant blue eyes were especially fetching when she challenged him. "If I say no," he began slowly, "you'll assume that I'm in favor of your burning in an everlasting lake of hellfire. But if I say yes, you'll accuse me of trying to manipulate you for my own selfish gain. So you tell me—which answer would you prefer?"

She grinned. "You're good. You know that?"

He grinned back. "Why, thank you. Care to make a donation?"

She laughed out loud. The sound of her voice was musical, and the knowledge that he had made her happy, if only for a second, affected him more deeply than he expected. He wanted to hear that laugh again. He wanted to hear it often.

But he knew it would never happen if he kept letting her distract him. "Sarah, I'm not trying to criticize you for the way you're handling things. But the fact is, if I was an old friend of yours—instead of being some smarmy minister you only met a week ago—we wouldn't be sitting here talking about our plans for tomorrow. You'd be venting your anger about how perfectly horrible this morning was, and you'd keep on venting until you felt better."

He wanted to ask her about her fear. He wanted to know the whole story of what had happened to her when she was young, and he wanted to make sure she had the proper help in dealing with it. But for right now, he would be happy if she shared anything she was feeling. Anything at all.

"So," he suggested. "Couldn't you just *pretend* that I'm an old friend? We can get back in the car, you can rant and rave all you want, and you'll feel better by the time we hit the state line. I promise."

He watched her as she considered. She was fascinating to watch no matter what she was doing. Her hair was dry now, as was her shirt. The latter was fortunate for his concentration.

"The problem with you extroverts," she said critically, "is that you assume that what works for you must work for everybody. But I don't like to babble about my feelings."

"Don't babble then," he suggested, undeterred. "Just state. But state the reality, not some sugar-coated nonsense you came up with for my benefit. I know you're furious. Why not admit it?"

"I'm furious," she said flatly.

"Excellent!" he praised. "So am I. It was ridiculously hot out there, and you should have warned me there was no running water for five miles in any direction. We could have at least brought drinks with us."

She leveled her eyes at him. "There was root beer on the stairs."

He wanted to laugh at that one, but he couldn't afford to get off track again. "And you're furious with whom, exactly? Your uncle?"

She paused. "No. I've got nobody to blame but myself."

"Why? Because you didn't check up on things more often? Force your uncle to sell?"

She threw him a hard look, making clear that she knew exactly what he was doing.

He stared back without apology.

She rolled her eyes with a sigh. But then, to his delight, she capitulated. "Because I should have realized that being so isolated made the house a sitting duck for vandals. Because I should never have left my family's belongings unguarded—I should have insisted on moving everything to a storage unit years ago. What happened happened because I didn't want to deal with it. Because I wasn't strong enough to face it." She stopped and looked at him. "There. How was that?"

Adam's heart thudded in his chest. *At last.*

"Fantastic," he praised. "But how strong do you expect yourself to be? Did you really think that you could go back there and not feel anything at all?"

"Of course not," she said sharply. "I knew it would be difficult. That's why I wanted your company. I thought having someone else there would distract me. It did, at first. But—"

She broke off.

"But what?" he asked quickly. "But then you saw the mattress?"

Too far. He wanted to catch the words in the air, pull them back. But it was too late. Sarah's eyes flashed with alarm, and her face paled.

"What mattress?"

Damn his loose tongue! "The mattress on the living room floor," he explained, trying to rid his voice of emotion. Perhaps he could tell her what he had observed, just not what he suspected. She wasn't ready for that. "Seeing it obviously upset you. I thought that's what you were about to say."

Her blue eyes searched his again. She didn't answer for a long time. When she did, her voice was contrite. "I yelled at you, didn't I?"

She looked so mortified, he couldn't help but smile. Of all the things for her to worry about! "Maybe a little," he said easily.

She didn't smile back. "I'm sorry. I didn't mean to. I don't know what I was saying. I was just so disgusted." She paused and took a breath. Her eyes fixed on the cup in her hands. "I suppose it was childish of me. But I think that was my mattress."

Adam's smile disappeared. She was lying to him again. She was skilled at thinking up quick, plausible explanations, but she could never convince him that her flight from that house had been motivated by anything but cold, raw fear.

"All of a sudden," she continued. "I felt like the walls were closing in on me, and I had to get out of there. I'm sorry if I upset you. I don't usually get so out of sorts."

"Don't apologize," he said softly. "You had any number of reasons to be out of sorts. You still do."

She stiffened slightly. "It was a long time ago."

"That doesn't matter," he insisted. "You feel what you feel. The kind of pain you suffered doesn't go away just because you want it to. Don't be so hard on yourself."

The effect of his last six words, so unexpected, so abrupt, engraved itself in his mind. Her expression clouded, and her muscles tensed. Her unspoken response was plain.

But I deserve it.

She stood up with a jerk and began collecting her trash from the table. "Let's go," she said without enthusiasm. "It's a long drive, and I want to make sure you have plenty of time in Atlanta."

Adam remained sitting, mired in disbelief. Seeing fear in Sarah was bad enough, but what he had just seen was worse.

Guilt. Guilt over more than just letting the house become a shambles. Did she feel guilty about what had happened to her family? Or about whatever else had happened within those walls? None of it could possibly have been her fault. And if she thought that it was, her wounds were even deeper than he imagined.

He rose. Sarah was good at pretending. But not good enough. Deep in her beautiful, tortured eyes, he could see a woman drowning.

And he was in way over his head.

Chapter 15

Sarah's grandmother's frail chest rose beneath the thin pink blanket, then fell again. Sarah realized that she had been regulating her own breathing to match. She wasn't surprised. There was little else to do.

Elayna Bird hadn't recognized her granddaughter in years; now she didn't recognize anyone. She wasn't able to speak. She rarely made eye contact. Alzheimer's disease had claimed her brain many years ago, but cruelly, the disease was taking its time with the rest of her. At seventy-eight, her stubborn heart was still strong.

Sarah held the older woman's hand beneath the blanket. Her mother's mother had been another casualty of the family tragedy, though at the time, Elayna's deterioration had gone largely unnoticed. What seemed a normal grief response had melded slowly into dementia, with no one, including Sarah, ever being certain which had come first. All she had known back then was that her once-strong Grandma was no longer someone she could lean on. Elayna had needed too much help herself.

Today she seemed no different, no better and no worse, than when Sarah had last visited five months ago. Sarah always checked on her at least that often, though Elayna's son was probably not aware of it. He certainly wasn't aware that Sarah also called the facility regularly to ask about him—had he been visiting? Did he inquire about his mother's care?—and that Sarah's watchdog at the front desk consistently reported in the affirmative.

Sarah's motives in wanting to know were selfish. She would prefer her grandmother be nearer to her, so that she could avoid driving even this far south. But Elayna had always lived in Georgia, and despite Dwight Bird's grating personality, she had always been close to her only son. As the granddaughter, Sarah didn't feel it was her place to separate them, even if she was picking up the tab.

The room was pleasant and bright, the atmosphere of the home, peaceful. It wasn't an unpleasant place to spend a Sunday morning, yet Sarah found herself feeling antsy. She wondered what Adam was doing.

The last twenty-four hours had been so bizarre, they seemed to have left her in a low grade of shock. The dichotomy between morning and afternoon had been extreme, and in the rational light of a new day, she couldn't help but wonder if both had actually happened.

She had dreaded the drive from Auburn back to Atlanta, certain that Adam would hound her with unanswerable questions every mile of the way. But after their discussion in the restaurant he seemed to undergo a curious change of heart. He didn't ask her anything. Instead he had hopped into the car and proposed that neither of them mention the ordeal the rest of the day. The proposal had been an easy one to accept, but whether she talked about the morning or not, Sarah was certain that nothing could remove the pall it had cast over her.

She had been wrong.

Adam had done it, somehow. Perhaps it was because she was too emotionally drained to fight him anymore, or perhaps it was some subconscious act of rebellion. Whatever motivated her, she had done what she had sworn she wouldn't do. She had let her guard down.

How could she not, when Adam's enthusiasm for a simple afternoon of sightseeing had been so contagious? All the rest of the day he had been like a kid in a candy store, delighting in every facet of the rich Southern scenery around him, packing as much activity as he could into every sun-baked minute. He had also been downright devious—always claiming he would take her to the motel after just one short side trip, then another. She knew what he was doing, but she didn't resist. He seemed to genuinely want to make her happy—to see her laugh. And after all she had put him through, she figured that, for one afternoon, she could oblige him.

She had lived in the area for seventeen years, but until yesterday she had never seen Northwest Georgia from the top of Stone Mountain. One idle mention of this fact to Adam had resulted in her being hustled onto the park's skylift, and as he stared wistfully out at the hikers below she got the impression that if not for her iffy health, he would have coerced her to scale the beast on the walk-up trail.

He had stopped the car at every historical marker and scenic viewpoint he could find—and some he only imagined—and when they had finally reached Atlanta he had begged for a guided tour of the Underground, then topped it off with a Jamaican dinner and some live reggae music. He hadn't returned her to the motel until after ten o'clock, at which time she had fallen into bed with her sides aching from laughter, feeling as though she had traveled to the Land of Oz, and that in the morning all would be black and white again.

When she awoke, she realized she was right.

"Sarah?"

A familiar male voice, high-pitched and nasally, met her ears. Her chin jerked up. There in the doorway, looking as shocked as she felt, stood her uncle. All five feet, seven inches of him. Portly and bald, except for a wispy, combed-over gray crown.

"I can't believe it's you," he said with a polite, yet self-conscious smile. "You should have told me you were coming."

She swallowed. She had gone to great effort to avoid such a confrontation. She had been informed he didn't usually visit on Sundays. "It was a last-minute trip," she explained.

He walked up to the other side of the bed. Sarah turned her eyes toward her grandmother. She could feel his looking at her.

"They tell me you come down every once in a while," he said, his voice stiff. "Guess I was lucky to catch you today. I check in a couple times a week, of course, but usually after work. Weekends are pretty busy for me."

Sarah did not take the bait. Her uncle's favorite hobby was cruising flea markets for old toy cars and Coke paraphernalia, and he could discuss the topic incessantly.

He cleared his throat. "Your grandma's holding her own.

She'd be healthy as a horse if it weren't for the Alzheimer's—at least that's what the doctors keep saying. But I just try to make sure she's comfortable."

Sarah nodded. "I think she is."

Another silence descended. Sarah knew the question would come eventually. The fact that it came before a "how are you" or "what have you been doing lately" was entirely in character.

"So," he began, moving to drop his pear-shaped form onto the window seat. "Have you sold that house yet?"

Sarah shifted in her chair. "As a matter of fact," she announced without enthusiasm, "Yes. I sold it to the county."

"The county?" he exclaimed with disdain. His voice was loud and sharp, and Elayna's hand tensed slightly, as if the sound had startled her. "Why in the devil would you do that? They won't pay you anything. Was it condemned?"

Sarah lowered her own voice to a whisper. She knew that what was left of her grandmother's brain couldn't follow their conversation, but if the woman could be affected by tones of voice, she didn't want to upset her. "In a manner of speaking. They're extending the bypass. They took it by eminent domain."

He swore. "Did you get anything for it?"

Sarah tried to control her ire. Her uncle wasn't an evil person, but for whatever reason, they had always been like oil and water. She couldn't be in the same room with the man for more than five minutes without wanting to strangle him. She had felt that way ever since she was a teenager, and the years hadn't changed a thing.

"The compensation was fair. I hired an attorney to make sure of it."

His eyes widened with surprise. "Well," he said finally. "That's good. What about the furniture and everything? Last time I drove by, the place was a wreck. I wasn't sure there'd be anything left."

Sarah cleared her throat. There wasn't much point in lying to him. Lying took brainpower, and what she had left of that, she needed to save for Adam. "I took some keepsakes, but vandals had already picked the place over pretty thoroughly."

He let out an exasperated sigh. "I told you that would happen, didn't I? I kept telling Karen we had to push you about selling, but she was as stubborn as you were. 'It has to be Sarah's decision,' she'd say. Now look what's happened."

"Nothing's happened," Sarah returned coldly. Keeping her temper was tougher when he started in on her aunt. She hated that. "I don't need the furniture, and money isn't an issue, so you don't have to worry about it."

He sighed again. "I just thank God your parents had good life insurance."

Her teeth gritted. For her uncle, "thank God" was an empty expression. None of her mother's relatives knew a mass from a bar mitzvah, but they all claimed to be Catholic when it was convenient.

"So," he continued, his tone brightening, "You moved to Pittsburgh, eh? How do you like it up there?"

She tried to calm her nerves. He was asking about her life. That was something new. When she had sent him the token change-of-address card, she wasn't sure he would read it. "I'm still settling in," she answered, "but so far I like it. The job is working out well. I'm a manager now—for older adult services."

He nodded, seemingly impressed. She realized she hadn't asked anything about his life, either. "Are you still working with the same firm?" she inquired. He was a CPA, and as far as she knew, he had had the same job since the eighties.

He nodded again. "Oh yeah. But I'm getting ready to retire in a couple years."

She smiled a little. "And be free to hit the flea markets seven days a week? Are you sure that's wise?"

He grinned back. "I'll take Wednesdays off. Got to do some fishing, too, you know."

She breathed a little easier. There was something she had wanted to ask him for a long time, and the moment seemed right. "Do you," she began tentatively, "ever hear from Karen?"

His puffy cheeks reddened. "No," he said with an artificial cough, hiding his face behind his hand. "Not directly. But I did run into a friend of hers a couple months ago. I thought she was getting married again, but apparently she didn't. The friend said she'd gotten a new job over in Charlotte."

"You don't have her address?"

He shook his head, then looked at Sarah suspiciously. "Why? You want to look her up?"

Sarah's eyes met his. "She was a good friend to me."

He didn't answer for a moment. He looked disgusted. "Karen didn't do you any favors, honey, catering to your teenaged whims. She handled things wrong from the start. If it had been up to me, I would never have let you girls stay alone in that house in the first place."

Red heat flashed behind Sarah's eyes. She felt the urge to fly up out of her chair, but she didn't want to let go of her grandmother's hand. It was the only thing keeping her calm.

Her parents had died in the spring of her senior year; her aunt and uncle had lived over two hours away. All she had wanted was to stay in Auburn long enough to graduate from high school, to be with her classmates, to feel normal. Dee was nineteen and had a full-time job. There was no reason to uproot them.

Her aunt had understood that. Right after it happened, Karen and Dwight had taken a week of vacation, moved into the house, and stayed with their nieces through the funeral. But afterward, the couple had had to return to Georgia. Karen had been concerned about leaving the girls alone, but Dee seemed to be taking everything as well as could be expected, and after much discussion they had agreed that Karen would come and stay with them on the weekends for a while. But Sarah's uncle had staunchly objected. He didn't want to spend his weekends alone, and he certainly didn't want to spend them in Auburn. He was adamant that the girls sell the house and move in with them.

Sarah's aunt had prevailed. But before the next weekend rolled around, Dee was dead.

"It was *not* Karen's fault," Sarah hissed. "She did what she thought was best. She cared about both of us."

He threw her the sort of look one normally reserved for an

uppity child. "She did care, but the woman had no backbone. She just did whatever you asked her to. I kept telling her you were just a kid—you didn't know what was best for yourself. If it had been up to me, you never would have gone to college so far away, either, I'll tell you that. I thought you should have stayed right here and been forced to deal with it all, but Karen let you run, and look what good it did you."

Sarah's muscles tensed. She tried to focus on her grandmother's hand. "Would you like to rephrase that?"

Her uncle had the decency to seem embarrassed. "I didn't mean to insult you. But for God's sake, Sarah, you weren't right for years. You'd come back from college and people would try to talk to you, and every time you'd go pale as a ghost. People were always asking me if you were in some kind of therapy. How the hell would I know, when you were all the way up in Illinois? If you'd stayed down here, we could have at least kept an eye on you."

"I was a financially independent, legal adult," she reminded. "It wasn't your decision."

He sighed with a groan, but said nothing more.

Sarah gave herself a moment to cool down. "For your information, I'm doing splendidly now. I have a successful career that I enjoy, and I've even bought a house of my own. I flew down for the weekend just to settle things in Auburn—I visited the cemetery and made sure the graves were being tended, and the house has been sold now. So everything's fine."

His eyes widened. "You *flew* down?"

She allowed herself a smidgen of pride. "That's what I said."

He pursed his lips. "Well, that's progress, I'd say. You have a boyfriend or anything?"

She stiffened again. The man seemed programmed to irritate her. She toyed with the idea of claiming to be a lesbian, just to watch the ensuing apoplexy. But she had listened to enough criticism already. "Not at the moment."

"That's too bad," he responded, seemingly genuinely disappointed. "Mother would want great-grandchildren, and there's no hope left for me." He surveyed her critically. "A pretty girl like you wouldn't have any trouble snagging a man if you'd lift your nose out of the books once in a while. Why would you want to work with older adults, anyway?"

She stole a glance at her watch. Adam was supposed to pick her up at noon. She hated to shorten her visit with her grandmother, but her patience was at its end. If she couldn't kick her uncle out of the room, she would be better off waiting in the lobby.

"I enjoy working with older people for a lot of reasons," she answered. She gave her grandmother's hand a squeeze and rose. "I should be going now, but I'll be back in a few months. If she needs anything in the meantime, let me know."

He bristled. "I'll take care of whatever she needs. I always do."

Sarah looked back at him. The care issue would forever be a thorn between them. He had wanted his mother's own money to support her. He was willing to chip in if her reserves gave out before she did, but only if the facility selected was a "reasonably priced" one. Sarah had wanted her grandmother to have the best, she could afford to provide it, and she had insisted on doing so. But in his mind, his niece's largesse was emasculating.

"I know you will," she responded. She bent down and kissed her grandmother on the forehead, then turned to leave. "Well, it was good to run into you again. I suppose I'll see you later."

"Sarah?" he said pointedly.

His tone stopped her. She whirled to face him.

He stammered, seeming uncomfortable. "I haven't talked to Karen in years, you know, but the last time I did, she asked about you. I was thinking maybe—well, if you wanted to give her a call sometime, I'm sure she'd be happy to hear from you. I don't have her number, but it's probably listed in Charlotte. She took back her maiden name. It's Karen Beaver."

An unexpected warmth pulsed through Sarah.

The man really did care.

"Thank you," she answered. "I would like to talk to her sometime. I'd like that very much."

He smiled. "Well, I hope you do. Goodbye, then."

She smiled back. "Goodbye."

She turned again and walked out the door, puzzling. For all her uncle's blame-casting, he did seem to understand how much his ex-wife had meant to her. Perhaps his defensiveness was born of the fact that he, too, felt partly to blame for Dee's suicide. Everyone involved back then seemed to, except for the one person who deserved it.

He had never felt a twinge.

Chapter 16

"There you are. Are you ready to head out?"

Sarah looked up, and her heart skipped a beat. Adam was standing beside her, and she hadn't even noticed his approach. She had been staring into the leaves of the ficus tree in the corner of the lobby, reminiscing about Stone Mountain's nature trail. Everything that had happened yesterday afternoon still felt surreal to her, and she felt strangely awkward being caught in the midst of pondering it.

"Yes," she answered, rising. He offered a friendly smile, and as she returned it, her discomfort eased. Their trip was almost over. She was actually looking forward to the flight home, and she owed that to him. She owed him for a lot of things.

She felt stronger today than she had felt in a long time, and she was sure that laughter had been her medicine. A few hours of sightseeing and general frivolity might be an ordinary occurrence for someone like him, but for her, the afternoon had been a rare treat. She wasn't the sort of person who traveled for fun. She wasn't the sort of person who did anything for fun. She didn't feel she deserved it, so she didn't seek it out. But he hadn't given her any choice.

"Did you have a good morning?" she asked hopefully. Realizing how difficult she had been in Auburn and how much mental energy he had wasted worrying about her, just paying his expenses didn't seem a fair trade anymore. She could only hope he had recouped some of the weekend's losses in the time he had spent alone.

"It was great," he answered cheerfully. "I did a little more driving around. How about you? Did your grandmother seem comfortable?"

She nodded appreciatively. Adam's line of work did bestow

him with some useful talents; knowing what to say when it came to ill relatives was one of them.

He glanced at his watch. "Well, let's head off then. The security lines can be pretty long on Sundays."

"Sarah? You still here?"

The nasally tone hit Sarah's ears like nails on a chalkboard. It was her uncle again, and he was heading their way.

He sidled up rapidly, his eyes fixing on Adam with an eager smile. He extended a beefy hand. He didn't even look at her. "Hello, there," he said pleasantly. "I'm Sarah's uncle, Dwight Bird, CPA. And who might you be?"

She cringed. The last thing she wanted to put Adam through now was some Southern gentleman's chest-beating routine. But it was too late. As her only male relative, her uncle felt responsible for her—no matter how old she was, and no matter whether either of them liked it. His familial duties could be discharged only by passing her off to another of his gender, and at long last, he had one in his sights.

"Adam Carmassi," the victim returned, his smile easy as he shook the older man's hand. "I'm Sarah's neighbor, from Pittsburgh. This weekend, I'm also her chauffeur. It's nice to meet you."

Dwight's smile faded. But only slightly. He considered a minute. "You helped her fly down, then," he surmised.

"She's a trouper," Adam said tactfully.

Sarah's uncle offered a lop-sided grin, still eyeing Adam like a piece of meat. "She seems to be doing much better these days," he offered, speaking as if she weren't there. "I sure was happy to hear she'd finally sold that house. That's a load off my mind, I tell you what." He shook his head. "Just wasn't healthy, her hanging on to it like that. But there wasn't anything I could do."

The blood drained from Sarah's face. She braced for a hefty glare from Adam, but he responded to her uncle's revelation without missing a beat.

"Oh, I think Sarah's handled the situation beautifully, considering the circumstances," he said smoothly.

"So, what line of work are you in?" Dwight belted, ignoring

the previous statement.

Sarah glanced at her watch. She had to get Adam out of this.

"I'm a Methodist minister," he answered proudly.

Her uncle's eyes widened. It was clear he couldn't decide whether that was good news or bad. "Sarah goes to your church?" he asked incredulously.

"No, I don't," she said quickly, not giving Adam a chance to answer. The interview was over. "We just met each other a few days ago. But right now, we're running late for our plane, so we'd better get going. Goodbye again." She turned to leave.

Her uncle cast a quick, irritated glance her way, then extended his hand to Adam once more. "Well, thank you for bringing her down. I hope you have a nice flight back."

"I'm sure we will." The men exchanged a courteous farewell, then Adam turned to join her. She studied his face as they walked away, expecting to see mortification at least, anger at worst.

What she saw, unaccountably, was a grin.

"I'm really sorry about that," she apologized as they settled into the car. "My uncle means well, but he's impossibly aggravating. I didn't mean to subject you to him."

Adam was still grinning. "You didn't think that little exchange was fun?"

She rubbed her face with her hands. "You have to understand the mentality. I could be President of the United States, and in that man's squinty little eyes, I'd still be a failure. A woman isn't a success in life until she snags a husband and has babies. I'm twenty-six, and I'm single. Ergo, he's failed as my guardian. I'm nothing but an albatross."

"You could never be anyone's albatross."

She looked up. He seemed to mean what he said, and she couldn't fathom why. If she were him, she would drop her carcass off at the nearest mental health facility and never look back. He knew now that it was her, and not her uncle, who had held on to the house until it crumbled. He also knew that she had lied to him about it. He should be confronting her, not saying something sweet.

She took a breath. "What happened to the house was my fault," she admitted without segue. "I inherited it outright after I turned eighteen. My uncle had nothing to do with it."

Adam kept his eyes on the road. The day was blistering hot, as expected. Waves of heat rippled over the concrete before them. "I kind of figured that."

She stared. His claim not to have believed her carefully crafted story disappointed her. It also made her nervous. "Oh?"

"What you told me didn't make much sense," he explained. "And I still don't understand. I'm sure you have some good memories associated with that house, but you also have some very bad ones. Why would you choose to hang on to it?"

She stiffened. This was precisely the conversation she had lied to avoid. "My reasons for not wanting to sell are personal. I didn't want to get into them, but I didn't want you to think I was a nutcase, either. That's why I tried to put the blame on my uncle."

"I see." He was quiet for a while. A long while.

She looked out the windows as they drove, but the scenery on this part of I-285 had little to recommend it. She was struggling to read the message on a faded bumper sticker ahead of her when it began. A queer, disorienting sensation, much like one feels when dreaming of falling. Her head felt light; her body, heavy. Her pulse began to race. Her heart thudded loudly against her breastbone.

She put a hand to her chest.

"I know that none of this is my business," Adam was saying. "But the truth is, I'm worried about you. Keeping secrets can be a huge burden, and despite what you told me about going to therapy, it's obvious that you've left some issues unresolved."

She whipped her head around to look at him. She wasn't sure which upset her more: what he was saying or the bizarre feeling that had come over her. But as she sat there staring at him, the extraordinary thumping stopped—as suddenly as it had begun. Her heart was beating plenty fast still, but not quite so urgently. The lightheadedness was gone.

She was fine. It was nothing.

"I appreciate your concern," she stammered, averting her eyes again. She didn't want him to see how frightened she was. The doctor had told her to call if anything unusual happened. But it was Sunday. The only doctor she could reach down here would be at a hospital ER, and she did *not* want to spend four hours sitting in some overcrowded waiting room. Adam would have to take her; then he would miss his flight, too.

No way. She was fine. In a couple hours she would be back in Pittsburgh. If it happened again, she would take care of it there.

She stole a worried glance at Adam, but they had hit a patch of heavy traffic, and he seemed not to have noticed her lapse.

He was, however, interrogating her again.

She settled against her seat back with a sigh. Her reasons for bringing him along had all been practical, utilitarian. She had never expected to enjoy his company so much. And even though it was contrary to her goal in moving to Pittsburgh in the first place, the idea of having a male friend appealed to her. Surely they could share a laugh once in a while without his getting too close. She could be honest with him about select things; he had no way of finding out the whole truth.

Not until construction begins.

Her hand flew to her chest again. Her heartbeat was still rapid, but she was fine. There was no accompanying funny feeling. Just a sickening image of backhoes and bulldozers, rolling through the weeds—

"But?" Adam asked.

She couldn't remember the reference. She looked at him. His eyes were still on the road. The traffic was horrible. "But what?"

"You appreciate my concern, *but*," he prompted. "*But* I'm a pain in the neck and you just wish I'd leave you alone, or *but* you're convinced there's absolutely nothing I can do to help you?"

The kindness in his voice sent a warmth through her, even as his earnestness made her squirm. "The latter," she answered softy. "You're not a pain in the neck, Adam. As hideous as yesterday morning was, you made me enjoy the rest of the day, which was a real miracle. I really do appreciate that."

His face lit up with a smile. "So, you admit it."

"Admit what?"

"That I can help you."

She squirmed even more. She didn't want to offend him, and she didn't want to hurt him. But he had to back off. "I do not *need* any more help," she stressed. "Of course it still bothers me to think about what happened to my family, and of course I still miss them. What else do you want me to say?"

He paused. A silence hung in the air. "I want you to deal with whatever else it was that happened to you. Besides losing your family." His voice turned deliberate. "The thing that frightens you so much."

Her heart seemed to stop altogether. Her limbs felt paralyzed. He could *not* know. He simply couldn't. She hadn't said anything. There was nothing to see. She hadn't—.

There was no way.

But he couldn't keep on frightening her like that. "I told you I'm not afraid of anything!" she said adamantly. "Why do you keep asking me that?"

Her reaction seemed to distress him. It distressed her too. Could she have done a better job of acting like she had something to hide?

"Sarah," he said calmly, almost penitently, "please don't—"

"What is it *you* think I'm afraid of?" she demanded.

He didn't respond. His face was red. The traffic was demanding a good deal of his attention, and she could tell he was frustrated.

"I don't know what you're afraid of," he said finally. "But I'll be honest with you. I don't believe the story you told me about getting accidentally beat up by a drunk. I know that you're afraid of something because I can see the fear in your eyes—and I've seen it more than once. Nobody can live with that kind of fear and be happy, Sarah. That's why I keep pestering you. I want to help you, if I can. To be happier. That's all."

She forced herself to breathe. In and out. Slow and easy. He didn't know. He didn't know anything. He was assuming that she was afraid of a person.

A person.

That was fine.

She collected herself. "My past hasn't been a bed of roses, and I suppose I do spook easy because of it. But I'm not in any danger now."

He turned his head to the side, as long as he safely could, to look at her. "Are you sure about that?"

She forced her eyes to meet his. "Yes."

He looked back at the road. She got the feeling he wasn't convinced.

"I don't need a bodyguard," she continued. "Or a shrink. I've been thinking that a friend might be nice, but only if he can restrain himself from giving me the third-degree every other second."

He smiled a little, but his jaw was clenched. "And what if he can't make any promises?"

Her heart sank. The man was more tenacious than she thought. Telling him anything would be a mistake.

She looked into his passionate, sincere face. Of course it would be a mistake. A person like him could bring her nothing but trouble. For nine years she had held herself emotionally distant from everyone and everything that could threaten her carefully constructed cocoon. Her world was temporary; everything about her was temporary. She had never so much as indulged in a pet. There had been no point in building relationships, putting down roots. Kansas City was the closest she'd ever gotten to having real friends, which was exactly why she'd had to leave it. She never wanted anyone who cared about her to learn the truth. She couldn't bear it.

She could not let Adam get any closer. In one weekend he'd found out more about her than people she had worked with for years. Could she convince him to stop the inquisition, or would he keep on pushing, regardless?

Had he not just answered that question?

Moist heat pressed behind her eyes.

She would have to stay away from him. Period. There could be no more carefree afternoons, no more witty repartee, no more laughter. Just her new job, her funky split-level house, her books, and her garden.

Her stomach felt like lead. She had had the nerve to really enjoy something. It figured it couldn't last. She had been foolish to think it could.

"Is that a no?" he asked.

Her insides churned. "You'd better get in the right lane now," she said without emotion, her gaze locked on the windshield. "Our exit's just ahead."

Chapter 17

The cab pulled out of Sarah's driveway, shifted gears, and sped out of the cul-de-sac with a loud squeal of its nearly bald tires. Sarah's eyes searched the empty front windows of Adam's house as they passed by.

Then she caught herself, and looked away.

She hadn't seen Adam since Sunday, when she had thanked him profusely for his services over the weekend and then politely dismissed him. He had called yesterday, but she had kept the conversation short.

"So how was your weekend?"

Sarah looked over the front seat to the back of her cab driver's shaved head, which was tattooed with a flying lizard. The man's name was Dustin. He had been her driver almost every day since she had placed the standing order, and he talked too much.

"It was fine," she responded dully. Politeness was admirable in a cab driver, but she found Dustin's continual chitchat unnerving.

"I went to the most awesome club on Saturday night," he continued eagerly, oblivious to her tone. "Komo's Dungeon, on the South Side. Ever heard of it?"

Sarah squirmed. She didn't drink, had never been to a "club" in her life, and did not care to hear—as she had last Friday—how many times he'd thrown up on his way home.

Dustin made her nervous. Men in general made her nervous, but this one was just young enough, strong enough, and creepy enough to set her teeth on edge besides. She kept hoping she would get somebody else.

Her lack of a response did not deter him.

"It's an awesome Goth scene. Crushed Meat is there a *lot*. I think they're playing again next weekend."

Sarah stared out the window and willed the cab forward. Dustin stopped at a yellow light and turned to face her. Reluctantly, she met his gaze.

He smiled lazily, revealing a chipped tooth—no doubt a casualty of his tongue stud. "If you're into it," he said slowly, "I could take you sometime."

Panic surged, bringing heat to Sarah's face.

Calm down!

No amount of experience in putting men off had ever seemed to make the task easier. She had no idea what attracted them. Didn't her modest wardrobe say enough? Her aloofness? Her outright rudeness? She never wore any makeup. Her hair was plain. She was a *librarian,* for crying out loud! But still, there were men like Dustin. Men who assumed she would take their leering as a compliment.

Even greater than her annoyance with them, however, was her frustration at her own anxiety—a reaction she couldn't seem to control, no matter how old she became…or how much time passed.

She summoned her resolve. She would *not* play the hunted doe. She would act like the mature, capable woman she had fought so hard to become.

"No thank you," she said, keeping her tone even. "All I need is a ride to work. And if you don't mind, I'd rather not chitchat on the way."

Dustin's head snapped forward. His face reddened, and the muscles in his jaw tightened.

He didn't say a word the rest of the ride.

When they reached the library, Sarah handed over his tip without making eye contact and stepped hastily out of the cab. She held her head high as she walked into the building, but she could not keep her knees from wobbling.

You're being ridiculous. Everything is fine.

Was it? She had no idea what kind of man Dustin really was. And *he* knew not only her name, but where she lived, where she worked, and exactly what hours she was in transit between.

She rushed into her office and shut the door behind her.

Her shoulders shivered.

Stop that! Just breathe…

There was no reason for alarm. She would simply cancel with that cab company and call another. She would never see Dustin again, and within five minutes he would forget she ever existed.

She would *not* overreact.

Her desk phone rang. She snatched it up immediately, grateful for the distraction.

"East Allegheny Library, Older Adult Services," she answered. "Can I help you?"

"Is this Sarah Landers?"

She recognized the doctor's voice, and her body tensed all over again. "Yes, it is."

She had taken off work the day before to have an EEG—the last of her assigned diagnostic tests. Her boss had been curious as to the reason for it, but Sarah had not explained. Her health concerns were nobody's business.

"This is Melissa Gardner. I wanted to let you know that the results of your EEG were normal. There's no indication here of any abnormal brain function, so that's good news."

Sarah let out a breath. "That means I wasn't having seizures, right?"

"It's highly unlikely. But I am still concerned about your heart. How have you been since Friday? Any episodes of lightheadedness or dizziness?"

Sarah twisted a strand of hair around her finger. She hadn't told anyone about the bizarre feeling she had experienced in the car on Sunday. Now it was difficult to remember exactly how she had felt, and why it had frightened her so. Her heart had raced, but her heart raced all the time. It was doing it again now. Could she really be sure she hadn't imagined the rest of it?

"No," she heard her voice answer. "I've been fine."

"That's good to hear," Melissa answered, sounding genuinely relieved. "But if you should have a dizzy spell, or anything you even *think* might be a dizzy spell, you should call the office and let me know right away. All right?"

It was the perfect opening. Sarah could backtrack now.

She didn't. "Am I cleared to drive, then?"

The doctor took a moment to answer. "I can't say I'd recommend it, no. Maybe with one loss of consciousness, but two still raises concern, even with normal tests. I think we need to watch you a while longer—be on high alert for any more symptoms. Do you have any other questions?"

"No," Sarah answered quickly, before she could decide otherwise. "Thank you."

They hung up. Sarah sat still, staring at the phone. She had lied to her own doctor.

Why?

She knew why. She had lied because she was a coward. She knew how the doctor would respond to the truth, and she didn't want to hear it. She wanted to be fine, so she pretended that she was. It was the same thing she had been doing for years. Sarah the Ostrich. Head in the sand.

She realized she was twisting her hair again. She quit.

She sank down into her office chair, unshed tears burning behind her eyes. Why did she always have to be so afraid? Why couldn't she stand up to things like other women—other *people*—could?

Did it even matter if she had a serious arrhythmia? Her last will and testament had been signed, sealed, and filed; her grandmother would be fine. The Alzheimer's Foundation would have a nice windfall coming, and her uncle could even buy a few more toy cars. No one would miss her anyway—she had seen to that.

She sat there, feeling sorry for herself, for a full five minutes.

Then she got a grip.

She had always known that the truth about her past would come to light eventually. She had expected it, waited for it. When the eminent domain case arose, she was certain that this, at last, was to be her final battle. She was also sure that by the end of it, she would be ready to accept her fate. Strong. Noble. Willing.

She was not.

She wasn't ready, and she could see now that she never would be. Living as a sitting duck wasn't living at all, and she wasn't going to do it anymore.

Whether it was noble, or not.

She rose from her chair and headed for the nonfiction section.

"Why did you change cab companies? Was there a problem with the first one?"

Adam's brown eyes searched hers. She remained standing at her front door, determined not to invite him in. It wasn't easy. Just the sight of him—so spirited, so vital, so alive—was enough to boost her spirits. She hadn't seen him in two days. It seemed like longer.

"Not a problem, exactly," she responded. "I just didn't want to party with the driver."

Adam's eyes hardened. Anger flushed his face, and he stepped forward. "What happened?"

She backed up, startled. She had been trying to make a joke, not to incite him. "Nothing happened," she said quickly. "He just asked me out. So I told him no and called another cab. That's all."

"Are you sure?" The wrath in his voice was not assuaged.

"I'm sure," she said quietly. She looked at him quizzically, and he averted his eyes. The incident had bothered her far more than she let on, of course, but she hadn't expected him to know that. The fact that he seemed to both moved and disturbed her. Clearly, he had noticed her wariness around men. But he couldn't know its source.

And he wasn't going to.

"Is that all you came by for?" she asked, employing her distant-polite voice.

His eyes searched hers again. "No," he answered. "Do you mind if I come in?"

She stiffened. She did mind. The last thirty seconds had only reminded her how vulnerable she was to him. He would come in and make himself comfortable, smile at her with that charming smile of his, and then resume prying into her past. And she craved his company enough to let him.

"I'm kind of in the middle of something," she responded.

He hit her with the charming smile up front. "It won't take long. I promise."

Cursing her weakness, she opened the door. He was already heading out of the foyer before she remembered the books. The volumes she had brought home from the library were lying exposed in the center of her coffee table.

Her breath caught. "Would you like something to drink?" she asked, moving toward the kitchen. If she could keep him out of the living room, he wouldn't see them.

"Sure," he responded, following. "Anything's fine."

She smiled with relief. "I'd offer you some of Rose's zucchini bread, but I ate it all in three sittings. That stuff is delicious. I've been thinking of hinting for some more."

"I'm sure Rose would give you as much as you want," he replied, sounding distracted.

She pulled out two cans of ginger ale, gave him one, and sat down on one of her kitchen counter stools. He joined her on the other.

He sat for a moment without drinking. "I wanted to apologize," he said finally.

She was in mid swallow, and she sputtered a little. "Apologize for what?"

He breathed out heavily. "For pestering you with questions about your past. I realize you don't owe me any explanations. I was only trying to help, but it's obvious I pushed too hard, and I'm sorry."

Her heart sped up again, but this time she didn't worry about it. She was too pleased with what she was hearing. Perhaps she could still enjoy Adam's company—in small doses—without an unacceptable amount of risk. The thought delighted her. She couldn't explain to him how much their outing on Saturday had meant to her—to do so would only highlight her inexperience, and she didn't want him to think her pathetic. But she would dearly love a repeat performance.

"Do you really mean that?" she asked seriously. "You can be happy with what I've told you and let it go?"

He looked back at her, his expression troubled, but sincere.

"I'll try."

She considered. The statement was hardly an oath; then again, oaths got broken. His words weren't absolute, but she did believe he meant them. She smiled. "Well, good. I was beginning to miss that rapier wit of yours."

He grinned, but his eyes were guarded. "So you *were* avoiding me."

"Yes," she admitted. "But I won't anymore, as long as you keep up your end of the bargain."

He smiled for real this time and raised his ginger ale can. "Deal."

She started to smile back, but a pang of guilt accosted her stomach. She hadn't left Kansas City just to find herself in the same mess somewhere else, but that's exactly where she was headed. Whether he asked any more questions or not, just being around him was courting disaster. She liked him too much.

She rose from her stool. "Would you like to see that book I was telling you about?" she offered, trying to entrench herself in librarian mode. "The one about historic landmarks from the Civil Rights movement?"

He said that he would. She walked toward her bookshelves, and he set down his drink and followed her. Her stomach still ached. She didn't want another library client. She wanted a real friend—someone her own age. As different as she and Adam seemed, she had learned in Atlanta just how many interests they shared, and she would love nothing better than to explore them with him.

But she would have to be careful. Their friendship would have to stay casual, light, and superficial. Then what he didn't know about her couldn't hurt either one of them.

She put a hand to her stomach. Her eyes drifted over the second shelf from the left, and she frowned. She always kept her travel books together. Could she have left that one unpacked, with her historical texts? After a moment's contemplation, she remembered that the book had been too tall for the top shelves, and that she had put it on the bottom. She stepped toward the lower shelf on the far right side, hand outstretched.

She looked up at Adam, and he looked awful. His tanned face was as pale as it could get, and he was breathing heavily.

"Are you okay?" he asked, his voice uneven.

She blinked. Was *she* okay?

Then, with a start, she realized where she was. She was lying on the couch, her head and shoulders in his lap. She struggled to rise, and he put an arm beneath her back to steady her.

Grim understanding dawned.

"I passed out again," she said miserably. "Didn't I?"

"Yes, you did," he answered, his voice unexpectedly gruff. "And I really wish you'd cut it out. I told you—I'm no good in medical emergencies. You almost gave me a heart attack."

His expression was deadly serious, but she couldn't help grinning a little. "Sorry."

His speech was only part of the reason for her mirth. The greater part was difficult to describe.

He was holding her, sort of. Not closely, but enough to support her from falling back again. She would have guessed that, finding herself in such a position, she would instinctively pull away. But that wasn't happening. She didn't want to go anywhere. To her surprise, she felt warmly, wonderfully comfortable.

"What happened exactly?" she asked. She didn't want him to move.

"You reached for a book, and then you just kept going down," he answered, his voice still strained. "I sort of caught you, but you banged your hip, I think."

The hip she had injured in her original fall was indeed sore again. But until he mentioned it, she hadn't noticed. Actually, she felt fine. More than fine.

Images filtered slowly through her mind, images from a part of her youth she could still remember fondly. She had had a boyfriend once. His name was Jimmy Jones, and his appeal had come from his simplicity. He was a farmer's boy, her neighbor across the highway, and not the type of person she had ever envisioned being with for long. But he had been tall, with wavy brown hair and large green eyes that sparkled when he laughed, and he had always been sweet to her. Their dates consisted of dinner, a movie, and an hour or so of parking at some quiet nook on his father's cattle farm, necking with relative innocence in the front of his fire-engine red mini pickup.

The romance had run its course as most teenage pairings did, moving from exciting to lackluster to over in a matter of months. It was the kind of dalliance most people forgot as soon as the next one blossomed. But for Sarah, there had never been a next one. She'd had nothing to do with any man since Dee died.

"You should call Melissa," Adam urged. "She may want you to go to the ER."

Sarah made no response. The ER was the last place she wanted to be. She felt safe right where she was, with Adam's benign, gentle touch bringing her a much-needed sense of serenity. With the exception of brief hugs from her aunt or female friends, her life since the tragedies had been devoid of affection. She had nearly forgotten how calming—how satisfying—such closeness with another human being could be.

She had been missing something. What happened with *him* had messed up her mind. But perhaps she wasn't a lost cause.

She looked up into Adam's kind, handsome face. And she wondered.

Chapter 18

"Sarah," Adam repeated. "Are you listening to me? Are you feeling lightheaded—or anything?"

"I feel fine," she answered softly. "I'm just not in any hurry to move, that's all."

His own heart skipped a beat. His breathing was still ragged. First she had fainted on him, now she——. Well, he didn't know what she was.

When she had fallen he had scooped her up and carried her to the couch, fully expecting that she would wake up uneasy, perhaps even upset with him for holding her. He had been halfway prepared to dodge a blow. But that wasn't what happened. Instead, she had relaxed into his arms.

He supposed he should take that as a good sign—that she was still capable of giving and receiving affection, that she felt comfortable with him, that she had finally begun to trust him. If she had been anyone else, he could accept her acquiescence as a victory and celebrate. But she wasn't anyone else. And that was the problem.

She was the woman with whom he had just spent one of the most enjoyable Saturday evenings of his life, and the one whose image had been plaguing his mind ever since. The one whose flowing hair and subtle curves now tortured him at every turn, monopolizing his thoughts and cutting into his sleep. He'd been working very hard, for the last forty-eight hours, to convince his brain that she was off limits, and he did not need an impromptu situation such as this playing havoc with his resolve.

A physical relationship with Sarah was out of the question. First off, because toying with a woman without any kind of commitment went against everything he believed. But even if he was ready to move on, even if he thought the relationship was right for him, there was no question that it would be wrong for her. She had been sexually assaulted, and that trauma was still unresolved. Heaven only knew what other demons she was fighting.

So why didn't she squirm from his grasp? She should be getting up right now, moving toward the phone. She should be talking about what had happened and apologizing for having scared him to death. She should be doing anything—*anything*—but nestling so comfortably in his arms, looking up at him with those beautiful blue eyes of hers. Looking at him so…

Damnation.

In one movement he lifted her off his lap and shifted her to a sitting position beside him. Then he backed away, perching on the edge of the couch to face her. "Either you call Melissa," he ordered, "or I will. What's your preference?"

She blinked at him, startled. She probably thought he was angry at her. Maybe he was.

"I'll call her in a few minutes," she answered. "I just talked to her this morning. There's no rush."

"No rush?" he challenged. "You just passed out again—cold. You don't think that's significant?"

The expression in her eyes changed from dreamy to defiant. He breathed a sigh of relief. The old Sarah was back.

"Of course it's significant," she retorted. "But it's not an emergency. I already know what she'll do. She said if it happened again she would have me come in for another Holter monitor—but for a longer period this time. It's not like I need to be hospitalized."

"I'm not so sure about that."

She stared at him with surprise, but then her expression softened. "Please don't worry about me, Adam. You really don't need to. I'll be fine. I promise."

He could tell that she was thinking about Christine. She thought he was being overly paranoid, overly protective, because his wife had died so young. She was right. But only partially.

He got up off the couch, went to the kitchen, retrieved

Sarah's cell phone from the counter, and placed it in her hands. "Call now."

"I don't have the number memorized. Besides, it's after hours."

Adam took the phone back. "I can get her home number from information. Her husband will be listed." He began to dial, but Sarah stood up.

"I told you I would call her," she said firmly. "But not now. Not this second."

"Why not?" he demanded. "What are you afraid of?"

The same, trite question hung in the air, heavy as lead. She stared back at him, her eyes angry. "I have to go to the bathroom first," she said stiffly. *"Do you mind?"*

He shut his mouth. She was good at getting him to do that. He just wished he knew when she was bluffing. She was quick-witted enough that he couldn't always tell. He sat back on the couch and set the phone on the coffee table. "Fine," he answered, allowing some of the humor to return to his voice. "The phone will be here when you get back. But don't try climbing out the windows. I know where you live."

She rolled her eyes at him. Then she rose and walked out of the living room.

He sat and stared into the air ahead of him, mulling her actions. Most likely she was afraid of what the doctor would say, afraid to face more tests. If he hadn't been here when she collapsed, would she have told anyone? Had it already happened more often than she was admitting?

He wished he knew exactly what had transpired at her last appointment. He had been assuming that Sarah's fainting spells stemmed from some past injury, and that Melissa was aware of the abuse. But what if he was wrong? What if Sarah hadn't been honest about her medical history? Or more frightening still, what if her problems weren't related to trauma at all? What if she was suffering from something else entirely, something even more serious? He rubbed his face with his hands. *No. Not that.*

What he had gone through with Christine had been sheer hell. She had suffered for weeks without telling him— headaches, blurred vision, all the way up to the first seizure. It was his job, his duty, to support her, but she'd been too much of a martyr to let him. She had tried her best to hide what was happening, telling herself she could handle it alone, that it would be wrong to worry him unnecessarily. But in her heart she had to want him to see it. She had to hope that he would read the signs, care enough to demand an explanation.

He hadn't. He hadn't realized how sick Christine was, how stressed she was, until it became impossible for her to hide it anymore. He'd done everything in his power to support her, then. But the end had come more quickly than anyone imagined.

He let out a muffled groan. He couldn't bear a repeat of that nightmare. He might not have been able to help Christine, but he was committed to helping Sarah, and he was *going* to succeed. He just had to keep his head straight. There were a hundred reasons why he should fight any romantic feelings for her in the process—and if he had to, he'd write every blasted one of them on the backs of his hands.

He stood up. Maybe the answer, for him, was to date again. He'd waited longer than necessary already, but the idea still didn't appeal. A single pastor was always prime quarry for a congregation's every spinster daughter, granddaughter, niece, and cousin, and exactly one year after Christine's passing he'd been deluged with third-party propositions. He had put them all off then, and he'd been doing so ever since. But maybe he was wrong. Maybe hanging on to celibacy was what had gotten him into this mess.

He glanced down at the coffee table. A stack of books, each tagged with library stickers, lay sprawled there. The top one showed a man driving a backhoe.

His brow furrowed. He leaned down and took the book in his hands. *Road Construction Fundamentals: A Handbook for Civil Engineers.* He flipped through the pages curiously. Excavation, grading, compaction, paving. It was hardly the sort of reading matter he would expect from Sarah. But hadn't she insisted she read everything? He replaced the book and looked at the others. *The Making of Our Nation's Highways. Surveying and Site Preparation: A Civil Engineer's Guide.*

His stomach knotted. Every one of the books was about road construction. There was no way such a selection could be a coincidence. She wanted to know something about the building of that bypass in Alabama. But why? Why would she care what happened to that wreck of a house now?

I tried to fight it, but I lost, she had told him. She had protested the eminent domain. She hadn't wanted to be anywhere near the house herself, and she had let it fall into complete ruin, but when it came to losing it for good, she had resisted. She seemed unduly interested in the survey stakes—in where the road itself might go. Was she seeking confirmation that the house would be destroyed, or was she, in fact, hoping for the opposite?

All at once he got the feeling he was being watched. He raised his head.

Sarah was standing in the doorway, staring at him. She looked petrified. She also looked furious.

He scrambled for a cover. "Well," he said with a smile, "you claimed you read about everything, but I wasn't sure I believed you. Now I do. But Civil Engineering? Please. Surely you can find leisure reading a little more exciting than this. Personally, I'd recommend Mack Stokes' *Major United Methodist Beliefs.*"

Her expression turned deadpan. "Sounds riveting."

He tried not to show his relief. She didn't realize he'd made the connection. If she had, she would be throwing him out now.

She walked on into the living room, then passed by him and headed toward her ginger ale. "I'm sure you'd find much of what I read to be on the dry side," she explained. "But it's not really—not once you get into it. I pick a topic, I delve in, and I almost always enjoy myself. You can learn a lot by not yielding to first impressions."

She sat down on her stool and took a sip, and he marveled at her forced nonchalance. In another minute, she might indeed be lecturing him on the Dewey decimal system. "Sarah," he said heavily.

She offered an innocent lift of her eyebrows. "Yes?"

He walked toward her and extended the phone. "Do you

really think I'm going to forget?"

She made no move to take it. "I was hoping."

He sat down on the stool next to her. "Do you *want* me to worry about you?"

"Of course not."

"Then call now." When still she did nothing, he growled low in his throat. "I'll call for you, then."

She took the phone from his hands and set it down on the counter. "I'm perfectly capable of managing my own health."

"You could have fooled me."

"Well, that's not saying much."

He fought a grin. How could she be so infuriating, and yet so blasted attractive, at the same time? "I'm not leaving until you call. You'll probably need a ride to the ER anyway, so let's get this show on the road."

Her blue eyes fixed on his, and for a long moment, she seemed lost in contemplation. Her gaze made him nervous. Either she was sizing him up to test another lie, or she was plotting a whole new defense strategy. He didn't care for either prospect.

"It's not fair to you," she said softly.

He drew in a breath. "What isn't?"

"Your feeling like you have to take care of me. I know how much you must hate dealing with doctors and hospitals after what you went through with your wife. I want you to stop feeling responsible for me."

A tide of warmth welled up within him. She was perceptive, and she was compassionate. Just two more reasons why her request was impossible to follow. "I'm used to dealing with doctors and hospitals," he assured. "It's a part of my job. And I appreciate your concern, but I'm going to continue to worry about you until you stop passing out, and there's nothing you can do about it."

He picked up the phone again. This time, he finished dialing.

Melissa Gardner's intelligent hazel eyes bore into Adam's,

and their unspoken message chilled him. "You know I can't share any of the details of Sarah's situation with you," she reminded. "At least, not unless she wants me to."

"Of course," he replied, certain that Sarah, who was out of earshot getting dressed, would agree to no such thing. But Melissa didn't have much of a poker face. "You're sending her home?"

The doctor nodded. "It's not my preference, but she's adamant about not being hospitalized—at least not yet. I've agreed to continue working with her as an outpatient, but only if she agrees to certain conditions, one of which is that she needs to have someone watching her."

"I see."

"Adam?"

"Yes."

"I hope you're not—" She broke off, then shook her head. "Never mind. It's not my business."

She started to turn away, but he grabbed her arm. "Sure it is. Tell me what you were going to say."

The doctor looked at him with a peculiar mixture of respect and sadness. He had only known Melissa for a little over a year, but he admired her tremendously. Not only because she was such a devoted church member, or even because she was a dedicated-enough physician to go back into her office on a Tuesday evening just to spare a friend a trip to the emergency room. He admired her because she was, hands down, one of the sharpest, most discerning individuals he'd ever met. "You do realize that Sarah's condition could be serious," she continued. "Don't you?"

His pulse began to pound. "Yes, I do."

She knows, he thought soberly. The doctor could tell that his feelings for Sarah were more than just neighborly. Was the depth of his distress that visible? Was there something about the way he looked at Sarah? He hadn't touched her again. He'd been careful about that.

"All right," Melissa responded, her smile still tempered with sadness. "I just wanted to make sure."

He couldn't ask her anything more. Sarah reappeared. She

walked out into the waiting room with an artificial grin and patted the black box at her waist. "Frankenstein's all set," she announced. Then she thanked her doctor and signaled her readiness to leave. Melissa showed them out, and they returned to Adam's car.

"Well," he asked as he buckled. "Did she say whatever it was you expected?"

"Precisely," Sarah answered, her tone falsely upbeat. "It's just a waiting game, really. I need to pass out while I'm wired. It's the only way I can get a firm diagnosis. But I will get a diagnosis, and then I can get it taken care of. There are treatments. It's not hopeless."

"Of course it's not," he declared, more forcefully than intended.

She was quiet for a moment. Then her voice turned meek. "Can I ask you something?"

He nodded.

"If you wouldn't mind terribly, I really could use a competent chauffeur for the next few days. Raoul wasn't as bad as Dustin, but he did ask me if my husband mowed our lawn himself. It's no big deal, really, but—"

"Of course. I'll be happy to."

He tried to halt the rush of heat into his face, but wasn't sure if he succeeded. No wonder the woman mistrusted men. Was she hit on by every one she came across?

Probably.

His temperature edged up a degree. He remembered the fear in Sarah's eyes as she gazed at that accursed mattress, and again he felt rage toward a man he'd never met. No doubt Sarah's attacker had walked away unpunished. Where was he now? Did she even know?

"You don't look happy to," she responded, watching him with concern.

He plastered an artificial smile on his face. "Sorry," he answered swiftly. "I was thinking about something else."

Chapter 19

Sarah propped up the pillows at the head of her bed and lay down, attempting to convince herself that it felt good to be alone again. Between Rose's and Adam's babysitting, she hadn't had a spare unwatched moment in which to begin the unpleasant task before her. Adam had hung around for hours after returning her from Melissa's office last night, leaving only when she insisted she was ready for bed. Even then, he had called back later to assure himself she was still all right. Had he not had a church meeting he might have stayed with her this evening too, but instead Rose had taken a shift, feeding her a mouth-watering Tex Mex casserole and then teaching her some line-dancing steps to go with it.

She should have hated their fussing; felt smothered. Instead, she had enjoyed every minute of it. So much so that her house now seemed strangely empty.

She glanced at the pile of books on her nightstand and drew in a heavy breath. She had no more excuses. It was time. Facing the grim reality of her situation would be difficult, but now more than ever, she was determined to fight. She had thought of little else the last twenty-four hours besides the feeling she'd had waking up in Adam's arms.

She knew it was selfish of her. But she wanted to feel it again.

She lifted the top book from the stack on her nightstand and pulled it into her lap. Her pulse pounded. *Road Construction Fundamentals: A Handbook for Civil Engineers.* A backhoe graced the book's cover.

Images roared into her head like a cyclone. A crumbling, decrepit house. A crane. A wrecking ball. The walls caving in in a choking cloud of dust. Men in orange vests standing around, everywhere. Surveyors, equipment operators. Swarming. Measuring. Sifting. Digging. Pushing mounds of earth. Smoking. Laughing out loud. Then suddenly, one of them would shout…

Her lungs shuddered. She slipped the book back onto the stack and slowed her breathing. She would read the book. She would definitely read it. Just not right this second, now, before bed.

She eased her head back onto the pillows, ashamed of herself. She knew what she was afraid of. She was afraid that the books would confirm her worst-case scenario—nip her fragile, new-found sense of optimism in the bud.

She could not let herself give up. Not if there was one chance in a million that the nightmare she envisioned *wasn't* a foregone conclusion.

She thought of Rose and Adam. She attempted to concentrate.

Was there a way out—even if the worst did happen at the farm? She had heard no one mention *him* in years. Granted, she had not stayed in Auburn long enough to hear much gossip. At Dee's funeral, his cousin had told her that he had skipped town, and she had found that comforting. But what had happened since?

With one determined motion, she swung her feet onto the floor and rose. She strode into what was supposed to be a dining room and sat down at her computer. Her finger punched the power button, and the machine whirred. Her heart was beating rapidly again, but at least its rhythm was regular.

Maybe she couldn't face the construction books—and the nightmares they would surely provoke—tonight. But there were other, less gruesome angles to pursue. A little background check on *him* would be simple. It was certainly long overdue.

Her fingers hovered over the mouse as the screen flickered to life. She clicked herself online and pulled up the search engine. Then she stalled.

She had never even known his last name. How could she possibly look him up?

All she had ever heard Dee call him was Rock. He might have shared the same last name as his cousin, but could she even remember that? They were a shiftless lot, all of them. Sarah's parents had hated Dee's hanging out at their place; the patriarch was in jail as much as not. What was their name?

She wracked her brain. She could come up with nothing that sounded right, but she did have a strong feeling that the name was a common one. Jones. Simpson. Something like that. Dee had dated so many lowlifes, Sarah never could keep up with them. She had always stayed two chapters behind—

Her mind snapped to attention. *Of course.* She might never remember Rock's cousin's surname, and she had probably never even heard his own. But Dee knew.

She withdrew her hand from the mouse and rose, then moved to the rear bedroom. The banker's box of her sister's things was packed carefully into a spare closet, along with several boxes of her own childhood mementos. She pulled it out and popped the lid.

Yearbooks. A fast-pitch softball trophy. The rest were all loose papers and journals. Dee had never been much of a collector, and her accolades had been few and far between. But what Sarah thought was most important to her sister, she had kept. And at the top of that list was her writing.

Dee had been a prolific writer, even in grade school. Most of what she wrote was fabrication—unlike Sarah, she had never cared much for facts. But as she grew older the one real thing that did fascinate her was her own love life, and she had taken great pleasure in dramatizing it. Their parents had become concerned, in Dee's later years, that such writing was a compulsion, perhaps even a sign of schizophrenia. But Sarah had disagreed. Dee was high strung; she was emotional. In retrospect, Sarah thought her sister might even have been bipolar. But Dee didn't write because she heard voices in her head. She wrote because she enjoyed it.

Sarah dug through the stack of once-blank, hardback books. Not for Dee the quintessential calendar diary—she preferred her exploits be in novel format. A fun date might be half a chapter; a dramatic break-up, two. Her social life had been a whirlwind after high school, and she had started filling books in a matter of months. Sarah had read them all religiously, at Dee's insistence, but she couldn't keep up. Dee was never still dating whatever guy Sarah read about, and the latest pregnancy scare had long since been resolved. Dee preferred writing to talking even, leaving Sarah's real-time questions answered all too often with the irritating *"you'll just have to read about it!"*

A flash of blue caught Sarah's eye. She grasped the book in question and pulled it out. It was the last one Dee had written in. Most of the books were red and plain, but she remembered this one. She had seen it in a store, admired its floral design, and bought it for her sister.

She sat down on the floor, the book in her lap. Dee had written nothing after their parents died. Sarah knew because she had checked the last entry shortly after Dee's death, hoping to find some small nugget of comfort. She had not. To her knowledge, the only words her sister wrote after the tragedy were those of her suicide notes.

Sarah flipped through the book, plunging in a thumb at the point where ink-covered pages met white. She did remember what Dee's last chapter had been about. It had been about him.

She fingered forward to the beginning of the chapter.

> It's not like I was looking for trouble. Okay, I might sometimes, but on this particular day I wasn't. I liked Tommy; we were still having a good time. I had no plans to break up with him. He was super hot for me, and I liked his body: tall, lanky, and smooth.

Sarah skipped ahead impatiently. Dee could write reasonably well for a teenager, but she had always gone on far too long with physical descriptions, particularly those of the opposite sex.

> We were out on his porch drinking some Cokes, and Brett and Toni were there.

Martin, Sarah thought with a flush of pride, the images

swiftly coming back to her. Tommy and Brett Martin. The Martin's farm was only a few miles from their own, and it was a renowned dump. Skinny chickens were always roaming onto the highway in front of it, and the yard was littered with rusted car and tractor parts.

It seemed like an ordinary Saturday. We were just kicking back, having some laughs. Then we heard a really loud engine.

Sarah averted her eyes. She could not read everything Dee had written; it was too likely to sicken her. She knew how the chapter would go. Dee would describe meeting the new guy, detail every inch of his physique, then lapse into some drivel about how he undressed her with his eyes. Dee would wallow in artificial guilt over whatever guy she was dumping—for all of a paragraph or so—then slide right on into another first date.

Sarah didn't need to read all that. All she needed was a name. Whatever details Dee might occasionally have fudged, Sarah knew that all her characters were real.

She returned her eyes to the page and skimmed.

He had the blackest hair, like he was foreign...

Clearly older than Tommy, though at the time I didn't know how much...

His stare moved down—

Sarah exhaled. She closed her eyes. Just a name, she told herself. Forget the rest. Don't think about it.

Tommy walked up and gave him a high five, but he didn't look all that happy to see him. He kept looking back at me like he knew there were sparks flying, and there wasn't much I could do, because there were. "This is my girlfriend, Dee," he said, with an emphasis on the 'girlfriend.' "Dee, this is my cousin Rock." I liked the name right away. It was strong and it was cool,

*just like him. He smiled at me, and gave a kind of a
wink...*

"Rock what?" Sarah said aloud, frustrated. She had already
known that much. It wasn't the kind of name one forgot easily.
But she doubted that it was his given name, and even if it was,
she could do nothing with it alone.

She skimmed further, her eyes touching each line as if it
were caustic. All Dee talked about now was Tommy, his
reaction to his cousin's bedroom eyes, his growing agitation.
Next followed the inevitable breakup scene, which dripped
with the high drama Dee was so famous for.

> *I was sure he was going to break down in tears on
> me, and I wondered, for a split second, if I was doing
> the right thing. But I didn't feel the same way about
> him anymore. I had to see how things went with
> Rockney, because I couldn't stop thinking about him.*

Sarah's eyes paused. *Rockney.* A full first name, or a last? She
leaned toward the latter. He probably had a first name he didn't
like. She continued to skim. No further names caught her eye.
Until she saw her own.

> *He took me home on his bike, and when we got there,
> Sarah was in the yard. She was doing something in
> the flower garden by the garage.*

Sarah's heart beat loudly. This part, she remembered having
read before. She remembered how much she had hated it.

> *Sarah looked gorgeous of course, like she always does.
> She's got hips and thighs as slim as a boy, but with
> just enough butt to make guys drool. And even though
> she's kind of flat-chested, she's got such great
> shoulders she's still totally hot. She was wearing a
> halter top and short shorts, and I just knew Rock
> would notice her.*

Dee knew that Sarah would read the story. She had written about her sister before, and always in flattering terms, perhaps because of that. But her words now brought nothing but nausea.

> *She didn't come out to see us, and I was glad. Rock stared at her and asked who she was, and I told him she was my straight-laced and boring little sister. [No offense!] I thought he might ask more about her, but he didn't. He just grabbed me and started kissing me, right there in front of her!*

Sarah slammed the book closed. There were only two paragraphs to go, and she could tell at a glance there were no names in them. What was the point of torturing herself? She knew how it ended. Dee mused about how good a lover Rock was likely to be, then ended the chapter looking forward to their next date. Except that their next date hadn't happened. The Landers' plane had crashed first.

Sarah breathed out heavily. She hadn't completely wasted her time. His name was probably something Rockney. Maybe he even went by Rock Rockney. Either way, it was an unusual name, and that would make tracking it easier.

She replaced the book and returned the box to the closet. Then she headed back to her computer and put her hands on the keyboard. Her fingers were less than steady, and she had to backspace twice to correct typos, but at last the hated words appeared clearly on the screen before her. "Rock Rockney."

She hit the enter key and the search engine churned, producing a list all too quickly. Her eyes scanned it with trepidation. There were indeed men with the last name Rockney who went by "Rock." But none were logical matches. They were either too old or too respectable. If she did come up with a hit for *him*, it was not going to be as part of a byline.

"Rockney Alabama," she typed. Then she held her breath. There were few entries, and her eyes zigzagged over them as if she were racing. Genealogies. Too old. Unrelated news story. That's a woman.

She released the breath. There was nothing.

She sat motionless for a moment, deliberating. Maybe no news, in this case, was good news. It was possible she had the wrong name altogether, or that she was missing a reference in another state. But there was nothing on the internet that tied him to Alabama. Wasn't that all that mattered?

She felt a tiny surge of jubilation. Had she not wished, more than once, that all traces of the man's very existence could be erased? That she could pretend he had never been born?

Perhaps she could. Evidently, nobody else cared about him either.

Her doorbell rang. As always, its volume caught her off guard, and she sprang from her seat in response. *Adam.* He had come over to check up on her again. He said he would call, but she had left her cell phone in the bedroom; if it had rung, she hadn't heard it.

She shut down the computer and made haste toward the door. She didn't want him to know what she was doing, but she didn't care to risk a 911 call either. "I'm fine," she said immediately, greeting him with a tight smile. "I just left the phone where I couldn't hear it. Sorry about that."

He appeared handsome in the porch light, as he did in all lights, and she could no longer look at him without recalling the sensation of being held. The memory—and the potential— tantalized her. There had been a time when she was certain she would never be attracted to a man again, but she had been wrong. Whatever else Rock Rockney had done to her, he had not robbed her of the capacity to appreciate—and desire— human affection.

Without hesitation, she reached out, took Adam by the hand, and pulled him inside. "Come in."

He acquiesced, but then stood stiffly in the doorway, seeming uncomfortable. She realized that she hadn't bothered with her robe, and wondered if her state of dress was disturbing him. But she was perfectly decent—well covered in a T-shirt and the sleep pants her Holter monitor was clipped to.

"You missed a great casserole tonight," she said, suddenly feeling awkward herself. She moved toward the living room and gestured for him to follow. "Too bad you were tied up. You could have had a free line-dancing class, too."

He smiled, but didn't move. "Rose has long since given up on me as a dancer. But I am sorry I missed the food."

Sarah stopped walking. She tried again. "Want some leftovers?"

He continued to stand in place, watching her from a distance. "No thanks. I can't stay long. I just wanted to check in. Are you going to sleep now? No more climbing stairs or operating the stove tonight?"

"Straight to bed," she responded, not bothering to cover the disappointment in her voice. "I promise."

He nodded. "All right, then. Good night." He turned toward the door.

Sarah moved to intercept him. "Thank you for checking on me," she said sincerely, blocking his path. She didn't want to be alone with her thoughts—alone with the books still sitting on her bedside table. Even if he did appear anxious to leave.

"You're welcome," he said softly.

She knew he was intentionally distancing himself from her, but regardless, she felt an overwhelming urge to touch him. "You know," she replied, being careful to keep her own voice light. "As guardian angels go, you're the best."

If it was a mistake, she didn't care. She put her arms around his neck, and she hugged him.

Chapter 20

A knock on Sarah's office window startled her. She jumped in her seat and swiveled around. Adam was standing in the hall. Confused, she gestured for him to come in. He had never come all the way into the library before; ordinarily she waited for him outside. Was he early?

She checked her computer clock. No, he wasn't early. She was late. She floundered with her mouse, quickly closing out the web site she had been combing. He hadn't seen it, had he? Her face reddened. She had been doing well today. She had vowed to do some online research as soon as she put her salaried time in, and she had kept that promise. But she'd found more than she bargained for, and she had lost track of time. He could *not* have seen the site. She couldn't deal with the questions.

She studied his expression as he entered. She couldn't tell if he were reacting to the website or something else, but he was clearly on edge again. He had departed at light speed after she had hugged him last night, and though he had acted more normal on the drive to work this morning, she was certain now that she had blundered. It had been an innocent embrace— much less than what she wanted. But perhaps he had sensed that. Perhaps that was why he had recoiled.

She sighed at her own foolishness. She had wanted to experience new emotions; she hadn't considered that rejection might be one of them.

"Are you hungry?" he asked.

"Of course," she answered, shutting down her computer and gathering her things. "Work always makes me hungry. But as I told Rose last night, I don't expect the two of you to feed me. I should be cooking for you."

"And I fully intend to let you do that," he countered. "But not tonight. Tonight the weather's gorgeous, and it's high time you saw the view from Mt. Washington. A trip up the incline is mandatory for all new residents, and if we don't get you up there soon, you'll be fined. Plus, I know a great little restaurant in Station Square that's right on the way. What do you say?"

Sarah blinked. Whatever had happened last night, he wasn't recoiling from her now. The proposal sounded heavenly, and she didn't care to analyze it. "Will you let me buy dinner?"

He considered. "Only if you promise to spring for dessert, too. They make an awesome cheesecake, and I'd hate to miss out because I was too polite to ask."

She grinned at him. "Like that's a risk." A flash of color caught her eye, and her brow furrowed. He had a trace of bright green along the side of his face, smeared into the roots of his black ringlets.

He followed her eyes and put a hand up. "I didn't get it all off, did I? Sorry about that. I was in a hurry."

Her eyebrows rose. "What exactly—"

"Vacation Bible school," he explained, opening the door for her. "I was the Jolly Green Goliath. You got a problem with that?"

"Um, no," she said with a smile. "No problem at all."

A gust of wind ruffled Sarah's hair, and she put up a hand to tame it. The breeze that rolled off the rivers was brisk, and in the warmth of the evening, delightfully refreshing. But she didn't want her hair in her eyes. She wanted to take in every detail.

The dramatic contours of Pittsburgh fascinated her. Unlike every other place she had lived, and contrary to her own preconceived notions, western Pennsylvania was beautifully mountainous. The steep cliff that was Mount Washington towered over the Monongahela River below, offering a spectacular view of its junction with the Allegheny River to form the Ohio. A cluster of skyscrapers filled the Golden Triangle where the three rivers met, and a flowing fountain punctuated its tip. From the concrete overlook on which she stood, Sarah could see downtown, both stadiums on the North Shore, and many miles' worth of the quaint city boroughs and suburbs that flanked the rivers' edges. New office buildings gleamed where the old steel mills had once stood, but many historic clapboard houses still remained, clinging with seeming impossibility to the sheer slopes flanking the Mon.

She leaned out over the iron railing. "Our houses are where, exactly? Over there?" She pointed.

Adam, standing beside her, adjusted her aim. "More that way."

"I see," she said with a smile. "And where's Kennywood? Isn't it right on the Monongahela?"

He stared at her a moment, smiling curiously. "It's that way," he pointed, "around the bend."

Sarah took in the view with satisfaction. She felt good tonight—as good as she could remember feeling. Just as in Georgia, Adam had managed to whisk her troubled mind out of its element and into a fantasy zone that was blissfully carefree. In the dream, she could be a normal person. A normal woman.

The rather noisy family of five that had been sharing the overlook with them decided to move on. Silence descended, and Adam looked over his shoulder. They had been in the midst of crowds all evening, but now, suddenly, they were alone.

Sarah liked the thought. She had read that the windswept overlook was a popular place for weddings, and now she could understand why. Its milieu was undeniably romantic.

Adam pulled his arms from the railing and straightened. He moved a step away.

Sarah frowned. They had had a fabulous evening. She had eaten pasta and cheesecake until her slacks were tight and laughed until her ribs were sore. Adam had laughed, too. And she didn't believe he was only humoring her.

So why should being alone with her now make him uncomfortable? "Is something wrong?" she asked.

He started. "No, of course not," he answered, his smile self-conscious. He leaned back against the railing—but farther away.

Sarah watched him, puzzled. She might be one of the least socially experienced twenty-six-year-olds on the planet, but even she was certain, after tonight, that he was as attracted to her as she was to him. She had been making no secret of the latter—at least not lately. So why was he fighting it?

She moved over next to him, their arms and shoulders touching. "This is a beautiful spot. Thanks for bringing me."

He straightened and stood up, his expression graduating from nervous to miserable. "You're welcome. We'll have to come again sometime. But for now, we should probably get going."

Disappointment slammed her like a blow. Why did the one and only man in the last decade who had managed to stir her interest have to be so noble? She wanted to be held again. She wanted that warmth, that comfort. She would be happy with even the smallest dose of it, at least for now. What was the problem?

He turned to leave, but she stood still. "Adam?"

He stopped and faced her.

"Can I ask you a personal question? Please?"

She saw his jaws clench. He deliberated a moment. "All right."

"Have you dated anyone since Christine died?"

His every muscle seemed to tense. "No."

"Do you think you will?"

He turned away from her. His shrug was stiff. "I'm not sure."

Sarah breathed out with a huff. She knew she had no right to ask for clarification, given how carefully she guarded her own history. But she was almost certain that his hesitancy had something to do with Christine. Whatever the source, she wished they could resolve it soon. Patience and forbearance took time she didn't have.

"I wish you would tell me more about her," she requested, her voice casual. "All I know is that you went to seminary together and that she was beautiful. But what was she like?"

He looked out over the vista rather than at her, and his gaze seemed troubled. But after a long pause, he put his hands back on the railing, relaxed a little, and complied. He smiled as he talked, but his tone was mirthless. "Christine was devoted, caring, resourceful. She loved working with kids. She struggled through seminary, but she enjoyed her work in Christian education, and she was good at it. She was an only child, and the way she was raised she could have been spoiled, but she wasn't. She never complained about anything. She was happy to keep her life simple. Her faith was very strong."

He stopped. He looked so unhappy Sarah's own stomach twisted. She didn't understand. She expected him to be melancholy, to miss the love of his life. But something didn't seem right. It was as if, over a year after his wife's death, his grief still had claws. She felt the same way when remembering Dee, and she knew she always would. But her situation was different. Christine's death had been tragic, but at least it had been due to natural causes. Her husband should have found more peace by now. The same peace Sarah had come to with her parents' passing.

"Then I'm sure she would have wanted you to be happy," Sarah stated, well aware of her brazenness. "She wouldn't want you to grieve forever."

He straightened again. His smile was superficial; tolerant. "Of course she wouldn't. She was quite adamant about that, in fact."

He backed off and took a step toward the street. "Enough about me. Are you ready to go?"

Sarah smothered another sigh and followed. She realized she was getting nothing more than a dose of her own medicine. But that didn't make it taste any better.

They were alone in the incline car on the ride back down the mountain. Sarah supposed Adam regretted that. He was sitting a good foot away from her on the bench seat; from the looks of him, he would have preferred the row behind.

She supposed she should be embarrassed—trying to

convince a man he should move on when her motives were so obviously self-serving. But she refused to be embarrassed. Adam's being lonely didn't serve anyone's purpose. Still, she suspected she should tread a bit easier. "I didn't mean to push you," she offered, breaking an increasingly awkward silence.

To her surprise, a glint of humor appeared in his eyes. "You, push me? I don't think that's a problem."

Sarah stared. Then what *was* the problem? He couldn't possibly think he was the one doing the pushing. If anything, he'd been treating her like she were made of glass.

A sour thought wafted through her mind, and her pulse began to pound, rattling her body in concert with the shudder of the descending incline. "Adam," she said earnestly. "Are you afraid I'm going to die?"

His face hardened. His eyes met hers. "You are *not* going to die," he commanded. "Don't even say that."

"But you are afraid of something," she insisted. She knew it was egotistical, assuming that something besides lack of interest was preventing the closeness she was suddenly so desperate for. But the chemistry between them tonight had been palpable. Why wasn't he acting on it? If it wasn't Christine and it wasn't her illness, what was it? He might be a minister, but he wasn't a priest.

"Tell me," she demanded.

He continued to look her straight in the eyes. His answer was slow and deliberate. "I'm afraid of hurting you, Sarah. You may think you're ready for more than a friendship, but I don't believe you are."

A flush of heat enveloped her. Her cheeks burned. What was he talking about?

She scooted away on the bench, twisting to face him. "What makes you think," she practically stammered, "that you know what I need?"

His brown eyes continued to hold hers, gentle now, but fervent. "I saw the way you looked at that mattress in the house. I see how uncomfortable you are around men. It's not hard to put two and two together."

When the light turned on in her head, it seared her like a

flame. She put a hand to the rail in front of her, half-standing in the quivering car. "You think I was *raped?*" she shouted, incensed.

Adam's eyes flickered over her shoulder. They were passing the ascending car on the opposite track. Two middle-aged couples, no doubt within earshot, eyed them suspiciously.

Adam lowered his voice, but its resolve didn't waver. "Yes. I do."

"Well, you're wrong!" she hissed. "You're just plain *wrong!*"

He said nothing. He remained sitting, his stance calm, sympathetic. She squelched a strong urge to throttle him.

"You don't believe me, do you?" It was rhetorical question, and she didn't give him a chance to answer it. She plopped back down on the bench with her back to him, working hard to regain her composure. Why was she so indignant? It was easy enough to see how he could reach such a conclusion. Yet she hated that he had even thought it—hated it so much that she had just come perilously close to blurting out the truth. The man was getting to her.

"Sarah, it's nothing to be—"

She whirled around. "Oh, spare me the recovery rhetoric," she snapped. "I have lied to you before, and you know that. I did it to protect my privacy, and I'm not apologizing for it. But I'm not lying to you now, Adam. I have *not* been raped. *Never.* Not even close!"

For several seconds, he made no response. The only sounds in the car were the clinking of the machinery and the swipe of a tree branch across its metal roof. "I didn't mean to upset you," he said finally. "I'm sorry."

Three more deep breaths cooled her ire. At least superficially. "I'm sorry I snapped at you. I know you're just trying to help."

They sat silently for the rest of the ride, staring out over the approaching rooftops of Station Square. They disembarked at the station and walked wordlessly to Adam's car. He opened her door for her, then turned.

"I had a wonderful time tonight," he said quietly. "At least, up until the last fifteen minutes. Sorry about that."

She grinned. Her eyes moistened. "Ditto."

His expression softened. Then he stepped forward and pulled her into his arms.

She wrapped her own quickly around his waist and pressed herself to his chest. The feeling she had craved so fiercely did not disappoint. It was soothing, peaceful, fortifying. She wanted to absorb his warmth, to capture it. She wanted to keep it with her.

But the embrace didn't last long. After a few, tantalizing seconds, he dropped a kiss on the top of her head, grasped her upper arms gently, and set her away from him.

His message could not have been clearer. "Well, it's back to work tomorrow," he announced lightly, moving toward his own door. "I suppose we'd better get you home."

Sarah turned onto her right side, jerking the sheet with her. She lay still for half a minute, then flopped onto her back again.

Rock Rockney. It was as if he were in the room. Laughing at her. Taunting her. She could not remove his heinous image from her mind.

He just grabbed me and started kissing me…

Dee had been so naive, so reckless. She had thought she was worldly, but she was deluded. She hadn't been afraid of him, but Sarah had been. From the first moment Sarah had laid eyes on him, straddled over that monstrous motorcycle, shirtless, her flesh had crawled. She didn't like the way he looked at her. She didn't like the way he handled her sister. But like an idiot, Sarah had said nothing. She never said anything to Dee about her promiscuousness, because she knew that any criticism could send her sister into a rage. Or worse yet, a profound and lasting funk.

Sarah had said nothing about Rock. Not then, and not when he next appeared at their door that first night after her aunt and uncle returned to Georgia. The first night she and Dee were alone.

Sarah hadn't wanted him in the house. She didn't want Dee to let him in. But the house was her sister's as much as hers.

Dee wanted privacy, and Sarah gave it to her. Even when Sarah heard Dee yelling at him, she had stayed upstairs. An argument with a boyfriend was nothing unusual; Dee yelled at everybody. Sarah had almost been rooting for such a spat, figuring if he got ticked enough, he would leave. But she never heard a door slam.

No sound had alerted her to the horror unfolding. It had been the opposite, the absence of sound, that had soon pricked the hairs on the back of Sarah's neck. That made her creep down the stairs, slowly, cautiously, to see exactly what was going on. She knew what explanation was likely. She knew the scene she was about to stumble on could be X-rated, and if that was the case she was prepared to return promptly to her room. Just as soon as she made sure that Dee was all right.

Sarah flopped back on to her left side again. Sleep wouldn't come. Her mind raced.

Adam thought that she had been raped. She could not remember that fact without a flush of heat forcing her into a cold sweat. It was almost as if his thinking it made it true. As if she and her sister had spun out of time and landed in each other's places.

She sat up and turned on the light. It had been years since she'd suffered a night like this. Dee was in her thoughts frequently, but over time she had learned to prevent reliving the worst of what had happened—at least when there was no provocation for remembering it. She knew that going back to Auburn would be difficult, and unexpected catalysts like her ER visit were always a threat. But there was no excuse for her tonight. Adam's accusation had disturbed her far too much. If she had any sense, if she had kept her wits, she could have told him that he was right. Maybe then he would have been satisfied, and the probing would end. What did it matter if he thought she had been raped?

She supposed it shouldn't matter. But it did.

"Sorry, Dee," she mumbled aloud, staring at the hands that clutched her sheets. "I almost lost it. But it won't happen again. I promise."

She reached over and pulled *Watership Down* from the

bottom of her book stack. Then she laid her head back on the pillows. She had no idea how long she tried to read, staring at the same lines over and over, or at what point her grip slackened and her eyelids closed. All she knew was that when she woke, it was with such a violent start that the book landed half a room away.

She had seen Dee. Seen her just as she had seen her then. Battered and bruised. Humiliated and angry. Frightened, livid, incensed. Dee's eyes had been wild, her lower jaw had trembled.

I did it, Sarah, she had declared, her words ragged and uneven, split with gulps of breath.

I killed him.

Chapter 21

When Adam arrived at the church office the next morning, only Ruby Reichenbach, the full-time secretary, was in, and she was on the phone. He was glad. He passed her desk with a smile and a wave, dodged into his own office, and shut the door.

He dropped into his desk chair and ran a hand through his hair. *Another sleepless night.* They were becoming the norm.

He pushed the button to boot up his computer, then sifted through his stack of phone messages. He had missed two calls yesterday, both when he should still have been here. Ruby had been careful to note the times. She had underlined them twice.

He could have told the secretary the reason for his irregular hours. He could have said he was driving an ill neighbor to work, and other than the famed Reichenbach single-eyebrow arch, he would have received no more comment. But he hadn't told Ruby—or anyone else in the office—anything. And if he was honest with himself, he knew why.

Because he wasn't driving an ill neighbor to work. He was conniving to spend more time with a woman he wanted desperately.

More desperately, in fact, than he'd ever wanted any woman in his entire life.

How stupid had he been to think that he could help Sarah without becoming emotionally involved? He should have known better, stopped himself sooner. He'd been in lust from the first moment he'd laid eyes on her, and now that her soul had bewitched him as well, the effect was excruciating.

When they had left Auburn that dreadful morning, all he had wanted was to make her happy. Everything else he had been trying to do for her seemed only to backfire, and he had wanted to give her something—a little bit of joy, a couple hours of fun—to make up for it. She had seemed to need that, and she had seemed to enjoy it. But it was supposed to end there.

He'd had no intention, when he picked Sarah up at work yesterday, of asking her out for another fun-filled evening on the town—certainly not after what had happened the night before. She hadn't meant anything by that first impromptu hug, and he had gotten himself out of it as soon as humanly possible, but that hadn't mattered. Three seconds of being next to Sarah in a T-shirt with no bra had cost him seven hours of sleep, and he had been determined not to repeat that agony. But his well-laid plans had gone up in smoke when he saw her in her office, her eyes glued to the website of the Alabama Department of Transportation.

He knew then that whatever was bothering her was only getting worse. And to think that he could back off—leave her hanging in the wind with that wretched fear still in her eyes— just to pacify his own torment was ludicrous. Whatever Sarah's problem was, he was in it with her now. And if that was the case, he had reasoned, if getting closer to her was a necessary evil, was it so wrong to indulge her in a ride on the incline and some cheesecake?

He had been an idiot. And now he was playing with fire.

Knuckles rapped tentatively on the glass panel in his door. He looked up and gestured for Ruby to come in.

"Good morning, Adam," she said crisply. "I have another phone message for you." She walked to his desk and laid the pink slip on top of the others. Then she paused, unabashed, to study him. "Is everything all right?"

He blinked. Why exactly was she asking? How transparent was he? "Everything's fine," he insisted, guessing that he must look tired. "I've just been having trouble sleeping lately. I think it's catching up to me."

The secretary smiled tolerantly. "Your hours have been a little irregular this week. I've wondered what was going on, but I didn't want to pry."

Adam breathed deeply. He knew that he had been cruising

for a lecture. Ruby was probably the world's most efficient secretary, but she could also be the most difficult. She had worked with his predecessor, Reverend Diller, for seventeen years, and from Adam's first day at work she had let him know just how impeccable her previous boss had been. Reverend Diller had always been on time. Reverend Diller had preached lovely sermons. Reverend Diller had always returned calls promptly, and he had never left a half-full cup of coffee on his desk overnight. Ruby Reichenbach had known Reverend Diller. Adam was no Reverend Diller.

"A friend of mine has been having some personal problems," he answered, bending the truth only slightly. "I've been trying to help, but I'm not sure I've accomplished much."

Ruby studied him another moment. "I'm sure you're helping more than you know," she said politely, her mouth drawing into her own peculiar, painful-looking version of a smile. "But you do have to take care of yourself in the process."

"You're right about that," he said appreciatively. "Thank you."

She smiled her tight smile once more, then walked out.

Adam took a deep breath. Then he turned to his computer. Why had Sarah been looking at the ALDOT website? He had promised he would stop pestering her with questions, but he had never promised to stay out of her business entirely.

He located the website and perused its contents for himself. Weather news. Emergency road closures. Alabama Homeland Security. Statewide Transportation Improvement Plan. He clicked into the latter and soon located a listing of construction projects in Lee County, including the bypass extension that affected Sarah's farm. But the information given online was scant, consisting almost entirely of coded numbers and letters. What was Sarah looking for?

A map, he thought grimly. It wasn't enough for her to know that the house would be razed. She wanted to know exactly where the asphalt itself would be laid. But why?

He closed his eyes. What he had first suspected when he saw the construction books in her house was seeming more and more likely. She didn't want the house destroyed. What she was doing was trying to save it. There hadn't seemed to be anything else in it that she wanted. But perhaps there was something else still there—something she was determined no one else should have.

He clicked around for more information, but the site didn't post specific construction maps. How would she get her hands on one? He clicked on *Project Letting*. The bypass was already underway; the maps would be in the hands of the contractors by now. *Proposal Letting List. Low Bid Sheet.*

His fingers paused. Sarah had undoubtedly been looking for what he had just found—the name of the contractor on the project. She would contact them; ask her questions. But what would she do with the answers?

He sat back in his chair, brooding.

Sarah had lived in or around Auburn for seventeen years, and she hadn't visited the area in five. It was a relatively small town, minus the university, yet while he was with her she hadn't made a single phone call or looked up a single friend. She hadn't even asked to stop at a familiar restaurant. She had liked the one that was new—and practically deserted. He believed all along that she was hiding from someone, and he still did. Was she afraid that the razing of her house might enable this man to find her again?

His mind jogged back to the day she had collapsed on her steps. She had practically had a conniption when he had picked up her mail. He hadn't meant to be nosy, but he couldn't help but notice that the one letter she had already opened had a legal-looking return address. He had wondered then if she were being divorced, or sued, and if the distress of seeing the letter was what had caused her to pass out. Looking back now, he suspected it involved the eminent domain case. But why was Sarah being so secretive about it, even back then?

A glimmer of an idea rose up in his mind. Perhaps there was something about the house itself. Something about the way it was built, something hidden within it or buried under it, the discovery of which would be sensational enough to attract public attention. Her name might be broadcast in the local media—perhaps along with her current location. It could lead the man right to her.

To what lengths had she already gone to separate herself from her past? Was Landers even her real last name?

"Adam?"

He started, nearly tipping his chair. Ruby was standing just inside the door of his office, watching him. He hadn't noticed her come in. "Yes?"

She stepped closer. "Robert Pearson is out of the hospital. His wife said you mentioned coming by again, and she didn't want you to waste a trip downtown. But he would love a visit at home if you have time."

Adam nodded. "Of course. Thank you."

"Also, Laurie is still waiting for your sermon title for the thirteenth. She needs to get *The Spirit* to the printer by Tuesday."

"I'll have it to her by the end of the day," he said optimistically, wondering just how generic a title he could come up with. He was behind on his sermons for August. He was behind on everything. He had lost control of his own brain.

Ruby stared at him for a solid ten seconds, not saying a word. Then she turned on her heel and walked out again.

Adam sat up in his chair, closed out the ALDOT site, and pulled the top phone message off his growing stack.

Then he put it down again.

How could he go about his normal life when Sarah was scrambling to stay hidden from a rapist? She had denied it when he had confronted her—denied it so fiercely and so convincingly that for a moment he had believed her. But he was afraid that taking her word for it would be wishful thinking. He shouldn't be surprised that she would deny it. Such a reaction was common, practically typical. And she had been keeping the secret for a very long time.

If only she would decide to trust him—to let him in. Why was she so convinced that no one else could help her? Why did she insist on fighting such a battle alone?

Guilt. The answer flashed in his mind like a neon sign. Whatever trauma had befallen Sarah at that house, she still felt guilty about it. She thought it was her fault, and she was ashamed of it. She didn't want anyone to know.

His eyes moved to the picture at the edge of his desk. It was a photograph of Christine and himself at their seminary graduation. His jaws clenched.

Guilt, at least, was an emotion he understood. Guilt at failing Christine when she became ill, yes. That was what everyone focused on. But no one knew about the rest of it, the worst of it. Not even Christine. At least that was what he had hoped. He could never bring himself to be honest with her; he had chosen to live the lie instead. He had ruined her young life, and then a brain tumor had ended it. That kind of guilt couldn't easily be washed away. He preached about forgiveness, he believed in it, he practiced it. But forgiving himself, when it came to Christine, wasn't possible. He could not bear even to think about it.

His intercom beeped. Apparently, Ruby was getting tired of walking back and forth. He pushed a button. "Yes?"

"Can you take a call from Hillary Phillips? On line two?"

"Sure thing."

Hillary Phillips, an attractive young RN who was interested in spearheading a church wellness program, reminded him of Sarah. At least in height and coloring. But Sarah was thinner and shapelier, with those mesmerizing blue eyes...

He punched a button on the phone. "Hello, Hillary?"

He heard nothing. He pushed two more buttons in succession. Then he realized he'd made a mistake.

Within seconds, Ruby appeared at his door again.

He looked up sheepishly. "I think I cut her off."

Ruby nodded solemnly. She approached his desk. "*Reverend Carmassi*," she began, arching her left eyebrow high. "I may look young, but I wasn't born yesterday."

He stared. Ruby was in her early fifties, but didn't look a day under sixty-five. "What do you—"

She raised a hand. "If you don't want to talk about it, that's fine by me. But don't go skulking around acting like it's some secret. That's not healthy. Besides, everyone in the office already knows."

He shook his head in confusion. "Already knows what?"

She let out a long, dramatic sigh. "That there's a woman in your life, of course." Her dour mouth flipped into a bona fide grin. "And personally, I'd say it's high time."

Adam stared at the clock on his desk, willing its stubborn hands to move. The entire day had proceeded at a crawl, but the afternoon had been particularly agonizing. He had caught up on his phone messages and made two house visits, but he could get nowhere on the August sermons. He could think of nothing but how to get through to Sarah, and despite his protestations that he was only helping a friend, every time Ruby or Laurie caught him staring at the walls, they grinned at him like schoolgirls.

In forty-five minutes, he was due to pick up Sarah at the library again. He would take her to Melissa's office to have the monitor removed, and then he would take her home. What he would do after that, he had no idea. But he was certain he would have to do something.

When the intercom buzzed again, he jumped on it. "Yes, Ruby?"

"It's Laurie. You have a call from a Cindy Tollison."

Her voice sounded practically gleeful.

"That rings a faint bell," he said honestly. "Is she Harriet Tollison's daughter?"

Laurie's voice sounded disappointed. "Oh, I'm not sure. Maybe."

He took the call, being careful this time to punch the right buttons. "Hello, Adam Carmassi, here."

"Reverend Carmassi?" a small voice squeaked. "Hi, my name is Cindy Tollison. I'm sure you don't remember me, but I've visited your church a few times with my mother—"

"Harriet. Of course. I remember you." He did, now. A petite, mousy girl—unusually shy. Her mother had obviously been matchmaking when she introduced them. He hoped that wasn't what this call was about.

"Okay. Well, the reason I'm calling is, you know Sarah Landers, right?"

His heart stopped. It took him a second to find his voice. "Yes, I do. She lives across the street from me. Why?"

"Well," Cindy continued, her tone even squeakier, "I work with her at the library, and I saw you drop her off a couple times, and I recognized you. I don't know how well you know her, but—"

When his heart started up again, its pounding threatened to break a rib. "Did something happen to her? Did she collapse?"

"Yes," Cindy replied, sounding relieved at his familiarity with the situation. "She was walking down the hall with one of the other staff, and she fell down. She woke right back up afterward, but she hit her head pretty good. She kept saying she was fine, that it happened all the time, and she absolutely refused to let anybody call an ambulance or take her anywhere. But her supervisor is really worried about her, because she's wearing that box thing, you know, and he told her to take the rest of the day off, but she wouldn't go. And she won't tell anybody what's wrong—"

"Of course she won't." He had shut down his computer while Cindy was talking. His keys were in his hand.

"She went back to work in her office, but she looks awful, very upset, and the supervisor asked us all confidentially if we knew whether she had family he could call, and I told him I'd seen her with you, and that you were a minister—"

He was standing now, one hand on the doorknob.

"Thanks for calling, Cindy. I'm on my way now."

Chapter 22

Sarah's fingers fumbled over the pushbuttons on her cell phone. She didn't use the device often; she didn't talk much on the phone, period. Lately she'd been keeping it close by, as Melissa had advised, but there had been no need to call for help today. This time she had awakened to see herself surrounded by half a dozen people just itching to summon an ambulance. But she wasn't going anywhere. Not until she made this call.

She looked from the keypad to the printout on her desk. Despite the time difference, she might have waited too late already. Contractors seemed to quit work mid-afternoon, and it was a Friday to boot. But her own day had been so consumed with meetings and public tasks, this was the first chance she'd had to be alone in her office. She had to make the call now. No way could she wait until Monday.

She finished entering the string of numbers and hit the call key. Her fingers trembled. She tucked the offending hand under her thigh.

After a few seconds, she heard ringing. Her eyes drifted to her door, reconfirming that it was closed all the way.

"Clifton Construction."

She cleared her throat. She had expended a great deal of effort in her college days to drop her Southern accent, but she could still reclaim it on demand. All it took was a little concentration and the sweet, lilting twang of the woman she was impersonating flowed easily off her tongue. "Hey there. This is Deb Jones calling. Our farm's over on Angus Road, across from where the bypass is cutting through. Y'all are doing that work, right?"

"Yes ma'am."

Sarah took a breath. She would beg her ex-boyfriend's

mother for forgiveness if the time ever came, but the scheme was the best she could come up with. The Jones' farm hadn't been condemned, but it bordered on several that had. Their interest would surely seem credible.

"Well, I was wondering if there was any way we could find out exactly where that road's going to cut, because my husband is thinking of putting up another house for my daughter and her kids, but you know we don't want to do it if it's going to end up too close to the new road and all."

There was a pause. Sarah swallowed hard. She knew she was making a lot of assumptions. She was assuming, first off, that the man she was talking to didn't actually know Deb Jones. She was assuming that if his phone had caller ID, he wouldn't notice the unfamiliar area code. And furthermore, she was assuming that this unknown man would be friendly enough to go out of his way to help a stranger.

Papers rustled. She could hear the man mumbling to himself. "Um…are y'all out west of Angus Road?"

Her pulse pounded. "Yes. We're right across from the Landers' place, and then our property wraps around the south end of the Hankmans' farm too."

Another pause ensued. Sarah felt herself break out in a sweat. "Is there any way my husband or I could take a look at the maps you've got? Or could you send us a copy, maybe? We'd be happy to pay for it."

"Um…"

She held her breath.

"Yeah, I guess we could do that. I've got the section that shows out by your place, but you'd have to see it yourself to tell what's what. You got a fax machine?"

She released the breath with a gush. "Well, I don't, but you can send it to my daughter. Her number's 412-555-5411. Name's Torey Braddock. That would be SO helpful. Thank you so much."

"No problem, ma'am. You have a good day, now."

"You too." Sarah hung up the phone. Good old Southern hospitality. The ploy about the daughter had been perfect. She hadn't said where Torey was supposed to live; surely he wouldn't think twice about the area code.

She would have the maps in her hands before she left today. Everything would work out fine. Really, it would.

She put her hand back up on the desktop and willed it to stay steady.

Sarah had just begun to make progress on some legitimate work when she caught sight of Adam out of the corner of her eye. She looked up, and their eyes met through the glass. Her pulse increased slightly, as it always did when she saw him. But this time he didn't smile at her. This time he opened the door to her office and walked straight in. He seemed upset.

Her own face showed confusion. She didn't think she was running late again, and a glance at her watch confirmed it. "Hello," she said tentatively. "You're early. Is something wrong?"

He pulled up her spare chair and sat down. He didn't say a word. He just looked at her.

All at once, she knew what was wrong. Her heart began to thump, and she cursed inwardly. Everyone's heart thumped now and then, but hers couldn't do even normal gymnastics without a ripple of panic shooting through her. "How did you find out?" she sputtered. "Who called you?"

His expression remained sober. "I have my sources."

She didn't like that thought. Then again, maybe she did. "You didn't have to come early," she insisted. "I might as well be here as anywhere else. Besides, in a way, it was a good thing. I was wearing the monitor, so I should be able to get a diagnosis now."

"You should have called me."

His tone made her breath catch. His dark brown eyes sparkled with moisture as he looked at her, and she felt a flush of warmth. The man really did care.

"I'm sorry," she apologized. "I didn't want to worry you—not when I knew we were going in to get the monitor off today, anyway."

He looked skeptical. "Would you have told me when I got

here?"

She didn't answer immediately. Lying to him was becoming more difficult. Knowing that he genuinely cared made it painful.

"Honestly, Adam," she began, "I don't know. Surely you can understand why I don't want you to worry about me. It's bad enough *I* have to worry about me. Why should anyone else suffer if they don't have to?"

He looked at her curiously. Then he stood and stepped closer. As his hand reached out toward her head, she realized what he had seen. She flinched, but his fingers were gentle as they drew back the curtain of hair on the left side of her face, revealing the monstrous goose egg on her temple.

He withdrew his hand with a sigh. "Come on. Let's go."

She tensed. "Go where? I have a half hour of work left."

"You know where, and don't give me that—your boss already told you to leave."

Sarah blinked. "How did you know that?"

"Divine revelation."

She narrowed her eyes at him. She didn't want to admit, even to herself, how much this latest episode had frightened her. Rationally, she had been expecting it; she had even been hoping it would happen soon, while the monitor was in place. But having it happen at work…when she was supposed to be in her element, in control…waking up to find every one of her coworkers staring at her…

She realized her limbs were trembling again. Somehow, when her health problems had been a secret, they had seemed more manageable. Now that the entire library staff knew, her own perception of their significance had magnified.

She rose and fumbled for her purse. "All right, we can go. I just need to check for a fax before we leave." She threw her bag over her shoulder and walked around the desk. She attempted to sidle past Adam in her haste to get out the door, but she didn't make it.

As their shoulders brushed something within her gave way, and without conscious thought she turned instead and leaned into him heavily, resting her cheek on his shoulder. Her eyes closed.

He wrapped one arm around her back.

"This one really scared me," she murmured.

His deep voice answered her in a whisper. "I know."

They stood still a few seconds more, then she drew in a shuddering breath and straightened. She didn't look at him. She couldn't bear to.

She knew that she deserved whatever punishment fate doled out to her—she had already escaped it longer than she could have expected. But knowing that didn't help. Why, oh why, did everything have to come crashing down around her just when, for the first time in her adult life, she'd finally gotten a taste of what it could feel like to be really, truly happy?

A wave of ire washed over her at the thought, tempering her fear. *Hang fate.* She was not going to give up. If her days were numbered, they were numbered, but she would not spend whatever time she had left lying in some hospital bed, idly wondering whether the grim reaper or the Alabama State Police would be the first to rip her out of it.

As long as her heart continued to beat, however erratically, she was going to continue what she had started, formulate a plan. All she needed was a little more time. Time *without* Adam hovering over her. He couldn't have any idea what she was doing. He could never know the truth about her.

Not ever.

"Thanks for that," she said softly, pulling away from him and moving towards her office door. "I suppose we'd better get going."

Chapter 23

"If I pass out again," Sarah insisted, her voice firm, "I pass out again. I survived it four times already and I'll survive it again. But I will not let you or Rose waste any more of your time babysitting me. You're going to go back to your house and do whatever it is you ordinarily do on a Friday night, and you're not going to worry about me anymore. That's an order."

Adam showed no reaction. He remained standing just inside her door, looking toward her kitchen thoughtfully. "How about if I order some pizza?"

Sarah sighed. She didn't want him to leave. But she had work to do, and she needed privacy. The fax she'd been waiting for had come through just in time, and it was practically burning a hole in her purse.

"Adam," she said, as seriously and intently as she could manage, "you know I enjoy your company. But right now, after three days of wearing that gnarly contraption and only being allowed sponge baths, what I really want is a long, hot shower. And if I also had the very comforting knowledge that you were, for at least one evening, getting to do whatever you wanted without worrying about me, I would have just the kind of relaxation I need right now."

He looked back at her with a studious expression, and she could tell he wavering. "And what if you pass out in the shower?"

She sighed. "Then I'll try to remember to dip to the right, so my goose eggs will match." She reopened her front door. "I'm going to take a shower whether you like it or not, so unless you're planning on taking one with me, you might as well be in your living room as mine. I'll call you at nine o'clock, on the nose, with a full report. Now get out of here."

He blinked at her, as if his thoughts were temporarily misplaced. Then he shook his head and turned toward the door. "All right, I'm going. But I'll expect that call at nine. And *don't* bolt the door. If I can't reach you by phone, doorbell, or window-pounding, I'm using Rose's key."

She nodded. "Understood."

"Goodbye for now."

"Goodbye. Thank you."

He walked out, and she shut the door behind him. Then she made a beeline for the kitchen, withdrew the folded papers from her purse, and spread them out on the counter.

Her eyes roved over the sea of blurred solid and dotted lines, cryptic symbols, and meaningless numbers that covered the assorted sheets of fax paper. Her brow furrowed. The pieces were photocopies of sections of a larger map, and after some manipulation of the various puzzle pieces, she managed to rejoin them in what she thought was some semblance of the original. But she was still hopelessly befuddled.

What was she looking at? Did the angled lines to the left represent Angus Road? If so, what were the lines with the crosshatches? The circled letters? All those abbreviations with arrows?

She let out a muffled groan. Evidently, construction diagrams were written in a foreign language. But the setback was only temporary. She had taught herself to read French, Spanish, and a little ancient Greek—she could figure this out, too. All she needed was a translation guide.

She snapped her fingers, then started for the bedroom. Surely one of the construction books she had checked out would explain how to interpret such diagrams. She reached the pile, picked up the top book, and thumbed through the table of contents. Chapter two was pay dirt. She sank down on the bed, switched her brain into gear, and began to read.

Twenty minutes later, book in hand, she walked slowly back toward the map on the kitchen counter. Her feet dragged on the thick carpet. Her heart was shifting into overdrive again.

She reached a stool, sank down onto it, and took a deep breath.

Calm. Just be calm.

She closed her eyes and counted to fifty. Her pulse seemed a little slower. She opened her eyes again.

She forced her gaze back over the patchwork diagram, and this time she found Angus Road immediately. She could also tell that the map was centered on the Hankman's farm, with her parents' land being up and to the left. But what she needed to see, she could see.

Her house and garage were small, nondescript boxes. The new, four-lane bypass was demarcated by a series of straight, bold lines. It swept across the southeast edge of her parent's property like a knife blade, forever chopping off the ruins of the old barn and the stand of pines beyond.

The bypass did not go near the house. But the house wasn't what Sarah cared about.

Her heart thumped against her sternum. She tried to slow her breathing again, but she couldn't. Her eyes were fixed on one thin, squiggly circle. One small, insignificant-looking symbol that held her fate solidly in its grasp. The new road did not go on top of it. But it came darn close.

She looked back at her book. The grid marks on the map. The numbers. She measured with a fingernail. She calculated.

Fifteen yards.

The book slid off her lap onto the floor.

Only fifteen yards separated the edge of the asphalt from the edge of the water. Only fifteen days might separate her life as she knew it from the disaster to come.

Fifteen hours.

Fifteen minutes?

The images stormed through her mind, torturing her. Punishing her. *Come on, Sarah!* Dee's shrill voice had commanded her. *Push!*

The ground had been wet. The motorcycle was amazingly heavy.

Use your legs!

They could never have made it if the pond were not downhill. They had barely made it as it was. She could still feel the ache that had plagued her arms, her back, her thighs. It was all that had kept her from going numb.

It had been dark, except for the moonlight. Moonlight that glinted off every inch of the bike's perfectly polished chrome. Every inch that wasn't smeared with blood.

He's slipping, Sarah! Stop a minute!

Bungee cords. Dee had strapped Rock's body to the motorcycle with bungee cords. Every which way—whatever worked. Ten, at least. Maybe more. She'd used every one Sarah could find.

Okay, now push again. Harder!

The wheels bogged down in the mud. The weight kept shifting. Sarah's muscles had felt like gelatin.

We're almost there!

Down toward the pond's edge. Steeper, soggier ground.

We're going to have to run it in, or it'll stop shallow. We'll need lots of momentum. Are you ready?

Sarah had nodded. She could remember nodding, over and over again. She remembered the slick feel of the bloodied leather seat, the awkwardness of looking for a hand hold.

Grab his leg, Sarah!

She had touched him then. His cut-offs were around his thighs, and she had grabbed the denim. She would not touch his cool, sticky skin. She couldn't bear to help her sister manipulate the stiffening limbs. She would look nowhere near the bloody mess that was his head. She had tried to look anywhere else.

Moonlight on chrome. Wheels in mud.

On the count of three, we head straight in. Keep running until you can't go anymore. Don't let it fall over! All right?

Concentrate. Keep it upright.

Three!

They had run down the steepest part of hill, plunging heavily into the stagnant water. Had the slope been more gradual, the bike would have bogged down before it was covered, but Dee had thought of that. Instead, their speed had propelled the grim load well past the shallows, sucking them along with it into the quickly deepening water.

Okay, Dee had sputtered. *Let go!*

Sarah struggled to find a footing in the shifting silt. She pushed her wet hair from her face, only to feel some slickness departing onto her forehead. Was it mud…or blood? She had whirled away and immersed every inch of herself in the dark water, scrubbing at her face, her hands. So much blood. She would never get it off.

She rose and took a breath. Dee was talking to her.

It's sinking, Sarah! Look at it!

She had submerged herself again. Underwater, it was quiet. Underwater, she could pretend she had left the insanity of the other world. Underwater, she was—

Underwater, she was with him.

Sarah had burst back above the surface. She had scrambled up the pond's muddy banks and dry heaved into the cattails.

It's going to be all right, now. Dee's hand had rested gently on her shoulder. *No one is ever going to know anything about this. Do you hear me?*

No one.

Not ever.

Sarah's eyes remained glued to the survey map.

Fifteen yards.

She stood with a jerk. She crumpled the faxed pages into a ball and propelled them into the trash can.

There's no hope now.

Of course there is!

They're going to find him.

Not necessarily. Maybe they'll just fill the pond in—bring in a load of dirt and dump it. Then no one will ever find him.

Sarah put her hands to her face. The warring voices would drive her insane, if she let them. She had to stay focused, stay on course. The first answer she'd gotten might not have been what she wanted. But there were plenty of other questions, and thanks to Melissa's fortuitous absence from the office earlier, Sarah still had the weekend.

The technician who had removed the Holter monitor hasn't asked specifically whether Sarah had passed out again, so Sarah hadn't offered that information. Nor had she bothered to inform Adam that she hadn't actually talked to a doctor. Without a rush on the results, Melissa wouldn't get a report until Monday at the earliest. Whatever therapy might be prescribed then, Sarah would be willing to cooperate, even if it meant time in the hospital. But not yet.

Not until she had explored every option.

She bent over and retrieved the construction book from the floor, then thumbed back to the table of contents. *Site Preparation.* She turned to the appropriate page. She took a deep breath. She started reading.

She didn't have to read for long.

Whole pages described the difficulty in working with wet ground. Ground that had too much clay, held too much water. It was unstable; it had to be properly compacted. Pockets of water required drainage. Trenching. Pumping. The work area had to be firm.

The pond was fifteen yards from the edge of the concrete. It was in a low spot. The whole area would have to be regraded.

Every drop of water would be drained.

Sarah closed the book again. Her brain felt spent. She reached up and rubbed at the itchy patches the monitor tape had left on her chest. Then she carried the book back to her room, returned it to the pile, and headed for the shower.

The tape had left red marks on her skin. She lathered her washcloth with soap and scrubbed at them. Rivulets of warm, soapy water ran down her body while steam filled the tile-walled bathroom like a cloud. But inside, she was frozen solid.

They'll find him. It's only a matter of time.

There seemed no point in questioning it. The body would be found, and soon. There was nothing she could do to stop it.

You could get it out. You've got money.

She smiled at the lunacy, even in her despair. How exactly did one go about advertising for the sort of person who could relocate a corpse? She could know half a dozen mob bosses, and it still wouldn't solve her problem. Right now, she was the only person alive who knew the truth. Letting others in on the situation would at best result in perpetual blackmail; at worst, provide additional evidence against her.

She needed to face the facts. Rock Rockney's body was about to be discovered. Plan A was no longer tenable. It was time to formulate Plan B.

Nine years had passed. Nine years of boiling hot Southern sun and humidity. Would there be anything left to find?

She had tried to answer that question earlier in the week, but she had not succeeded. The only forensic pathology books in her library either covered basic techniques, described real-life cases, or both, and the internet had been no more helpful. Decomposition was an inexact science, and water added an infinite number of variables to the equation. She had managed to identify one book she thought might help, and she had promptly ordered it through interlibrary loan. But she had no idea when it would arrive.

She needed it now.

The heat in the shower made breathing difficult, and she opened the glass door just long enough to let a wave of cooler air rush in. She wasn't ready to end the shower yet. She couldn't bear to leave its warmth.

They'll know who it is.

Sarah's jaws clenched. Whatever Plan B rested on, it could not be Rock's anonymity. The motorcycle would be found too, license plate and all. Would the number still be readable? It hardly mattered. There would be other clues, like engraved serial numbers on the engine, not to mention the potential for plastic ID, which he could have had either in his pocket or in some storage compartment on the bike.

What she had to focus on was the timing. She had found no reference to him on the internet; there seemed a good chance that he was never reported as missing. Dee had insisted that he was a drifter with no close kin, just extended family he dropped in on from time to time. A sudden loss of contact would hardly raise red flags with those who knew him, even if they had cared. And if the attitude Tommy Martin had displayed at Dee's funeral had been any indication, no one did.

It could have happened after Dee had died and Sarah had

left. How could anyone prove it hadn't? The farm was abandoned; anything could have taken place out there. Who was to say Rock hadn't gotten drunk and driven the bike into the pond himself?

With bungee cords?

Maybe it was a suicide.

Sarah turned off the shower. Nausea swelled.

It felt wrong, looking for a way out. She should call the police herself, right now, and get it over with.

And then what would happen?

Shivers rocked her body as she toweled off. She could feel the moist heat of the room against her skin, but it had no effect. The chill was inside.

What could she tell them? That she had only been a teenager, that she wasn't responsible for her own actions? She could see now how foolish her decisions had been, but back then, she couldn't see anything. All she knew was that the one person she cared most about was falling apart, and that if she didn't do everything she could to pacify her sister, she would wind up completely alone.

The worst had happened anyway. All of Sarah's efforts had failed, except one. Her word. She had promised her sister that she would never tell anyone about the rape, ever. Dee had preferred taking her own life to the horror of living with what had happened that night, and her last request was that she be allowed to rest without the shame of it.

It had all happened a long time ago, true. But the years that had passed would only make the story more prurient, more sensational. If the truth were to surface now, the legacy of Deanna Elaine Landers would no longer be a tasteful tombstone, but a full-blown media blitz dripping with gory details of rape, murder, and abuse of corpse that would resonate with the community for decades to come.

And it would all be Sarah's fault.

No.

No matter what happened when the body was found, the whole truth could never be known unless she let it. She could think of something else, another explanation, that would fit the evidence just as well.

Just as soon as she knew what the evidence was.

She walked to her closet and began to reach for a sleepshirt. But when she saw the furious trembling of her arm, she drew it back.

Enough.

She could not do this anymore. Not tonight. She couldn't think, couldn't plan, without remembering. If she had any hope of sleeping tonight, she would have to switch gears now; distract herself. She would have to compartmentalize the past, as she had done so many times before, and concentrate on the present.

But that was harder now. The threat was real, and the images were vivid. No mere novel could pull her mind out of its spiral. Soothing her soul would require a far more powerful remedy—something interactive, something vital. What she needed tonight was Adam.

She turned and reached instead for a regular shirt and shorts. She owned nothing that could be classified as sexy, but the shirt in question had a relatively low neckline, and it had shrunk a lot in the wash.

In a matter of days, it would all be over. She would figure out a way to deal with the consequences she had wrought without breaking her promise. What would happen after that, she had no idea. But one thing was for sure. She would not have much time left with Adam. No matter what version of the truth came out, he would soon want nothing more to do with her.

In the meantime, she could only make the best of it.

Chapter 24

Adam saw Sarah coming the moment she walked out her door. He rose immediately and moved closer to the window.

What was she doing? Only an hour ago she had seemed desperate to be rid of him. He had obliged her, again. But not without reservation. Particularly not given his theory as to why she wanted privacy in the first place.

He had tried to get a good look at the fax she was so anxious to collect, but she had stuffed it into her purse as hastily as she could—with her back to him. Nevertheless, it had taken only the briefest of glances to confirm his suspicions. She had indeed managed to finagle a copy of the construction diagrams. And she had done it amazingly quickly.

What had she found out?

She reached his front porch, but didn't need to ring the bell. He opened the door as soon as she approached it. "See there?" he said lightheartedly, even as his pulse pounded. "I knew you'd miss me."

Sarah smiled back at him and walked inside. Her shirt was tight and her shorts were short. He began to break out in a sweat.

"I changed my mind," she said quietly. "After I took a shower I decided that some pizza might be nice after all. My treat. Unless you've already eaten."

He studied her face. She seemed drained, somehow. Almost defeated. Her shallow smile seemed designed to conceal that, but it failed.

"No, I haven't eaten. Pizza would be great. What kind do you like?"

He took her noncommittal answer; converted it into a large half-pepperoni, half-sausage pizza order; and settled her comfortably on the couch in his basement.

Still, she seemed unusually somber.

What was he supposed to do? Confronting her again would be risky, but perhaps now was the time. Had she not, for once, sought *him* out?

"You're obviously upset, Sarah," he said from his position on the recliner several feet away. He didn't trust himself any closer than that. "Are you worried about passing out again, or is it something else?"

She paused before answering. She didn't look at him. "Isn't passing out enough?"

Her voice was thin. She looked so fragile as she sat there, still as a statue, her face ghostly pale. As he watched, her hands began to tremble.

He couldn't bear it. He got up and moved to a position beside her on the couch. He refrained from touching her, but even the close proximity made him feel warmer; he hoped it had the same effect on her.

"Why don't you tell me what's really bothering you?" he suggested gently. "I already told you, I'm a great listener. And whatever it is, it won't leave this room."

Her trembling seemed only to increase. She turned to face him. "I don't want to talk about it," she answered, her voice barely above a whisper. "But I would like it if you would hold me."

His eyes widened. She couldn't have asked him for anything easier—or more difficult. Keeping his touch platonic was nothing short of torture, but declining a direct request from a trembling woman was beyond him. He wrapped an arm around her shoulders and pulled her to him, and she nestled her head against his shoulder.

"You've been so good to me," she murmured. "Thank you."

He made a desperate attempt to lighten the mood. "I have invested in you pretty heavily as a neighbor. But don't worry, I'm expecting a big payoff. Mail collection when I'm on vacation, fish feeding, that sort of thing. Oh, and it's important that no one at the church find out about my mob connections, either. Can you handle that?"

He could feel her smiling.

She didn't answer, but after a moment, she asked a question of her own. "Do you still want to debate theology?"

He blinked. The woman never ceased to surprise him. "Sure, any time. What would you like to start with? The Methodist social principles are topical, or would you prefer something heavier, like the nature of divinity?"

Her voice was impassive, almost deadpan. "Actually, I was wondering if you believed in hell."

Adam swallowed. Anxiety swelled. Though she was trying not to show it, he could tell the question was not an idle one. She was asking for a reason.

He drew in a breath. He tried to keep his voice casual. "If you mean a real physical hell, with fire and demons and pitchforks, then no, I don't."

She lifted her head and met his gaze. "Then what do you believe?"

Looking into her tortured blue eyes, he felt suddenly ready to explode with frustration. Sarah was afraid she was going to die, and she felt horribly guilty about whatever had happened in Alabama. She wanted his help, but she wouldn't help him. She wouldn't tell him the truth. It was as if she had tied both his hands behind his back and was now informing him, oh so calmly, that she was drowning.

"I believe that hell is a state of being," he began, quoting his well-worn position with half his brain, thinking a step ahead with the other. "A separation from God. It's not a punishment people have foist upon them. It's a decision they make themselves."

Sarah was quiet a moment. Then she settled back into his shoulder. "So you're on the liberal side of Methodism," she said thoughtfully. "My grandparents went the other direction—completely off the scale. They were into some wacko charismatic church that messed up my dad so bad he practically became an atheist. We had no contact at all with them when I was growing up. They showed up at his funeral just long enough to tell Dee and me that he was with Satan now, and that if we wanted to escape the same fate, we should acknowledge our depravity and come and live with them."

Adam's stomach soured. At least that answered one question. Sarah had come by her cynicism honestly. But if she knew enough to know that he was on the liberal side of Methodism, she had managed to educate herself despite her biases.

"And what about you?" he asked. "What do you think hell is?"

She said nothing for a long time. "I don't really care," she said finally, determinedly. "I think it's more important to live in the present." Then she shifted her position, bringing her eyes level with his, her face close.

The clang of warning bells in Adam's head was deafening. Sarah was frightened, vulnerable, and miserable. She was curious about his opinion of her fate, but she had no interest in give and take. All she wanted from him, as she was making apparent, was physical comfort. Why she would seek out male attention after being raped, he had no idea. Nor did he know how much comfort—and of what type—she had in mind. But he had a hard time believing her choice of such a snug, low-cut shirt was an accident. And if it wasn't, he was in trouble. In trouble on so many fronts, he couldn't begin to count them.

He moved away from her and stood up. "The pizza should be here any minute. Should we go back upstairs?"

Sarah didn't move. Her perceptive blue eyes stared him down. "I know you don't believe me, Adam," she said softly. "But I told you the truth. I was never raped. You're looking for a problem that isn't there."

He could think of nothing to say. Every fiber of his being wanted to believe her—wanted to believe there was one chance in a thousand that eventually, things could be right with her. That she would open up and be honest with him. That she would let him help her work through her past, her fears. That her health problems could be treated. That she would begin to look at him as more than just a convenience. That she could come to terms with and respect everything that was important to him in life. That she could commit herself to him for the long haul.

Or that the planets would align the day after tomorrow, the rain would turn pink, and the daffodils would sing Ave Maria.

It wasn't going to happen. And no matter how much he wanted her, he couldn't settle for anything less. He had set his course on that score a long time ago, and he wasn't changing direction now.

No matter how good she looked in that damnable shirt.

"I'd like to believe you, Sarah," he answered. "But we both know that honesty isn't your strong suit. If you want my unconditional trust, you'll have to earn it."

She stared at him curiously. She didn't seem offended so much as intrigued. To his surprise, she stood up and faced him. "I really would prefer not to lie to you anymore," she insisted. "But I can't answer the questions you want me to answer."

He met her gaze. "Can't? Or won't?"

She considered. "Both. It's about keeping promises. Surely you can understand that."

He studied her for a long time. He couldn't take his eyes away. How could she lie to him so coolly, over and over, and yet at times like this act so forthright? He was used to women who played games, who never said what they meant, who expected him to guess what they were thinking. But Sarah didn't do that. He was beginning to believe, despite his every self-protective instinct, that her true nature was indeed forthright—that her lies were the aberration.

Could he test his theory? If he asked the socially awkward question he wanted to ask, would she hide her eyes and talk around it, or would she give him a straight answer?

"I can respect a person who keeps their promises," he replied. "Provided those promises don't hurt anyone. But there are some things I'd still like to get straight."

She braced herself, her eyes wary. "Like what?"

He took a breath. "Like why you were so anxious to get rid of me earlier. And why you changed your mind."

She replied with a level gaze. "I had something I needed to do, and I wanted to be alone. When I finished, I was upset. I was hoping you could cheer me up. You're terribly good at that, you know."

She smiled at him, and he smiled back. But he wasn't finished. His eyes held hers. "What is it you really want from me, Sarah?"

She looked uncomfortable, but after a moment's thought, she answered him. "Most of my motives are selfish. You make me laugh, and I need to laugh right now. And when you hold me, I feel safe. I like that feeling, and I'd like more of it. But on the unselfish side, I'd like to think that you enjoy my company, too. That being with me makes you feel a little less lonely."

Damnation. His heartbeat quickened. She *was* being honest with him. He could feel it. Maybe her lies did all relate to keeping promises. Maybe she hadn't been raped. Maybe hidden behind her soft language about companionship lay an attraction—both physical and emotional—that was as strong as his.

Maybe there was hope.

He stepped forward and took her hands in his own. He couldn't hold back everything that was on his mind much longer. He had to confront her with what he knew.

"Sarah, I know that you've been trying to figure out exactly where the bypass goes," he began. "I think you're afraid that something at the house will be discovered, because you're afraid it will put you in danger. I want you to tell me what that is."

The effect of his words hit him like kickback from a pistol. Sarah's eyes widened with terror. Her beautiful chest heaved with rapid, heavy breaths; her shoulders shuddered. She pulled her hands away as if he had burned them. Her low voice cracked on the single syllable she managed to utter.

"*No!*" She whirled away from him and started toward the steps, but she didn't get far. He was behind her in an instant, taking her hand again, pulling her back.

"Sarah, wait! I'm sorry," he apologized. "Please, don't leave now. I won't ask you anything else, I promise."

She turned to face him. Her eyes were moist even as they flashed with aggravation. "You promised that once already."

He took a deep breath. He continued to hold her hand. "I said I would try. And I did. But whatever is torturing you, I want to help you get past it. Can't you understand that? I can't just sit back and watch it eat you alive. And don't think my motives are all ministerial and noble, because they aren't. Not by a long shot. I'd love nothing better than to hold you all day long—and all night too, for that matter—but the fact is, I'm not that easy. I want more from you, Sarah. I want you to tell me what's bothering you. I want you to let me help!"

Her eyes moved to the floor. She stood still a long time, her breathing still rapid. He had no idea what she was thinking, but he was glad that, at least, she did not pull back her hand. Finally she managed one long, slow breath. Then she turned to face him.

"So what you're telling me," she said, her voice still hoarse with emotion, even as her face brightened to half a smile, "is that the milk isn't free. Prospective customers have to buy the cow."

His eyebrows rose. The woman did cut to the chase. He liked that.

He really liked that.

He grinned back. "That's about the size of it, yes."

She narrowed her eyes. "Bit of a role reversal, wouldn't you say?"

"What are you, sexist?"

She studied him thoughtfully. "My loss," she whispered.

She was about to say something else when the doorbell rang. He had never been less happy to see a pizza man.

"So you see," Adam continued, polishing off the last piece of sausage, "for a mainline Protestant denomination, Methodism is very inclusive."

"Unless you believe in reincarnation as a cactus."

"Yes, well, then I would refer you to my fine colleagues over at the Unitarian church," he offered, smiling at her. He couldn't help but smile at her. They'd just had one of the more enjoyable theological discussions he'd ever experienced over take-out pizza, and he had experienced quite a few. Why she had suddenly become so willing to engage in shop talk, he had no idea. But the more she dragged out the meal, picking at her pizza and taking only minute sips of her slowly disappearing drink, the more certain he became that she didn't want to leave. Or that she was afraid to go back home.

The distinction might be significant.

All of a sudden she stood. "Well," she said with undisguised chagrin, "I guess I've wasted enough of your time. I'd better be going."

He stood with her. "You're not wasting my time. What's the hurry?"

She didn't answer. She took her glass into his kitchen and set it on the counter by the sink, then moved into the living room, gazing out the window that faced her own house. "Thanks for having dinner with me. And for giving me the chance to get your theology straightened out."

He grinned as he joined her. "You wish."

He was standing there beside her, watching her, admiring her long lashes and the soft curve of her cheekbone, when her face suddenly blanched. He thought at first that she was passing out again, but her eyes didn't close. Instead they widened to saucers, and she drew in a breath with an audible shudder.

His eyes followed hers out the window.

A police cruiser from the township was drifting by. It made a one-eighty in the cul-de-sac, then came to rest just short of Sarah's driveway. The patrolman inside rested his left arm out the open window. He fidgeted with something in the seat.

Adam looked back at Sarah. She was staring at the car as if it were a monster.

His head began to swim. An icy chill pervaded his chest. "Sarah?" he asked quietly. "Is something the matter?"

She didn't move. Didn't answer. She barely even seemed to be breathing.

"Sarah?"

A motor revved, and Adam returned his gaze to the window. The policeman had both hands on the wheel again. He was driving away. He cruised slowly back up the street and out of sight.

"I'm sorry," Sarah answered, her voice artificially light. "My mind wandered. Did you say something?"

Adam's chest felt heavy. As heavy as if his heart had just been wrenched out and replaced with solid lead.

The patrolman hadn't been stopping at Sarah's house. He had been stopping to light a cigarette, unwrap a piece of gum, pick his teeth—any of the six million reasons that cops on patrol pulled over now and then. Adam had seen them pause in the cul-de-sac many times before. Often he'd gone out to chat with them.

But Sarah had thought the car was stopping at her house. And the prospect had terrified her.

No. It couldn't be. Sarah's secrets, her "promises," could *not* be about a crime. Not a real crime. She had been a victim. She was running from a person, not the law.

Nausea enveloped him. What had happened in that accursed house of hers? How had her sister died, and what exactly was Sarah afraid the construction would reveal?

What had she done?

"I'd really better go now," she said in a clipped tone, turning away from him. "I could use a good night's sleep."

For several seconds, he couldn't move. She had his front door open before he caught up with her. But he did catch up with her, wresting the door from her grasp and closing it again. He put his hands on her upper arms and turned her to face him.

He looked straight into her exquisite almond eyes, and he kept looking into them. He looked as deeply as any mortal could possibly look, and he didn't stop until he had noted every nuance, scrutinized every glimmer. He wanted to find something; he had to find something. He could *not* be wrong about her.

"Why are you looking at me like that?"

Adam relaxed his hold on her arms. He realized he'd been gripping too tightly. But she hadn't complained. Not about that.

"What's wrong?" she repeated.

He let out a long, slow breath. It was all right. He hadn't

been wrong about her. Whatever horrors had ravaged her young life, whatever guilt and fear she'd been carrying ever since and whatever delusions that burden had wrought, he was sure of one thing. Sarah Landers' heart was right. For all her lies, all her bravado, the spirit inside her was gentle. She had a conscience. She knew love.

She was a good person.

Right now, it was the only thing that mattered.

"Nothing's wrong," he answered. His voice sounded unsteady. He fixed it. "I'm just trying to think of a way to get you to stay longer."

She smiled a little.

The sight warmed him.

She might think she had something to fear from the police. But she had to be mistaken. She was young when it happened, now she was confused. She needed to confide in someone who could help her sort it out.

That was all.

"I've been analyzing you," he continued, making his tone playful. "And I've decided your weakness is your competitive streak. So how about I crush you at backgammon?"

She smiled sadly. "Sorry. I don't know how to play."

"Perhaps a game of chess, then? I figure I could polish you off in twenty minutes, tops."

Her smile broadened. "I'll take you down in ten."

Chapter 25

"There you are! I hope you're feeling better this morning. They told me you had a rough afternoon yesterday."

Sarah smiled at the retired professor who worked the library's reference desk part-time. He reminded her of her long-deceased maternal grandfather. "I'm feeling much better today, thank you."

"Good, good." He turned around in his swivel chair and lifted a book from a shelf behind him. "I thought you'd want to know as soon as this came in. I saw you'd put a rush on it."

"I appreciate your calling me. Thank you." Sarah extended her arms, breath held. He placed the thick, spiral-bound book into her hands.

"Interesting stuff, there. You writing a novel?"

She let out a nervous laugh. "Now, don't let that get around. It's a secret."

He chuckled. "No one will hear it from me. I've got a few half-finished books in my own desk drawers."

She slipped the book into her briefcase and cast a glance over her shoulder. Adam was nowhere in sight. He had stayed in the car as she'd requested, thank goodness. If she'd had her druthers he wouldn't be here at all, but when she'd warned him she would be out for a while he had absolutely refused to let her call a cab.

She thanked the man once more and headed back outside. She had been up for hours, but her mind still seemed oddly detached from her body. A late night of competitive gaming with Adam, a glass of warm milk, the maximum dose of allergy medicine, and twenty billion jumping sheep had failed to produce the sound sleep she had so desperately needed. Instead she had woken up repeatedly, plagued with nightmares she was still trying to forget.

Adam's car was waiting for her at the curb. She stepped in, and he pulled away. "Did you get it?"

She started, still adrift in her fog. "Get what?"

"Whatever it was you needed," he answered, his voice heavy.

Her own heart sank. He knew that she had been lying to him again. Not lying exactly, but withholding the truth. She had told him she needed to pick up something at the library, but she had refused to say what, or why. She had no reason to feel guilty about that, but seeing the hurt in his eyes felt like taking a fist in the gut, regardless.

They had had a wonderful evening together last night. She had worked hard to make it so, and it had ended amicably, if not as affectionately as she might have liked. But this morning he seemed unusually preoccupied—and discouraged. She reminded herself, over and over, that her secrecy was for his benefit as well as her own—that the truth would only hurt him more.

"Yes, I got it," she answered, taking a stab at cheerfulness. "It looks like I'll be spending a quiet day reading. You should approve of that. What's on your agenda?"

"I have a wedding," he answered, his eyes on the road.

The dullness of his tone disturbed her. "You don't sound too excited about it. Don't you like marrying people?"

"Of course I do."

He did a better job of sounding enthused the second time, but Sarah was not convinced. "I suppose weddings must be hard for you," she said sympathetically.

He turned his head and looked at her. She could tell he understood what she meant. Despite all that she was keeping from him, she had noticed how easily he seemed to read her now, and vice versa. It was a curious phenomenon.

"I'm always happy to see a couple who's right for each other get married," he insisted. "It's harder when that doesn't seem to be the case, but as an outsider, you can't really judge something like that. It's hard enough for the couple to know."

The continued melancholy of his voice was out of character,

and Sarah wondered, suddenly, if he'd gotten any more sleep than she had. She also wondered whether his last statement referred to any couple in particular. But she didn't have the chance to ask.

"In any event," he finished, "I'm afraid I won't be around most of the day. But Rose is all set to harass you in my absence, so don't get any ideas."

Sarah smiled superficially. She did have ideas. But they were hardly pleasurable ones. The research she had to conduct today might very well deepen her ulcer to the bleeding point.

The trip home passed quietly. Adam walked Sarah to her door, where she thanked him for the ride and made her standard, token effort at convincing him not to worry about her. He then made his at convincing her that wasn't possible. All too soon, she was alone again.

She settled onto her couch and unfastened the briefcase. Adam had looked at the worn black case suspiciously, but though she was certain he had guessed its purpose, he hadn't said anything.

She opened the lid and lifted out the book. Its loosely bound pages buckled in her hands, and a faint brown stain marred its plain white cover. *Guide to Underwater Investigations.* She could not risk Adam's having so much as a glance at that title, not with everything he had pieced together already. She knew now just how much sharper he was than his happy-go-lucky manner would indicate. If he could defeat her in a fair game of chess—which, much to her annoyance, he repeatedly had—she could not put anything past him.

She closed her eyes a moment, steeling her resolve. Then she opened the book and began to read.

Sarah held the closed book in her lap. For a long time now she had lain motionless, staring at the ceiling. She had tried to sit up once, but the room had spun, and she had no need of additional nausea. The information she had gleaned from the text had already provided the equivalent of ipecac.

Soft tissue decomposition… autolysis… putrefaction. She had tried to keep her mind on the hypothetical, the abstract. But that had proved impossible. *Discoloration… bloating… crepitus.* Nine years underwater would leave nothing recognizable to the eye as Rock Rockney, that much the book had made abundantly clear. But on one important question, it had been stubbornly indecisive.

Bones. Skeletal remains did decay underwater, with time. But how much time was affected by far too many variables for comfort. Had the body remained exposed to the water, or had the entire mass sunk deep into the muck, encasing the bones in a blanket of silt that could preserve them almost indefinitely?

She didn't know.

There might be nothing left of Rock Rockney. But there could just as easily be bones. And bones, in even half-decent condition, might be all it took to establish a cause of death.

She no longer bothered trying to banish the images. They had become rooted in front of her eyes—agitating her heart, souring her stomach. The back of Rock's head had been covered with a sea of blood, but still, she had seen the indentation. The onyx elephant had fractured his skull. And there was no way such a wound could be self-inflicted.

Timing. Sarah forced her brain to work, forced the gears to turn. She had learned one assuring thing, at least. The timing of Rock's death would be almost impossible for the authorities to determine—at least from the evidence underwater. Even if something did narrow down that window of possibility to within a week or so, no one could prove he hadn't died *after* Dee's suicide.

Sarah also realized that if she admitted any knowledge of his disposition, there wasn't a tale she could tell that could protect either her or her sister. Even if she was willing to sacrifice everything for Dee's sake—claim that she had acted alone, that her sister had already died—the authorities would not be convinced. No 110-pound seventeen-year-old girl could have done such a deed without help. No tweaking of facts, no tearful confession, could prevent the nightmarish publicity, the speculation, the charges.

The punishment.

She could not say anything. Anything at all. The truth might be found out anyway. But then again, it might not. For now, silence seemed her best gamble, if not her only hope. Her only chance to preserve any semblance of the life she had built for herself.

Assuming she deserved it.

The doorbell rang. For once, she didn't startle at its volume. Her nerves seemed past such a normal, healthy response; dispassionate analysis was all she could muster. Most likely, Adam had dropped over on his way out—perhaps to admonish her once again not to leave the house alone. Or else, Rose was checking in early.

She roused herself from the couch. She carried the book into the bedroom, buried it on the bottom of her bedside stack, and closed the door behind her. Then she crossed to her front door and opened it.

Before her stood an unfamiliar middle-aged man in slacks and a button-down shirt. Behind him stood two uniformed policemen.

Chapter 26

Sarah's response surprised even her. For nearly a decade she had lived in fear of precisely this moment. She had imagined it unfolding countless different ways, but the upshot was always the same. Her secret was out, and her life was over. Perhaps it was this ceaseless practice that allowed her to absorb the situation before her with so little emotion. Or perhaps it was the depth of her fatigue, both mental and physical. However it came about, she found herself facing the visitors not with the expected guilty panic, but with all the detached studiousness of a theater director watching an oft-practiced, yet still unsatisfactory, scene.

"Hello," she greeted.

The man in plain clothes offered a tight smile. "Hello. My name is Thomas Mayburn. I'm an investigator with the Alabama State Police. These two gentlemen are with the Allegheny County PD. Are you Sarah Landers?"

She allowed her eyebrows to rise. Her brain raced to play the part she had assigned herself. She had never acted in front of an audience, but she was familiar with the methods. She must become who she wanted them to think she was. She must allow her every expression and gesture to match. Not force it, but *believe* it.

"Yes, I am," she answered, her voice faltering. "What's wrong? Is this about my grandparents?"

The tight smile returned. "No, ma'am, I'm not here about a family member. I came to discuss an issue relating to your former property in Lee County. Can we come in?"

What issue? What could they be talking about? Sarah pushed herself into her role. She could do it.

"Of course." She admitted the policemen and directed them

to her living room. She sat on the couch, and the detective joined her. The two men in uniform settled silently into her armchairs.

"What's the problem with the property?" she asked. "I thought the sale was finalized."

"It was, ma'am." The detective opened a notebook and pulled out a pen. He was an unremarkable man, of medium height and weight, with brown hair and nondescript brown eyes. His air, if he gave off one, was of beleaguered competence. "I'm sorry to disturb you about this, but I'm afraid it's very important. I'll explain in a minute. First, would you mind telling me how long that property had been in your family?"

He launched into a long series of benign, factual questions about her family and their history with the farm, and she cooperated with what she judged to be an appropriate amount of impatience. But he got to the point all too soon.

"I understand that it was your reluctance to sell that held up construction on the new bypass. You mind telling me why you were so intent on hanging onto the place?"

Sarah's heartbeat surged, but an answer came to her quickly—a better answer than she'd given Adam. She feigned a slight embarrassment. "That was stupid of me, I know. I spent a fortune on attorney fees and still got nowhere. But I felt like I had to try. I knew I could never live in that house again, but I did want to keep the land in the family, because that had been my father's plan when he bought it. He was very sentimental about the place. I suppose he affected me."

The detective watched her closely. Sarah sensed neither disapproval nor suspicion in his reaction, but she was not at all sure that precluded their existence.

"What is it?" she repeated, acting out the anxiety she knew she should feel regardless. "Did something happen with the house? I was just there last weekend—I know it's probably some kind of safety hazard. Is that what this is about? Did someone get hurt?"

"Please," the detective said calmly—almost maddeningly calmly. "I promise I'll explain everything in a just a minute. But

I would like to know a little more about your family first. I understand your parents were killed in an accident?"

Sarah answered the next string of questions as she had always answered them. Her parents' plane had crashed. She and her sister were both devastated. Dee, who was already emotionally disturbed, had been unable to cope and had overdosed. Sarah had gone to live with her aunt and uncle for the summer, then enrolled in college the next fall. She had not lived in Alabama since. She had visited only rarely.

The detective nodded, seeming satisfied. Then he reached into a pocket of his notebook, extracted a small square of paper, and held it out toward her. It was a copy of a photograph. "Do you recognize this person?" he asked matter-of-factly.

Sarah did. She would recognize that person anywhere, under any circumstances. His every feature was burned into her memory like a cattle brand. But she could not allow the detective to know that. The picture was an old one, obviously a class photograph from high school. Rock looked young— fifteen or sixteen. He had probably dropped out before any more were taken.

Sarah concentrated. To a less jaundiced eye, the boy in the picture would look little like the man she had met. The boy's hair was softer, not so greasy. His cheeks were still puffed with baby fat, and he offered an impish grin suited to an even younger child. If her only exposure to the adult Rock had been a few insignificant encounters, she was certain she wouldn't recognize him.

"I don't think so. Should I?"

The detective didn't answer. He extracted another piece of paper. "How about this one?"

She peered into the small mug shot, most likely gleaned from a driver's license application. Her heart skipped despite herself. The image was dead on. Oily black curls. Dark skin, long nose. Half-squinted, hostile eyes. A smirk where a smile should be.

Her pulse quickened. She was not at all certain she could mask the surge of adrenaline his hated visage could evoke. But perhaps she wouldn't have to. "Maybe," she answered, allowing her voice a fitting amount of tumult. "What's his name?"

"His name was David," the detective offered. "David Andrew Rockney."

She looked up. She hadn't missed the change in verb tense. She had been careful to watch her own. "David?" she repeated meaningfully. She disliked hearing his given name. It made him seem, somehow, more human. But the man who had raped her sister, an unbalanced teenage girl who had been orphaned only days before, had had no humanity.

She looked again at the picture. Then she decided it was time. "Rock," she announced. "Did he go by Rock?"

The detective nodded. He seemed pleased. He also seemed to be hoping Sarah would say more without prompting. She decided she would cooperate.

"My sister dated him. At least I think that's him. I only saw him a few times."

The detective sat up. "Can you describe your sister's relationship with him? When it started, when it ended, that sort of thing?"

Sarah hesitated. She had to be careful not to divulge any more information than was necessary, but she also wanted to appear helpful. She covered her lapse with a shrug. "They weren't seriously involved. She met him shortly before my parents died; he didn't come to their funeral or anything. The only reason I remember him is because he was such an—"

She broke off. She was speaking ill of the dead, and she didn't want to seem callous. But was she supposed to know she was speaking of the dead? Surely any halfwit would suspect as much by now.

The detective offered no particular reaction. "Go on."

She took a breath. "He showed up at the house right after my aunt and uncle went back to Georgia, as soon as Dee and I were alone. I don't think he'd even talked to Dee since the accident, but then he waltzed in like the two of them were an ongoing item and starting harassing her about using the house for a party. Dee told him no, and they ended up in a shouting match."

The detective scribbled on his pad. He looked up. "And then what happened?"

Sarah covered her thumping heart with another shrug. "Nothing. He left. That was the last we saw of him." She swallowed. "Why is all this significant? What happened to him?"

The detective said nothing.

A sharp ache accosted her middle. The last thing she had wanted was for her story to implicate Dee, but if she wasn't careful, that was exactly what would happen. She opened her mouth, but quickly shut it again. No—the story was sound. Rock *had* come over that night to talk Dee into giving a house party, and Dee had gotten furious with him. He just hadn't left afterward. Sticking as close to the truth as possible had to be the best course—in fact, any incidental inclusion of incriminating information about Dee would probably make Sarah's story all the more credible. She shouldn't feel like her sister had anything to apologize for. If she felt the need to defend her, the detective would wonder why.

He stopped writing and looked at her again, his mouth drawn. "Are you certain that your sister didn't see this man again, after that argument?"

Careful, Sarah. She pretended to consider. "I wasn't with her every minute, but if she did see him again, she didn't mention it. She wasn't—"

She stopped to think. Every word was so important. Too important. "You have to understand. Those last few days, guys and dating were the farthest things from her mind. She was depressed; she hardly left the house. She was in a spiral from what happened to our parents, and she never got out of it."

The detective was silent a moment. He tapped his pen on his notebook. "And did you see Mr. Rockney again after the night he and your sister argued?"

"No," she replied, realizing she'd already answered the question once. *Don't expound. Why would you?*

He allowed another uncomfortable silence. Then he caught her eyes and held them. "Mr. Rockney's remains have been uncovered at the bottom of a pond on your former property,

Ms. Landers. I was hoping you might be able to shed some light on how that could have happened."

A look of shock was not difficult to feign. If she hadn't known until now, how would she feel? She took several seconds to find her voice. "*My* pond?"

"Yes."

She paused again, staring out into space. Then she asked another question. "How long had—" she stammered. How did one refer to such a thing? "How long have the remains been there?"

"We don't know for sure," the detective answered. "That's one of the things we'd like to pin down."

"Did he drown?"

She couldn't help but be pleased with herself. She had no reason to suspect foul play, and she wasn't going to show any.

The detective remained coy. "We're not sure about that yet, either. We're still waiting for the autopsy report."

He proceeded to have Sarah walk him through a series of specific dates—when Dee had met Rock, when the Landers had died, when Rock had come to the house, and when Dee had died. Last but not least: when Sarah had moved out, leaving the house and grounds vacant. When he finished, he leaned back into the cushions of the couch, his expression contemplative.

He said nothing else, and as the silence grew increasingly awkward Sarah longed to say something herself, to further explain the things she wanted to get across. But she managed to hold her tongue. Nervous, babbling suspects were a gold mine for an investigator. He was probably being quiet for just that reason. She had to act as if this were all just a curiosity—and a nuisance.

"Is that all?" she asked finally. "Is there anything I need to do?"

He sat back up suddenly. "Did Mr. Rockney own a car?"

Sarah blinked. "I don't know. I think he had a motorcycle."

"Do you know where he lived?"

She shook her head. She could offer that she remembered he was a relative of the Martins, but that would be going too far. If her story was true, she wouldn't remember because she wouldn't have cared.

The detective allowed another uncomfortably long pause. The two uniformed officers, other than shifting in their seats occasionally, might as well have been mannequins. Sarah was certain she was being watched for nervousness, and she was determined not to show it. Increasing agitation, however, would seem appropriate.

"Do you know if Mr. Rockney had any enemies in Auburn?" the detective spouted suddenly. "Did your sister mention any of the people he hung around with?"

"I don't remember," she answered. "But he must have had friends. He wanted to invite somebody to a party."

"Were you present when Mr. Rockney and your sister had the argument?"

The detective was talking faster, throwing out questions without segue. Sarah resolved she would not get flustered.

"I heard the beginning of it, but then I went upstairs to my room. My sister had a habit of ranting and raving at people; I was used to tuning her out."

"Then how do you know that a party was all they argued about?"

"Because that's what she told me."

"When?"

"Right after he left. He slammed the door so hard the house shook—I remember that." *Nice touch, Sarah.*

"So you don't know for a fact that a party was the *only* thing they argued about, other than that's what your sister told you."

She looked at him as if the question were silly. "I guess not."

Yet another silence followed. Sarah decided that even an innocent person would be getting upset by now. "Why is all this important?"

The detective's voice was calm again. "It might not be, Ms. Landers. We're just collecting all the information we can."

"Well, I don't know what else I can tell you," she said irritably. "I can't believe this. When did—" She looked pointedly at the detective, allowing her voice to assume a new sense of horror. "Just when do you think he died?"

The detective offered a half smirk. "As far as we can tell, Ms. Landers, the last people to see Mr. Rockney alive were you and your sister."

She allowed her eyes to widen. But she remained careful. "You mean it could have happened while we were still living there?" Appearing sickened wasn't difficult. Today, the response had been her status quo.

The detective merely shrugged.

She looked down at her feet. Real nausea swelled. *Don't implicate Dee. Don't defend Dee. Just keep your mouth shut.*

The detective watched her for a long time. Then he rose.

"I think that will be all for today, Ms. Landers. But I may need to ask you some more questions later. Will you be staying at this address?"

The uniformed officers rose also. Sarah joined them. Her legs were unsteady. "Yes, I just moved here."

"Thanks for talking with us."

"Of course. Is there—" she faltered. "Is there a problem with the county now, I mean, about the sale? Does this put me in any legal trouble? They didn't notify me—"

The detective smiled. He was a hard man to read, but Sarah could swear that his amusement was real. "Well, you are supposed to declare human remains when you sell, but that's kind of hard if you don't know about them." He tucked his notebook back under his arm. "Don't worry, Ms. Landers, I don't think the county will come after you. They're plenty annoyed about the construction being held up again, but I don't imagine they're anxious to go another round with your lawyers."

Sarah held her breath. They were leaving. He had believed her, and they were leaving.

But the detective hadn't gone anywhere yet. He remained standing in place, glancing around the room.

A thought struck. What if they asked to search the house? Was there anything incriminating in Dee's keepsake box? Sarah didn't think so. Dee's legitimate suicide note had said plenty, but Sarah had flushed that, as instructed. Dee had been clever enough to write two of them. Dee had always been clever.

But Sarah was not. Because all the policemen had to do was walk into her bedroom and they would find three books on road construction and one on underwater investigations.

No.

She could not let them search. She would demand they get a warrant. Then she would look guilty anyway.

"Thank you again, Ms. Landers," the detective reiterated. The uniformed policemen moved toward her front door. The detective followed. "I appreciate your cooperation. You have a good day, now."

Sarah let out her breath with a gush. *Don't act so relieved!* "Will you keep me informed?" she asked, sounding nervous again. "I would like to know what happened."

The detective stopped in the doorway, handed her a business card, and stepped out. "If you don't hear from us again, give a call."

And then, as suddenly as the men had come, they were gone.

Sarah stood for a long time, her weight braced against the back of the closed door, her breathing shallow and jerky.

She had done it. She had pulled it off.

She should feel relief. Maybe even elation.

Instead she felt dead inside.

All the fear, all the guilt that had haunted her for so long had at last reached a terrifying crescendo. And still it wasn't over. She had merely shifted her suffering into a new phase. A phase in which she had even more to feel guilty about.

She had lied to the police, and she had done it to save her own skin. Her sister's memory might have been protected in the process, but she had done it for herself.

Her nightmares last night had not been of ponds and corpses. They had been of prisons. Of her being forced—at long last—to face the consequences of her actions. She deserved to be punished. What made her think that she had any right to escape? To be happy?

She had always envisioned herself standing up to the truth—

someday. When that time came, she had promised herself, she would admit exactly what had happened, and she would accept whatever punishment justice meted out. As long as she suffered eventually, it hadn't seemed so wrong to switch the timetable, to enjoy her young life as a free woman—put off the rest until later.

But she hadn't stood up to anything. The time had come, and she had lied again. She had changed her mind, broken the deal. She was a coward.

She returned to the couch and sat down, then fell on her side, her face buried in the cushion.

What would happen now? Would this be the end of it?

That seemed unlikely. The detective might have believed her; but then again, he might not. Who else had he questioned? Had he already talked to Rock's cousin, Tommy Martin?

A hot wave of nausea rolled through her middle. *Tommy.* Dee had only just dumped the guy to be with his cousin—and he had hated Rock even before that. Sarah remembered how angry he had been at Dee's funeral, as if he blamed his cousin for that, too, without even knowing why.

The poor man had motive wrapped up with a bow.

What if the police blamed Tommy? What if they prosecuted an innocent man?

Sarah's nausea was hardly bearable. She tried to breathe slowly.

There is no evidence against him. It won't happen. Stop borrowing trouble.

But there was evidence against her, if the detectives bothered to look for it. If her lawyers in Alabama heard about the body, they would surely suspect that she had known all along. Would they say anything? If the library employees who processed her request for *Guide to Underwater Investigations* knew, how hard would it be for them to connect the dots? What if the detective subpoenaed her library records? Her phone log? What if he questioned Adam?

She sat up again, queasy. Her thoughts were going in circles, and she had to stop. Either she would get away with her lies or she wouldn't. At this point, neither outcome would be a victory. All she could do was cope.

Her doorbell rang.

She didn't move. A part of her wished the detective was back—wished she had a second chance to do the right thing. Maybe this time, she would be stronger.

But the larger part of her quaked at the thought. It could not be the detective. He had believed her. He had to believe her.

She rose with a rolling motion and stumbled toward the door. Once again, she didn't bother with the peephole. She merely turned the knob and pulled, unable to avoid thinking, in the back of her mind, that fate had made this moment pivotal—that the identity of the caller would determine her next move.

It wasn't the detective. It was Rose.

The older woman's already lined face crinkled with worry. "Sarah, dear," she said tentatively. "I saw the police car leaving. What's happened? Is everything all right?"

Sarah couldn't answer. She stepped back, encouraging Rose to enter. She closed the door.

Rose's sharp eyes studied her. "Bad news? About your family?"

Sarah shook her head. She wanted to speak, but she didn't know what to say. No words could describe what she was feeling. Her stomach ached as though it had been wrung inside-out; the swirl of conflicting emotions within her neared the boiling point. She was beginning to believe she would explode.

Rose didn't ask any more questions. All she did was hold out her arms.

Sarah fell into them. Then, for the first time in more years than she could remember, she broke down and cried.

Chapter 27

Adam hung his car keys on the hook by his garage door. He was tired, and he was drained. He felt bad bugging out of the reception early, but wedding dinners went on forever, and he was worried about Sarah. He was also worried about himself.

I knew she was the right one for me after we went on that hiking trip, the groom had remarked. *I mean, how many women can you be around constantly, for six straight days, without getting on each other's nerves, and still want more? I figured if that wasn't true love, nothing was. You know?*

Adam had smiled. But he hadn't known. Rather, the groom's words had disturbed him.

He scooped up the foam basketball from the floor and tossed it over his shoulder toward the basket. *Almost.* He collapsed into a rose-covered chair and closed his eyes.

I can't believe you beat me, Sarah had exclaimed last night. Her eyes had been shining with pleasure, even as she maintained an affronted facade. *Nobody beats me at chess. This was just a fluke. Let's play again.*

She had been a formidable opponent, but he had been on a roll. He would have played all night as long as he could hear her laughter, admire her slender form from across the board. He hadn't wanted her to leave. He had wanted her suitcases unpacked in his bedroom.

Why was he doing this to himself? What did he think could possibly come of it?

Whatever he was feeling, it was obvious Sarah didn't share the sentiment. She enjoyed his company, but she didn't trust him. He wanted to be angry at her for using him, but he knew that wouldn't be fair. Not when she had refused his offers of assistance at every turn; not when he had insisted on forcing them on her anyway. She had never asked him for anything except physical comfort, and he had chosen to deny her that. Her only sin was her own self-destructiveness.

And his was his irrepressible desire to play the hero. From the beginning he had fancied himself her protector, her savior. He would rescue the damsel in distress, pat himself on the back, and accept her accolades. Then he would go back to whatever else he had been doing.

He was an idiot.

He had done everything he could think of to help Sarah Landers, yet she was no better off than when he had started. All he had accomplished, it would seem, was the hijacking of his own brain.

He heard a noise outside, and his eyes flew open. Someone was on the porch. The bell chimed, and he sprang to open the door. He looked out eagerly—and failed to hide his disappointment.

Rose chortled good naturedly. "Well, I'm delighted to see you, too."

Adam flushed. "I'm always thrilled to see you, Rose. You know that. I'm sorry, I was just…"

"You were hoping I was Sarah," she interrupted, stepping inside. "But she happens to be resting at the moment. At least, I hope she's resting. One never knows with that girl. Can we talk?"

Adam's pulse began to pound. "What happened? Is she all right? Did she pass out again?"

"No, no, nothing like that," Rose said calmly, picking her way toward her favorite wing-backed chair. She settled into it without awaiting an invitation, then with a sweep of her hand, invited him to join her.

He did.

"I am worried about her, though," Rose continued, her brow creasing. "Very worried."

He sat perched on the edge of his seat. "So am I. What happened?"

She dipped her chin, and her gray eyes bore into his. Rose always moved her head, rather than her eyes, since she could only focus forward. It made her seem birdlike, and he could not help likening her to an eagle. Smart, strong, and noble, but not above a certain ruthlessness when necessary.

"She had some visitors earlier. County policemen."

Adam's breath caught in his throat. For a second he imagined what Sarah must feel like when she collapsed—as if her body had disappeared out from under her.

"They—they went into the house?" he stammered. "They weren't just passing by? Do you know what it was about?" An image of Sarah in handcuffs flashed in his mind, but he beat it down. That was insane. Sarah had done nothing criminal. She couldn't have. She didn't have it in her.

Rose's eyes softened as she looked at him. "All I know is what she told me. She said it had to do with her parents' farm in Alabama—and her sister. She was being intentionally vague, and I didn't push her. But she said something about her sister having been mixed up with the wrong people, and how it was all coming back to haunt her now."

Adam stood up. He crossed to the window and looked out toward Sarah's house. The wheels in his brain turned furiously.

Dee. So, it was Sarah's sister who had been at the crux of it.

Stop hitting me! Dee, where are you?

Her sister had attracted trouble, and Sarah had suffered for it. But she had loved Dee, he was certain of that. He could see it in her eyes every time she talked about her. He should not be surprised that Sarah would try to protect her sister, even now.

It's about keeping promises, Sarah had told him. *Surely you can respect that.*

Adam whirled around to face Rose again, but she was no longer sitting. She was standing at his elbow. "Did she say what the police had found?" he asked hastily.

"It would appear you know more than I do," Rose remarked. "What I've already told you is all I got out of her, and then some. Mainly, I let her cry on my shoulder."

He tensed. In all he and Sarah had been through together, both in Alabama and since, he had never seen her cry. She had always been far too guarded. Too proud. Maybe the police visit had been too much for her—the straw that broke the camel's back. Or maybe it was him. Maybe she didn't trust him enough to be that vulnerable.

"How is she now?" he asked weakly.

"Exhausted. I tried to convince her to take a nap. She didn't look like she had slept in days, so I turned on some Sinatra and poured a couple glasses of Zinfandel into her. I think it worked. But she won't sleep forever, and when she does wake up, her troubles will still be there."

Adam stepped away from the window and sank back into a chair. Rose stood above him and cleared her throat.

"Oh, sorry." He moved from her favorite seat back to his original.

Rose sat down, then affixed him again with her eagle eyes. "I take it you don't know the whole story, either."

He could not repress a sigh. "No. She won't tell me."

"I see." The eagle eyes bore deeper. He was certain she could see the back of his head. Her expression softened again.

"Adam, my dear, she does care for you. Any fool can see that. If she didn't, she wouldn't have been so adamant that I *not* tell you about the police car."

His eyebrows rose. "But you did."

She smiled. "Because I'm old enough to know the difference between what someone says they want and what they're aching for. Sarah doesn't want you mixed up in her affairs because she's ashamed of them. She probably thinks you'd look down on her, you being a high-and-mighty minister and all."

He bristled. "I'm not—"

Rose lifted a hand. "No need to defend yourself to me, young man. I've heard you cursing at that wreck of a car of yours, remember? Not to mention all the times I covered for you so you could wriggle your way out of a perfectly harmless blind date. Sick elderly neighbor, indeed!"

He cracked a tired smile. "And your point is?"

"My point," she said sharply, "is that whether Sarah knows it or not, she needs you. I have a feeling about all this, and that feeling is telling me that today's police visit wasn't the end. There's worse to come for her, and she's scared to death."

Hearing his own worst fears spoken aloud was too much.

"And what exactly am I supposed to do about it?" he countered, rising to his feet in a rush. Frustration swelled within him, and he could not keep the ire from his voice. "I've tried everything I can think of to get her to open up to me, and she won't! She doesn't *want* my help!"

He began to pace. "I've already gone above and beyond the call of duty with her, don't you think? I've changed vacation plans, lost office hours, begged favors from friends—and for what? She's in worse shape now than when I met her! Why should I meddle more? It's not like she's even a church member. What I should do is hand her off to a therapist, or an attorney…hell, *anybody* who actually knows what they're doing, and then just back off!"

He stopped pacing. He looked tentatively at Rose.

She grinned.

"And what does that look mean?" he asked irritably.

She smiled wider.

"Rose!"

The older woman laughed out loud. "Sorry, my dear, but I can't help it. You are so touchingly pathetic."

He frowned.

"For heaven's sake," she continued mildly. "You're a grown man who's been married before. One would expect you'd know when you were in love."

Her words hit him as if she'd thrown a rock. He could only stand still, stunned. Rose could not be that deeply inside his brain. How could she be so glibly certain about something that was still such an enigma to him—a question that seemed so impossible to answer?

He found his voice. "Rose, I don't even know where my wallet is."

She chuckled again. "Well now, that's a common enough symptom. Nothing to worry about there. What you do need to worry about is Sarah. I'll support her all I can, but a woman like her needs a man, too. She needs some strong arms around her, someone steady, who'll be there when she finally does decide to talk. Trust me, it could make all the difference."

Adam's jaws clenched. "But I can't just—" He broke off.

Rose stared at him. Then she rolled her eyes. "Oh, don't be such a coward, Adam. It's terribly out of character. You're already in love with the woman. You can either admit defeat and nurse a broken heart now, or you can jump in with both feet and hope for the best. You have to nothing to lose."

She rose. "Now, if you'll excuse me, I have a bus to catch. I need to teach some twenty-somethings the proper way to do the Cotton-Eyed Joe."

He walked her wordlessly to the door. She turned and smiled at him, then stood on tiptoe to plant a kiss on his cheek. "Chin up, dear. Sarah will come around. No red-blooded woman can resist your charms for long." She stepped out and looked back at him with a wink. "You're just lucky I'm not thirty years younger."

He returned a warm—yet slightly nervous—smile and closed the door behind her. He stood a long time, contemplating, his hand still resting on the knob.

Whatever he felt for Sarah, it seemed that right now his course of action should be the same. He was in a unique position to help her, and despite his outburst, he was still determined to do so. Rose was right about one thing—he could not allow himself to become discouraged.

He had to concentrate on a solution, because clearly, Sarah's problem was not all in her head. The police did not concern themselves with legal, insignificant events occurring halfway across the country a decade ago. Someone somewhere had committed a crime.

A serious one.

But what? If what Sarah had told Rose about Dee being mixed up with "the wrong people" were true, it could mean Dee had invited them into the Landers' home. Perhaps things got out of hand, a crime was committed, and some evidence of it was left behind.

But what sort of evidence would remain in a thoroughly looted house after nine years? And why would Sarah be so determined to keep what had happened a secret? Her sister was dead. He could understand not wanting to sully a loved one's memory, but such a desire hardly explained the depth of

Sarah's fear.

He tried to think of what might.

His stomach soured.

Sarah was in real trouble. And her evasiveness had to end.

Chapter 28

The rapping on Sarah's door was so quiet, it wasn't audible from much farther than her living room. But she happened to be in her living room, and despite the sound's inherent eeriness, it filled her with a warm sense of hope.

She rose and looked out her peephole, and a flush of heat moved through her. It was Adam, being considerate as usual. The hour was late, and if she was asleep, he didn't want to wake her. She had slept a few hours, but Rose's ministrations had only pacified her for so long. Now she was awake again. Awake and plagued by gruesome images no amount of willpower could quell.

She opened the door.

"Good," he greeted softly. "I didn't wake you. I saw your light on and thought I'd give it a try."

She moved back, and he stepped inside. She closed the door and looked at him.

He was still dressed up from the wedding. But his collar was loosened, and his tie was gone. Her pulse quickened as she admired the set of his shoulders, the smoothness of his dark skin, the soft black curls that framed his kind, striking face. His dark eyes twinkled in the dim light.

How could she have ever seen any resemblance between this man and the brute who had ruined her life? There was no resemblance. Nothing. The two were of different species. Rock had driven her sister to madness. Adam was the only thing keeping her from it.

"I'm glad you came," she uttered. Her voice was still hoarse from crying. Once the dam had broken, she had been unable to stop.

He smiled at her, and the sight made her battle-weary

stomach flip-flop yet again. There was something in his eyes—something new. What she said seemed to have pleased him.

She smiled back. It felt good to please him. She only wished she could do more to make up for her lies, to take back all the grief she had caused him. She wanted him to be happy. He deserved that.

"How was the wedding?" she asked lightly, rubbing a hand across her cheeks. Her last tears seemed to have dried, but there would be no remedy for the puffiness. She could only hope she just looked sleepy.

"Fine, but I didn't come here to talk about that," he said softly. He was gazing at her with his intent look, the one that so often caused an unsteadiness in her knees. "I came to talk about the police being here."

The image loomed large again. Rock's bloodied skull. Broken. Lifeless. Its specter had been haunting her all evening—a wispy veil of red dancing before her eyes.

She was not surprised that Adam knew of the police inquiry; she had suspected Rose would tell him. What did surprise her was the sudden surge of elation she felt at that thought. She was glad that he knew.

Never mind that such a reaction made no sense. Her aim had always been to shield him, to prevent his getting any further involved. She shouldn't be happy; instead, she should be feigning nonchalance, assuring him that the interview was all some irrelevant misunderstanding.

She couldn't. She didn't want to insult his intelligence anymore, and she certainly didn't want to hurt him. All she wanted was to thank him—to show him how much she appreciated his being here. She stepped forward and wrapped her arms around his neck.

She leaned into him and held him close, resting her chin over his broad shoulder. He was such a strong person; everything about him was strong. He had been as good to her as any person could possibly be, and he had asked for relatively little in return.

His arms closed tenderly around her, and she relaxed at the bliss of it. No wonder people got married. It wasn't just about the sex. It was about what she was feeling now…the warm, safe sensation that came from being held by someone who cared about you.

All he had ever asked of her was the one thing she could never give him. Honesty.

The images returned with brutal force. She could see Dee hooking a foot under Rock's shoulder and flipping him over. His face had been bloody, too.

Sarah pulled back. She was taking advantage of Adam yet again, and she was ashamed. She let her hands rest loosely on his shoulders as she looked into his face.

"Sorry about that," she whispered. She expected him to release her, but he didn't. His arms still encircled her waist, and one look in his dark eyes told her why.

He wanted her. Despite all his protestations about cows, milk, and commitment, he wanted her very much. And though there had been a time when she thought she would never desire any man ever again, she realized she had been wrong. What she felt for Adam now had nothing to do with what had happened to Dee so long ago. It was about wanting to make him—and by extension, herself—happy. She wanted to forget everything else in her life and simply enjoy being close to him.

She wanted him. Period.

Without restraint, she flung herself forward and pressed her lips to his. She clung to him as if she were afraid he would escape, taking all his warmth and goodness with him. She didn't want to be alone anymore. She wanted to crawl inside his very soul, warm and safe and satisfied, and she wanted to stay there.

At the first touch of her lips, she could feel his resistance, but then suddenly, swiftly, he pulled her against him, deepening the kiss with a desperation that flooded her with joy. When she was close to him, everything that tortured her soul was obliterated—absorbed by his strength, his energy. He was the one and only thing that could take her pain away. He was everything that she needed, and she wanted more of him. So much more…

Abruptly he pulled away.

"No, don't!" she cried, holding onto him. Why did he have

to be so blasted noble? Two men in a hundred wouldn't act this way!

He took her hands and held her away from him. His face glistened with perspiration, and his voice was rough. "This is *not* why I came over here, Sarah."

"I don't care!" she cried. "I want you, and you want me. I'm not asking for anything more than that!"

His eyes burned with frustration. "I know you're not! That's the problem!"

He took several steps away from her, then walked down into the living room. She watched miserably as he stood, facing away from her, breathing slowly, deeply—obviously fighting hard to collect himself. It was a long time before he turned around.

"The police were here today," he repeated finally, heavily. "You fell apart afterwards, crying on Rose's shoulder. I know you're scared to death, and I know it has something to do with what happened in Alabama. I want you to tell me what's going on."

Images. Sounds. Memories. They returned to her in a sickening rush.

Is he breathing? Her own voice had exclaimed. *I don't see his chest moving.*

Who cares? Dee had shrieked. *I hope he is dead! I hope he rots in hell!*

Sarah's own hand had reached down, felt along Rock's bloody throat...

She focused her eyes on her coffee table and stepped down into the living room like a zombie. She could not begin to think straight. For a few, blessed seconds, her mind had been at peace... but Adam had dragged her back. Straight back to hell on earth.

She collapsed onto her couch and dropped her face into her hands. She knew he didn't mean it. He didn't realize what he was doing.

"Answer me, Sarah," he pleaded. "Why were the police here? What did they want from you?"

She lifted her face from her hands. But she didn't respond.

I don't feel a pulse!

Dee had paused then. Turned around. Her voice had held an eerie placidity. *Really?*

Adam sighed with exasperation. "You're not going to tell me, are you?"

Sarah shook her head.

"And why not?" he demanded angrily.

She swallowed. "Because I don't want to lie to you anymore."

Sarah wasn't looking at Adam. She couldn't. A part of her feared that if their eyes met, he would see everything that she could see. She kept her gaze on the table, but with her peripheral vision, she saw him turn his back. She was afraid he was heading for the door, but instead he paced a few steps, then returned and sat down beside her.

"Sarah," he began roughly, struggling to regain control of his temper. "I know that whatever this is, it's not pretty. You're ashamed of it, and you have this idea in your head that I'm going to judge you. But I promise you, that's not true. I'm not in the judgment business. All I want to do is help you through this."

He put his hand under her chin and turned her head to look at him, and his touch—even a fingertips' worth—sent a shudder through her. "I know this involves your sister," he said gently, "and I know you were trying to protect her. You probably still are."

He's dead, Dee.

Sarah's heart thudded in her chest. Adam was too close to the truth. Way too close. How had she let this happen?

"But no matter how things may look," he continued, "no matter what evidence you're worried about the construction uncovering, I know that you're a good person. I would never believe the worst of you. You have my word on that."

Heat welled behind her eyes. She could picture the onyx elephant in the air. Descending.

"Whatever happened," he continued. "I know that you were young, and that it was a horrific time for you. For you to show bad judgment is almost a given."

Her breath caught. For the briefest instant, a flicker of hope surged through her. Was it possible? Could he understand?

But then he finished. "But I know that, whatever choices you made, you would never intentionally hurt anyone. You were a victim of circumstances, that's all. You have a good heart, Sarah. And in the end, that's all that matters."

The onyx elephant came down. It made contact with a sickening thwack. Her hand went numb. She dropped it.

Sarah closed her eyes, and a single tear rolled down her cheek. Tremors rocked her shoulders. No, Adam could never understand.

She wasn't who he thought she was. She wasn't normal, she wasn't good, and she wasn't redeemable. He was sure she could never hurt anyone. He was no doubt also sure that she could never bludgeon a man to death, conceal his corpse in a watery grave, and walk away as if nothing had happened. But he was wrong about that, wasn't he? And if he ever found out the truth, he would condemn her just as she already condemned herself. Perhaps he thought he could forgive her—but whether he realized it or not, he had already limited his imagination to things he *could* forgive.

The truth was beyond his imagination.

"Sarah?" He lifted her hands away and forced her to look up at him again. "I'm asking you to trust me. I swear I'll do whatever I can to help. But you have to tell me the truth. Now."

His brown eyes were warm. His expression was earnest. The combination made her body feel limp with misery, and she wished at that moment that she could melt herself to liquid, seeping straight down into the couch cushions, never to be seen again.

She hated what she was about to do. Her very bone marrow cried out against it, but she could see no other way. Telling Adam the truth would accomplish nothing. Not only would he be repulsed by her, not only would he feel betrayed by her duplicity, but he would forever after question the worth of his own judgment. He would regret ever having befriended her. Knowing he had touched her would make him sick.

Adam wanted to believe she had done nothing wrong. And if he needed to believe that, then maybe he should.

"They found drugs," she croaked, her voice barely discernible. "In the walls. I knew they were there, but I wasn't sure where. I tried to find them once and couldn't."

She pulled away from him and stood up. She collected herself. When she spoke again, her words were clearer. Her gaze was on the air; on nothing. She could not look anywhere near him.

"Dee fell in with a bad crowd. She was in deep, much deeper than I realized. After my parents died she agreed to use the house as some sort of storage place. That's when she got into trouble. Her boyfriend stole something. Some men broke into the house one night and tore the place apart looking for it. They told Dee they would kill her if she didn't return it. But she didn't know where it was. Only her boyfriend did, and he had disappeared. Whether he ever resurfaced or not, I don't know. Dee killed herself, and I left."

Sarah took a breath. She was good at lying. It had been a skill borne of necessity, honed over many years. But she could take no pride in this fabrication. Every word of it gnawed at her gut like acid.

"I knew that if the house was demolished it would only be a matter of time before someone found the drugs, and I was afraid I could be in serious trouble—legal or otherwise. I didn't know if Dee's boyfriend had been murdered, and I didn't know if there was anyone still out there looking for revenge. They threatened me too, that night. It scared me. But I didn't go to the police. Dee begged me not to, and after she died I couldn't stand the thought of everyone thinking the worst of her—plus I was afraid that reporting it could put me in even more danger."

She stopped. For the first time, she hazarded a glance in Adam's direction. He wasn't looking at her. He was looking at the floor. His face seemed flushed.

"The men roughed me up a bit," she finished, quieter. "I'm still a little gun shy when it comes to muscles."

She continued to watch him. When it became apparent that

she had finished, he rose. Without a glance in her direction, he headed toward the door.

"Adam, no!" she said quickly, rushing to intercept him. She was confused. He looked angry, and she wasn't sure why. The story made her look like a victim of circumstances, just as he wanted her to be.

She grabbed his arm. "Where are you going? What's wrong?"

He stopped. He turned and faced her. The look on his face was horrifying. He was livid, but it was more than that. Behind his eyes, where a twinkle should be, she saw a pain that seared her.

"What's wrong?" he repeated, his voice laden with bitterness. "Nothing's wrong, Sarah. That's the best one you've come up with so far, and that's saying something. Congratulations. Maybe you can make a career of improvisation someday. But you can stop practicing on me, because I'm done."

Sarah's stomach turned to lead. She dropped his arm, and he whirled toward her door. But in the next instant she stepped into his path again.

"I don't *want* to lie to you," she explained weakly, her voice cracking. "You just aren't leaving me any choice!"

He stopped. He met her eyes. "The truth isn't a choice?"

Another image. Rock landing face down, blood oozing through his oily curls. She hadn't cared about the blood then. She hadn't cared about him, period.

Sarah's lungs weren't working properly. Her breath came in gulps. "I don't want to hurt you," she said softly, desperately. "Please don't make me. You've got to let it go. You've got to let me handle this myself."

His expression softened. His anger was defusing, but that left him with only sadness. "But you're not handling it, Sarah," he said in a low voice. "And if you would open your eyes, you would see that."

He turned away again. He put a hand on the doorknob.

She put her own hand on top of his. "Please don't leave," she whispered, her voice barely holding together. "I don't want to be alone tonight."

The look in Adam's eyes was close to agony. "Neither do I." He took another long, searching look into her face. Then his voice turned as uneven as hers. "I would do anything for you, Sarah. If you would only trust me enough to tell me the truth."

Something inside of her seemed to break. A part of her soul she didn't know she had. It had only just come alive—and now it was dying. She was destroying it.

"I wish I could give you what you want," she exclaimed, frantic to hold on to it—whatever it was. "I would do anything to make you happy. But I *can't*. What you're asking just isn't possible. Please try to understand."

He grasped her arms and set her away from him. "I understand perfectly," he said, his voice still strained. "That's why I have to go."

He opened the door. He was on the other side of it before she caught his hand again. "Please don't leave like this," she pleaded. "Stay with me!"

His eyes flashed hot with desire, and for a brief instant, she thought his baser instincts might rule. But just as quickly, his expression returned to melancholy.

His answer was a hoarse whisper. "I'm sorry, Sarah. But I can't."

He freed his hand and walked away.

Chapter 29

Sarah clutched her robe around her and leaned heavily against the window. She was tired. Every muscle in her body ached; her mind was mush. She hadn't slept all night.

Trying to contain the images was hard enough when she was awake. In fitful sleep, she knew it would be impossible. Hence, she had whiled away the night hours with television, books, cleaning, and cooking—spending two full hours doing nothing but keying the words of a novel into a computer file she had then deleted. She believed that if she waited long enough, exhausted herself enough, she could at last fall into the kind of deep, dreamless sleep that she so badly needed. But it was mid morning now. And that hadn't happened yet.

The cul-de-sac was still and lifeless. It was warm outside, apparently too warm for the locals to seek any more of the plentiful sun. Rose had checked in earlier, but Sarah hadn't been in the mood to talk. She had explained that her plan was to sleep now, and Rose had retreated. But there was worry in the older woman's eyes.

Adam wasn't home. He would be at his church now, getting ready for the Sunday service. What that entailed, Sarah had no clue. But she couldn't stop wondering if he was all right. What happened between them last night had affected her profoundly. She could only imagine what he might be feeling.

She thought back on her plan in coming to Pittsburgh and let out a rueful laugh. Isolation, indeed. Privacy. Lack of emotional ties.

She couldn't have failed more spectacularly. In a matter of weeks, Rose had become more dear to her than any of her elderly friends in Kansas City. If the worst happened to Sarah now, the poor woman would be both shocked and hurt—

precisely the sort of grief Sarah had been trying not to cause anyone.

When her thoughts turned back to Adam, she could hardly bear them. Her downfall would hurt him most of all, and she had only herself to blame. She had let him get too close, and she had done it out of selfishness— because he had made her laugh. Brought her joy. Made her feel normal again.

She wanted desperately to spare him. But in his case, the law was only half her problem. No matter whether she was prosecuted or not, the guilt of what she had done would always haunt her. And if Adam could see it, it would haunt him, too.

She put a hand to her forehead and massaged her right temple. Her head hurt, like the rest of her.

I wish I was Catholic.

The spurious thought made her smile. Catholicism did seem to have her problem covered. She could simply walk into a confessional booth, shock a priest sworn to secrecy, do a little penance, and be done with it.

But she wasn't Catholic, was she? She wasn't anything. She had always figured that what her father taught her was all that truly mattered—that the most important thing in life was to love and be loved. Living right wasn't about keeping ancient rules and regulations; it was about respecting all people, and alleviating suffering wherever one could. Her father's beatnik philosophy had always made sense to her, and she had never blamed its lack of structure for the mess she'd made of her life. But neither, frankly, did it offer her any comfort now.

She closed her eyes and pictured her father. He had always worn a long, shaggy beard, and he delighted in the most outlandish of cheap plastic glasses. If at least three students didn't insult a new pair, he would promptly buy another. Sarah smiled to herself at the thought. Her father's approach to life had always been happy-go-lucky. Even when he blew a fuse and yelled, the unpleasantness wouldn't last long. In ten minutes, he would be smiling again. In that way, he had been much like Adam.

She opened her eyes. She wondered, as she had done so often before, what her father would have done in her place.

Either of her parents would have done whatever it took to get Rock off of Dee. She didn't blame herself for that reflex, even now. But her father would have stopped there. He would have called the police—and an ambulance. He wouldn't have let a hysterical nineteen-year-old dictate his actions. He wouldn't have done anything else to feel guilty about.

But she had. And she always would.

She turned from the window and walked to her bathroom. Then she extracted two more antacids from her medicine cabinet, chewed them up, and looked in the mirror.

The visage that looked back at her was ghastly. She wondered if she had appeared equally gruesome to Adam last night. If she had, he hadn't seemed to mind. That was the kind of man he was, always looking under the surface. Trying to see the beauty in her, whether it existed or not.

She couldn't help but love him.

That battle she had lost, finally and forever, somewhere in the middle of their second chess match. Never mind that her love was as good as poison—destined only to hurt them both. If she had been stronger, she could have shielded him, kept him from getting too close. Instead she had let her own desire drag him deeper into her abyss.

She regretted that now. She had been trying to use him, and he knew it. Still, he had done his best to stand by her.

He deserved better.

Much, much better.

She stared at her miserable reflection for another moment. Then abruptly, she straightened. She pulled open the drawer that held her makeup and snatched up her concealer. She repaired her eyes. She drew out some blush.

She smiled.

More than anything, right now, she wanted to see Adam happy again—wanted to give back some small portion of the joy he had brought to her. There was precious little she could do for him, under the circumstances. But she had the perfect idea where to start.

The sun was hot, but the air was only mildly humid. Sarah walked across the dry grass of the cemetery, hoping that her one and only dress—which she ordinarily reserved for job interviews, library galas, and funerals—was appropriate. She was lucky Adam's church was within walking distance. Its proximity to the parsonage was no accident—the minister's backyard was contiguous with the cemetery, and the church building was on the other side. Adam could walk to work every day if he wanted, but he often needed his car on the job.

She wondered what he actually did on that job, not just on Sundays, but day to day. She wondered everything about him. What sort of life had he had with Christine, and why had he been so reluctant, after her death, to move on? Sarah could testify to the passion pent up within him—yet he'd been alone for well over a year before she met him. Why? A man like him needn't be alone for five minutes if he didn't want to be. She had thought there was something odd about his reaction to any mention of his wife, but she hadn't been able to put a finger on it. With everything else that had been on her mind, she had taken little time to ponder what might be on his.

That was going to change. Whether her available time consisted of days or years, she was determined to atone for the grief she had caused him. It was her new personal mission, and it started this morning.

She saw other people entering the sanctuary, and she smiled with relief. At least there would be a crowd to hide in. She would slip in discreetly and position herself in the back. He might not see her until it was over, but he would be surprised when he did. It was the last thing he would expect, and she was certain it would please him. It would also please her. Not that she expected to get much out of a bunch of rites and ritual—in fact, she rather dreaded that aspect—but she was fiercely curious to hear the sermon. She wanted to see Adam in his element. She wanted to understand him.

She reached the steps of the sanctuary and walked up. Her heart began to thud again, and she groaned with annoyance. The last thing she wanted now was to pass out in front of a bunch of strangers. She reminded herself that the previous episodes had never happened when she expected them. But that was small comfort.

She entered a vestibule area. She looked around.

The church building was an old one, and it seemed small for the crowd. People of all ages—the majority dressed far more casually than she—were in all directions, most sitting in sanctuary pews already, but many still milling about. She was surprised by the noise. Lively conversation abounded, complete with an occasional guffaw of laughter. A pack of children plowed past her, one accidentally stepping on her foot. The offender, an orange-headed boy of seven or eight, paused to offer a quick "sorry," then caught up with his friends. An organ began to play. No one seemed to notice.

Sarah breathed slowly. The scene before her was introvert hell, and her feet itched to do an immediate about-face. But one thought steeled her: the look that would be on Adam's face when he saw her there. She bucked up and headed for the sanctuary entrance. She hoped to move straight to a seat at the back, but the elderly usher who met her at the door had other ideas.

"Well, hello there," he said affably, his blue eyes twinkling with delight as he pumped her hand in greeting. "My name's Bob Storm; I don't believe we've met. And I'm quite certain I would remember any young woman as gorgeous as you if we had. Is this your first visit?"

"Yes, it is." Sarah smiled back, but she was certain her nervousness showed. A little friendly flirtation from an octogenarian didn't bother her in the least, but personal questions did. She didn't want to talk to anyone. She only wanted to observe.

"Fabulous!" the man beamed. "And what brought you here to this particular church, if I may ask?"

Sarah squirmed. "I just moved here—to a house on the other side of the cemetery. Your minister is a neighbor of mine."

The man's blue eyes danced with delight. "I see," he said meaningfully.

Sarah's eyebrows rose slightly. She wasn't sure what the man was implying, but it was clear he approved. He put a hand on her elbow and guided her forward to a pew that was almost full already. She tensed, looking wistfully toward the back, but those pews were no less crowded. To her dismay, he proceeded to introduce her to the couple she would be sitting next to.

The woman, who was about Sarah's own age, held a drooling infant on her lap. Her husband sat beside her. They greeted Sarah warmly, making chit chat while the organ music swelled and still more people filed into the sanctuary. Sarah conversed on autopilot, her heart threatening to leave her chest. What was she doing here? What had she been thinking?

The infant began to cry, and the woman's attention was diverted. Sarah quickly buried her nose in her program. The instructions might as well have been written in a foreign language. *Proclamation of Faith. Doxology.* She scanned down and saw the sermon title. *"When All Seems Lost." Reverend Adam Carmassi.* Her stomach churned. *Reverend.*

Then she saw him. He had appeared at the front, sitting on a bench. The organ music swelled to a crescendo, then stopped. He stood up and walked to a podium.

A giant lump rose painfully in her throat. He was wearing a robe. He didn't look at all like the Adam she knew. He looked like a minister. He *was* a minister.

Her hands clutched the program so tightly it crumpled. What had she been thinking? She didn't belong here—she wasn't like these people. They had greeted her as if she was welcome, but that was only because they didn't know her. She was only pretending to be some nice young acquaintance of the minister—in reality she was a criminal and a fraud whose plan was to seduce him and leave him hanging. How could it possibly be otherwise? Had she really thought, even for one second, that she could ever be a minister's wife?

No, she hadn't. She had never thought that far ahead. All she had wanted was to be with him. She never thought anything through that far ahead.

Adam was talking. He was welcoming the crowd, making announcements. She couldn't focus on the particulars. She wanted to slide down in her seat, out of sight. She wanted to disappear.

But then he saw her. She could tell the exact moment. His eyes moved over the crowd and stopped. He was in the middle of a word. He stammered.

She wished she could smile, but she couldn't. All she wanted to do was run away. He recovered quickly and continued his address, but his gaze kept coming back to her. Each time it did, his eyes sparkled.

It was exactly the reaction she had wanted. But she had been wrong to seek it. She could never make him happy. She wasn't Christine. She wasn't even close to what he needed. She was as wrong for him as any woman possibly could be.

Organ music swelled once more. The congregation stood.

Sarah bolted.

Chapter 30

Adam pulled into his garage so fast he almost overshot and ran into his work bench. Of all the days for him to be tied up after a service, today was the worst. He paused in his house just long enough to hang up his keys, remove his tie, and toss it through—or rather at—the basketball hoop. Then he set out across the lawn to Sarah's house.

His spirits were buoyed, and nothing was bringing him down. Sarah had come to church.

He didn't think for a moment that she had come to get religion. Her biases against the organized side of things were strong, and they would take some time to mellow. But he wasn't worried about that. Their theological discussion had assured him that they already agreed on the basics, whether she realized it or not. Disagreeing on the specifics was a matter of upbringing. Sarah had fled from the service this morning because its unfamiliar trappings had made her feel out of place, but that's all they were. Trappings. He could have warned her, if he had known, but she hadn't told him she was coming. She had wanted to surprise him.

He smiled.

Sarah had come to church for only one reason. She had done it because she cared about him. And with that knowledge in hand, he was prepared to face anything. Even the unpleasant showdown that was about to occur.

He rang the doorbell.

It took a long time for Sarah to answer.

"Hello," she said flatly. She looked tired, drained. Perhaps as if she'd been crying again. But even with blotchy skin and bags under her eyes, she still looked beautiful. She couldn't look any other way.

"Hello yourself," he said with a smile, stepping in. He wanted to touch her, hold her, but her body language wasn't amenable. Perhaps she was embarrassed. That was all right. He could wait.

They moved into the living room. He turned toward her and caught her eyes. "Thank you for coming this morning. I can't tell you how much it meant to me."

Her eyebrows rose. Her voice was hoarse. "I left before it even started."

He grinned. "Yes, I noticed that."

Her eyes widened. "You're not upset?"

He couldn't stand it as long as he thought he could. He laid his hands gently on her upper arms. "Of course I'm not upset. The coming is what's important. The leaving was immaterial. It was an overwhelming experience for you, I'm sure. I'd have been shocked if you made it through the offertory."

She said nothing. She seemed almost in a daze. Tired, and stunned. He wondered if she had slept last night. He knew he hadn't.

"So," he said cheerfully. "What did you think of the congregation? I trust you were greeted warmly at the door?"

She blinked at him. "Everyone was very friendly. I just wasn't comfortable. I'm sorry I missed the sermon. I really did want to hear it."

Her words warmed him. But there was tension in her arms. "So, how did it go?" she asked stiffly. "The sermon, I mean."

Reluctantly, he dropped his hands. She was putting distance between them again. He supposed he should have expected that. "It went swimmingly," he replied. "All I could think of was getting back to you. I lost my place three times. At least thirty people came up to me afterwards and asked if I felt all right. A couple mothers even put their hands on my forehead."

He was speaking tongue-in-cheek, but Sarah looked mortified. "I'm sorry. I didn't mean to throw you off your stride."

He chuckled. "It's a little late for that."

An awkward silence ensued. Sarah's eyes left his. She turned away and stared out her back window. Then in one motion she spun back around and spit out her next words like pistol shots. "I don't think we should see each other anymore, Adam."

Her tone stung him, but he was able to steel himself. He knew what she was doing, and he had no intention of letting her succeed. He took a step closer to her. He held her eyes.

"That's unfortunate, because you'll find me very difficult to get rid of." He took her hands in his and held them tight, even as she pulled away. "There are some things we need to get straight, Sarah. Number one is that I think you're a wonderful person, and you're not going to convince me otherwise. Number two is that I'm not going anywhere, and you can't make me. Number three is this: I came over here to ask you a question."

Sarah's eyes turned moist. She looked miserable, haunted. The fear in her expression was as sharp as he had ever seen it, only now it was accompanied by a gut-wrenching look of pain. For a second, the sight chilled him, but just as quickly, it bolstered his resolve. *Enough.* Sarah would not keep her problems from him any longer. It would end now.

"Do you trust me?" he asked, his voice firm.

Her breathing quickened. "Yes," she said weakly. "Of course I do."

He squeezed her hands. "Then tell me the truth. Tell me what happened in Alabama and why the police came to question you."

Her face flooded with anguish. She ripped her hands from his and turned her back to him. "I *can't!*" she roared at the window. "Don't you get it? It's not going to happen! Why can't you just give up and go away? You'd be better off if you never even met me!"

Disappointment surged, but Adam was determined to rise above it. He had known the odds. He knew what he was probably going to have to do—still, until now he had hoped to avoid it. "Apparently," he said, keeping his voice level, "you weren't listening to numbers one and two."

He backed away from her, then glanced around the living room. There were no books on the coffee table. He saw nothing suspicious on the shelves. He moved toward the dining room. He had seen her computer sitting on the table. Perhaps it was there.

"What are you doing?" Sarah demanded, watching him.

He didn't answer. He fingered through the papers that lay scattered around the computer. Nothing but gobbledygook. A date book. A novel. Nothing significant. He stood up straight again and glanced around the kitchen.

"What are you looking for?" Sarah protested, the pitch of her voice rising with distress. "Stop that!"

He crossed back to her and laid his hands on her shoulders. "I'm finished playing this game of ours, Sarah. I will not stand by any longer and watch you self-destruct. Either you tell me what's going on, or I'm going to find out on my own."

She paled. Her shoulders trembled beneath his hands. Her voice was plaintive. "Please don't do that."

He pulled her to him and hugged her tightly. Perhaps there was still another way—a way that wouldn't be quite so traumatic. He knew that she was afraid of something, but he also knew that whatever had happened in Alabama, guilt was playing a large role in her response to it. He smiled to himself suddenly, thinking that—irony of ironies—he was now the perfect person to help her with that. The lightening of his own load, just this morning, had taught him volumes.

"Come sit down." He led her to the couch and sat, and though her manner was stiff, she joined him without protest. "I want to tell you something," he began. His heart pounded anew at the prospect of saying what he was going to say out loud, but he was certain the time had come. For him, as well as for her.

"You may think I don't know what guilt feels like, Sarah. But you're wrong. I've been tortured with it for a decade."

She looked up at him, her brow furrowed. For a moment she seemed sympathetic, even disturbed. But then a stony cynicism took over. "What, you coveted your neighbor's Lexus? Didn't give up enough for Lent? I thought Christianity had an easy remedy for the whole guilt thing."

He let the impact of her mocking tone roll off him. She was trying to push him away, and he wouldn't be suckered. "Oh, it does, indeed," he answered. "But forgiveness is a cooperative effort, and until this morning, I refused to cooperate."

He had her attention again. "This morning?" she asked, her voice still rife with skepticism. "What horrible sin could you possibly commit that you suddenly got cured of this morning?"

He held her gaze. His pulse pounded in his ears. "It's about Christine. About how I ruined her life."

Sarah's blue eyes widened as she looked at him. Her voice softened. "What are you talking about?"

He drew in a deep breath. Then he continued. "When I first met Christine, we were teenagers. I thought she was the most beautiful creature God ever created, and as I got to know her, I realized she was every bit as beautiful inside, too. She was an amazing person in so many ways: she was sweet, she was caring, she was unselfish, and though she was loaded with creative talent and ambition, there wasn't an arrogant bone in her body. Half the guys on campus had their eyes on her, but from the beginning, she chose me. I couldn't believe how blessed I was; she was everything I could ever ask for. We wanted all the same things out of life—seminary, a career in the church, a family of our own. All our friends called us the perfect couple. I asked her to marry me, and she accepted. We got married two weeks after graduation. We were both just twenty-one."

He paused and looked at Sarah. She seemed to have questions, but was refraining from asking them. He appreciated that. His tone dropped. "Everything seemed right at the time. I admired her more than I had ever admired any woman, and I never had the slightest doubt about her devotion to me. I was certain getting married was the right thing to do."

He paused. Sarah was listening intently. Her eyes drank him in as she prompted for more. "But?"

He breathed out sharply. "But it was a mistake. A huge mistake. And the fault was all mine."

He drew back from her. Saying the words out loud was a needed release, but hearing them spoken still caused an ache in his chest. His voice fell quiet. "I wasn't in love with her, Sarah. I thought I was, but I was wrong. All the elements seemed to be in place. I was very fond of her, and I was certainly attracted to her physically. But there was always something missing. Always. I never had what other people talked about: the butterflies, the nervous excitement, the jolt of elation you were supposed to get just from seeing the person, the desire to be with them constantly. At the time, I thought all that must just be romantic nonsense—something that happened to some people, maybe, but not everyone. I had any number of perfectly valid reasons for making Christine my wife, and I couldn't come up with a single logical one against it. I convinced myself that our relationship had everything that really counted."

Sarah had moved closer to him. Her nearness created an instant heat—the hand she placed softly on his arm was like a flame.

"But I was wrong," he repeated. "And I was miserable. I can't begin to explain to you just how miserable I was. How trapped I felt. How much of a fraud. Christine loved me very much; she was wonderful to me. I was sure at first that there was nothing really wrong between us, that what I felt was normal, that I would grow to love her more. But every year that passed only made things worse. Despite myself, I grew resentful. Christine wanted to be near me all the time. But what she meant as devotion, somewhere along the line, I began to perceive as clinginess. Without intending to, I started to distance myself—to stop the constant pressure to *make* myself feel what I thought I should feel."

He rubbed his face with his hands. "I tried so hard to love her. I tried everything I could think of to make things right, to make us both happy, but I couldn't. She knew that something was wrong, even though I denied it. How could I possibly explain? The truth would have devastated her. Christine took responsibility for everything—I knew she would blame herself. She would think she'd done something wrong, that *she* wasn't good enough. I couldn't begin to be honest with her about how miserable I was.

"So I didn't do anything. We just went on. I pretended. I was determined that I could make things work out—that I owed that to her."

Adam looked at Sarah. Her eyes were moist. What he was

saying was affecting her, though he wasn't sure how.

"I'm sure she must have known," she offered, her tone mild.

He turned his own eyes away. "I think she did know," he replied soberly. "But she pretended, too. She couldn't deal with it any more than I could."

He stiffened. "We both just went on, hoping against hope that things would get better. The days turned into years. First we were busy with seminary, then with our jobs. But a few years ago, it came to a head. Christine told me she wanted a baby."

He blinked, remembering the scene. It still hurt. He had always cared enough about Christine that her pain seemed like his own. "I realized then that my resolve to make things work wasn't as strong as I thought. If I were truly committed, having a child would be the next logical step. But I didn't want that. I didn't want it because in the back of my mind, I was still holding on to the possibility that the marriage might not be forever. I had been leaving the back door open, and I knew that starting a family would close it for good. I would never leave Christine if there was a child involved. She knew that."

He paused again.

"So you told her no," Sarah offered softly.

He nodded. "But I didn't tell her the truth. I just kept making up excuses. We weren't in the right place in our careers; we needed more money first. I knew it hurt her, but she never argued. She said that we both had to be ready. Yet she kept bringing it up. Every time she did, I knew I should be honest with her. I wasn't sure I would ever be ready, and if that was the case, she had a right to know. I should have made a decision, one way or the other. I should have either committed to her wholeheartedly or let her go."

"But she didn't want to go."

"No," he replied, his voice cracking. He made haste to strengthen it. "That's why she didn't push me any more than she did. She just kept hoping I would change my mind. She knew I'd always wanted children, and I think she was convinced that a child would change things between us—make things right."

"It wouldn't have."

"Of course not. But Christine wanted a baby. Being a mother meant everything to her." Adam stood up. He couldn't bear to look at Sarah. He was telling her things he'd never told anyone—not even the wife he'd shared his life with. But though the words were painful to say, he knew they would also be liberating. Perhaps for both of them.

"She could have gotten pregnant 'accidentally' if she wanted to," he admitted. "But she didn't do that, because that's not the kind of woman she was. She put her own desires aside and respected my wishes, and that selflessness cost her dearly. She developed a brain tumor, and she died. She died without ever having the chance to be a mother." His voice turned solemn. He had—at long last—forgiven himself, and the bitterness he had once felt was gone. But the sadness would always remain. "She died without ever even knowing what it felt like to be loved by her own husband. *I* did that to her, Sarah."

She was watching him, her eyes intent, her voice firm. "It wasn't your fault that she died so young, Adam. You know that."

"No, her illness wasn't my fault. But I believed that everything else that went wrong in her life was. I lived with that guilt every day of our life together, and after she died, it became unbearable. I let that guilt bury me, Sarah. I wasn't interested in forgiveness. I wanted to suffer. I'd made her suffer; why shouldn't I? What right did I have to go on and lead a happy life, after the way I had ruined hers?"

His pulse went back to pounding. He had said the words, released the demon. The bitter memories had brought back plenty of pain, but the feeling was tempered by something new—an invigoration he hadn't felt in years. The confession had helped him immeasurably, but he hadn't done it just for himself. He was convinced he could use his own experience to get through to Sarah. And at this moment, he had her right where he wanted her.

She rose and faced him. "You have every right," she asserted, her blue eyes blazing. "You never intended to hurt her. You were young, and you made a mistake in judgment. But so did she. She chose to hang on to you when she knew you weren't happy. She chose to play the odds and hope for the best, because she would rather be with you, knowing that you didn't love her, than be without you. That was her choice, Adam."

Sarah's voice turned gentle, soothing. "She was probably suffering from some guilt of her own at the end. If she told you that she wanted you to be happy after she was gone, then you have to believe she meant it. She wouldn't want you to stay miserable, brooding over the past."

He caught her eyes and held them. His breath came fast and heavy. "No, I don't believe she would," he said slowly. "Nor would your sister want you to."

Sarah drew back. Her eyes narrowed. "We weren't talking about me."

He caught her arm. "We are now. You feel guilty about what happened in Alabama. You don't think you deserve to overcome it. You made a promise to your sister and you're determined to keep it, no matter how much it ends up costing you."

She looked at him as if he were some sort of seer—the sort that gathered power from the dark side. Her gaze hardened.

Adam pressed on. "What you're doing is wrong, Sarah. And if your sister loved you as much you loved her, she would tell you the same thing I'm going to. She's gone now. She's been gone for a very long time, and nothing that happened back then can possibly hurt her anymore. But *you* are alive, and keeping these secrets is tearing you apart. Dee wouldn't want that. She would want you to get past it. She would want you to do whatever you had to do to be happy."

All color had left Sarah's face. Adam stepped closer, half fearing she would collapse again. But her eyes remained alert. They seemed at first wondering, then crestfallen. When she had been trying to help him, she had garnered strength. But now she was drained again. Drained, and weary.

"You don't understand," she whispered, almost too low to hear. "It's not just about Dee."

He pulled her to the couch and sat her down again. "Then

make me understand. What *is* it about?"

She was quiet for a long time. Her voice, when it returned, was pleading. "It's about me. No one else. I know you want to help me, and I thank you for that. But you can't. And I care about you too much to keep dragging you down. I meant what I said before. You'd be better off without me. Please believe that."

Discouragement threatened, but he beat it down quickly. Nothing was going to break his resolve—not this time. "Sorry," he told her firmly. "No sale." He stood. His gaze panned the room, then fixed on a location.

Sarah's voice quivered with panic. "What are you doing?"

"I already told you," he explained. "I'm going to stop this."

In a few long strides, he was at her bedroom door.

"No!" she screamed, leaping up after him. "Stay out of there!"

He moved quickly. He wasn't worried about her thwarting him, but he was worried about upsetting her. He had no idea how much agitation her heart could take. But he knew things couldn't get better until they got worse.

"Adam! Stop it!"

His eyes rested on the stack of books on her bedside table. He reached them and extended a hand. *Watership Down*. He'd liked that one, too. *Road Construction Fundamentals*. He had seen that one before. All three of these. What he wanted was whatever book, fax, or printout she had made a special trip to the library to pick up yesterday. What she had hidden from him in that ridiculous briefcase.

"Adam, *No!*"

Sarah's hand reached out and grabbed his arm. Her short fingernails scratched his skin, but the pain had no effect on him. All he could see was the bottom book in the stack. *Guide to Underwater Investigations.*

Sarah's hand left him. She sank down onto the bed, silent.

Adam's brain seemed to shift into slow motion. He slid a hand into the book and opened it to a random page. *Postmortem Physiology.* He shut it again. His mind flashed a picture of Sarah after her flight through the field, nervously fingering a survey stake…

The pond.

His breath left his lungs. He turned to look at her, but her face was hidden behind her hands.

Not that. No.

There could not be a body in the Landers' pond. That was insane. Not for all these years. She would have to have known about it all along, thought about it sunk there in the muck, decomposing…

He looked at her again. She hadn't moved. Her sides shook as her breath came in in heaves.

It was true. It was worse than he'd thought. Whatever had transpired at that farm, at the end of it, somebody had died. And that somebody's body had been in a watery grave ever since. Drowned? Shot? What the hell had Sarah's sister gotten her into? Had Dee actually killed a man? Could that be the real reason behind her suicide? How dare she swear her little sister to secrecy, then leave her to deal with such a mess alone!

Good God.

He sank down on the bed beside the huddle that was Sarah. He wrapped both his arms around her and held her tight. "It's all right," he murmured, having trouble finding his voice. "It's going to be all right."

Her own voice came back low, but surprisingly steady. "No, it's not," she protested bitterly, her hands still covering her face. "It can't be, now. You've ruined everything."

He didn't think he could feel any more shock, but he was wrong. He stared at what he could see of her. "*I* have?"

"Yes," she returned, her voice terse. "I was trying to protect you, and you wouldn't let me. You had no right."

He withdrew his arms and pulled her hands from her face. She wasn't making any sense to him, but that was nothing new. "You don't need to protect me from anything. No matter how bad this is, I promise you, it will be all right. I told you already—I know that you're a good person. Whatever happened is not going to change my mind about that." He forced her gaze to meet his. "I know you, Sarah."

She sprang up as though he had struck her. "You *don't* know me!" she said harshly, stepping away. "You don't know me at all. And I don't want you to!" She glared at him, and her tone turned venomous. "I'm only going to say this one time, Adam. I want you to leave. *Now.*"

She was turning pale again, despite her agitation. A flash of fear shot through him. Her getting this upset had to be risky.

"Take it easy, Sarah, please," he said softly. "If you really want me to go, I'll go."

She held open the bedroom door. *"Go!"*

He rose slowly, then moved through it. Leaving her alone now was the last thing he wanted to do. He wanted to hold her, to comfort her. He knew that she was angry with him, but she wouldn't stay angry. As hard as this was for her, it was still a step forward.

"Get out of here!" she cried, her voice faltering.

He swallowed, then hastened his steps. He couldn't be stupid. Sarah needed to calm down. He would leave and send Rose over. There was more to talk through—so much more he wanted to say, to know. But there would be plenty of time for that later.

He reached the front door and opened it. "Take care of yourself," he said over his shoulder, softly. "Please."

She made no response.

He walked out the door and closed it behind him.

Chapter 31

The cab pulled to a jerky stop in the parking lot by Melissa's office. "You want me to wait?" the unkempt, middle-aged woman driving it barked.

"No, thank you," Sarah answered, handing over the fare. She jumped out quickly. Another thirty seconds of the odor of cigarette smoke mixed with pastrami breath and she would lose what little she had choked down for breakfast. The cab rolled off, and she headed toward the office door.

Her steps were anything but lively. She had no desire to be here, facing what was sure to be a thorough berating by her doctor. Calm, professional Melissa had sounded nothing less than furious on the phone. She had demanded that Sarah come to the office immediately, and she had refused to even estimate for how long. If Sarah cared about her health, she would be shaken. But she didn't care.

No sooner had she opened the door to the waiting room than the receptionist caught her eye and leaned forward. "Ms. Landers? Dr. Gardner wants to see you right away—in her office."

Sarah nodded, then followed the designated assistant blindly through a maze of narrow hallways and doors. She felt numb.

When she had awakened before dawn this morning, it had taken some time for her to remember what had transpired the day before. The pall of hopelessness she had arisen with could have come from another nightmare, but it hadn't. Its source was all too real. Adam knew about the body. He might not have figured out the specifics before he left, but he would soon enough.

She couldn't bear to see him again. She had fallen into an exhausted sleep early yesterday, thanks to more of Rose's ministrations, and she had slept straight through to the wee hours. At first light she had left a note for Adam on her front door, then taken a cab to the library. She had been attempting to bury herself in work when she had received the dire call from Melissa.

The assistant opened a door and ushered Sarah inside a nondescript office. A mahogany desk dominated one corner, a cluster of comfortable chairs occupied the other. "Just have a seat," the girl said pleasantly. "The doctor will be with you in a moment."

Sarah obliged. The "moment" turned out to be five seconds. Melissa stormed through the door and plopped her stout body into the chair beside Sarah, one edge of her white lab coat stuck out and pinned to the armrest.

"I really wish," the doctor began without introduction, "that you had bothered to tell me about collapsing again on Friday."

Sarah didn't relish having upset anyone. But she was too apathetic to feel embarrassed. "I'm sorry," she said dully. "I didn't know if it mattered. It was just like the others. I figured it would show up on the monitor."

Melissa was clearly struggling to control her temper. "Oh, it did," she replied curtly. "There's no question about that. I only wish I had got the results back prior to an hour ago, so that I could have done the competent thing and admitted you to the hospital ASAP."

The doctor's tone and words were ominous. Sarah supposed she should care. "So, what did the results show?"

Melissa took a deep breath. Her patient having been properly admonished, she now went into comfort mode. "You have an arrhythmia, Sarah," she announced. "An episodic malfunction of the heart that causes it to beat very rapidly. The technical term is paroxysmal supraventricular tachycardia."

Sarah tried to focus. "That's what you suspected, right? You said there were treatments."

The doctor leaned forward. "Yes, there are. I've already contacted a cardiologist. You'll be admitted to the hospital today; he'll finish the work-up and recommend therapy—most likely a procedure called radiofrequency catheter ablation. It's essential that we locate the source of the arrhythmia and eliminate it as soon as possible. Do you understand?"

Sarah's mind drifted. Hospitalization. Alone in a bed, surrounded by strangers. Maybe she would go home healthy afterward. It would be nice to drive again. Or maybe she would never go home at all. Maybe the detective would track her down at the hospital, and she could be cured just in time to go to prison.

"Sarah?" the doctor prompted. "I know you must have questions. Just ask them."

Sarah looked up. "This arrhythmia—how serious is it?"

The doctor put a hand to her chin. "For most people, not life-threatening. But your case isn't typical. You've lost consciousness four times in two weeks, and the latest monitor reading showed several irregularities. The cardiologist can tell you more, but suffice to say, we need to address the problem immediately."

The fog in Sarah's brain showed no signs of lifting. But as she listened to Melissa's words, a ray of brightness did appear in its midst. "Do you mean that if I don't have the treatment…"

The doctor's lips pursed. "We don't know what would happen, because we don't yet completely understand what's causing the arrhythmia. I don't mean to scare you, Sarah, but with symptoms this severe, there is a risk—small, but still significant—of sudden death. There is absolutely no reason to take a chance with something like this."

Sarah sat, silent, as her weary brain ruminated over what lay before her. The best that could happen would be for her to be cured, and for the investigation over Rock's death to be closed without incident. But even if both those things happened, her life here was still over. Adam was relentless; he would figure out what she had done. What she *was*. And once he and Rose knew the truth, they would want nothing more to do with her. Living so close then would be torture. She would have to move again; start all over. Alone.

And if the investigation wasn't closed? If the detective realized she was lying? She could be prosecuted for murder.

She hadn't set out to kill Rock Rockney, but in light of everything that had happened afterward, why should anyone believe that? Why had she not called an ambulance? Why had she not, at the very least, come to her senses later and informed the police?

Guilty.

Sarah closed her eyes. She was woefully ignorant on the topic of criminal law, a weakness she now regretted. Despite her boasts of having read about everything, violent crime and its repercussions were subjects she had never been able to stomach. She could not even watch second-rate TV dramas without nausea. What had ever made her think she could stand up to such a nightmare in real life? Trotting off in handcuffs with resignation, content in the knowledge that justice was being served?

"Would you like me to call Adam?" the doctor asked, her tone softer now. "He can come and pick you up, then you can collect some things and check in to the hospital."

Sarah's brain flashed the dreaded image—the one that threatened more, with every passing second, to tear her in two. Adam's beautiful brown eyes looking at her, not with their usual tenderness, but with repulsion.

Maybe even hatred.

"No," she answered firmly. "That won't be necessary. I'll just take a cab back to work for now. Then I can give the matter some more thought." She smiled superficially, attempting to convince the doctor her judgment was sound.

She should have known better. Melissa rose up in her chair, her hazel eyes blazing. "I'm afraid that's not an option, Sarah," she replied coolly. "My recommendation is that you be hospitalized immediately. I have to insist on that."

Sarah rose. She tried to keep her voice firm, but polite. "I understand your position, and I don't blame you for being irritated with me. But this is my choice. I don't want any treatment. Not right now."

Not ever.

"If you won't follow my recommendation," the doctor continued, her voice grave, "I'll be forced to dismiss you from the practice. You're taking your life in your hands, Sarah, and I can't have that kind of disaster on either my professional record or my conscience."

"I understand," Sarah returned quickly, grabbing her purse. "I don't blame you at all. You've been wonderful. Thank you. Just send me a bill."

Melissa's face changed. The frustration and annoyance was still there, but it was tempered by something else. "And what about Adam?" she asked forcefully. "How do you think he'll take your decision?"

Sarah averted her eyes. "My wellbeing is no longer his concern." She stepped toward the door, but Melissa, who was in her path, showed no signs of moving.

"Is there anything I can say to change your mind?"

Sarah looked back at the doctor's face, and guilt pummeled her. The poor woman truly did care, if not about her, then at least about Adam. Melissa was speaking as a woman now, not as a doctor. "I'm afraid not," Sarah replied mildly. "But thank you for trying."

Melissa offered a slow nod. Still, she didn't move. She contemplated for several seconds, her mind seeming to race behind her eyes. When she spoke again, her tone was level. "There is one more thing that might help. If you won't go to the hospital, there is a lesser treatment, very safe, that might at least help you with the driving issue. If you'd be willing to give it a try, I can have the materials ready in twenty minutes."

Sarah considered, but not for long. She was in no hurry to return to another smoky taxicab, now or in the future. "All right," she agreed.

Melissa smiled tightly. She led Sarah out of her office and into an exam room down the hall. Then she closed the door.

Chapter 32

Without so much as a hello, Melissa grabbed Adam's arm and pulled him through the waiting room and into the reception area behind.

"I don't know *what* she's thinking," the doctor began, expanding on what little information she had given him over the phone. "But you've got to talk some sense into her. Letting this arrhythmia go is tantamount to suicide. I'm compromising any number of ethical principles by bringing you down here and telling you all this, but it's for her own good." She paused, her sharp eyes resting sympathetically on his. "And yours."

Adam swallowed. Melissa's phone call had frightened him. He had waited all afternoon and evening yesterday for another chance to talk to Sarah, but Rose had insisted she was asleep—and needed to be. When he'd shown up at Sarah's door this morning, she was already gone, leaving nothing but a terse note explaining that she would be taking cabs to work from now on. He had planned to confront her at the library at lunchtime, but he'd barely gotten settled in at his own desk before Melissa had called to demand that he come to her office—ASAP.

"She's refusing treatment?" he asked, his thoughts muddled. All he had learned yesterday was still not enough to explain Sarah's present actions. He understood her mortification, her anger at him for invading her privacy. But he had tried his best to be supportive, rather than judgmental. Shouldn't *some* part of her be relieved? Anxious to talk it through? No. She was running again.

"She's waiting around because I told her I wanted to try one more thing," Melissa explained, leading him down a corridor, then stopping short of an exam room door. "I didn't tell her it was you. Good luck, Adam."

The doctor put her hand on his arm and squeezed. Then she pulled a chart from the wall and disappeared into another room.

Adam took a breath. He knocked on the door.

"Come in," Sarah's voice called.

He obliged. He watched her eyes carefully as she recognized him, and he was not disappointed. All too soon, they were filled with nothing but the indignation he knew would be coming. But she couldn't hide what happened first. At the unexpected sight of him, their blue depths had lit up like sunshine.

She averted her gaze. Her tone was cool. "I'm beginning to think you just like seeing me in hospital gowns."

He grinned. "You're not in a hospital gown now."

"No, but you didn't know that."

He walked up to where she was sitting on the exam table, her shapely legs dangling over the edge like a child's. He hopped up and sat down beside her. The table issued an ominous creak.

"We didn't finish our conversation yesterday," he said lightly.

"Oh? I thought we had. You realized you were wrong about me, and I realized I needed to get on with my life."

He turned his head to look at her. The woman was maddening. What was she thinking? He tried hard to keep his voice in check. If she insisted on playing this emotional deadpan, at least she was calm. He had no desire to see a repeat of last night's hysteria.

"Well, neither of those is accurate, I'm afraid. I've never been wrong about you—at least not about anything important—and you're not getting on with your life at all. Melissa seems to think you're trying to end it."

She showed no visible reaction. Her tone chilled him. "And what if I am?"

He sat still for a moment, stunned. Then he slid off the table and turned to face her, his voice heavy. "Don't even joke about that."

Her eyes met his. Miserable. Remorseful. "I told you before, Adam," she said quietly. "I don't want to hurt you. My life is a complete mess, and it's only going to get worse. Do the smart thing and cut your losses."

Adam's face burned with heat. She wasn't joking. She wanted to die. And judging by Melissa's sense of urgency, she might do just that—unless he could get through to her. But how could he? He was no miracle worker. All he ever did was pray hard and fly by the seat of his pants, and this time nothing was working. What else could he possibly do? Yell at her? Shake her? Kiss her?

"I won't give up on you, Sarah," he blurted.

"I don't know why not," she answered. "You already know enough about me to send you screaming into the hills. I don't even understand why you're here."

He held her gaze, his tone even. "That should be obvious. I'm here because I love you."

She stared back at him, her eyes wide. Her face paled, even as a flush of heat flared in her cheeks. "No," she said stubbornly. "You can't."

He took a much-needed breath. "I assure you that I can. And I do. It took me a while to recognize it, seeing as how the feeling is a first for me. But when I saw you sitting there in church yesterday and all two-hundred or so other faces faded into the woodwork, I knew. You were all I saw—all I could think about. You still are."

She slid off the table, her eyes fixed on the floor.

"I'm telling you," he continued, "I'm hooked. And there isn't anything you can do about it. So I would appreciate it if you would stop wasting your energy trying to get rid of me and resign yourself to the fact that I'm going to help you through this. All of it."

Sarah stepped away from him. She was attempting to restrain tears, but she was failing. "The only fact here is that you're going to get hurt even worse than I thought. I'm sorry. I didn't want that. I'm sorry I ever moved to Pittsburgh."

"Don't say that!" he answered roughly, struggling to keep his composure. She was scaring and infuriating him at the same time.

"I'm leaving, Adam," she announced with sudden fortitude.

"I'm…moving back to Alabama."

"You are not!" he fired back, the struggle lost. "You're going to check into the hospital and get this arrhythmia treated. *Today.*"

She whirled around, her eyes blazing. "I'm not going to get it treated at all! I'll sign whatever forms Melissa wants me to sign, but I won't do anything else."

Adam grabbed hold of both her arms and pulled her to him. His voice rose. "You could die from this, Sarah! Don't you get that? Don't you care?"

Her own voice rose to nearly a shriek. *"No! I don't!"*

Adam released her, stunned. She turned her back on him.

Her voice seemed to come from far away. Faint, wispy. "I've never wanted to die as much as I do right now. You're the most wonderful man—the most wonderful person—I've ever met. And I've brought you nothing but grief. You have to let me go."

Adam's pulse pounded. He stepped around to face her again. He let a hand drift down her jawbone, then lifted it, forcing her to look at him. "Don't do this to me, Sarah," he warned, his deep voice beseeching. "Don't do it. It's not fair."

"I *know* that," she answered, her voice cracking.

"Then cut it out!" he ordered. "If you insist on trying to walk out of my life, the least you can do is tell my why. You owe me that."

He watched with bated breath as, deep in her eyes, something crumbled. He saw within her a look of final defeat—defeat tempered with a queer sort of relief. The sight was a long-desired one, but he was far too alarmed now to feel elation.

"Yes," she answered quietly. "You're right. I do owe you that, don't I?" Her eyes welled up with tears again, and she swiped at her cheeks to stem them. "We might as well get it over with now. Maybe it will be easier for you."

Adam winced at the tone of her voice, the bitter edge to her words. He had never seen any person so contorted with guilt, including himself.

"You want to know what really happened in Alabama?" she

asked, her voice high, unnatural.

"You know I do," he answered.

Her blue eyes went blank. Her limbs grew stiff with tension. "That's because you think I'm an innocent victim of circumstances. But I'm not. What I am is a criminal. I've been running for over nine years now, trying to amuse myself the best I could until it all caught up with me. Well, now it has, and I could be arrested at any time. I didn't want any of my friends to have to witness that spectacle, which is why I left Kansas City in the first place. I wasn't supposed to make new friends. See what a great job I did of that? See how gallantly I put everyone else's interests ahead of my own?"

Her voice was unsteady; her lips quivered. Adam was worried about her heart, but the more she spoke, the more worried he became about the rest of her. It could not be as she was saying. It simply couldn't. She wasn't seeing the situation clearly. She was exaggerating.

"Arrested for what?" he asked softly.

"What do you think?!" she railed, her voice nearing a scream. Any second Melissa or one of the nurses would open the door to check on her. Once they did, the moment would be lost. He had to finish this.

"What do I think?" he answered boldly, taking a chance. "I think that a man assaulted your sister in that house, and I think you were there and watched it happen. I think she fought back, and somehow or other, she killed him. Then she convinced you to help her cover it up. And you did, because you wanted to protect her."

Sarah's eyes were wild. Her entire body trembled. "Well, you're wrong!" she shouted. "Dee didn't kill him, Adam! *I did.* Do you hear me? *I killed him!* I smashed his skull in, and I left his body to rot! *That's* the kind of person I am! Do you *get it now?*"

Melissa stormed through the door. She threw Adam a sharp look as she went to Sarah. "What are you yelling about?" she chastised with a fury.

Sarah didn't answer. She was breathing heavily. Too heavily. Adam's own heart had ceased to beat. Melissa lifted her stethoscope and placed it on Sarah's chest. She didn't listen for long. "Lay down, Sarah," she said sternly, leading her patient back to the exam table. An assistant appeared at the door, and Melissa barked out more orders.

Adam didn't hear the specifics. He stood obediently out of the way, but his eyes were on Sarah. She was pale. Deathly pale. When she lay down, her eyes closed. Her chest was heaving.

Melissa was speaking to him. "You'll have to wait outside. What just happened here? What were you thinking?"

He didn't answer. His voice wasn't working.

Sarah had killed a man. He had attacked her sister, and she had killed him. She had done it in Dee's defense. She had to have. Yet she had spoken of the act as if it were murder.

Had she never shared her story with anyone else? Never had any help to distinguish concrete fact from the distorted impressions of an overwrought seventeen-year-old girl? Was she so traumatized then, so ashamed, that she couldn't see the events even halfway objectively, even now?

Or was there more to the story? Was there some malevolence, some darkness in Sarah that he had willfully failed to see?

Melissa looked up at him, then softened her tone. "I'm sorry for snapping at you, Adam. I'm sure you were doing the best you could. But for now, just go back outside and have a seat in the waiting room. Please?"

He hesitated. His eyes filled with the sight of Sarah's thin frame stretched out on the table, and the grim possibilities spun uncontrollably in his head—a fierce, furious tornado of horrors that seemed bent on buffeting his hard-won confidence.

Then he clenched his jaws tight.

He straightened his shoulders, and he nodded.

Chapter 33

Sarah heard the door open and shut. She sensed that someone was standing in the room, watching her, but she kept her eyes closed. She felt light-headed. Dizzy. Disconnected from the irrelevant body that lay on the exam table, once again tethered to a machine by a series of pesky, taped-on wires.

The visitor approached her bedside. She felt a hand touch her shoulder, and she knew without opening her eyes that it was Adam. Her face flushed with heat.

He shouldn't be here. He should be gone by now. Whatever the Methodist version of last rites was, she wasn't interested. She especially wasn't interested in hearing him explain—oh, so tactfully—how very much he cared about her soul, but that she had to understand, whatever had been between the two of them before, well, now it just wasn't feasible…

"Sarah?"

She swallowed. She kept her eyes shut. "I'm awake. What do you want?" There was a pause. She could picture him in her mind. He would be clenching that little muscle in his cheek now—biting back whatever sharp retort had sprung into his mind, replacing it with something ministerial.

"I want you to open your eyes."

He didn't sound ministerial. He sounded rather forceful. Not angry, exactly—but determined.

"And I want you to leave," she shot back.

"Open your eyes."

She took in a deep breath, then let it out slowly, as Melissa had coached her. Sarah knew that if she lost consciousness now, the doctor would whisk her straight to the hospital. She could only refuse if she were lucid.

"Why?" she asked calmly.

The exam table squeaked as Adam leaned his weight against it, resting one arm above her head and the other at her side. She could feel his face close to hers.

"Because I want you to look at me."

Sarah's eyes burned. She might have cried again, but there didn't seem to be any tears available.

She didn't answer.

"I know what you're afraid of, Sarah," his deep voice rumbled, softly. "It took me a while, but I figured it out."

His tone had turned tender now, beguiling. But she would not be suckered as to his intentions. No minister worth his vestments would let her commit suicide without a fight.

"I don't want to go to the hospital, Adam," she asserted. "And I know enough about my rights as a patient to know that no one can make me. I hereby absolve you of all responsibility—you did your best. Now please, just go away and forget about me. I want you to be happy."

"You really mean that?" he said, his voice oddly optimistic.

"Yes!"

Her only warning was a creaking of the table. In a flash his position shifted, and his lips were pressed to hers. Shocked, she reached up to push him away, but the kiss was as gentle as it was unexpected, and she felt herself melting to it, her arms encircling his waist, her affection-starved senses clamoring for comfort.

She forgot about keeping her eyes closed.

When at last he lifted his head and looked at her, she stared straight back at him.

He smiled. "You thought my feelings would change if I knew," he whispered. "You were wrong."

Her heart beat fast as she searched his face, his deep brown eyes. She had been so sure she would see revulsion. Regret. A patronizing sort of pity.

All she could see was love.

His warm hand picked up her cool one. He held it close to his face, his moist breath tickling her fingers. "We never got to finish the conversation I started last night—about my guilt over Christine. You missed the important part."

Sarah could only stare. She didn't understand why he was talking about Christine now. She didn't understand anything.

His eyes held hers. "When I saw you sitting in that church pew yesterday, I finally understood what it meant to be in love. Raw, full-fledged, gut-twisting, butterfly-fluttering love. I realized that the feeling has nothing to do with appropriateness, much less hard work. It's something one has no control over.

"All this time, I thought that I had sabotaged my marriage by yearning for some fanciful feeling that didn't exist, or worse yet, that it *did* exist, but that I hadn't tried hard enough to get it. Yesterday, I finally understood. I know now that there was nothing more I could have done. I loved Christine as much as was within my power to love her."

Sarah's lips curved into a smile. He had indeed seemed happy, after church. Had she been able to do *something* good for him, after all?

"I can't tell you what a wonderful sense of peace that revelation brought me," he continued. "And I owe that to you."

Her smile broadened. "Well, I'm glad I'm not totally worthless."

He threw her a meaningful look. His voice dropped lower. "You're anything but worthless, Sarah. I tried for a decade to fall in love with Christine, and I couldn't do it. I tried *not* to fall in love with you, and it happened anyway. So if you think you're going to ruin this whole love thing for me on account of your own petty problems, you can forget it. For all I know, you're the only woman on earth who'll ever have this effect on me. I like this love business, I intend to indulge myself in it, and I'm not going to let anyone—including you—mess it up for me. Got that?"

Sarah's brow furrowed with confusion. Either he had lost his mind, or she had. Had he heard a word she'd said earlier? Had she only imagined saying it?

"I killed a man!" she cried, her voice catching in her throat. "Didn't you hear what I said?"

"I heard every word," he answered calmly. "And I still love you. Deal with it."

Sarah's mind raced. What had she not told him? "You don't know everything that happened," she began anxiously. She couldn't bear to believe what he was saying, only to have him retract it later—when the full horror of it finally penetrated. "You can't possibly love a murderer."

"I should be able to," he said without humor. "But you aren't a murderer, Sarah. You know that."

"Do I?" she blurted, her voice rising. "I *hated* him!"

The door opened. Melissa hurried in, took a quick look at Sarah, and studied the paper strip on the bedside monitor. "You need to stay calm, Sarah," she said firmly, even as she threw Adam a look of desperation. "EMS should be here any minute."

"I'm not going," Sarah repeated.

Adam cleared his throat. "She'll be ready, Melissa."

The doctor's eyes held his. She pressed a hand on his shoulder, then walked out.

Sarah started to speak, but Adam shushed her.

"Don't talk anymore; don't relive it," he ordered. "When you're better, we'll talk through everything. We'll find a good defense attorney and we'll figure out where we stand. But right now, none of that matters. All that matters is getting you healthy again."

Sarah stared at him, still disbelieving. The confession she had resisted making so strenuously, for so long, had left her feeling oddly transparent. Hollow. As if a large part of her had been ripped forcefully from its cocoon, dragged out and exposed to the light of day, to shrivel. She felt weak without it. Unnatural.

She was silent for a long time. Adam sat quietly beside her, her hand still clasped in his.

"Do you really believe I'm worth saving?" she asked slowly, her voice barely above a whisper.

When Adam said nothing, she caught his eyes.

His answer was there.

Sarah looked away. She didn't deserve what he was offering her; she didn't deserve him. Accepting his help, his love, seemed somehow dishonest.

Was it really what *he* wanted?

She met his gaze. "You still don't know the whole story, Adam. There could be worse things I haven't said yet—things that would disturb you even more." But were there? In her heart, she doubted it. She had told him the worst already—without even explaining all the circumstances. "I just don't see how you can be so sure about me. How you can be so sure that I—"

She struggled for the right words. "That I'm worth it. I'm not convinced of it myself. How can you be?"

His dark eyes moistened. There was a twinkle behind them.

"I know," he answered, "because the boss man told me."

Sarah's brow furrowed. Then she got it. Adam *would* bring everything back to religion, wouldn't he? She supposed that was allowable. After all, it was who he was.

"I see," she returned with a grin. "And I suppose you have a direct line?"

He smiled back. "Of course. Everyone does."

Sarah could picture it clearly—on the desk in Adam's office. An old-fashioned rotary telephone, complete with metal bell. Bright red, naturally. *"God"* written across the dial—punched out with plastic label tape.

Despite herself, she chuckled.

"What are you laughing at?"

She met his eyes. She knew he wasn't teasing her; he had meant exactly what he said. There was an undeniable light in him, a strength, that she had never quite been able to qualify. A vitality that kept him running strong, no matter what blindsided him. Through all the sadness and guilt he had suffered over Christine, all the torture and frustration she herself had put him through—it had always been there.

Whatever it was, it worked for him.

Who was she to argue with results?

"I can't promise you a life with no problems, Sarah," he continued. "There may be repercussions from what happened in the past. Making things right might not be easy. But I'm asking you to take a chance. On *life*. On how much better it could be. Living openly, without the guilt and the fear. Feeling free to love—and be loved."

The exam room door flew open. Melissa stepped inside. "EMS is here," she announced.

Adam squeezed Sarah's hands.

A chance.

It could be one chance in a hundred million.

She considered.

She squeezed back.

"All right," she proclaimed, feeling suddenly, oddly, hopeful. "Let's do it."

Chapter 34

Sarah drifted in and out of consciousness. Something was trying to make her wake up, but she didn't want to. She wasn't ready yet.

There was water all around her, and it was murky. She couldn't see more than a few feet before her face, where wispy green vegetation swayed in rhythm with the motion of her arms. She was rapidly running out of breath. Cool, clear sunlight filtered through the water above her head, and she swam anxiously toward the surface. But something had hold of her ankle.

It was Rock.

"Adam!"

Her eyes flew open. She took in the unfamiliar ceiling, walls, and doors as if one nightmare had been switched for another. Where was she?

"I'm right here, Sarah."

Adam was beside her, taking her hand. She was awake. She was in the hospital.

She let out a breath of relief. Her heart rate slowed.

"Are you all right?" he asked anxiously.

"I'm fine," she responded. "I just had a nightmare, and…I got confused."

"You called me."

Sarah struggled to clear her head. His voice sounded faintly amused. "What?"

He was grinning at her. "I said, you called *me*. I like that."

Sarah tried to smile back, but the nightmare still had a hold on her. Rock still had a hold on her. Pulling her down.

"It's about time you woke up," Adam continued, still smiling. "You were less than coherent when they brought you out of recovery last night, and then you slept straight through till this morning."

She surveyed his rumpled shirt and unruly hair. Had he stayed here, with her, all night?

"The procedure went perfectly," he continued. "The cardiologist believes they were able to 'ablate' whatever was causing the arrhythmia. He anticipates a full recovery."

Sarah absorbed the news slowly. "Just like that?"

"Just like that."

She could think of nothing else to say; cold pond water continued to cling about her.

"What was it about?" Adam asked.

She blinked.

"The nightmare," he clarified, sitting down on the edge of the bed. "Do you want to tell me about it?"

His nearness chased away some of the chill. But he wasn't near enough. She wanted him to crawl under the covers, lay down beside her, pull her to him…

She tried to concentrate on his question.

She had never told anyone about the nightmares. She had always suffered through them alone. Yet here he was, asking. He knew the worst already, and he was still here.

Her eyes teared up. She prided herself on not being a crier, but perhaps she could blame the anesthesia.

The events of the last twenty-four hours had rocked her from the inside out, and she knew it was for her ultimate good. But along with her newfound willingness to hope had come a vulnerability she hadn't expected. She could scarcely remember a time when her loathsome secret had not been the bulk of her, defining her every move, her every reflection. Now that core of her was gone. What she was left with was naked. Fragile.

She wanted to hide her tears; she wanted to be closer to Adam. In one motion she sat up and wrapped both her arms around his neck, straining the leads on the monitor wires attached to her chest. He held her as she was for a moment, awkwardly, then he moved to sit alongside her instead, maneuvering carefully around the wires until he could wrap his muscular arms around her middle. She nestled eagerly into his side, savoring the feel of him—his warmth, his strength, his tenderness.

"Talk to me, Sarah," he urged, his voice soft in her ear.

She swallowed, willing herself not to tremble. Her heart was fine now; the time had come. She needed to get it out—to get it over with. Being held, yet not having to face him, was nice. It would be easier this way.

"The nightmare was about Rock," she said quietly. "I've had the same one a million times. But I don't want to talk about that. What I need is to tell you what really happened."

Her limbs trembled.

Adam's arms tightened around her. "I'm listening."

She took a breath and began her story with what was closest to her heart: her sister. Dee's journals, her emotional problems, her promiscuousness. How Sarah had loved her dearly, despite everything. With a cracking voice, she went on to explain what had happened when Rock Rockney came to their house that night. The horrific scene that met her eyes as she walked down the stairs into the living room. Dee's clothes, crumpled on the floor. Her mouth, stuffed with cloth—his handkerchief. Her eyes, fraught with terror, seething with hate. The muffled whimpers that were meant to be shouts of outrage, or pain.

Sarah told how she had screamed at Rock to stop, slapped him, pulled at him. But he was too strong. He had thrown her off with one apelike arm, her frail presence no more worrying to him than a gnat. Her eyes had come to rest on the elephant statue. Her hands had snatched it up…

Her voice trailed off.

Adam waited a moment before speaking. Up to now, he hadn't uttered a word. "You hit him to defend your sister," he said gently. "You didn't intend to kill him."

She shook her head. "But when I did it, I hated him—I told you that. I wasn't paying attention to how hard I hit him. I didn't care if he did die. When I saw him crumple, I was glad—"

"Well of course you were!" Adam broke in, his voice rising. "How could you feel anything *but* rage toward a man who was—at that very moment—raping your sister? If it had been my sister, don't you think I would have pounded him into the floor?"

Sarah tensed. Adam's flares of temper didn't disturb her—in fact, she found his particular brand of righteous indignation charming. But the images his outburst provoked were hard to see.

Adam let out a remorseful groan and softened his voice. "For heaven's sake, Sarah, you're only human. As for your not caring whether the man died, I don't believe you. If you had the chance to choose between his dying by your hand or spending a decade enjoying the company of his own kind, he would be behind bars right now. You never *chose* to kill him. You chose to strike him in defense of your sister. His death was an accidental consequence."

She shook her head again. "I could have done more. Once Dee was out of danger, I could have called an ambulance."

"So why didn't you?"

"Because…" the horrific scenes pounded her mind mercilessly, and she let them out in a rapid tumble of hastily chosen words. "Because when he fell, I honestly thought I'd only knocked him out. All I cared about was Dee. She was hysterical. Screaming. Throwing things. I tried to calm her down, but she wasn't hearing me. She started kicking him as he lay there on the floor, in the face, in the ribs…everywhere. Then she was jumping on him, pummeling him. She beat at him with her sandals, the brass picture frame from the coffee table, the art books—whatever she could grab. She was wild—I couldn't get her to stop. She kept striking out at him until she was exhausted. Then she was crying, sobbing, and I was trying to comfort her. I don't know how much time passed before I even thought about him. When I did, my only concern was what he might do to us when he woke up. I was afraid of him; I wanted to call the police. But Dee wouldn't let me—she didn't want anyone to know what he'd done to her. She wanted to drag him outside the front door and just leave him there, on the lawn. But he—"

Her voice gave way.

"He didn't wake up," Adam finished.

"No," she replied hoarsely. "And when I finally got the nerve to check for a pulse, there wasn't one. When we realized he was dead, everything changed. Our roles reversed. I was the one who broke down. I guess I cried—I don't even remember that part of it clearly. What I do remember is that Dee took charge. All of a sudden, she was my big sister again. She kept telling me I hadn't killed him, that *she* had—that it was her beating that did it. She was saying that because she wanted to spare me—and perhaps because she hated him enough to want it to be true. But I didn't believe her. There was so much blood in his hair, on the floor…I knew it was my blow that killed him.

"I still wanted to call the police—at one point I had the phone in my hand—but I let Dee stop me. She kept saying that *she* would go to jail—that Rock was unconscious already when she attacked him. That unlike me, there was no excuse for what she'd done. Mainly, she was ashamed. She didn't want anyone to know about the rape. She just wanted to make Rock Rockney and everything that had happened that night go away."

Sarah told the rest without stopping. The bungee cords. The motorcycle. Those few horrific moments underwater. The scrubbing and the cleaning; the trips to the county dump. The silence in the house. The empty bottle of antidepressants beside Dee's bed. The realization that she was completely, finally, alone.

When she finished, she felt limp. Exhausted.

But also strangely empty. Happily, blissfully empty.

Adam said nothing for a long time. When he did speak, his voice was even. Strong.

The very tone of it comforted her.

"Thank you for telling me," he said slowly. Then he shifted position to face her.

"What you have to realize, Sarah, is that your view of events is distorted. You're still seeing everything through the eyes of a traumatized, panicked adolescent. But what I see—what any objective adult would see—is different. You made some serious errors in judgment, that's true. Not calling for help was a mistake. Hiding the body was a mistake. Certainly keeping it a secret all these years has been a mistake. But your actions are more understandable than you seem to realize. You were only a teenager—a teenager who had been orphaned just days before. You were put in a terrifying situation, you reacted rashly, and then you panicked. Losing your sister on top of everything else was too much—it no doubt put you in some kind of shock."

She had turned her face away from him, but with a hand under her chin, he brought it back.

"You thought I would be horrified, Sarah, and I am. But not because I misjudged you. I'm horrified by the thought of your spending the last nine years suffering through such tremendous guilt. Believing you were some kind of monster, living in constant fear of being discovered and punished—"

"I'm still scared," she exclaimed. "You know that I could go to prison."

His gaze locked on hers. "That's not going to happen, Sarah."

"You don't know that!" she argued, her voice thin. "You can't. What Dee and I did after I hit him will make us look guilty of murder, even if we weren't. And I lied to the police, just the other day. I told them that Rock left the house that night and that I never saw him again."

A flicker of distress crossed Adam's eyes. Sarah could tell that the admission worried him, even as his voice remained steady. "I'm no expert on the law," he replied. "But I suspect the police might overlook that lapse if you come forward with the real truth voluntarily—and immediately. You are *not* guilty of murder. You can't even be sure that you *did* kill him, Sarah! The fatal blow could very well have come from Dee; after this much time, there's probably no way of ever knowing. As for whatever lesser crimes were committed, you have to remember that you were only a juvenile, and there were certainly extenuating circumstances. Not to mention statutes of limitations running out."

Sarah said nothing. Her mind seemed, suddenly, a blank.

Adam pulled her against him and hugged her tight.

"You don't have to suffer through this alone anymore. And we don't have to speculate. We'll hire an attorney and we'll take his or her advice. Maybe we'll have a fight on our hands; maybe we won't. Maybe the authorities will be happy enough just to put a lid on the case and let it go."

Sarah shivered. If the detective had believed her lies, he would not be letting it go right now—he would be pursuing Tommy Martin. Even if she had nothing else on her conscience, there would always be that. Yet it was within her power to clear him completely.

If she were strong enough.

"Whatever happens," Adam continued, "we'll deal with it. You, me, Rose… and whatever other friends and family you'd like support from."

Friends and family. Support. The words had an almost whimsical ring to them.

Sarah had accepted her isolation along with her guilt, but she hadn't enjoyed being alone. Not really. She realized now that she did want other people around her. That she needed them. To love and be loved, just like her father had always said—

An alarming thought penetrated her brain, and she pulled away from Adam with a start. "You didn't tell Rose?!"

"I most certainly did," he said sternly. "She was here, you know. During the procedure. She told me she would be back this morning."

Sarah stared at him, unbelieving. "She's still…she doesn't–"

"Better watch what you say," he chastised. "She'd be furious if she knew you gave her so little credit. Of course she doesn't hate you, Sarah. There's no reason why she should. If anything, she's irritated at you for being so hard on yourself."

Sarah felt as though the world had turned on its head.

Your perspective—it's distorted.

"But I lied to you," she insisted. "I lied to you both."

"That was annoying, yes," he agreed. "But we forgive you. Provided you cut it out."

The tears were back again, hovering. Sarah had lost control of them. "I can't believe that you and Rose… that you can know everything and still… I don't deserve that from you. It's too easy."

Adam sat back from her a bit, studying her face with a

melancholy expression. "Forgiveness is a wonderful thing, Sarah," he said quietly. "It's a shame you're not more familiar with it."

Forgiveness.

Sarah considered. Adam's ability to forgive her had saved her life. Her inability to forgive herself had nearly cost it.

Maybe there was something to all this theological mumbo jumbo, after all.

Suddenly, inexplicably, Sarah felt herself smiling. The chill of her nightmare seemed finally vanquished. Her body felt oddly warm. "There seems to be a lot I'm not familiar with," she said slyly, catching Adam's eyes. "But I could learn, don't you think?"

She had expected the implication of her words to please him. She did not expect that after his gorgeous brown eyes lit up like beacons, he would pull her to him with such momentum that they both fell back against her pillows.

"Do you mean that?" he whispered, his face an inch from hers.

She relaxed against him; her smile widening. *Bliss.* "If I say yes, will you kiss me?"

She didn't have to say yes. He didn't seem able to wait. He kissed her with the same unbridled, heady passion he had succumbed to once before, and for several dizzying, heat-filled moments, she thought that—hospital bed or no—this time he might *not* stop, a prospect which didn't disturb her in the slightest.

But he did stop. Suddenly, abruptly, and with no warning whatsoever, he wrenched himself apart from her, sat up, and turned away.

She sat up with him; pressed herself to his side. The absence of him was agony. "Will you please," she said between halting breaths, "stop teasing me like that? A girl can only take so much!"

He looked back at her, but didn't smile. His faced was flushed with heat, his eyes—much to Sarah's distress—radiated a queer sadness.

"Adam," she said pointedly, with fear as much as

frustration, "what is it? What's wrong with you? Or should I say, what else is wrong with me?"

He shook his head; put a hand to her cheek. "Nothing's wrong with you," he answered roughly, winded. "It's just that… I've had a chance to think this through already. But you haven't. You've only been thinking in the short term. Looking at the long term… well… you might feel differently."

Sarah's brow furrowed. The man was talking in riddles. He looked nervous as a school boy.

"I haven't been fair to you, Sarah," he said suddenly, standing up. "There are some things I should have explained to you before, but I… There is no excuse."

Her stomach turned to lead. It was happening, exactly as she feared. She had known all along that Adam was the marrying kind; hadn't she also known that no man in his position could possibly consider someone like—

"I know you think I'm a great catch," he continued, making a weak attempt at humor. "But you aren't familiar enough with what I do to understand."

He tried to catch her eyes. Sarah looked away.

"I'm afraid I come with a very high price tag. It might not be fair, but it's the way things are, and I can't change it. I don't have an ordinary job, Sarah. Being a minister's— Well, being *with* me means taking on an unofficial job you'd never get paid for. Making friends and setting up house, only to be moved to a new church every few years. Having well-meaning people pry into your personal affairs 24/7; sometimes publicly judging you. Living with just enough money to get by—never much more. Not to mention competing with a passion that consumes a great deal of my time and attention, including evenings and weekends."

He paused. He returned to the bed and sat back down beside her. "I'm some salesman, aren't I?" he said miserably. "I know. It's a deal no sane woman would take. Even another Methodist. But for you, feeling like you do… I'm sorry, Sarah. I should have explained before."

Sarah sat still, bewildered. He couldn't possibly be serious. Could he?

He wasn't telling her she wasn't good enough. He was worried she didn't want *him* enough. As if accepting him for who and what he was, tolerating a little minor aggravation and inconvenience along the way, was too much to ask of her.

Her heart leapt in her chest—this time, in a good way.

She pulled him back against her; kissed him gently on the cheek.

"Adam," she chastised playfully, "Stop being ridiculous. Just tell me the truth. Do you really think I could make you happy? *Me*, as messed up as I am, with all my baggage and my inexperience with churches and my hundred and one other problems that would make any man with a neuron in his brain run as far away from me as he could possibly get?"

His answer was immediate. "Yes. Absolutely."

A warm joy surged within her, sending a fiery heat to the very tips of her fingers. She was about to thoroughly pounce on him when his qualification stopped her in her tracks.

"That is," he said tentatively, "if…"

"If what?" she cried, frustrated.

"If you love me, too," he finished.

A lump rose in Sarah's throat. How could he possibly doubt that? How many times had she—

Never.

Oh, my!

She wrapped her arms around his middle, hugging him so tightly she was pretty sure two monitor leads popped off her chest. "I do love you, Adam Carmassi," she declared loudly. "I love everything about you, and I intend to keep on loving you as long as I live, no matter what your damned job is, and no matter how long it takes me to break down your defenses and seduce you."

His face turned slowly toward hers. "Are you saying you're willing to—"

"You heard me, Rev," she interrupted, nuzzling her nose against the curve of his solid, black-stubbled jawbone. "If by some miracle I do become a free woman…"

She kissed him softly on the earlobe, her voice lowering to a whisper.

"I'm buying the cow."

Epilogue

Six Weeks Later

It was hot. The September sun was blazing, but Sarah's hands felt cold. She could see her right wrist tremble as she held it out of the woman's way. Her knees were trembling too.

She wasn't supposed to be so afraid. She had told Adam she wouldn't be. But now that the moment had come, her old bravado seemed a distant joke.

The woman tightened the straps at her side with a sharp tug and clicked the remaining restraints into place. "All right," she announced gruffly, her tone slightly bored. "That's it. Stand by for your instructions."

Sarah looked up tentatively. She wasn't supposed to be reacting like this. She had fancied herself as strong now—far stronger than she had ever been. Her healthy heart could race with the best of them, and at the moment seemed trying to prove it. There was no excuse for her cowardice, not when she had brought such a predicament on herself. No one had made her do it. It was her own decision. She had insisted she could handle it. She had been determined—no matter what.

A man whose name badge said Sean stepped up before her. "All right," he said forcefully, clapping his hands together. "Are you ready?"

Sarah swallowed. The man looked twenty-one, tops. She would feel better if he were older. But she had no choice about that now. She had no choice, period. She had opened up her mouth and let her overconfidence do the talking, and now she had to pay. There was no turning back.

Not if she wanted to save face.

And saving face was everything.

"Sure, we're ready," Adam answered, his deep voice booming beside her. He squeezed her left hand. "Aren't we?"

She nodded. "Oh, sure. Ready."

"You're not chickening out on me, are you?" he teased, smiling at her. "Because as I'm sure you recall, this was *your* idea."

She groaned. "I remember, I remember!"

"But, if you can't practice what you preach—"

"Will you *shut up?*" she snapped, kicking him sideways in the shin. It was the best she could do. Their body harnesses prevented her from moving much more than that. "Just listen to Sean."

The man grinned at them. "Yes, listen to Sean. Here's how the Sky Coaster works. First, you'll be pulled up to the tower..."

Sarah's mind wandered. Adam was the one with the frequent flier account. He could pay attention to the directions. She had to concentrate on her nerves.

She had nothing to be afraid of. Not really. The Sky Coaster hadn't lost anyone yet. It was perfectly safe. She had said so herself.

She had said a lot of things, hadn't she? The last few weeks, she'd become a regular chatterbox. The relief of Rock Rockney's case being closed—once and for all—had manifested itself in any number of odd ways. Like her actually wanting to spend some extra time in Auburn afterward, looking up old friends. Like her voluntarily calling her father's crazy parents, just to check in. Like her actually enjoying getting to know Adam's friends—even giving out her phone number.

She had been determined to tie up every loose end, and she had. She had told the whole truth, all the truth, and nothing but the truth, and though it was hardly an enjoyable experience, with the help of her excellent attorney she had come through it just fine. The county was quick to exact a financial penalty for her failure to disclose human remains before a sale, but the state of Alabama had showed no interest in prosecuting a nine-year-old accidental-death case against a juvenile who was now a law-abiding adult. The criminal justice system—it appeared—

had bigger fish to fry.

No charges were filed.

Rock Rockney, Sarah discovered, did have a criminal record of his own. He had been the only child of a single mother from whom he had become estranged, and who, perhaps unbeknownst to him, had died of a drug overdose shortly before his visit to Auburn. No one had ever reported him as missing. Sarah had located where his mother and grandparents were buried, and she had paid for his remains to be laid to rest there. She liked to think she had laid him to rest, period.

Sean had finished talking. Sarah's heartbeat quickened again.

"Did you get that?" she asked Adam as the operator walked away.

Adam laughed. "Weren't you listening?"

"No."

"Well, I'm not going to help you. You knew the risks."

Machinery whirred. Sarah's harness tightened. Her feet left the ground.

"I've got news for you, preacher man," she said through gritted teeth. "We're in this together. If I go down, you go down with me."

He squeezed her hand again. "I wouldn't have it any other way."

Sarah breathed deeply as the wires pulled them higher. They were clear of the platform now, moving over the lake. She looked wistfully at the wooden roller coasters that—mere hours ago—hadn't seemed quite exciting enough.

Had she lost her mind?

Certainly, some euphoria could be expected. For the first time since the tragedies, she was finally free to be happy. She loved her job, she loved her house, and she loved Adam. His work situation hadn't been completely smooth sailing, but they were managing it—together. As he had anticipated, a few church members seemed to disapprove of their relationship, but most had gone out of their way to welcome her. Her favorite piece of encouragement had come in the mailbox: a simple card, hand-written and unsigned. *Thank you*, it had said, *for making Reverend Carmassi so happy. We like him this way. Keep up the good work!*

She couldn't think of that card without smiling.

She couldn't look down on Kennywood without smiling, either. They were almost to the tower, and the view was breathtaking. People scurried about beneath them like ants, many pausing to look up, voyeurs to their imminent doom.

"Why did I let you talk me into this?" Adam lamented, his voice suddenly weaker.

"Because you can't resist me," she answered, knowing the reverse was also true. He had talked her into flying—all by herself—to visit her aunt in North Carolina. He had talked her into attending a theology discussion group at his church. He had talked her into attending any number of Pirates games, and he had talked her out of dragging him to Phipps Conservatory for the summer flower show.

Most importantly, he had talked her into accepting some professional counseling. Good as life was, she did understand now what she was facing. Rome had not been built in a day, and nine years of emotional upheaval could not be erased overnight.

But she was convinced she had made a pretty good start.

They stopped. The harnesses suspended them, limbs dangling, 180 feet above the park below. In a matter of seconds, the contraption would release them into a harrowing drop straight down, then swing them out in a giant arc over the water and up into the air again.

It would be fabulous.

Really.

She held Adam's hand in a death grip. "Thank you for doing this with me."

He squeezed back. "My pleasure. First, Kennywood. Next, the Sydney Harbour Bridge."

"Thrill seeker."

"Takes one to know one."

"Okay," she acknowledged. "But even thrill seekers are allowed to get a little nervous."

"Just as long as you don't scream in my ear."

She frowned. "I told you, I don't scream. I'm the silent,

internalizing type."

"Well, in that case—"

The anchor line released them. They tilted, heads down, and dropped into freefall.

Sarah screamed at the top of her lungs.

About the Author

USA-Today bestselling novelist and playwright Edie Claire was first published in mystery in 1999 by the New American Library division of Penguin Putnam. In 2002 she began publishing award-winning contemporary romances with Warner Books, and in 2008 two of her comedies for the stage were published by Baker's Plays (now Samuel French). In 2009 she began publishing independently, continuing her original Leigh Koslow Mystery series and adding new works of romantic women's fiction, young adult fiction, and humor.

Under the banner of Stackhouse Press, Edie has now published over 25 titles including digital, print, audio, and foreign translations. Her works are distributed worldwide, with her first contemporary romance, *Long Time Coming*, exceeding two million downloads. She has received multiple "Top Pick" designations from *Romantic Times Magazine* and received both the "Reader's Choice Award" from *Road To Romance* and the "Perfect 10 Award" from *Romance Reviews Today*.

A former veterinarian and childbirth educator, Edie is a happily married mother of three who currently resides in Pennsylvania. She enjoys gardening and wildlife-watching and dreams of becoming a snowbird.

Books & Plays by Edie Claire

Romantic Fiction

Pacific Horizons

Alaskan Dawn
Leaving Lana'i
Maui Winds
Glacier Blooming
Tofino Storm

Fated Loves

Long Time Coming
Meant To Be
Borrowed Time

Hawaiian Shadows

Wraith
Empath
Lokahi
The Warning

Leigh Koslow Mysteries

Never Buried
Never Sorry
Never Preach Past Noon
Never Kissed Goodnight
Never Tease a Siamese
Never Con a Corgi

Never Haunt a Historian
Never Thwart a Thespian
Never Steal a Cockatiel
Never Mess With Mistletoe
Never Murder a Birder
Never Nag Your Neighbor

Women's Fiction

The Mud Sisters
Soccer Mom in Galilee (as Rachel Stackhouse)

Humor

Corporately Blonde

Comedic Stage Plays

Scary Drama I
See You in Bells

www.ingramcontent.com/pod-product-compliance
Lightning Source LLC
Chambersburg PA
CBHW050558190726
48283CB00007B/2186